A GLORIOUS LAND OF NATURAL WONDERS AND TERRIFYING SAVAGERY BECKONS THE FIRST AMERICANS TO A BOUNTIFUL PARADISE . . . OR THEIR DOOM

Cha-kwena—As headman of the People, he possesses the magic and spirit of the great white mammoth. Driven by a vision of a new land, he leads his tribe beyond the dark forest even as they beg him to turn back before they reach "the edge of the world."

Mah-ree—As Cha-kwena's woman, she worries that he will discover her defiance of the ancient ways and blame the People's misfortunes on her determination to be like First Woman, adept with the spear and in the hunter's arts.

Shateh—Virile and powerful even in middle age, the foremost war chief of the People desires one thing more than any other: a son of his blood to carry on his spirit . . . no matter what it costs.

Warakan—Saved from cannibals, he now calls Shateh father. But an enemy within his adopted tribe will cause the boy to be cast into the wilderness, where he will become something to be feared . . . or worshiped.

Ban-ya—Abandoned and believed dead, this astonishing woman survives in the sacred valley where the great mammoth go to die, vowing to raise the twin sons she has borne in exile and take revenge on those who betrayed her: Shateh and Cha-kwena.

BANTAM BOOKS BY WILLIAM SARABANDE

THE
FIRST
AMERICANS

THE EDGE
OF THE
WORLD

WILLIAM
SARABANDE

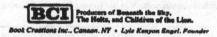

BCI Producers of Beneath the Sky,
The Holts, and Children of the Lion.

Book Creations Inc., Canaan, NY • Lyle Kenyon Engel, Founder

BANTAM BOOKS
NEW YORK • TORONTO • LONDON • SYDNEY • AUCKLAND

THE EDGE OF THE WORLD

*A Bantam Book / published in arrangement with
Book Creations Inc.*

Bantam edition / December 1993

*Produced by Book Creations Inc.
Lyle Kenyon Engel, Founder*

ISBN 978-0-553-56028-2

Published simultaneously in the United States and Canada

To Les Grant, for more than I can say!

Great Bear

THE GREAT LAKE

EDGE OF THE WORLD

© BOOK CREATIONS INC. 1993

The Watcher

Twin Brothers

Great Snake

········ Tundra
ᐱᐱᐱ Forest
᎐᎐᎐ Grassland

LAURENTIDE
ICE SHEET

Laurentide Ice Sheet

Area shown
in main map

North America
c. 12,000 years ago

RON TOELKE '93

They come,
    Hay yah! On the wings of North Wind
They come,
    Hay yah! Raven is their brother.
Bear says this,
    Hay yah! First Man and First Woman turn away.
They are coming from the sky,
    Hay yah! They will eat your children!

PART I

TOTEM SLAYER

"What I am trying to say is hard to tell and hard to understand . . . unless, unless . . . you have been yourself at the edge of Deep Canyon and have come back unharmed. . . ."

—TEWA ELDER
Seeking Life by V. Laskin

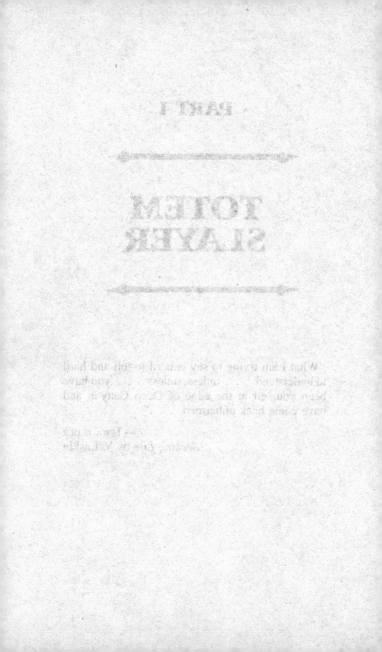

1

They came like wolves across the land. Slowly, cautiously, into the wind they came, lean men and youths painted black and red with ash and ocher and their leaner dogs, the color of storm skies and late-summer grass.

In the pure, savage light of the Ice Age noon, Cha-kwena looked down at the dog closest to him. He held no affection for its kind; nevertheless he envied it. Like the others with which it ran this day, the dog was among the best of the tribe's hunting pack, and Cha-kwena knew that it would instinctively do what was needed when the moment came to signal it into action.

May I do as well as you this day upon the hunt, Dog, brother of Wolf and Coyote! He exhaled a tight, inaudible sigh of hope and longing. *For if I do not, there are those among this man pack who would have the meat of my bones roasting on the spits tonight!*

Cha-kwena had not spoken aloud, but somehow the dog sensed his thoughts and turned up its head. Cha-kwena took little notice. His dark, angular eyes were now fixed on other animals.

He moved forward with the others, soundlessly insinuating himself around boulders and sidestepping loose stones. Cha-kwena was a young man, small and spare of frame, but as strong and agile and quick to react to his

3

surroundings as the tawny little pronghorn antelope of his distant homeland. Downslope and perhaps as many as a thousand paces ahead, a small herd of striped, broad-bellied brown horses grazed at the base of high bluffs and at the neck of a dead-end draw toward which he and the other hunters had been maneuvering them since dawn.

At last we have them where we want them! Cha-kwena was so tense with anticipation, he could barely breathe. *Too long have my fellow hunters gone without man-worthy meat and a kill that will make our women sing with pride!* As he looked down at the horses, his youthful face split with a wide, white grin of satisfaction. Earlier in the day he had feared that the hunt might be over before it had a chance to begin. Fresh bear sign had made the horses skittish. The hunters had tethered the dogs and proceeded warily, realizing that they must not fail to walk wisely or take every precaution to remain in favor with the spirits. Otherwise they might lose the herd and themselves fall prey to a carnivore of infinitely greater and more terrifying magnitude than man.

At this moment Cha-kwena remembered that he was a shaman with a considerable reputation to maintain. With his medicine bag around his neck and his sacred owl-skin headdress securely upon his head, he reminded himself that once—and not so long before—he had led his followers to victory in a great war against their enemies. Secure in this knowledge, he uttered a special chant to Bear, reminding Walks Like a Man that if he were wise, he would avoid confrontation with so powerful a shaman as Cha-kwena of the Red World. "If you are looking for sweet roots and season-end berries and mouse tunnels to dig," he added, "you are going in the wrong direction, for the land through which my hunters now travel offers none of these."

His invocation must have been heard, for after a while the hunters lost all sign of the bear and gratefully pursued the horses into long, weather-eroded hills that were as dry and barren and creased by time as an old woman's genitals. The others called it bad land, but they continued on, following the horses across country that offered nothing more threatening than rodent droppings, owl casts, and occasional mammoth spoor. Now, at last, the herd reached its destination. There were grass and water at the neck of the draw. The horses were almost within spear range. Thanks to the rocky terrain, the constancy of the wind, and the skill of the hunters in using both to their advantage, the horses detected no sight, sound, or scent of the human and canine predators that were about to make meat of them.

Cha-kwena sighed with relief. It was going to be a good day, after all! Soon the chase would be over. Soon his fellow hunters would have cause to smile at their shaman once more while they rejoiced in the taking of much meat to their hungry women and children. Then they would settle into a temporary butchering camp and rest before they began the long journey back to the village. For this Cha-kwena was supremely grateful. The overland trek had not wearied him; but his feet hurt, and he longed to take off the new moccasins that his woman had made for him. She had done something wrong with the seams, and several grass seeds had penetrated the sinew stitching to prick mercilessly at the soft skin between his ankles and the hard, thick rime of his callused heels.

Cha-kwena frowned. As soon as he returned to the village, he was going to have a serious talk with his headstrong little girl-of-a-woman about her careless workmanship. Mah-ree remained stubbornly disdainful of the complex sewing skills and customs of the People of the Land of Grass with whom the recent war had placed their little band in uneasy but beneficial alliance. Despite her status as a chieftain's daughter of the southern tribes of the distant Red World, where they had both been born, and her considerable gifts as a medicine woman, many of the hard-living northerners looked askance at her these days.

Cha-kwena's frown became a scowl under his beaked, stone-eyed headdress. It was all he could do to resist the urge to reach down and rub the soreness from his feet, but resist he did. It was dangerous for a shaman who claimed to walk strong in the power of the totem to suffer sore feet on a hunting expedition upon which everyone was depending for winter meat. If the onetime warriors from the Land of Grass lost faith in their shaman now, only the Four Winds could say what would happen to him and his small band of followers. He had led them all into this land with bold promises of a new and better life, but so far they had suffered hunger and discouragement.

Now, just ahead of Cha-kwena and slightly to his right, Shateh, leader of the hunt and warrior-chieftain of the combined bands of the People of the Land of Grass and the People of the Red World, raised his spear arm as he came to a halt. Cha-kwena stopped midstep. Everyone else did the same. No one moved. Even the dogs were frozen in place. All eyes, including Cha-kwena's, were on Shateh. Like nearly all of the hunters from the Land of Grass, the chieftain was tall and visibly powerful. The irregular vertical stripes of his body paint made him seem even larger, and his scars and graying, hip-length hair marked him as a survivor of many hunts and battles. Around his neck was a magnificent collar of golden eagle flight feathers.

Cha-kwena, forgetting all about his aching feet, positioned his bone spear hurler and long, wood-shafted, stone-tipped lances in anticipation of the kill. He could see tension in the chieftain's broad back and upraised arm. The final phase of the hunt had begun.

The young shaman held his ground as others readied their weapons and fanned out to assume prearranged positions along the high, bare, boulder-strewn ground. As shaman, his place close to Shateh was one of great prestige, and Cha-kwena knew it. The hunters were watching him now, taking slow, thoughtful measure of him from beneath lowered brows as they waited for him to begin the final invocation to the spirits of the hunt on their behalf. Whatever happened from this moment on, be it good or bad, he knew that the men would hold their shaman accountable.

Sobered by the weight of responsibility, he sent his sun-browned left hand rising to enfold the leather medicine bag that hung by a braided sinew cord around his neck. As he did so, he saw an immediate change in those around him. There was an ancient and all-transcendent magic in the sacred stone that lay within. His hand flexed around the talisman, which had been in the possession of the holy men of his band since time beyond beginning. It was a little stone, no larger than his thumb. Only its hooked shape— like a stabbing fang ripped from the mouth of a saber-toothed cat—gave any indication of its latent power. Yet all knew that the keeper of the stone walked strong and invincible in the protective power of the ancestors as he commanded the spirits of earth and sky to guide his people to victory in war and to all good things upon life's path.

Cha-kwena's hand tightened around the sacred stone. He felt neither strong nor invincible nor particularly commanding. If the hunt was to succeed, he knew he must command the forces of Creation to heed the needs of his followers. It seemed an unfair responsibility to be heaped upon one man. Resentment made him glower. He had never wanted to be shaman. By right of inheritance, through war, and because of circumstances too terrible to recall, the spirits of the ancestors had chosen him to be the one through whom they would speak to the People.

And so the sacred stone had come into his protection. Now it was his to guard with his life, just as his beloved grandfather, the old shaman Hoyeh-tay, had done before him. Many had fought and died to steal it from him and turn its powers to their own ends. All had failed . . . except Shateh.

The chieftain was looking at him now, waiting patiently for him to form his prayer upon the stone. Their eyes met and held. At one time Cha-kwena counted this man among his mortal enemies, but Shateh had chosen to stand with him in battle. Together they had broken and scattered their enemies upon the Four Winds. When Shateh had named him Brother and insisted upon uniting their two peoples, Cha-kwena had been unable to refuse. And so now Shateh claimed the sacred stone *and* the young shaman who went along with it, not by force but because Cha-kwena owed the chieftain his life, his loyalty, and the favor of the spirits upon at least one hunt in all these many moons.

Spirits of the stone, you must *hear this man!* A tremor went through Cha-kwena as he closed his eyes and raised his head high. With his medicine bag still gripped in his hand, he silently invoked the elemental spirits of all things, both animate and inanimate, and shared his hopes and fears with them. *Life is hard and hungry for the people of Shateh and Cha-kwena in this new land to which war has brought us. Now our enemies are vanquished. Those who have hunted the sacred mammoth and profaned the way of the Ancient Ones have been slain. Now the people of Shateh and Cha-kwena are one. Together we keep the way of the ancestors and follow the sacred mammoth ever eastward into the face of the rising sun. But until this day the land has yielded no man-worthy meat. So you must speak to these horses! You must tell them of our hunger. You must ask them to be meat for us. Spirits of the stone, for the sake of my people, you* must *grant this man a good kill, or the tribesmen of Shateh will lose all trust in me and faith in your power!*

"Perhaps that would not be such a bad thing?"

Cha-kwena's eyes flew open. Who had spoken? He knew that none of the hunters had asked the question. It had come from within himself or from within the sacred stone; he did not know which. The others were still watching him, waiting for him to give the signal that would tell them that his prayer for a successful hunt was complete. He stared straight ahead, unblinking and suddenly unseeing. As some-times happened when he attempted to commune with the powers of the talisman, the intensity of his prayer shifted reality, and without warning, his mind plummeted through the labyrinthine inner corridors of perception into which only a shaman may wander. Through the vast canyons of his interior self, Cha-kwena coursed with the blood in his own veins, felt the powerful pull and push of his lungs, and heard the massive, steady drumbeat of his heart. Then the corridors of his inner vision led out of darkness as, borne on the exhalation of his own breath, he left his body and, spreading his arms wide, ascended back into reality.

With a start he saw that the other hunters were still watching him expectantly from their various positions of readiness. They were frowning, and Shateh was looking back at him, waiting and scowling. When his eyes again met those of the chieftain, a surge of awareness rushed through Cha-kwena. The chieftain was displeased with him.

"You have been too long at your prayer, Shaman!"

Cha-kwena swallowed hard. Flustered, he released his medicine bag and gave a single quick nod to indicate to the others that his invocations on their behalf had been offered. Only the Four Winds could say if they had been heard.

Shateh lowered his head in stern-eyed but otherwise expressionless acknowledgment, then turned away and gestured the others forward as he began to advance once more into the wind. Cha-kwena quickly positioned the butt end of his newest lance into the barbed end of his spear hurler and followed. The narrow, slightly arched back of the hurler rested on his right shoulder, and his stone-headed lance was at the ready, gripped between his thumb and the first two fingers of his right hand. The young shaman's heart began to race, and he found it almost impossible not to tremble with nervous excitement at the prospect of the kill and long-yearned-for feast to follow.

And then it happened. The favorite among the chieftain's three dogs was overcome by the thrill of expectation. One moment the animal was obediently walking to heel; the next, it was slobbering and whining and straining to be free of its tether. In less time than it took to draw a single breath, the chieftain smashed its skull with the blunt end of his spear, and the dog fell over dead. Shateh released the animal's tether and led his hunters on without breaking stride.

Cha-kwena stopped. Sometimes, as now, the ways of Shateh and his people stunned him. He understood that the dog had been on the verge of barking and alerting the horses to the presence of the hunters; but the cool, offhanded ease with which the chieftain had just slain the erring animal disconcerted him. Memories pricked his gut more intensely than the cursed seed coats pricked his ankles. Shateh always did what he deemed best for his tribe, no matter who or what it cost him. If the hunt did not go well today, Cha-kwena knew all too well that Shateh was capable of cutting down a favored but no longer effective shaman with the same ease that he had just displayed to slay a favorite dog.

Suddenly the wind turned. Like a viper twisting in a wooden snaking trident, it whipped around from behind and stung the bare portions of Cha-kwena's skin with airborne grit and sand carried from distant dunes and surrounding badlands. Staggered, the young man gasped from the unexpected, unseasonable cold. The wind snapped the fringes of his moccasins painfully against his lower legs, then ripped his owl-skin bonnet from his head and carried the headdress and his scent—along with the scent of every man, youth, and dog in the hunting party—to the herd of horses.

Cha-kwena sensed rather than heard the ragged exhalations of disappointment that came from those who had also been brought short by the wind. Shateh, standing just ahead of him, was shaking his spear at the sky as long, wind-whipped lengths of hair blew like tattered skeins of storm cloud before his face. Cha-kwena backhanded his own hair out of his eyes and squinted past the chieftain just in time to see the stallion raise its head and, with a shrill, imperative whinny, alert its bristle-maned mares and young to imminent danger. As one, the horses, tails up, ears back, hooves ripping the earth, were off at a gallop through shallow grass. The beasts raised a cloud of grit-laden dust as they sped away from the draw and away from the hunters.

"Ay yah!" Shateh cried out in anger and frustration, his deep voice as explosive as the single stone-tipped hardwood lance loosed from his spear hurler.

Without awaiting the chieftain's command, Cha-kwena hurled a lance of his own. As a shaman who had just failed to foresee the turning of the wind on a hunt that was critical to the survival of his people, he felt obliged to do something. Never had he thrown a spear so hard. Given the distance between him and the horses, he knew his effort was a waste of a perfectly good projectile point. As it flew from his spear hurler, though, the balance and heft of the throw felt right—so right that he was not quite as amazed as every other man and youth in the party when his spear arced high over Shateh's lance to embed itself in the shoulder of one of the mares. The horse went down hard, rump over head, hooves flying skyward while the rest of the herd scattered and vanished into the eastern hills.

"Hay yah!" The cry of triumph burst from Chakwena's lips. The spirits of the stone had heard his prayer. "This *is* going to be a good day, after all!"

Many miles away, a small, sun-browned, naked young woman stood knee-deep in a wide, stony creek at the base of the bluff-top village from which the hunters had departed at dawn. Facing into the sun, Mah-ree cast no shadow upon the water when she drew out yet another fish from the looped end of her fishing stick and flicked it into the basket of woven reeds balanced on her narrow hip. At this moment a twig snapped within the unseasonably yellowed willow thickets that lined the south-facing shore. Simultaneously, a rock wren flew from the scrub growth to the sunstruck boulders of the embankment to her right.

Mah-ree stiffened. Images of lions and dire wolves, of snarling bears and cougar-sized leaping cats with stabbing fangs the length of a grown man's forearm, flared within her mind. She held her breath. So did the other women who had come with their children, babies, and dogs to the creek's edge to bathe, fill waterskins, and gather what they could of an almost nonexistent crop of summer's-end berries and roots.

Ready to flee from danger, Mah-ree noted with relief that the dogs seemed unperturbed. Only two of them had raised their heads to listen and scent the air. She copied them and breathed in the strong, familiar smells of the little valley within which her people had raised their skin lodges nearly a moon before. Then she listened to the low, constant sibilance of water over the midstream gravel bar, the wind rustling erratically in shoreline trees and shrubs, and the atonal singing of addled, deaf Kahm-ree as she sat naked and splay legged in the shallows. Pity for the old woman touched Mah-ree's heart; but if there was something threatening in the scents and sounds of this place, she could not smell or hear it.

High above, a teratorn uttered a shrieking cry. Startled, Mah-ree looked up. The rare, condorlike bird flew across the face of the sun. She frowned at the resultant shadow, but in a moment the broad, dark wings banked away upon the wind, and the sun was bright once more.

Mah-ree dared to breathe again as her eyes strayed to the largest of the streamside boulders. Young Gah-ti was sitting cross-legged on the lichen-colored stone. Sunlight glinted on the massive purple scar that covered the right half of his head. She frowned again, as she always did when she saw the results of the terrible mauling he had endured by the lion that had also taken his arm so many moons before. But his wounds were healed, and Gah-ti was strong again, hawk eyed and ready to sound an alert to the closest bluff, where the seasoned warrior Teikan kept watch with a young man called Ishkai. Mah-ree relaxed. If danger was lurking in the woods beyond the creek, the sentries would have alerted the women long before now.

She slid her gaze toward Teikan and Ishkai. Both men stood tall, talking together while several boys armed with slings sat around on the bluff top and played bone toss. Teikan was looking at her. Bold sexual appraisal gave heat to his stare. She glared up at him, wanting him to see her displeasure; indeed, she found his behavior insulting. Only a man with trouble on his mind would look with hungry eyes at another man's woman. She was Mah-ree, Medicine Woman, and could not be enticed to spread herself for the pleasure of a common hunter when she alone shared the sleeping mat of Cha-kwena, keeper of the sacred stone, shaman of the People of the Red World and of the People of the Land of Grass! With a tilt-nosed exhalation of disdain, she turned her back to the presumptuous Teikan and resumed fishing with her loop stick.

Her thoughts drifted with the current. She wondered where Cha-kwena was now. Was he thinking of her with love and a warm heart, as she was thinking of him? Heaving a wistful sigh, Mah-ree wished her man many horses upon the hunt this day, then daydreamed of how it would be when he and the others returned. There would be feasting. There would be a great fire around which the people would dance and sing. All would be as it had been in the days immediately following the great war, when the People of the Red World and the People of the Land of Grass had rejoiced in their victory and vowed to be brothers and sisters forever. All of the tension and distrust, the ruinous rot of malice and suspicion that had been growing between the two bands, would blow away upon the wind like the spores of some malignant fungus.

Mah-ree's imaginings ended with a shiver. The wind had turned and grown cold.

"We should have worn warmer clothing!" shouted the matron Wehakna from the shore. "East Wind of morning has blown away across the land. North Wind is with us now. Come in from the water and dress yourself, Shaman's Woman. You have taken enough fish for one day, and surely you know that only you and your Red World people will eat it!"

Mah-ree exhaled in annoyance. Wehakna was the first woman of the chieftain and had to be obeyed. Irritated, Mah-ree drew her fishing stick from the water, placed it in her basket along with her sizable catch, then turned and waded to the small stretch of sandy beach upon which she had left her elk-hide cape and skirt. With the exception of old Kahm-ree, who was still in the water, overturning rocks and looking for larvae and crayfish, the other women were gathered there with the children now, pulling on their

clothes and combing their long hair as they prepared to
return to the warmth of their lodges.

"When so many complain of hunger, all will be
welcome to eat of these fish after I have stuffed them with
seeds and pine nuts and slowly roasted them over a fire of
sweet grass and sage," Mah-ree offered as she picked up her
skirt and stepped lightly into it.

Her mother, Ha-xa, and her sisters, Ta-maya and
Tla-nee, came to admire her catch. They were joined by her
mother-in-law, U-wa, and Cha-kwena's little half sister,
Joh-nee.

Wehakna, tall and stern eyed, made a face of revulsion
as she looked at the contents of the basket. "Fish is not
fitting food, especially for the women who carry new life!"
she exclaimed.

Her sentiments were promptly echoed by Cheelapat,
the chieftain's youngest wife. "Would Mah-ree have us give
birth to scaled, tailed, gill-breathing babies?"

U-wa laughed. "What would be left for you to eat,
life-making women from the Land of Grass, if you truly
believed that every animal you consumed passed its looks
on to your babies?"

"Not camel," Ha-xa said merrily.

"Nor sloth!" added U-wa, her sense of humor leading
her to huff and grunt and amble slowly around, pawing at
the ground in a fine imitation of the animal of which she had
spoken.

The children were delighted.

The three wives of Shateh and the other women from
the Land of Grass were not amused.

"Mock us if you will, Red World women, but we know
that Mah-ree does not care about babies," remarked Senohnim, second woman of the chieftain. She was seated
upon the ground, leaning against a backrest of painted
buckskin stretched across a frame of woven wood. Looking
up, she smirked at Mah-ree and ran her hands proudly over
the distended mound of her drum-tight pregnant belly.
"Mah-ree is a shaman's woman and a maker of medicine,

but together she and her man have not been able to make the right magic to put a baby in her belly! Here, Khat and Tinah, help your mother to her feet and bring me my dress. The wind has grown cold. I would return to our lodge. The sight of so much unfit food offends my spirit!"

Mah-ree was stung. The offer to share her fish had been made generously and sincerely. Her slim arms enfolded her basket. Her long, heavily lashed dark eyes scanned the beach where the children were now fussing around the cradleboards of the infants.

Ta-maya had predictably taken it upon herself to manage the little ones. Mah-ree watched her older sister moving with calm, easy authority among the children. Even with her blind little stepdaughter, Doh-teyah, hefted on one hip, she had no trouble gently shooing off an old dog that had failed to follow the rest of its pack. It was now up and off, sniffing and whining after only who knew what. In minutes Ta-maya had the children eagerly picking up their scattered playthings and complying with her every wish. Mah-ree sighed as she looked at her beautiful older sister. Ta-maya, like Senohnim, was big with child.

Mah-ree fought back the urge to cry. How she longed to swell with life for her own man! She wanted babies—*many* babies! Cha-kwena had assured her that her time to be a mother would come; but she was sixteen and growing old, and still her belly remained flat. Her breasts did not engorge with milk, and her moon blood came with dauntless regularity. In a village within which many women were either nursing a child or in some stage of pregnancy, Mah-ree was ashamed. Worse, she was worried. She had overheard old Lahontay whispering behind Cha-kwena's back that a man who could not put life into a woman was no man at all—and surely not the shaman he claimed to be. Again she shivered, with longing for babies and with fear that her failure to conceive was sullying her beloved man's already seriously waning reputation.

"Here, Daughter," said Ha-xa, placing Mah-ree's cape around her shoulders, then slinging on her own cloak of jaguar skin. Although it was ragged and much mended, she wore it proudly. It had once been a headman's garment and, along with her daughters, was all Ha-xa had left to cling to of lost status and a long-dead, much-loved husband. "Do not listen to them, Mah-ree. When they have need of the healing ways, then they will remember to speak kind words to Shaman's Woman!"

"Shaman's Woman thinks she knows all!" snorted Vral, woman of the hunter Teikan. "Shaman's Woman thinks she *is* a shaman, maybe even another Sheela or barren-bellied Ysuna!"

The women and girls gasped as one.

Wehakna's eyes blazed. "Do not speak their names lest the spirits of those Watching Star women come back from the world beyond this world to live and feed once more upon the People!"

Mah-ree looked up at Vral with open resentment. Like nearly all of the females from the Land of Grass, the woman of Teikan was big boned, handsome, and noticeably pregnant. Proud of her body, she had left her garments behind when she had come from the village to bathe. Now she stood naked before Mah-ree. In the cold wind her nipples stood up and out like sun-puckered purple chokecherries. Mah-ree stared at them and said, not without a smile at Vral's expense, "At least I know enough to bring garments to protect my body from the cold when I come out from the village. You had best hurry back to your lodge, Vral, before your nipples fall off. And if that happens, upon what will your new baby or your man take suck?"

Cheelapat smirked at Vral's discomfort. "Do not worry about Teikan; that man has an eye for young girls these days. I do not think he will wait until you are able to open yourself to him or his newest bride comes to him in the spring. He will bury his man bone between someone's thighs long before then."

Standing close together, a threesome of adolescents giggled, and Eira, daughter of Lahontay and bride-to-be of Teikan, flushed.

Vral chose to ignore the girls and Cheelapat's slur. "Who knew that the wind would turn?" she asked haughtily as she crossed her arms before her breasts.

"Out there . . . on the hunt . . . my shaman will have known!"

Wehakna was now visibly angry. "Is that so? My Shateh was the chieftain *and* shaman before war drew us from our land. In that war Cha-kwena was so strong in the power of the totem and of the sacred stone that my Shateh named him Shaman above himself. But where are Cha-kwena's powers now? Look at this land into which he has led us! Where is the tall grass? Where are the great herds of bison and elk and other man-worthy meat?"

"They are here," replied Mah-ree with absolute certainty. "My shaman will find them."

Wehakna's piercing eyes fixed the young woman. "If he does not, my Shateh will be the shaman again, and we will return to the Land of Grass."

"And you and your Red World people will be our slaves," added Senohnim with obvious satisfaction.

"And Land of Grass men will take Medicine Woman and teach her the baby-making man magic that her 'shaman' cannot make on her!" Cheelapat was leering as she looked toward Vral. "I have heard your Teikan say that he would like to try."

Vral lunged at her for the remark, but Cheelapat only skipped out of the way and laughed maliciously.

"Beware of what you say, women of Shateh," said Mah-ree quickly, "lest my shaman hear and turn the forces of Creation against you! Where is your loyalty? You have chosen to walk with Cha-kwena! His power made you invincible against our enemies. You must have faith in the one who walks strong in the favor of the ancestors, or you will soon know remorse. Forget the Land of Grass. It is far away!"

Now Vral had caught Cheelapat by the hair, and the two women were going at each other with flailing arms and limbs.

"It is not as far as you think, Shaman's Woman, if Cha-kwena dares lead our hunters to the village again without man-worthy meat," warned Wehakna.

Mah-ree made no further comment. She knew it would be a waste of words. Suddenly, Vral and Cheelapat were on the ground, screeching and tangling and biting like a pair of battling lynx.

Even the Red World women and children were noisily and excitedly closing ranks to watch the fight while the sentinels on the bluff were cheering on their favorites. Disgusted by such violent—but, as she had come to learn over the past few moons, typical—Land of Grass behavior, Mah-ree raised her head high. Still balancing her basket on one hip, she turned and walked disdainfully away.

It was not until she was well along the uphill creek-side trail and more than halfway to the village on the bluffs that Mah-ree was brought up short by a sudden change in the sounds that reached her from the beach. The dogs were barking. The women were no longer shouting; they were screaming. The children were no longer laughing; they were squealing. And above the howling of the boys, Teikan roared, "Run wide! Scatter! *Now!*"

Mah-ree whirled around. Downstream of the beach, a great, high-humped yellow bear had already broken through the willows and begun its charge.

Cha-kwena was painfully aware of the passing of time as he stood dead still in the cold wind. No one spoke. No one moved. Breathless with exhilaration, he counted the moments, measured them by the beat of his heart until he was forced to take a breath. Still no one moved. Still no one spoke. Puzzled, he waited, wondered why no one praised his successful strike. Then, with a grunt—of acknowledgment or disgust, Cha-kwena could not tell—Shateh started downslope. Without a word, the others followed. Cha-kwena stared after them, taking advantage of the moment by rubbing his ankles until he sighed with pleasure at the relief he found. Only after the others had reached the fallen mare and formed a circle around it was he moved to join them.

"This kill is Cha-kwena's," conceded Shateh, picking up the owl-skin headdress from where it had lodged against the body of the downed horse and handing it to the young shaman.

The hunters muttered incomprehensibly.

Despite the chilling bite of the wind, Cha-kwena burned with the sweet heat of pride and put the bonnet back on his head. The hunt chief's spear had fallen short; his own had struck true. The spirits of the sacred stone *had* heard his prayer! He *had* made a good kill at last.

Even though the shaft had snapped when the mare had pitched forward, it had never looked more beautiful to him. The mare's fall had broken her spine below her head and well above her withers. She was still alive, but not for long; her eyes were already glazing.

Now, while Shateh pulled the young shaman's ruined spear from the quivering shoulder muscles of the downed horse and held the lance high for the other hunters to see, Cha-kwena could barely control his elation. Everyone would recognize what was left of the red shaft with blue banding as his: Red honored the distant Red World of his birth; blue acknowledged his rank as a shaman of that sunburned country. Holy men from the scattered villages of his drought-stricken clan had once gathered upon sacred mesas to paint their skin the color of the sky, so that the sky spirits would recognize them as worthy intermediaries when they wished to commune with the People out of the wind and clouds.

They were nearly all dead now, those proud, wise grandfathers in towering headdresses of tufted grass and collars of sacred sage and cloaks of rabbit fur that covered bodies as tough and dry and loose of skin as the lizards that formed the major portion of their diet. What would they say if they could see him now?

You have done well, Cha-kwena.

He flinched at the sound of long-unheard voices. His

eyes met Shetah's steady gaze, and as the chieftain extended
the spear to him, Cha-kwena saw not the chieftain at all, but
other men: skinny, gap-toothed Shi-wana of the Blue
Mesas; stolid, humorless Naquah-neh of the White Hills;
and his own irascible, bright-eyed grandfather, Hoyeh-tay of
the village by the Lake of Many Singing Birds. A molting,
yellow-eyed owl perched upon Hoyeh-tay's bony shoulder.
The raptor had been his grandfather's constant companion
and helping animal spirit. Cha-kwena wore the skin of that
owl upon his head.

He found himself smiling in fond recognition, even
though the bird and all three men had been slain by their
enemies, the People of the Watching Star. As the ghostly
figures faded from his vision, he was certain that they were
the spirits who had heard and answered his hunt prayer.

"I thank you," Cha-kwena said to the ghosts of the
past. With his head held high and his spare, muscular young
body painted in the hunting colors of his new people, he
proudly accepted his lance from Shateh.

A murmuring of resentment went up from the hunters
of Shateh's tribe. They exchanged guarded glances and
then, still grumbling, stared at Cha-kwena out of measuring,
wolfish eyes.

Cha-kwena was startled. Not understanding the cause
of their unexpected display of animosity, he chose to ignore
it. Intoxicated upon his success, he threw out his chest and
declared boldly, "This man, Cha-kwena, offers thanks to the
chief, Shateh, for leading the hunters to meat!"

The words were a statement of fact, but they were in no
way a concession; they were mandatory prologue to the
traditional litany of thanksgiving expected of any man—
especially a shaman—after a kill. He looked down at the
dying mare and continued boldly, "This horse will live
again in those who take its flesh into themselves. The blood
of this horse will make the eaters of its meat strong and
swift. The People will live because this horse has consented
to die. This man thanks this horse. And this man thanks the

spirits of the ancestors, for they have looked upon him with favor this day and sent his spear straight upon the wind."

The silence was deafening.

Cha-kwena's head was high again, but his brow was down. Why was everyone staring at him as though he had said something unforgivable?

Even his few fellow hunters from the Red World—Xet, K-wok, Tleea-neh, Hah-ri, and bold Kosar-eh and three of his equally bold sons—did not appear happy. Their lack of enthusiasm was troubling. Cha-kwena knew he had spoken eloquently. Perplexed, he stared back at them until he found his eyes caught in the belligerent glare of the stripling Warakan.

Cha-kwena was annoyed. Hostility from this boy was to be expected, even though he had no idea why Warakan disliked him so intensely. Unlike many others, he had never been unkind to this foundling spawn of his enemies, the People of the Watching Star. Warakan was brave and forthright, and since Shateh had honored the child by naming him Son, Cha-kwena had respected his place within the chieftain's fire circle despite his inability to look at him without reflecting upon his despised ancestry. Perhaps Warakan sensed this. Cha-kwena could not be sure. But now—although the boy was easily the smallest member of the hunting band and would need only one hand plus two or perhaps three additional fingers to count the number of his years—the animosity in his obsidian black eyes was so venomous and powerfully fixed that Cha-kwena actually winced. Irked, he broke eye contact with Warakan and looked down at the mare again.

She was dead.

He knelt, set his sacred headdress aside, and twisted the thong necklace with his medicine bag so that the talisman lay across his back and out of the way of the bloody work to which he must set himself now. This done, he took his round, palm-size stone skinning dagger from the leather hunting sack that he carried looped to the braided thong waistband of his buckskin loin cover, then bent to the task at hand. He opened the neck of the slain horse with ease. Then, after wiping bits of congealed horsehair and tissue from the edge of his skinning dagger, he skillfully removed the tongue before, adhering strictly to the hunting custom of the northerners, he rose to his feet and offered this most prized cut of meat to the chieftain.

The tongue steamed in the now bitterly cold air. Blood oozed from the mutilated stem and ran in hot rivulets down Cha-kwena's wrists and forearms. For a moment Shateh eyed the bleeding, purplish mass as though it were not a long-yearned-for delicacy but a vile thing. Then he snorted with disdain. "I, Shateh, first found sign of the horses that Cha-kwena has sent running away over the edge of the world. I have led you to your kill, 'Shaman'! I will not deny myself this meat!" This said, he snatched the tongue from Cha-kwena's hands in the manner of one taking tribute from an unworthy adversary.

The other hunters and their dogs closed ranks like a pack of hungry wolves around Cha-kwena. He knew what they wanted and gave it to them. Slitting the mare from throat to urethra, he gestured them forward so they could remove the organs of their choice while he set himself to freeing the skin from the carcass. The youths, knowing their place, fell back and pulled the dogs with them while the men surged forward. It was all Cha-kwena could do to keep out of their way as, like dogs, he thought, they snarled and snapped and jostled one another to obtain the best feeding positions. In moments the strongest among them had forced back all comers and were reaching into the belly cavity of the mare to take what they would of the man-worthy meat within.

"Ho! Foal!" exclaimed a man named Ranamal, raising the unexpected treasure high for all to see. "Shateh! Come! Shaman has taken *two* horses this day!"

Cha-kwena scowled—and not only at Ranamal's sarcastic parody of a compliment. The soft, tender meat of unborn grazing animals was a special delicacy to the men from the Land of Grass; like tongue, it was chief's meat. No one could eat of it until it was first offered to Shateh. Cha-kwena, inexplicably disturbed by the realization that he had slain a pregnant animal, squinted off into the wind to where the chieftain stood with Warakan before an audience of adoring dogs with whom he was generously sharing the tongue.

"Our women and little ones have gone long and uncomplainingly without meat that is worthy of them," said Shateh to Ranamal. "Set the fetus and the female glands of this horse aside as a special treat for them!"

With a shrug of disappointed acquiescence Ranamal obeyed, then returned his attention to the innards of the mare. Cha-kwena watched him elbow himself into the position of first butcher. The others moved aside and allowed him his place as, cutting and slicing and gorging himself, he began to hand out portions of heart and kidney, liver and intestines, to those who had not yet had a chance to eat, all the while tossing unwanted segments to the dogs.

Cha-kwena felt disgust. Unlike the others from the Red World, he had not been able to bring himself to share the northerners' appreciation for raw blood meat ripped hot from a kill. On one knee, he faced over the mare's rib cage, leaving the others to feed where he could not see them. He leaned into his work, putting his back to the wind, resenting the fact that no one saw fit to help him peel back and hold the skin of the horse while he sawed away the connective tissue beneath.

"We thank our shaman from the Red World for this gift of *one* horse," said Lahontay sarcastically, coming to stand close with a dripping slice of raw liver in one hand. "Perhaps, even now, the spirit of this *one* horse runs upon the wind with the *many* horses that will not be meat for the People on this day in which only our shaman's spear has tasted blood."

Cha-kwena looked up at the hostile old man. All pride bled out of him and was replaced by anger. "We will follow the herd. We will—"

"And how many sleeps will we have to spend upon the

trail before we catch sight of them?" demanded Lahontay. "And how many more sleeps after that before we find another suitable ambush site?"

"What kind of shaman makes the wind turn against Shateh and causes the horses to run away over the edge of the world?" pressed Warakan.

"A shaman who is strong in the power of the sacred stone and of the totem," Shateh responded slowly, as though he were not sure he believed his own words.

"And I say that the totem is dead!" Lahontay snarled as he pointed an accusing finger at Cha-kwena. "This Red World shaman has boasted that he has slain the great white spirit mammoth, Life Giver, and taken the power of the totem into himself. This was a great deed! Many, including Shateh, have dreamed of accomplishing it! All know that the Ancient Ones have told that the man who slays the totem and eats its flesh and drinks its blood will *become* totem! So we have followed this Cha-kwena, this Totem Slayer, and have named him Shaman so that his power would be our power! So we have taken his band into our tribe and said that we will be one people. But how can the power of the totem be with this Red World shaman when the land into which he has led us is as barren as the belly of his woman, and the wind turns against him, and the first man-worthy meat that this man has seen in many a long moon runs away from the spears of those hunters who walk at his side?"

Cha-kwena was savaged by the accusation. "I *have* slain the great white mammoth," he assured hotly. But inside he was as cold as the wind, for this slaying had come about not as a display of supreme bravery—as he allowed the hunters to believe—but as an act of mercy after he had come upon the totem of his ancestors disemboweled by predators and mired in a vast lake that filled the lowlands of a place that men now called the Valley of the Dead. He tensed from the memory and against Lahontay's continued stare; the old man's eyes were as sharp and invasive as the stone spearhead with which Cha-kwena had opened the great heart vein of the white mammoth.

Cha-kwena lowered his head and half closed his eyes, as though his lids and lashes were enough to shield him from the hostility directed at him from every man and boy of Shateh's tribe and his own. They had lost all faith in him. If only he could share the wondrous truth that he had kept secret from them all these long moons! Yes, he had killed the totem and taken its blood and flesh into himself when he had nearly drowned in the bloodied, gore-fouled lake. But the power of the totem did not live in him.

The great white tusker had mated before its death. Even now the immortal life spirit of the totem was growing within the matriarch of the small herd of mammoth that Cha-kwena had been steadfastly following eastward since the last days of the great war. As soon as the totem was reborn into the world, everything would change: The forces within the sacred stone would fully awaken . . . mammoth and bison and horse and elk would return in great numbers to a greening land . . . those who followed the keeper of the sacred stone would be invincible in the power of their shaman, who would heal all wounds and sickness and see to it that many male children were born to his followers.

Cha-kwena's heart quickened just to think of it. He longed to proclaim his knowledge to the others, but the spirits had allowed only him and his little Mah-ree to bear witness to this wondrous truth, and to speak aloud of a greatly desired thing was to invite malevolent spirits to destroy it before it ever came to pass. And this Cha-kwena would never do.

And so he raised his head and stood resolutely, feeling strong and secure in the knowledge that soon the others would understand why his powers were not what they had been before the death of the great white mammoth. But now the organ meat of the mare had made their blood hot, and knowing that because of him they would have no more of it this day, they were angry and disappointed.

"The sun is still high," he said reasonably. "We dishonor this horse with our angry words. Come, let us draw

lots to see who will stay and guard this meat while we
follow the brothers and sisters of this mare to the east
and—"

"No!" The angry shout came from Lahontay. He was
facing Shateh now, gesturing broadly with his bloody,
meat-filled hand. "I say that we have already come too far
into this bad and unknown country." He jabbed a finger
eastward. "The land ends there! All men know this! By now
the horses have fallen over the edge of the world and have
been burned up in that part of the sky out of which the sun
is born! Why would Shaman have us follow? Perhaps he is
not Shaman at all, but Enemy!"

Shaken, Cha-kwena tried to sound calm as he replied,
"Beyond the dry land are grass and good water and plentiful
food for hunters and gatherers alike. I speak true words to
you, Lahontay. If there were not good country ahead, the
mammoth would not lead us in that direction. Their kind has
more need than man of water and browse. Since time
beyond beginning, when Life Giver, the great white mammoth totem, led First Man and First Woman out of the spirit
world and into the world of the living, wherever the
mammoth kind have walked, there, too, have the People
always found much meat and drink and all good things. So
will it be for us. You must believe this."

Lahontay, shaking his head, chewed on the words, then
spat them out again. "So it was in the Land of Grass when
Shateh was our chief *and* shaman. In that far land we hunted
mammoth until there were no more. The spirits of the
ancestors sent many bison—high horned, short horned, long
horned, all kinds! The land was black with bison until the
People of the Watching Star came into our land seeking
captives taken in war with old enemies and—"

"The power of Cha-kwena led us to victory over those
enemies!" The coldly defensive reminder came from Kosar-
eh.

Cha-kwena was grateful and surprised. The big hunter
from the Red World had changed since leaving their
ancestral village by the Lake of Many Singing Birds. And

Cha-kwena did not need the power of a shaman to know that it was not only the love of Ta-maya, Kosar-eh's beloved woman, that had changed him. In keeping with the customs of the northerners, Kosar-eh had not cut his hair since the last days of the great war. After winning the names Lion Slayer and Man Who Spits in the Face of Enemies, he had warmed so completely to the ways of the warriors of the Land of Grass that it was sometimes difficult for Cha-kwena to remember that Kosar-eh had not been born to their tribe.

"Shateh was at Cha-kwena's side!" Lahontay countered Kosar-eh's reminder. "As were Shateh's warriors! Who is to say if Cha-kwena would have been victorious without Shateh and the fighting men from the Land of Grass?" His hawkish face turned to Shateh again. "I say it was better for us when Shateh was both our chieftain and shaman. These past moons since we have agreed to follow the mammoth east with this Red World man, Cha-kwena has shown no more power than the stone he wears."

The repudiations and insults were coming so fast and furious that Cha-kwena felt pummeled. He was speechless until Shateh, staring fixedly at him through narrowed eyes, said quietly, introspectively, "Together against our enemies we *were* a storm upon the land."

Relief struck Cha-kwena like sunlight strikes a man emerging from icy water on a winter day. "It is so! And together we *will* hunt again this day!" He had to be emphatic. To show weakness would only invite further disdain, and then only the forces of Creation knew what the hunters might do. Thinking of the dog that Shateh had killed with such apparent ease, Cha-kwena stood to his full height and wished he were taller as he declared boldly, "Our women and children will not hunger when the White Giant Winter comes upon the land. I, Cha-kwena, Totem Slayer, say this!"

"Lizard Eater!" Warakan snapped the insulting name contemptuously.

Cha-kwena looked down at the boy and was suddenly so angry that he completely forgot that this child was the adopted son of the chieftain. He snapped defensively, "Yes! In a hard and hungry land my people ate lizards when there were no bison, elk, camel, or horse. Also they ate ants and grubs and serpents. But they did not eat one another, and that is more than I can say of those who once named you Son. Where are your people, Warakan? Where are your man-eating, mammoth-hunting people, who sought to devour all who dared to stand against them? I will tell you where they are—scattered upon the Four Winds until there are not enough of them left alive to threaten those who name me Shaman! Strong in the power of the sacred stone and of the great white mammoth totem of our ancestors, I, Cha-kwena, have led the warriors of Shateh to drive your people from their stronghold! With the Four Winds at my side, I have led the warriors of Shateh and of my own band to send your people to walk the wind forever."

The boy's face went blank. Several youths smirked at Warakan's expense.

The other hunters nodded, approving Cha-kwena's words and the strength with which they had been delivered. Even Lahontay appeared momentarily mollified. Cha-kwena felt better, but the feeling was not to last. When he met the gaze of the chieftain, he saw that Shateh was not smiling.

"Shaman speaks too boldly. Shaman has forgotten that Shateh is chief!" His voice was sharp and cold. "And no man—shaman or otherwise—has ever led Shateh where he has not chosen to go!"

"But the horses . . . if we follow them now we can still—"

"Silence, Shaman, if you *are* still a shaman. I, Shateh, say that we will hunt no more this day!" This said, the chieftain turned his broad face skyward and squinted at thin streamers of cloud sweeping in from the northwest. His long mouth flexed. His brow expanded, then furrowed. When he looked at Cha-kwena again, his face was set, inflexible. "Winter is moons away, but the cold breath of the White Giant is heavy on this wind. There will be snow before the sun sleeps tomorrow. With a storm at my heels, I will not lead a hunting party into unknown country. We have made no preparations for winter travel. No, we will butcher this horse, then return to the village and take the meat that our shaman's spear has given to us to our hungry women and little ones. It is not much meat, but it will be enough to ease their hunger until the coming storm is over." Again he paused and turned his face upward. "You did not foresee this wind, Shaman, or this coming storm! What else have you failed to foresee this day?"

Mah-ree did not scream. Her eyes were wide. Horror burned her senses. With her fishing stick still in her right hand and her gathering basket braced against one hip, she stared down from the heights of the trail and tried to rid herself of the image of Ishkai leaping boldly from the bluff and landing wrong. His leg had snapped. He had fallen sideways, into the path of the bear. The animal had stopped, stood straight up on its hind legs, swung its head, and clacked its slobbering jaws. For one incredible instant Mah-ree had been certain that it was going to turn away. Then the first of Teikan's spears found its mark just as the dogs swarmed upon the beast. In that moment Walks Like a Man had taught the dogs how to fly as it swiped two of them straight off the ground and into the trees. The next swipe found Ishkai. He had not moved after that, save to twitch and spurt blood from a stump of a neck to which his head no longer remained connected.

The bear was moving again, full out now, with two of Teikan's spears protruding from the high hump of its shoulders and one of the boys' lighter-weight lances buried in its side. Impervious to its wounds, it kept coming. With the dogs racing after it, Walks Like a Man surged straight up the middle of the creek bed toward the women.

Mah-ree stared, unable to look away, grateful only for the fact that its attack on Ishkai had won the women and girls precious time in which they had managed to put good distance between themselves and the marauder. With their babies and toddlers in their arms and on their backs, they raced up the trail toward her. Mah-ree looked past them to the bear and wondered how an animal of such size and girth could be so graceful, so fluid in its movements, and appear so appallingly beautiful to her after what it had just wrought.

"Run, Daughter! Turn around and *run!*" shrieked Ha-xa as she came to a breathless stop with three-year-old Tla-nee clinging to her back. The others scrambled uphill past them on their way to the village on the bluffs. "Mah-ree! Wake up!" Ha-xa took hold of her daughter's slim shoulders and shook her. "What is the matter with you, girl? Run, I say!" The command given, she was off after the others.

Mah-ree did not follow. She could not move. In their mad rush to take the babies and little ones to safety, the women had failed to notice that deaf old Kahm-ree still sat in the shallows of the creek, happily plucking crayfish from the rocks, and that the chieftain's second woman had fallen behind with her two daughters. Senohnim and her girls were in the direct path of the bear, while Teikan was desperately retrieving ill-spent spears. Gah-ti was rallying the boys into howling, stone-slinging, lance-hurling ranks along both shores.

What brave men and boys! thought Mah-ree as she watched them advancing behind the bear, calling it to themselves. Gah-ti was forbidden the use of a spear lest his deformity dishonor the weapon and the prey for which it was intended. The others hurled their spears, but the lances fell short or glanced off their target as the bear kept coming up the creek bed, slowed only by the dogs.

Mah-ree's heart leaped at the valor of the pack. No longer were they beasts of burden, bred and trained to carry side packs and to drag sledges from one hunting camp to another; they were what untold millennia had made them— wild, kindred of wolves and coyotes, working together with no need of Man to tell them what to do. Racing behind, ahead of, and on both sides of the bear, they leaped to the attack, confusing the marauder, nipping and biting, hurling themselves onto its sides and shoulders and snapping at its face. With dogs all over it, Walks Like a Man stopped again, stood tall, and made a quick and bloody finish to a yelping, hapless rider that had failed to leap away in time.

It was the sharp, high squeal of the dying dog that caused Senohnim to look over her shoulder as she ran. It was a mistake. Terror-stricken, she stumbled. Brought low by the great mounded weight of her belly, she fell to her hands and knees. Khat and Tinah screamed as they tried to pull their mother to her feet. Failing, they left Senohnim on all fours and ran for their lives.

In only a few moments the two fleet-footed adolescents ascended the trail and, pushing Mah-ree aside, raced frantically past her. Her fishing basket tipped, spilling her fine catch onto the ground. She did not notice. Teikan, with Gah-ti at his side, was closing on the bear from behind and howling like the boys as he approached with Ishkai's spears in hand.

"Ho, Bear!" taunted Teikan in a fury over the death of what had been one of his favorite dogs. "Are you so old and unfit a hunter that you seek the meat of women? Ha! You have killed my dog! Now come for this man *if* you dare!"

The bear, still standing upright and slapping at harrying dogs, looked down at the warrior. The beast's upraised snout and lips offered an awe-inspiring display of teeth as it shook its massive head and roared in anger.

At that moment, old Kahm-ree looked up and, for the first time, became aware of the danger standing in the creek bed between her and the hunters. The haze through which she viewed her world instantly cleared. Eyes popping, she was on her feet, stark naked, skinny legged, sag teated, and scrambling for safety with a dread-inspired agility that soon had her out of the water, off the beach, into the willows, and out of sight.

"Ho, Bear!" Gah-ti danced away from Teikan and waved his arm, keeping the bear's interest focused downstream, away from the movement of the naked old woman. "This man is not afraid of you, Bear! There is not so much to eat of me as of my brother hunter, but come, not to where he stands, but here . . . over here . . . come, eat me, if you can!"

As the bear watched the wild gesticulations and whirling of the one-armed young man, Teikan loaded the spear hurler that he carried looped by a thong around his wrist. In a matter of moments, one lance, then another and another arced toward the bear's exposed throat and midsection. Two found their mark. The third, with the added impetus of desperation, overshot the bear to such an extent that it landed just down trail of Mah-ree and came bouncing and clattering along the stony ground until it rested, remarkably undamaged, at her feet.

Mah-ree caught her breath because, somehow, she shared the pain of the bear. Overwhelmed by the shock of its injuries, it bit and pawed at the offending lances, then fell to its side with a *woof* and was immediately leaped upon by the surviving members of the dog pack.

Teikan and Gah-ti shouted in triumph. All along the creek boys were yip-yipping with pride and relief. Old Kahm-ree was peeking from the willows, and from the bluff to which they had fled, the women and girls were cheering.

Mah-ree wondered why. The bear was dying, but it was not dead. Shaking off the dogs, Walks Like a Man was rising, standing upright again, and—with the muscles of its great neck torn and weakened—straining to hold its head upright as it turned and stared back up the creek to where Senohnim, on her feet now, was hurrying forward along the trail.

And suddenly, impossibly, it seemed to Mah-ree, the bear was charging again. With Teikan's spears fixed in its body, it was making one last defiant run. Mah-ree knew that if it was not stopped, it would take Senohnim's life with its last breath.

"Aiyee . . ." wailed Senohnim, looking back. She flailed her arms forward, seemingly reaching for helping hands as, once again, the weight of her belly brought her to her knees.

No one can help you now, Second Woman of Shateh!
thought Mah-ree. *Your life is Walks Like a Man's, if he
wants it! Unless . . .*

It was in this moment that Mah-ree remembered the
spear. She looked down at it. It was a big spear, long of shaft
and heavy of head; even if it were not a weapon forbidden
to her gender, she knew that it would take a man of Teikan's
size and strength to hurl it with any accuracy. But this was
no time to worry about such restrictions. In long-gone days
before Cha-kwena had allied with Shateh, Mah-ree, fearing
the vulnerability of the band and wanting to be of help, had
secretly learned the ways of the spear. Kosar-eh had helped
her until Cha-kwena discovered what they were doing and
angrily put an end to it. Even though she had broken a taboo
of the Ancient Ones, the ancestors had apparently not been
offended, for her people had been victorious against their
enemies. And now Mah-ree wondered if the forces of
Creation had not sent Teikan's spear to her for a reason. Yes,
she thought, surely it must be so, for I am all that stands
between Great Paws and Spirit Sucker now!

With a deep, steadying breath that set the searing,
white-hot blast of pure resolve racing in her veins and heart,
Mah-ree picked up the spear and, hefting it like a man, ran
forward, screaming.

2

It was late. The sun was long down. The moon had yet to rise. Stars sprawled across the vast, black robe of the night as the hunters paused and stared toward the village. Later there would be those among the hunting party who swore that they heard Spirit Sucker calling to them long before the lamentations of the women reached their ears, but Chakwena knew that the hunters lied. No one had anticipated what awaited them as they came across the land, moving quickly to keep warm in the increasingly cold wind, taking turns carrying and dragging the meat and usable bones of the butchered horse on pallets contrived of the slain animal's hide.

Teikan came toward them, holding high an oil-impregnated torch that defined his face and form in a strange, otherworldly glow and made it seem as though he moved within a lake of molten light. When he paused he said nothing at first but looked long and hard at every man and youth in the hunting party.

At last he spoke. "Walks Like a Man has come to our people. He has sent the life spirit of Ishkai to walk the wind."

Lahontay stiffened at the news of the death of his youngest and only surviving son.

Teikan continued, "Bravely did the son of Lahontay

leap to defend the women and children of the People. Bravely did he meet Spirit Sucker as it came to him in the body of Walks Like a Man. Never has Teikan seen such a bear! In silence came Walks Like a Man. As big as a mammoth and robing himself in the wind, he has caused many brave dogs to die. And he has caused Shaman's Woman to forget that she is a woman. Mah-ree of the Red World has dishonored Walks Like a Man by placing the final lance in him! Before I could stop her she wantonly broke the commandment of the Ancient Ones and—"

"She is . . . unhurt?" Cha-kwena was light-headed with fear as he whispered the question.

Teikan's face twisted as he nodded in affirmation. "She awaits you in your lodge, Shaman, whole and unblemished and alive, while the spirit of Walks Like a Man roams the village, ashamed to join his brothers and sisters in the world beyond this world because he has lost his life to a female hand. Now, in his anger, he feeds upon the life spirits of the People. Ishkai and the dogs have not been enough for him. He has called to Senohnim and made her bring forth to him the spirit of the male child that was in her belly."

"A son . . ." Shateh's words were barely audible over the wind and the snapping flames of the torch. "Senohnim has given me a son on a night of mourning?"

"It is so, Shateh," replied Teikan. "Yet again it is so."

The chieftain sucked air through his teeth and hung his head. Cha-kwena's heart bled for him. The other hunters looked away lest they shame Shateh by glimpsing the pain he must be feeling now, for among the People of the Land of Grass, no infant born into a village or encampment during a time of mourning could be allowed to live lest its new life make jealous the spirits of the dead.

The chieftain stood unmoving in the wind as though Teikan's words had leached the life from him. No one spoke. All knew how much Shateh wanted a male child. The chieftain was strong and powerful, but he was an aging man who had outlived his many sons. Only Warakan named him Father these days, but although a heart link could be made with an adopted child, a man needed male offspring of his own blood if his spirit was to be reborn into the world of the living. Without a son or grandson to take his name at the time of his death, when Shateh died, he would die forever.

"Wehakna has done what had to be done," Teikan went on. "Before life could become life, it was denied with a gentle hand that allowed it no intake of breath. I have had the boys prepare the burning pyre for Ishkai and the dogs, and for the son of Shateh who might have been. Now the women raise songs of mourning and ask the forces of Creation to allow the spirit of our sister Senohnim to remain within her body so that she—who intended no dishonor to Bear—may live to give birth again to the son whose spirit is now meat in the ghost mouth of Walks Like a Man."

A tremor went through Shateh as he nodded. "And the body of this bear?"

"With my own hands I have brought the skin and head and heart of Walks Like a Man into the village," said Teikan. "Now that Shateh has returned, we will mourn our dead and honor the courage of this bear that has been dishonored by the shaman's woman."

"It is Shaman who has brought this bear upon us!" Lahontay spoke in a soft hiss of loathing. "In the light of morning we saw sign of this bear! In the light of this morning we all heard Shaman's words to this bear! 'Walk not in the path of the hunters, Brother! Go! Seek what you will of food elsewhere!' With the sacred stone in his hand he raised his voice to Bear and sent it out of the country of the hunters to feed upon our women and unborn children and sons and dogs!" His voice had risen to a tirade; now it broke, and the old man broke with it. "Ishkai!" he wailed. "Ishkai!"

"What Lahontay says is not so!" Cha-kwena protested. "Why would I do this?"

Shateh looked at him coldly. With a weariness that seemed to border on death, he reminded, "You have not foreseen the turning of the wind. You have driven the horses that were to have been winter meat beyond the edge of the world. You have crossed the path of Bear and not looked back. Had we returned to the village this morning, Ishkai and many dogs would still be alive, and my unborn son would still be sleeping within the belly of his mother! Why *have* you done these things, Shaman? Unless you are *not* a shaman, after all?"

"He is our enemy!" cried Lahontay.

"We will soon see what he is," replied Shateh. "But now there are dead to mourn and a bear to be honored before—"

"*I* will make the songs!" interrupted Cha-kwena. "I will raise the sacred smoke! I will—"

"You will go to your lodge and wait there with your lawbreaking woman until I, Shateh, call you forth and tell you what you will do!" The chieftain interrupted in his own turn. "For four days and nights we will fast and keep the death vigil for the spirits of our dead in the way of our ancestors. Then I will call a council. In the meantime, make your songs and your smokes as you will. Call back the herd of horses that you have driven away beyond the edge of the world. Call off the storm that will soon come to us on the back of North Wind. Chant to the spirit of Bear and to the forces of Creation and ask them not to hunger for the life of my woman! Do all this, 'Shaman,' *if* you are a shaman! For at dawn of the fifth day, if you have failed, then I will know that one who once walked strong in the power of the sacred stone and of the totem possesses power no more!"

"The power of the stone is mine, Shateh, and I alone can speak for the totem. But I can only *ask* of the spirits. I cannot *command* them."

"No? Then why should I follow you, Totem Slayer? My enemies are vanquished. The bones of the great white mammoth lie in the Valley of the Dead, and I see none of its power living on in you. I am Shateh—chieftain *and* shaman. When the time of mourning is over, if you have failed to obey my commands, you will be cast out of this band, and I will set my hunters to pursue more man-worthy meat than that which you have allowed to run away beyond the edge of the world!"

Ranamal nodded enthusiastically as he informed Tei-kan, "Earlier this day we found sign of the tuskers grazing in the badlands. One of those great cows would make enough meat to—"

"Mammoth are sacred!" Cha-kwena cried out, appalled. "Their meat is forbidden!"

"To your people, not to mine," replied Shateh.

Cha-kwena was so shaken that he stared, gape mouthed, completely unaware of the fact that he was rubbing one ankle against the other as he reminded the chieftain, "Since bringing your band to live with mine, the people of Shateh and of Cha-kwena have been one people, sworn to respect and honor each other's traditions!"

Shateh's eyes narrowed. "Today your woman has forgotten this. Today Ishkai is dead. Today a son of mine has died before he had a chance to draw breath, and Senohnim lies confined within the women's lodge too weak to rise and mourn for him! You have led my people into a barren and hungry land, Cha-kwena. I will not stand aside and allow you to welcome Spirit Sucker to feed upon them. If you *are* still a shaman and if the power of the totem lives in you, you must prove it. And prepare your lawbreaking woman to answer to the spirits for her offense to Bear!" He paused. His features convulsed. "Why do you wait? Why do you stare? Go! I, Shateh, have spoken. I am chief! And until the rising of the fifth dawn, I will be shaman as well!"

Cha-kwena was afraid. The night pressed down on him as he walked alone to his lodge. The wind mocked him as he leaned into it and tried not to shiver from its ever-increasing cold. He stared upward, through long, thin veils of cloud at the star children of Moon. He saw the vast sweep of the Sky River. Allowing his eyes to wander, he soon found the bright little multicolored cluster of Many Old Women; the cold, glinting, malevolent eyes of the ever-battling Twin Brothers. Not far from the Great Bear and shining pale and steadily toward the north in the hunting grounds of the Great Snake he saw the Watcher, the one constant star around which all the others seemed to turn.

Cha-kwena's right hand rose to his throat as he continued on and, suddenly, with the sacred stone clenched within the curl of his fist and starlight shimmering in his eyes, Vision flared red with warning at the back of his brain; it was like a tattered patch of storm sky glimpsed through scudding fair-weather clouds.

"North." Cha-kwena spoke the word aloud. Everything dark and having to do with disaster in his life had always come from the north. His jaw tightened. *Including Shateh!* he thought. He paused in the cold, fixed, and bitter light of the North Star before entering the firelit peripheries of the village. He had reached his own lodge and was glad that it stood well apart from the others. He was in no mood to confront anyone but Mah-ree.

"Cha-kwena!"

He looked up. The cry had come from Mah-ree's mother. Cha-kwena saw Ha-xa break from the women and girls who danced around the fire that had been raised within the open area between the well-spaced, circling lodges. She was the last person he wanted to talk to. Ha-xa had never allowed her daughters to forget that they were the children of a chieftain; he blamed the woman for Mah-ree's stubborn arrogance. With a furious sweep of his hand, he gestured her back and away, then turned, brushed aside the elk-hide door flap of his lodge, and entered angrily.

Mah-ree was waiting for him. "If I had not run forward to place Teikan's lance, Senohnim would be dead now!" She spoke a defensive rush of words. "They have no right to be angry! They should be thanking me instead of banishing me to our lodge!"

Cha-kwena could see her clearly in the gloom of the stone oil lamp. A small, nearly naked figure kneeling dejectedly on their neatly laid bed furs, she looked so young and vulnerable that he could not bring himself to tell her that Shateh had just commanded him to prepare her to answer to the spirits for her offense to Bear. What would be asked of her? he wondered. *Her life.* He was sure of it.

"I tell you, my shaman, the forces of Creation sent that spear from Teikan's hand to mine! I did not seek it!"

"You have broken the law of the ancestors, Mah-ree!"

"And saved a life," she said petulantly.

"Have you?"

She pouted and shook her head. "The forces of Creation would not have sent the spear to me if they had wanted Senohnim to—"

"Will you never stop guessing at the wishes of the spirits, Mah-ree?" Cha-kwena was suddenly furious with her as he bent, pulled off his moccasins, and threw them at her. "Here! Take these! Thanks to your carelessness and stubbornness, these boots have nearly been the end of me this day!" He turned away from her startled stare and, rubbing his suppurating, abraded ankles, stood with his back to her. In one hand he held the door skin partially open and across his body; the other hand curled around the sacred stone as he stared into the wind across the darkness that lay between his feather-festooned lodge and the main body of the village.

The scene that met Cha-kwena's eyes burned his senses. Shateh and the others had returned. They had joined the dancers around the fire now. Men, women, children— his people and Shateh's—one people now, moving together, howling and wailing and raising funereal rhythms upon flutes and drums while they circled the wind-whipped flames beneath the effigy that Teikan had raised of the bear.

Cha-kwena had been too distraught to notice it when he had first returned to the village. Now the sight of it was overwhelming. On a frame of erect, cross-braced poles planted securely in the earth, Teikan had mounted the head and stretched the skin of Walks Like a Man so that the animal appeared to look down at the dancers with its forelimbs spread wide, its heart in its mouth, and its neck adorned with garlands of sacred sage that the women and children had made for it.

"You could say that you are glad that Walks Like a Man did not eat me," Mah-ree said peevishly. "He could have, you know. I was *that* close before I hurled the lance. And then I pulled Senohnim away just before he fell dead at our feet!"

Cha-kwena imagined her racing toward the living presence of the monster that now hung upon the poles before the fire. Although he was amazed and impressed, he refused to feed her arrogance by admitting either. He stared at the bear and wondered if he would have had the courage to face it down. With the claws of its back legs touching the ground, the animal towered well over eleven feet above the mound of its own meat and bones that had been piled beneath it. Anger flared within him. How could Mah-ree have so wantonly risked her life and broken the law of the tribe to save the life of the chieftain's smug, self-serving second woman?

Cha-kwena frowned. The people were hungry, but when their fast was done he knew they would consume the four-day-old meat of the slaughtered mare before they would eat the flesh of a man killer and dog slayer; nevertheless, because a woman of their band had shamed this bear in life, they would honor its spirit by sending it to the world beyond this world through fire. Soon they would feed its meat and bones to the same flames to which they had already consigned their own beloved Ishkai and Shateh's newborn son. *But first they will come for my Mah-ree.* He felt sick with dread as he watched their ritual.

Now, led by Shateh, the members of Ishkai's family were mutilating themselves with stone daggers while his widow gave her man's belongings to the flames. Old Lahontay, as naked and bloody as in the moment of his birth, raised his arms to the night and howled like a gut-wounded wolf.

"Come away from the sight of it, my shaman, and close our lodge to their music and howling and the stink of their offerings! At times like this, their ways are not our ways. I do not understand how those who have come with us from

the Red World can join with them . . . even my own
mother and sisters!"

Cha-kwena scowled. Not one of the men or boys from
the Red World had spoken to defend him. And now they
danced and wailed with their women, sliced their skin in the
ultimate gesture of respect for the dead, and howled until
they were indistinguishable from Shateh's warriors and
women.

"They are of the Red World no longer." He breathed in
the stench of burning flesh and bones and fat and hair.
Suddenly Vision took him—seared him—and then left him
sick and shaken. Blood welled thick and hot at the back of
his throat, eyes, and nostrils. He could taste it, see it, smell
it. It was the blood of his Vision. Numbly he let go of the
door flap and faced his woman. "We must go from this
place," he told her.

Mah-ree held up his moccasins. "I will need time to
repair these."

"We have no time. We must go *now*!"

"What are you saying, my shaman? No one may leave
the village until the grieving time is over—four days, four
nights. The spirits of the dead will walk the world of the
living until then. If they find us alone, outside the protection
of the village, in their hunger for life they will eat us!"

Cha-kwena could feel her soft brown eyes questing
worriedly over him in the mellow light of the stone lamp.
He could not reply. How could he tell his little girl-of-a-
woman that he had seen Death flying ahead of him in the
guise of Raven, while painted, faceless men in the skins of
wolves ran wild as they hunted a sacred mammoth? Beneath
a bloodred sky they ripped the unborn totem from its belly
to savage and consume it. How could he admit that he had
seen himself impotent and cowering naked within the mists
of a great black canyon while an enormous bear stood
upright like a man to challenge his progress along a dream
path that was littered with mammoth tusks and skulls and
dismembered bones? He knew those bones. They gleamed
like shards of ice in the cold light of a compassionless

winter moon. They were the bones of the unborn totem. They were *Mah-ree's* bones. And *his* own.

"We cannot stay in this place," he said. "Gather up your traveling things. Hurry. I will wear the hunting shoes that I brought with me from the Red World. We must not be here when they come for you."

"Come for me? *Who* will come for me? *Why?*"

He realized then that he must tell her—simply, directly. "Shateh has told me to prepare you to answer to the spirits for what you have done."

She made a face of annoyance that did not quite mask her fear. "I have risked my life to save his woman! Let *him* answer to *me* for that!"

With a huff of righteous indignation, she rose and went to her man, bringing his sleeping robe and wrapping it around his shoulders and her own. Beyond the wood and bone-braced walls of the little shelter, a mammoth trumpeted nearby, to the east, and dire wolves began to sing in high, shifting harmony with the wind and the wailing mourners.

"Listen," she whispered, snuggling against him. "The mammoth have come close to the village. I am never afraid when they are near. I will go to Shateh. He will listen to my words and understand."

"His unborn son is dead, Mah-ree. He—" Cha-kwena tensed. The mammoth trumpeted again, much closer this time. The young shaman listened, transfixed. Vision, bright and transcendent, flared again. He drew his woman close and spoke as though out of a dream. "It has been said by the Ancient Ones that in time beyond beginning, a great white mammoth led Father and Mother of all the generations of People out of the world of spirits and into the world of the living. Across a sea of ice they came, through corridors of endless storm, across forbidden lands. And always the great mammoth walked before them—Life Giver, totem to them and to their children forever. . . . And so it shall always be, until the day when the last of the mammoth kind walk no more upon the earth, for on that day Man and all of his children will perish!"

"It is a tale known to all. Why do you tell it to me now, my shaman?"

Cha-kwena shivered. The warmth of his little lodge embraced him, as did his woman; neither brought comfort to his ravaged senses. "For all we know, Mah-ree, the mammoth that trumpet out there in the night *are* the last of their kind. If you do not fear for your own life, you must fear for theirs."

"I do not understand. There are no mammoth hunters in this land."

"Shateh was a mammoth hunter once. He will be a mammoth hunter again."

Her eyes were enormous as she looked up at him. "But he has sworn not to do this! He has named you Brother. He has taken our little band into the protection of his great hunting circle and has made our people his people. I know that his women and some of his hunters complain about this bad country, but Shateh has turned his back upon the land of his ancestors because he believes that the power of the totem lives in you and—"

"He believes this no more. Listen to them, Mah-ree. You have said it with your own mouth: Their ways are not our ways. It was a mistake for me ever to have imagined that our two peoples could live as one. Before the time of mourning is over, Shateh will make you answer with your life to the spirit of Bear. Then his people will hunt mammoth, with their new brothers from the Red World at their side. I will not be able to stop them unless . . ." He paused. His hand sought his medicine bag. With the sacred stone held tightly within his fist, Cha-kwena knew what he must do. "North Wind speaks in the voice of the White Giant Winter and promises early snow that will cover our tracks. Now, while others mourn, we will leave this village. We will drive the mammoth ahead of us, over the edge of the world, where they will be safe from those who would hunt them."

Mah-ree, aghast, caught her breath. "We cannot go alone over the edge of the world with a storm coming after us! There are no people in that land! There is no game! You must tell Shateh our secret, my shaman! He will not lead others to hunt mammoth after he learns that the life spirit of the totem lives on not in you but within the—"

Cha-kwena struck her. It was a hard, openhanded, downward slap across the lower half of her face, and as he held his hand pressed against her mouth he saw tears well in her eyes. But he was not sorry. "You have half crippled me this day with your careless sewing! You have dared to use a weapon forbidden to your gender! And now your tongue runs like a river at spring flood! Someday your words and your willfulness will overflow the banks of caution and drown us both! To speak of a much-wanted thing before it has happened is to risk bringing dark spirits against it! You know this as well as I!"

She nodded penitently.

He released his hand.

Snuffling to keep back tears, she sent the tips of her fingers questing upward to press her split upper lip gently. "If we go now, alone, without a word to the others, what will happen to our people?"

"They are Shateh's people now!" he told her impatiently, turning away from her frightened face; it was bleeding and swelling with a hurt that he ached to kiss away. "This they have chosen. Tleea-neh and Xet have taken Land of Grass women. Ghree and her daughter are the women of Land of Grass men. Ranamal has looked at my mother and asked her to be his woman. They will come to no harm after we are gone."

"But when will we see them again?" Her throat was constricted, her voice a mere croak.

"Never," he said, and tried not to hear her sniffling and sobbing softly as he hurriedly began to assemble the garments and belongings they would need in the long, cold days and nights ahead.

"Never is a very long time, Cha-kwena."

He rolled his eyes as he worked. "For once in your life, Mah-ree, do as you are told. I will not leave you behind to betray our secret to Shateh!"

"Or to answer to the spirit of Bear?"

"That is no more than you deserve!" he snapped. "Then at least I would be free of you!"

The intake of her breath was the sound of one who has just been stabbed in the heart. "I am your woman, my shaman. I would not let you run away over the edge of the world without me! But never to see my sisters or my mother again—"

"Forget them! You must look to your skin now, before you are asked to offer it to the spirit of Bear!"

3

Clouds were obscuring the stars when Wehakna emerged from the lodge of blood in which Senohnim lay.

"The spirit of Shateh's second woman still fights to remain within her body! But Senohnim is weak from baby birthing, and the calling power of the spirit of the woman-shamed Bear is strong."

The fire was still high. The dancers stopped. All stared toward Wehakna, then to their chieftain. He stared back, tall, silent, haggard. Several moments passed before his eyes found Ha-xa among the women and girls.

"Go! Bring your lawbreaking second daughter to the fire! Shaman's Woman must speak for the life of Senohnim to the spirit of Walks Like a Man. Lawbreaker must answer to the one she has shamed. If Bear must have the meat of woman this night, it will be the meat of the Red World woman who has—"

"Shateh . . ." The tight, tremulously formed interruption came from Ta-maya, who was among the women and girls. Stepping forward, she faced the chieftain. "My sister meant no—"

"Silence, Daughter of the Red World! I will hear no words from you tonight!" The chieftain's voice was as hard and uncompromising as his expression. "You! Ha-xa! You will obey!"

47

With her jaguar-skin cloak around her shoulders, Ha-xa held her head high. Ever since Cha-kwena had refused to hear the words of warning that she had so desperately longed to speak, fear had been living within her. But she would allow no one to see it. All through the dancing, her eyes had strayed toward the shaman's lodge in hope of seeing the solitary cone of pollen-yellow light grow dim when the oil lamp within guttered from lack of attendance; this would have been a sure sign that Cha-kwena and Mah-ree had run away. But even now the shaman's lodge glowed softly in the wind-whipped night, and she could see a silhouetted form moving within.

Ah, Second Daughter! You were brave enough to break the laws of the ancestors in your challenge to Bear! Why have you not been brave enough to challenge the spirits of the dead and run away this night? Why has Cha-kwena not made you run?

"Ha-xa!" Shateh shouted her name.

She unflinchingly met his gaze. She understood his predicament. He was chief, shaman. He was father, husband. Ha-xa knew his heart and saw pity for her in his hard eyes. Her head went higher. She pitied him as well. She had lived among his people long enough to know that Shateh was a good man, a fair man. He was doing no more than he must do as chief. A daughter of her body had broken the law, and now the ghost of Walks Like a Man was feeding on his people. He had no choice but to yield to the spirit what it must have—the meat of the one who had broken the law of the ancestors and shamed the spirit of Bear. Unless . . .

The idea had been forming in Ha-xa's mind all through the dance. Now, as she stared across the pyre to where Shateh stood with the other men beneath the effigy of Bear, the notion flared to a brightness that sang within her as she threw her arms wide and cried out to the forces of Creation and to the ghost of Walks Like a Man, "I am Ha-xa! I am mother of Mah-ree! Her shame is my shame! Her blood is my blood! Her flesh is my flesh! Take my meat, Bear! It is Red World woman's meat! It is the meat of a chieftain's woman who has borne life in her belly and is more worthy of your great spirit than the meat of the barren-bellied little one who has shamed you! Look! This woman is not afraid! Bravely comes Ha-xa to Walks Like a Man in Mah-ree's place!"

"Mother, *no!*" screamed Ta-maya.

The voice of her eldest daughter was not the last sound that Ha-xa heard as she raced to the pyre and hurled herself into the flaming embrace of Fire.

"Ha-xa!"

Was it Shateh's cry, or was it the ghost voice of Bear? She could not tell. Others were shouting, calling, but their voices were far away, beyond a cracking, hissing, all-encircling wall of explosive heat and light.

Ha-xa . . . Ha-xa . . . Ha-xa . . .

It was the voice of Fire, welcoming her with pain, searing her, devouring her, taking her into itself until, despite her best effort at control, she was screaming and screaming and . . .

Mah-ree stopped dead in her tracks. "Did you hear that, Cha-kwena?"

Pausing, he turned on his heels to scowl at her in the darkness. They had come far since leaving the village, but not far enough to satisfy him. "You must stop looking back, Mah-ree. It will be snowing soon. The mammoth are near, moving ahead of us. I can smell them. We must keep them moving."

Mah-ree tried to swallow her apprehension; it lodged in her throat and burned upward along the back of her palate to sear her sinuses. The wind was very cold. It blew steadily from the north except for occasional erratic gusts that came from the east, bringing with them the strong, glandular scent of mammoth; it was a smell unlike any in the world, she thought, but her heart was too heavy to think of mammoth now. "But someone was screaming, Cha-kwena, and it sounded like my mother!"

He could not deny the truth. "The wind still brings us

the sounds of the village. No doubt Shateh has asked someone to summon you to the fire, and Ha-xa, realizing what he has in mind for you, has cried out in fear for your life. Come, I say! She has stopped screaming now. They will be after us soon!"

"On a night of mourning? With the spirits of the dead still—"

"They will follow us, Mah-ree, to capture you so that they can *appease* the spirits of the dead!"

She knew that he was right. Still facing into the gusts of wind, she heard the high ululations of bereft women and caught the essence of charred flesh, stronger now than it had been for some time. "They must be feeding the meat of Bear to the fire."

"It may be," he said evasively, doubting very much if they would do this before they had the meat of the Red World woman to send to the spirit world alongside Bear. The thought was distressing. What, then—or who—were they burning?

"It is not like my mother to scream. She is brave, Cha-kwena, a chieftain's woman!"

A terrible wave of awareness swept through Cha-kwena. It was not Vision. It was acknowledgment of a possibility that he would not voice to his woman, but one that he should have considered before now. Suddenly the night felt colder, darker, more full of threat than before. "You are a chieftain's daughter and a shaman's woman," he reminded Mah-ree. "Come, I say! Obey your man! Do not look back again!"

The sound of a woman's soft, happy humming caused Shateh to pause before the shaman's lodge. The other men were at his back.

"How can she sing while the other women keen as her mother burns?" exclaimed Teikan.

"She will soon sing another song, one that will sound more like screaming!" vowed Lahontay.

"Be silent, old man!" demanded Kosar-eh. "Have you no pity? She sings in fear and in remorse!"

"Please, Shateh," implored Gah-ti, "Ha-xa has given herself to Bear. Let that be enough!"

The chieftain ignored them all. He was shaking with anger and frustration. *Ha-xa!* What a proud, brave woman she had been! If she had been a son maker instead of one who birthed only daughters, he would have welcomed her to share his bed furs many a long moon before. Thinking of her leaping into the flames to keep the spirit of Bear from feeding upon his smug, petulant Senohnim was more than he could stand! With a furious sideward sweep of his hand, he slapped the door flap of the shaman's lodge aside and glared in at the daughter whose lawbreaking had caused the death of her own mother. The girl deserved to die, and her powerless, death-bringing "shaman" deserved to die with her. But, with a start, he saw that they were not there.

"They are gone!" informed Kahm-ree with a knowing and well-satisfied chuckle. "Long gone. Gone away!"

Shateh stared into the gloom of the lodge to see the old woman sitting alone before the warmth of the stone oil lamp. Wearing a hideous cloak of pieced red-squirrel fur draped over her head and shoulders like a molting tent, she sat with her knees bent and her moccasin-clad ankles crossed demurely in the manner of a young girl. Humming softly, she rocked slowly forward and back.

"What are you doing here, old woman?" he demanded.

She cocked her head. "What?"

He repeated his question hotly, impatiently remembering that Kahm-ree's ears received sound about as well as a rock.

"Ah," she replied. "I am hiding. Waiting for the dancing to stop. Keeping warm and away from knives. The firestone in the shaman's lodge is bigger than my own. It gives more heat to old bones on a cold night." She hummed a little before peering fixedly up at the chieftain out of a time-ruined face. "They took their winter things but left these behind for me. Such thoughtful children!"

Shateh scowled when the woman indicated the appro-
priated moccasins. Even in the dull light of the oil lamp, he
recognized them as Cha-kwena's and could see bloodstains
at the ankles. He nodded to himself. Cha-kwena *had* been
rubbing his feet on the hunt and, now and then, making
excuses to pause. With a snort of disgust, the chieftain
released the last residual faith he had left in the young
shaman's proclaimed invincibility.

"And the firestone, they left that for me, too," old
Kahm-ree babbled. "So kind of them, too, to keep a light
burning. I saw them go. Yes. And I knew that they would
want me to keep warm beside their lamp and—"

"Which way did they go?" Shateh interrupted.

"Into the dark."

"Which *way*, old woman? And how long ago?"

Kahm-ree frowned. With one hand she gestured out
and then up, and with the other she motioned around, before
shrugging and confiding in a whisper, "They have gone to
find my Ban-ya. Yes! They will bring my beloved granddaughter back to me. Shateh will forgive her. He will take
my Ban-ya to live with him again as a chief's woman. She
will suckle once more her little Red World son, Piku-neh,
and this poor woman will not be afraid of growing old with
no one of my blood to care for me except a four-summers-
old child."

Frustrated, Shateh shook his head at Kahm-ree's pathetic longing for her treacherous, long-dead granddaughter.
His mouth tightened as he thought of Ban-ya. What a
brazen, big-breasted, son-making, man-pleasing woman she
had been—and as deadly as a coiled viper. He had honored
her, a lowly lizard eater, by taking her to share his sleeping
furs along with his other wives. All he had asked of her was
a son to take his name in his old age, but she had given him
no son; instead she had conspired against him, shamed him
with a Red World man. And when Atonashkeh, the last of
Shateh's sons, had seen the viciousness of her ways, she had
baited his meat as though for a wolf and then had stood

aside and watched him die screaming. And now Shateh had no sons at all.

The chieftain's hands tightened into fists as he growled against memories. If Ban-ya were to walk into his life again, he would welcome her only to savor the pleasure of strangling her slowly. But this would never be. At his decree she had been cast out of the band. Abandoned alone within the Valley of the Dead, denied weapons or tools or the makings for fire, she could never have survived the previous winter. And yet old Kahm-ree held fast to her belief that the cursed Ban-ya still lived and, more incredibly, dared to hope that someday Shateh would take her back. Kahm-ree had lost her wits to bereavement many a moon before; asking her questions about Cha-kwena and Mah-ree was as foolish as talking to a dog and expecting answers.

Disgusted with himself for wasting time with the old hag—and for having failed to post a guard at the shaman's lodge to prevent Cha-kwena from fleeing with his woman—Shateh turned and stomped out into the night.

Snow had begun to fall. Wolves were once again singing with the wind. The others were waiting. The chieftain stared at them, and although it was dark, he could see enough of their faces to know that they had overheard every word.

"We will go after them!" declared the hunter Rek ferociously. "We will bring the Red World woman back to the village. If we are to save the life of Shateh's second woman, we *must* feed the lawbreaking lizard eater to the spirit of Bear through fire!"

"It is so!" affirmed Teikan. "We will take the sacred stone from the lizard eater! We will place it around the neck of a true and *worthy* shaman! It will be for *Shateh,* as it has been intended since time beyond beginning. Come! Let us go now!"

"No! It cannot be!" Lahontay's statement was an agonized wail of frustration. "Do not listen to Teikan! He could not save my son from that which Cha-kwena called down upon the village! How can he tell us what to do now?

Do you not see what Totem Slayer has done? Have you forgotten the other names by which he is called? He is Yellow Wolf, the spirit brother of Coyote! He is Trickster! I tell you, once he stood with us in war against our enemies, but he is Enemy now! Today he failed to lure us over the edge of the world to our death! Now, by running away with the sacred stone, he hopes to trick us into leaving this village before the time of mourning is over. If we do this, we will have spurned the laws of the Ancient Ones, and the spirits of our own dead will feed upon us! Tell them, Shateh! Tell them all that this is so!"

The chieftain did not reply. The fury that had driven him from the scene of Ha-xa's burning had passed. His senses felt battered, both by the assault of the old hunter's words and by the cold wind that made his lacerated skin ache—he had come naked and bleeding from the fire. He stood still, listening to the song of the wolves and to the keening of women, and when he drew in the scent of the funeral pyre, a terrible fatigue swept through him. How many sons and warriors and women had he mourned in his lifetime? How many wolves had he trapped and slain, and how many storms and enemies had he survived? A sigh of bitter acquiescence went out of him. *Too many,* he thought. *Far too many.* And now, once again, death and sorrow and betrayal blew on the rising wind of a coming storm.

"The spirits of the dead will not eat Shateh or his hunters! They will understand our need and lead us to the lawbreakers! And if they do not, we will fight them!"

Shateh was startled by the outcry and by its source. His brow came down as he saw little Warakan elbowing his way through the ranks of men and youths to stand before him.

"If Shateh hunts Trickster's lawbreaking woman, this boy will not be afraid to stand with his father against the spirits of the dead!" declared the boy, small and proud and brimming with bravado.

"I will come, too! I am not afraid!" The proclamation came from Namaray, eldest of Teikan's aggressive pack of broad-bodied, sturdy sons.

Shateh scowled down at both boys. He was impressed by their audacity, but he was also angered by it. "Since when do untested youths speak as men to their chieftain or assume that they have the right to tell Shateh or any other man what to do? Take yourselves from my sight!"

Scalded by the hotly spoken rebuke, Warakan and Namaray shrank obediently into the ranks of the other youngsters.

"The boys are rude, but they are right, Shateh," said Teikan. "We must hunt the lawbreaking woman. She must answer to Walks Like a Man for what she has done. If she does not, how will the ghost spirit of the shamed Bear be satisfied?"

"How do you know that he is not satisfied?" asked Kosar-eh in grim allusion to Ha-xa's sacrifice. "A chieftain's woman has come to him tonight in fire."

"The Red World woman of a lizard-eating chief?" Teikan's exclamation revealed his contempt. "She was not the one who shamed Walks Like a Man! He does not want her meat! She was *old!*"

The weariness in Shateh was growing. *Old?* The word bruised him. Ha-xa had not been old. Her face had been only a little furrowed. Her hair had only just begun to gray. She had cared for her youngest daughter, done her full portion of woman's work without complaint, gone with regularity to shed moon blood in the women's lodge, and, when he had now and then claimed his right as chieftain to penetrate a manless widow, their coupling had been good, easy, a mutual giving and accepting of pleasure—nothing more, nothing less. He would miss Ha-xa. And he would never think of her as old, for if she had been aged, what, then, was he? The question disturbed him.

"I tell you, Shateh," Teikan was still pressing earnestly, "now, before snow obliterates their tracks, we must hunt the lawbreakers! We must bring them back to the village and to the fire!"

Shateh had had enough of Teikan's unsolicited opinions. "It seems that Cha-kwena is not the only one to forget that Shateh is chief!" The clear warning and command for silence and obedience were in his tone.

Only Gah-ti failed to heed it. "Let Ha-xa's sacrifice be enough! Mah-ree risked her life to save the chieftain's second woman! Shateh cannot hunt such a brave heart with the purpose of offering her spirit to Bear through fire!"

Shateh was stunned as the one-armed young man rushed boldly from among the Red World hunters to place himself directly in front of him, so close that they might have touched noses had they been of equal height. Appalled by Gah-ti's unprecedented disrespect of rank, the chieftain took a backward step, only to find the shaman's lodge skins pressing against his heels.

"You should have seen her, Shateh!" Looking up at the chieftain, Gah-ti brazened on with his impassioned plea. "You cannot give Mah-ree to Fire or to the spirit of Bear! Neither are worthy of her! When Walks Like a Man came for Senohnim, no Land of Grass woman was as bold as Mah-ree, Medicine Maker of the Red World. When Teikan's spears failed to bring down the—"

"You are not fit to speak among men when the mourning fire burns high and the spirits of the dead walk my village!" interrupted Shateh. Suddenly energized by a surge of pure outrage, he struck out at Gah-ti with the full force of his right fist, dropping the one-armed man where he stood before he could offer further insult to the spirits of Fire and Bear, to Teikan, or to himself.

Staring down at the sprawled offender, Shateh, livid, massaged the bruised knuckles of his right hand. Gah-ti's breath had touched his face and invaded his nostrils. He could still smell it. Revolted, he wondered how a maimed, one-armed man had dared to presume such intimacy. Breath was spirit! Breath was the invisible blood of life! Breath was exchanged only in mutual accord as an expression of respect among equals or of affection between lovers, hunt brothers, hearth sisters, and between parents and children. Gah-ti was none of these things to Shateh! Even in the darkness, the chieftain could see the stump that was all that

remained of the young man's right arm and the scarred half
of his head as, levering with his left arm, Gah-ti fought to sit
up and then to stand.

Shateh's emotions were in turmoil. It was all he could
do to keep himself from knocking the offending cripple
down again. Of what good to the tribe was such a man as
Gah-ti? He was useless on the hunt. No woman would have
him. Children mocked him. Men and boys were sobered by
the sight of him and, fearful of ending their days looking
like Gah-ti, sometimes suffered dreams that threatened to
weaken their courage when they were called to prove their
valor on the hunt. In the Land of Grass such a man would
have been granted a quick death at the time of his injury; to
have allowed him to live would have been considered a
danger to the band as well as an affront to the forces of
Creation and to the man himself. Yet the Red World people
had not killed this mutilated son. They kept him alive as
surely as they nurtured his blind little sister, Doh-teyah, and
the addled old deaf woman, Kahm-ree. *Why?* Glaring at the
shaken Gah-ti, Shateh realized that he did not understand
the Red World people any more than he understood what
had possessed him to allow a maimed youth, a blind child,
and the deaf old grandmother of a murderess a place within
his own tribe when he had agreed to join forces with
Cha-kwena.

Cha-kwena. The name of the runaway shaman soured
the chieftain's mouth. *Cha-kwena possessed you. Cha-
kwena made you believe in his power. But now that the
totem is dead and the war is over, Cha-kwena has no more
power than the stone he wears. Yet still you follow him. You
have yielded to Red World ways. You have turned your back
on the land and the customs of your ancestors. How could
the forces of Creation not punish you? You have forgotten
the truth that first impelled you to be chief in the days of
your youth—that in changing times men must learn new
ways or die, and that true power lies not in stone talismans,
in the flesh and blood of totem animals, or even in the magic
of the wisest of shamans, but in the strength and courage of*

*the man who is not afraid to act for the good of his people,
no matter what the cost!*

Shateh's eyes narrowed. Rage had left him. He was
calm now and no longer tired. In the cold wind, with hard
pellets of snow stinging his skin and with the stench of the
funeral pyre in his nostrils, the song of wolves overrode the
wailing of women. He knew their song: It was the high
summoning of the winter pack, the calling of brothers and
sisters to come together with the lead wolf, to run before the
storm in search of meat to be cached and carried across the
land into winter dens. He half closed his eyes and listened,
feeling stronger, sure of himself again, recalling winter
hunts and gatherings of his own tribe. *You are so like men,
my brothers,* he thought, and he knew what he must do: He
must now reaffirm his position as lead wolf of his own pack
and retake the power he had so mistakenly yielded to
another.

"The wolves speak to warn us that the White Giant
Winter will come early and stay long in this far land into
which Cha-kwena has led us," Shateh said in a strong,
measured voice that fully conveyed his newfound sense of
power and commitment. "Snow flies, and game runs away
from the spears of our hunters in this bad country. In the
land of our ancestors, the Dry Grass Moon rises, and the
many bands of our people gather to welcome the bison as
they come down from the high country. The hides will be
prime for lodge making. The hump steaks will be thick with
fat. Too long has it been since my people have tasted such
meat! Too long have we listened to the Red World shaman,
who has lied to us about his power and led us from the land
of our people so that his little band of lizard eaters would be
safe and protected within the greater hunting circle of
Shateh!"

Kosar-eh had not moved from his place among the Red
World men to protest when Shateh had struck his son. Now,
though, he stiffened and stood defensively tall. "It is the
greater hunting circle of Shateh that chose to follow
Cha-kwena over the edge of the world."

"No more will we follow him!" Shateh eyed the Red World warrior sharply even as he added in the way of conciliation, "You have proved yourself in battle and on the hunt many times, Man Who Spits in the Face of Enemies. You and your youngest sons and your Red World woman are welcome among my people. This, also, do I say to the other brave fighters from the Land of Lizard Eaters. You are welcome to return with your Land of Grass women to the country of Shateh's ancestors. The People *will* be one—but not here, not at the edge of the world. In four days' time, after we have mourned our dead in the way of our ancestors, we will leave this bad land and return to the country of our grandfathers—all save One Arm and Blind Daughter and the old woman Kahm-ree. They will stay behind."

"I cannot abandon my son and daughter!" Kosar-eh's voice and broad, hunt-marred face convulsed with emotion.

"You have other sons! You can make other daughters!" Shateh was adamant. "On the day you earned the name Lion Slayer, you should have let the one-armed son die! And when the fever spirits took the sight of the girl-child Doh-teyah, so, too, should the child have been given to the spirits. This is the way of the People of the Land of Grass. On this night in which the bodies of my newborn son and Ishkai and Ha-xa of the Red World burn in fire, I, Shateh, say that no longer will I tolerate the unfit to live among my people! Only when we have cast them out and returned to the ways of our Ancient Ones will the forces of Creation smile once more upon us. All save One Arm will go back to the fire. He is forbidden to return to the village. He will go with the old woman into the night. He will go now. If I or any man or woman among my people is forced to look upon his face again, I will kill him where he stands! Come now, we must prepare to hunt the lawbreakers, and Kosar-eh must do as he should have done long ago with his blind child."

Shateh paused and, staring at Kosar-eh, waited for further protest. The man stood like a tree; whatever his emotions now, his face was set, expressionless. Gratified, Shateh nodded. The big warrior from the Red World was a valuable asset to his band; he would not want to lose him over a cripple and a sightless child.

The others—all save young Warakan, the stunned Gah-ti, and old Lahontay—were turning away, obeying their chieftain's command.

"Beware," warned the elder. "The spirits of the dead roam the wind this night, and Enemy will try to trick Shateh into following him over the edge of the world!"

"Let him try! It cannot be done!" snorted a proudly confident Warakan.

Shateh's brows expanded. "I will be wary, old friend," he assured Lahontay just as a mammoth trumpeted somewhere to the east. "Listen," he urged, noting that the song of the wolves was intermittent now and still coming from the same direction. "You forget that I am also a shaman, Lahontay. Cha-kwena will be moving eastward with his woman, attempting to drive his totem animals before him and out of the range of our spears." He shook his head in disparagement of the attempt. "I tell you, Lahontay, since the death of the great white mammoth totem, the Red World shaman has no power. Let him run where he will. Soon there will be other wolves at his heels than the ones you hear following him now. And from the wolves of Shateh, he and the mammoth will find no escape."

"He will know you are following!" cried Gah-ti. "He will—"

"The dead do not speak!" interrupted Shateh, and for the second time in one night, he struck the young man down. Then, with head held high, the chieftain returned to the village with Lahontay and Warakan.

It took Gah-ti a few moments to get to his feet. He stood alone, working his jaw back and forth, surprised to find that Shateh had not broken it. One way or the other, he did not care. He wanted to die. Kosar-eh had walked on with the others with never a backward glance.

Behind Gah-ti, within the shaman's lodge, old Kahm-ree was singing about days gone by, about happy times, about the sacred stone and the great white mammoth totem and the legendary powers of a young shaman who led his people ever eastward into the face of the rising sun. Gah-ti did not turn as he listened to her song. The totem was dead! The sacred stone was gone! The shaman had no power! Poor old Kahm-ree had no idea of what lay ahead for her, or she would not be singing. If she had knowledge of the tragedies of this day, neither her tone nor her lyrics gave hint of it. Perhaps it was a good thing that she lived in the past, he thought. Perhaps the past was all that was left to him, too.

Gah-ti frowned. The movement of his brow tightened his scalp; the scarred half, already stiffened by the cold wind and falling snow, began to ache. Listening to Kahm-ree's song, he found himself thinking that the scabs of forgetfulness dulling her mind were not dissimilar from the scars protecting the raw, tender flesh that still lay beneath the surface of his wounds. The observation depressed him. He felt no affection for the old woman, but as Gah-ti listened to her lapse into a light, childish, breathy chant, he could not help pitying her . . . and himself.

He continued to stare after the others. They had reached the pyre. Their bodies stood in silhouette against the flames. Gah-ti trembled, longing for warmth. His heart ached so badly, he could barely breathe. Maybe Kosar-eh would turn and come back for him! Maybe all of the Red World men would do the same! They would come and face him and say that it was better to part company with Shateh's great tribe than to leave a single man, woman, or child of the Red World behind to die. But they did not turn. They were talking low with their women or going off to their various lodges now—all save one. Kosar-eh stood alone, staring toward the little lodge within which the elderly Land of Grass women, Xama and Unal, kept watch over the babies.

Shivering violently in the wind, Gah-ti knew that his little sister, Doh-teyah, slept within that lodge. Would Kosar-eh now obey Shateh's command? Would he go to that soft, sweet-natured, sleeping baby, take her into his big hands, and do with her as Wehakna had done to Shateh's newborn son? Gah-ti's heart leaped in agony. His love for his sister shook him more cruelly than did the idea of his own abandonment. Unlike the others, little Doh-teyah could not see his stump or the hideous scar that marred his head; she smiled at the sound of his name and reached for him with eager arms whenever he came near.

"I will take Doh-teyah from the lodge! I will not let my sister die!" proclaimed Gah-ti as he took an angry step forward, and then another before being brought up short by the realization that he could never reach any of the lodges without being seen. If he was seen, he would be killed. Saving Doh-teyah had given purpose to his life. The awareness that he did not want to die surged through him. Now he could see his father moving toward the lodge in which Doh-teyah lay. Someone was with him—a pregnant woman, clinging to his arm—trying to stay his progress. Gah-ti knew that it was Ta-maya. Once again he felt pity for another. She had lost her mother and sister this night. Now her man was turning his back forever upon his firstborn son and was about to smother her beloved little stepdaughter.

As Gah-ti saw several women hurry to pull Ta-maya away from Kosar-eh, he heard her cry, "Kosar-eh! Man of My Heart! No! Please, no!"

Kosar-eh continued on without her.

Gah-ti felt sick as he realized that even if he were to race forward, he would not be able to deter his father. He would be stopped by others—he, a one-armed man with no spear and no hope of saving his sister or himself.

Tears stung beneath his lids. He tried to blink them away, but they pooled, then spilled and ran in scalding rivulets down his cheeks. With the snow-pebbled wind in his face, it did not seem possible that tears could burn his skin, but burn they did, as though juiced from the fibrous leaves of stinging nettle. Gah-ti's fingertips moved to wipe them away. His shame, frustration, and inner pain were more devastating than any he had ever felt before. His hand moved from his jaw to the necklace of lion's claws and fangs, which Kosar-eh had given to him when he had lain near death after being mauled. Gah-ti could still remember his father's words when Kosar-eh had presented it to him:

The spirit of the lion that has taken Gah-ti's arm lives in these claws and teeth! I have cut them from the great maned cat and strung them on a thong of sinew taken from that lion's body. May they sharpen and strengthen the spirit of my son in the days and nights of healing to come. The spear of Gah-ti has slain this lion. Brave is the son of Kosar-eh!

"Too brave!" Gah-ti cried as he recalled stalking the lion and venturing alone into its cave, vowing to prove his valor to Mah-ree so that she would look at him, instead of at Cha-kwena, with the favor he so desired. At the time, she had not yet officially become Shaman's Woman, and although Gah-ti was younger and viewed by many as a boy, he had been so sure that if he could slay the lion and come away with its skin as a gift for her, she would . . .

He swallowed down the rest of the supposition. The old longing still hurt. Gah-ti could not remember a time when he had not loved Mah-ree, and he could not remember a time when she had not loved Cha-kwena. The latter obstacle to his intentions had never seemed insurmountable. Even when Mah-ree was with her shaman, Cha-kwena always seemed to have his mind on other things. And so, desperate to prove his love and daring, Gah-ti had ignored all warnings and, unaware that his father was following, tracked the great maned cat deep into the dark, labyrinthine hollows of a cavern. The lion, taking advantage of Gah-ti's inexperience and lack of skill, had swiped off his arm and half scalped him before he even had a chance to place a spear. Kosar-eh had done that for him. His father had made the killing thrust with one of Gah-ti's lances, but not before the lion had done its worst. And now no man, woman, or child except Doh-teyah could be in Gah-ti's presence without feeling disgust or pity.

He pulled the necklace roughly over his head, tempted to hurl it into the darkness. His life seemed a wasteland.

"Shateh was right. I should have died that day! Of what good to the tribe is a one-armed man?" Self-pity burned Gah-ti as hotly as his tears. It was an emotion that did not sit comfortably with him; it made him restless, uneasy with himself as he saw Kosar-eh pause before the lodge in which Doh-teyah slept. "Of what use is a blind child? She, too, is better dead. She—"

Gah-ti cut off any further attempt to justify the smothering of a child. Righteous indignation flared within him, and as he put the necklace back over his head he shouted, "Bring me the one you call Blind Daughter! I, Gah-ti, eldest son of Kosar-eh, will take her with me from this village! I, Gah-ti, was not afraid to stalk Lion! I, One Arm, was not afraid to call Bear to myself and away from Teikan so he could throw his spears and save the women and children. I, whom Shateh calls Unfit to Speak among Men, speak now! Kosar-eh! Do you hear me, Kosar-eh? I, Gah-ti—who no longer names you Father—will take Doh-teyah with me from this village. It is not a fit place for Red World people!"

Kosar-eh remained as he was, very still, his back to Gah-ti. Then, without turning, he bent and entered the lodge.

Breathless, Gah-ti waited. He could hear the sound of the fire, the low hiss of the wind, and the distant howling of wolves. Then two figures emerged from the lodge. Kosar-eh was not one of them. They were small, covered in fur, like ambulatory little tents advancing to the chieftain's lodge. Ta-maya ran to them. A communication was given; whatever the words, Gah-ti was too far away to hear them; but in a moment Kosar-eh's woman could be heard wailing, and Gah-ti knew that his words to his father had been in vain.

A sob escaped him. The scene before his eyes burned his senses until, distracted by the recurring howls of wolves, he remembered that his beloved Mah-ree was out there in the wind and snow, alone with Cha-kwena while the spirits of the dead roamed the night with wolves.

"Why do you stand naked in the cold wind, Gah-ti, son of Kosar-eh?"

Startled by Kahm-ree's voice, Gah-ti turned. The old woman had come from the shaman's lodge, which had now gone dark. Her face, however, glowed in the light of the circular stone oil lamp, which she cradled in the fold of one arm. Gah-ti frowned. This time when the movement of his brow awakened pain in his scalp, he took no notice; he was too taken aback by the woman's appearance. Her face, with its seams and cysts and shrunken features, was not a pretty sight, and to his amazement, she was dressed for traveling. Gloved and booted and covered from head to midcalf in her hooded, moldering squirrel-skin robe, she was bent in half under the weight of several rolled furs that she had bound to her upper back. In her free hand she held a heavy, mud-colored, long-haired camel-skin robe and, draped over her forearm, several lighter-weight furs as well as the looped ends of a pair of men's moccasins.

"Here," she offered. "Cha-kwena and Mah-ree left these few warm things behind. I thought the moccasins were for me, but I know now they were meant for you. Why do you gawk, One Arm? Before the spirits of the wind and snow sap the life from you, cover your body and put these good, high winter boots on over your camp moccasins. You cannot go naked into the night any more than you can go into the village to gather your belongings."

Gah-ti was stunned. Kahm-ree looked predictably old and ugly in the light of the oil lamp, but she also looked unexpectedly commanding and intelligent. Disbelieving, he continued to stare at her.

She stared back, winked, then chuckled. "When men stand in the wind and shout at one another in front of a lodge in which old Kahm-ree is warming her bones, even these old ears can make out an insult and a threat. Unfit, am I? Addled, am I? Hmmph! We will show them, One Arm! We will go after Cha-kwena and Mah-ree, you and I. We will be with them when they find my Ban-ya! Then Shateh will know that my—"

"Ban-ya is dead."

"No. Ban-ya lives. In my heart I would feel if her spirit

were no longer in this world. Cha-kwena and Mah-ree have
gone to find her. I have seen the way they have gone. We
will follow. Why do you stand and stare at me, Lion
Stalker? Is Bear Baiter afraid to go into the night, as Shateh
has commanded? Do not worry. Kahm-ree will take care of
you. This woman is not afraid. In her haste to run away,
Mah-ree has left behind skinning daggers and awls and
many deadly blades that will keep us both safe from
sharp-toothed hunters that pad the night on four paws. And
the light of Mah-ree's lamp will guide us and keep the
wolves away . . . as long as the oil lasts."

4

Wolves were on their scent. Cha-kwena had no idea how long they had been following or when he had first sensed their eyes boring into his back, but he knew that they were there now, padding silently, concealing themselves in the snow-ridden wind and utter darkness of the night. He paused and looked nervously back and down, glad that he had placed Mah-ree and himself upslope of them; in this, at least, they had some small advantage.

"What is it, my shaman?" asked Mah-ree, brought up short beside him by worried curiosity. "Are the spirits of the dead following us?"

"Spirits . . . or wolves."

She heard fear in his voice and looked back.

And then it happened. Either Mah-ree saw the wolves or thought she did. Exhaustion coupled with fear to birth panic within her, and suddenly she turned and bolted like a terrified rabbit down the opposite side of the hill.

"Stop, Mah-ree!" cried Cha-kwena in dismay, for even as she ran, she was slipping on stony ground made dangerously slick by a thin, rapidly accumulating layer of new snow. For a breathless moment he was sure that his woman was going to regain her footing, for she was as light and agile as any female he had ever known, and her boots were soled, as were his, in the Red World way, with raised strips of rough cording specially made to hold purchase upon the ice and snow of winter terrain. But the slope was precipitous. Now, with the weight of her antler-framed backpack pressing her forward, she fell, arms out, slid down the slope, and vanished along with a small avalanche of snow and loose scree into the darkness.

Cha-kwena followed, leaping into thin air and coming down hard on the sides of his feet. Digging in with each long, aggressive downward stride, he braced and balanced his upright posture with his spear until, at last, he was at the bottom of the hill and standing over Mah-ree's prone and motionless form. He held his breath, hoping that her heavy winter garments had broken the impact of her fall, yet he hesitated to speak her name lest silence answer the question he was afraid to ask: *Is my little girl-of-a-woman still alive?*

She did not move.

He knelt, touched her with a gloved hand, and only after what seemed forever, summoned the courage to whisper her name. "Mah-ree? My Mah-ree?"

She sighed.

Cha-kwena was so relieved that he nearly swooned. She was levering up on gloved palms. He helped her to sit up. Feeling the strength of life still strong in her and watching the fluidity of her movements, Cha-kwena knew that she was in no pain that would indicate broken bones or seriously strained tendons. In seconds she was shaking her fur-hooded head, looking feverishly around, and demanding to know if spirit wolves were still following.

"They are, and they are real enough," he told her. With snow and wind conspiring with the night, he could not see more than a few steps ahead in any direction and had yet to set eyes on the wolves. Nonetheless he could feel them watching him from the top of the slope.

"Then give me a spear, my shaman!" she cried. "Who is here to see or care if I use one now?"

He was suddenly furious with her. "*I* am here! *I* care! And even in the dark and storm of this far land, the forces of Creation see and know all things!" He was on his feet, pulling her with him. "Get up!" he commanded. "And do not run again unless it is your wish to invite wolves to chase us!" He looked around nervously. "We know you are there, my brothers and sisters!" he called to them. "We know that you follow. I am Cha-kwena, grandson of Hoyeh-tay, guardian of the sacred stone and of the totem of the People! I am Brother of Animals, Yellow Wolf, kin to you and to Coyote. Would you feed upon your own kind? If so, I warn you, my spears are sharper than your teeth, and I will take some of you with me if you loose my spirit to walk the wind forever this night!"

Mah-ree checked herself for bruises, then readjusted the weight of her pack frame with its many rolled furs and hides, a thong-attached fire horn, and fur sacks that contained the necessities of life. "If we had brought some of our dogs with us, we would have no need to fear wolves, and our pack frames would be lighter by half!" she muttered peevishly, wiping snow from her gloves, traveling robe, and leggings. "But you said that the wolves would not follow us. You said that they would be drawn to the meat of the horse that was slain this day!"

"Shateh must have set men to guard the meat and keep wolves away."

"And now *we* are the meat the wolves are seeking."

Cha-kwena did not reply. She was right. He stared into the wind, trying to see through the falling snow to the animals that were stalking him. He failed. And yet he felt them closing the distance. If the beasts managed to circle, then spring unseen to the attack, he and Mah-ree would have no chance against them. Cha-kwena put one hand on his medicine bag, wrapped the other around the haft of his spear, then prayed for strength. With his sacred owl-skin headdress worn over the hood of his traveling robe and bound securely beneath his chin by thong ties attached to the tightly crossed, withered feet of the bird, he raised his head and shouted, "Owl, spirit helper of Hoyeh-tay and now of Cha-kwena, hear me! Grant this shaman your vision in the night so that I may see those of my brothers who would make meat of me and of my woman!"

And suddenly, as though the eviscerated, feathered remains of the long-dead owl had heard and heeded the young shaman's plea, the substance of the night and snow became like water, thinning, pooling, and parting before the invasiveness of Cha-kwena's stare. The wind dropped. The snow fell straight to the ground. Mah-ree caught her breath in amazement.

Cha-kwena continued to stare toward where he thought the wolves might be. He scanned upward along the hill, following the long, snow-free tracks of Mah-ree's fall and his descent. The crest was bare of all but patches of scrub growth and occasional boulders grouped like gatherings of fat old women so pitted and ravaged by time that not even newly acquired robes of snow softened their appearance. If wolves were hiding among the shrubs and monoliths, Cha-kwena could not see them. He turned, surveyed the surrounding land, and saw long, rolling, barren sweeps of whitened plain broken only by a short run of high bluffs that stood along what seemed to be a dead-end draw.

Recognition flared. Cha-kwena knew this place! He had been here before! It was across this plain that the horses had scattered and fled from the draw within which he and his fellow hunters had hoped to trap and slaughter them. He looked around again, squinted back along the slope down which Mah-ree had tumbled, and realized that somewhere along the base of this hill, the mare had fallen with his spear in her shoulder.

His gut tightened. Now, at the top of the slope, emerging from the cover of boulders, the wolves were staring down at him in exactly the same way that he and the other men had stared down at the horses earlier in the day. With cold, sinking dread, Cha-kwena realized that he and Mah-ree had been driven to this place by the wolves as surely as he and Shateh's hunters had driven the horses. The only difference was that the wolves were the predators now. He and Mah-ree were the prey.

"Stand behind me," Cha-kwena said to his woman, and positioning his spear, fixed his eyes on the lead wolf. It was big and black and as shaggy as a bison in winter. The others were almost as large, gray or mottled tan, except one that was nearly white. Then there were the adolescents, long-legged yearlings nearly as large as the adults, and one as black and long-haired as its sire. "So many of you!" he exclaimed.

"Do you see them, Cha-kwena?" Mah-ree whispered tremulously.

"Get behind me!" he commanded again, and as she complied immediately to the imperative sharpness of his tone, he realized that she could not see the wolves; only his shaman's eyes had the power to penetrate falling snow and darkness.

He frowned. The lead wolf had stopped and raised its head. The rest of the pack now imitated the stance of their hunt chief. Cha-kwena knew that they had heard his exclamation. But what had they made of it? There had been awe in his tone. They must have taken it as a sound of weakness because they were coming forward again— slowly, cautiously, still unsure of just what sort of prey they faced.

Instinctively, Cha-kwena stood to his full height. He threw back his shoulders. He wanted to appear bigger than he was, bolder than he felt. He drew in a deep, chest-inflating breath. Now, thinking like a wolf, he extended his head. If he had been able to raise the fur on the back of his robe, he would have done so. If he had possessed a tail, he would have tucked it between his limbs and curled it over his genitals, not as a sign of submission but in warning to every member of the advancing pack that he was protecting his precious parts in preparation for attack and was fully ready to rip to pieces any foolish comer that dared move against him and his female. Snarling and showing his teeth, he began to growl as loudly and viciously as was possible for a man.

Surprised, the wolves stopped, their heads out, tails

tucked, bodies as tense as lances poised and steadied in
spear hurlers.

Cha-kwena knew that one wrong move on his part
would send them flying to the attack.

"Do you see them, my shaman?" Mah-ree quavered,
pressing so tightly to Cha-kwena's back that she could only
have come closer had she slipped inside his traveling robe.
"I see nothing but the night and falling snow! Are wolves
coming for us?"

Cha-kwena heard fear in her voice and knew that the
wolves would hear it, too. "Be still. Stand boldly. If you can
easily reach your skinning dagger, do so. But move slowly.
Do not let them know that you are afraid."

Mah-ree obeyed.

Surprised, Cha-kwena knew that she must indeed be
terrified if she gave him no argument. He could hear her
slinging off her pack, fumbling amid the rolled furs. And
then, suddenly it seemed, she was standing at his side with
a fully armed, trithonged birding sling in her hands. Before
he could utter a word, she was stepping lightly ahead of him
and to one side, the short haft of the sling held in her right
hand as she raised her arm high and set the long, stone-
tipped thongs whirling above her head until they sang in the
air like some sort of screaming spirit of destruction. In
seconds she released the weapon. Spinning, it flew forward
and upslope, still screaming, until, with a quick series of
thuds that sounded like one, its weighted arms wrapped
around the neck and snout of the lead wolf. The animal gave
a surprised *yarf* of pain, then whirled and, with its clan,
vanished among the boulders and over the far side of the
slope. Amazed, Cha-kwena nearly dropped his spear with
relief.

"Are they still there?" asked Mah-ree, stepping back to
stand close beside him again.

"No . . . they have scattered and run away."

She trembled with satisfaction and moved closer still.
"You see? It is good that you are not free of me. Are you not

glad that you have taken me over the edge of the world with you?"

Cha-kwena did not reply. He *was* glad—and sorry, sorrier than he had been about anything in his life since he had been forced to slay the great white mammoth totem. A sense of terrible loneliness and desolation nearly staggered him as the press of Mah-ree's body made him realize how small she was, how young, and, despite her bold nature and willfulness with weapons, how vulnerable. What would have happened had her sling failed to find its mark? He had one spear in hand, and three more at the ready across his upper back. Would they have been enough against so many wolves? And would they be enough if Shateh and his warriors found them?

Deeply troubled, he stared into surrounding darkness. The clarity of vision that had been a gift from the spirit of Owl had faded along with the immediate threat from the wolves. Cha-kwena viewed the night as before, not as a shaman boldly pursuing mammoth eastward into the stormy dark but as any other man would view it—his sight limited, his body weary of travel, his spirit chilled by the grim prospects that lay ahead for him and his condemned woman, venturing alone beyond the edge of the world.

Cha-kwena's jaw tightened. He told himself that they would not be alone. If they continued to follow the sacred mammoth and kept the traditions of the Ancient Ones, the spirits of their ancestors would be with them. But Mah-ree had broken the laws of the Ancient Ones that day, and he had detected neither sign nor scent of mammoth in hours. What if old Lahontay was right? What if the world did end, out there in the dark? What if all men and beasts who ventured beyond the rim of the eastern plain were doomed to fall off the edge of the world and plummet to burning oblivion in the face of the rising sun?

Cha-kwena's free hand went to his throat, pressed his medicine bag, defined the shape of the sacred stone to his palm; somehow his heart seemed to be beating there, captive within the talisman. He could barely breathe as he imagined the mammoth plodding on, blinded by snow and dark, unaware of danger until they fell off the edge of the world into the sun. *No!* he told himself. *It cannot be! Mammoth are wise and wary and walk always with a spirit armed with knowledge of the way ahead. They will not fall away into the sun or lead those who name them Totem over the edge of the world to their death!*

Taking a deep, willful breath, he steadied his nerves with the age-old assurance of the storytellers of his youth— that since time beyond beginning those men who chose to follow and protect the great tuskers always found game and grass and good water for their people. *It will be no different now!*

"We must go on," Cha-kwena said to Mah-ree. "We must seek the mammoth."

"Yes," she replied, and with uncharacteristic obedience dropped to her knees and began to reassemble her pack frame.

Cha-kwena turned his back to the wind. It was rising again and blowing hard from the northwest. It moaned eastward past him toward the open plain and sent subfreezing tides of hissing, stinging snow against the cold-stiffened feathers of his headdress and the ice-rimed guard hairs of his winter traveling robe. The mammoth were out there somewhere. He knew it. He sensed it. Cha-kwena visualized them, moving ahead of the storm and toward some mystic destination that not even a shaman sworn to protect their kind could imagine. And safe within the protection of the herd, the spirit of the great white mammoth totem was alive, growing, preparing for rebirth.

Cha-kwena's eyes narrowed. Was the wind pointing the way to the herd and to the totem? *Yes!* He was sure of it. He felt this truth in his blood and heart and spirit. He smiled—until wolves began to howl on the far side of the slope. He could have sworn that he heard them calling his name. Startled, he whirled around.

"Cha-kwena?" Mah-ree was on her feet in an instant, abandoning her pack frame as she bolted to his side and snuggled up against him like a frightened little burrowing mouse. "Did you hear, my shaman? Did the wolves speak your name?"

Squinting into the wind, Cha-kwena was no longer smiling. He listened, rapt. Not wanting to reawaken panic within Mah-ree, he replied, "A trick of the wind!" But he was not sure. His hand tightened on his spear. The deep, sporadic ululation of the wolves continued. There were no voices in the sound now, but Cha-kwena was not relieved. His body was rigid with dread. He was certain that Shateh and his warriors were tracking, following in the dark, closing the distance between themselves and their human prey as surely as the wolves had done.

He recalled his earlier vision of blood and death and human bones lying like shards of ice in the cold light of a compassionless winter moon while painted, faceless men ran wild in the skins of wolves as they hunted sacred mammoth beneath a bloodred sky. He looked up. The sky was not red. And if the moon had risen, he could not see it. Above the overhanging beak of his owl-skin headdress, there was no sky at all. There was only snow—long, laterally falling clouds of white; it was like trying to see through a frozen fog. Yet see he must, if the premonition was to be forestalled. "Hurry," he said to Mah-ree. "Let me help you with your pack. We must find shelter from the storm."

"And from wolves!"

"Yes," he replied evasively. He did not want to tell her that the wolves he most feared now walked on two legs, not on four.

She knew. "No harm will come to us from Shateh! Let him follow! He will not find us. The spirits of our ancestors will protect us as we walk strong in the power of the totem and of the sacred stone. The mammoth are out there, my shaman. Like First Man and First Woman, we will follow them into the storm, eastward into the rising sun."

Shateh paused. Wolves were howling again. Following their song, certain that in this bleak and hungry land the beasts would be trailing the lawbreakers, Shateh had led the search party out of the village and into the night. Now, no longer sure, with fatigue growing in him, the chieftain narrowed his eyes and stared ahead.

Darkness . . . inferences of land seen through wind-driven snow . . . since the last of the torches had been extinguished by the freezing wind, he could see no more than this; but the wolves were still out there, and the long, sonorous monotone of their song told him that they were no longer hunting. Had they found their prey? Had they made a kill and settled in to boast of it? And if so, over what were they gloating? Shateh scowled. He doubted if it was human meat, for the occasional male and female moccasin tracks that Ranamal, the best of his trackers, had found shortly after leaving the village had veered away from the trail of the wolves entirely. Invisible to the eyes of his hunters under the cover of darkness and a rapidly thickening layer of ankle-deep snow, he knew that the trail would still be clear enough to the dogs.

Ranamal shouted to be heard above the wind. "To this place the wolves were following. Here they went ahead." Then, balancing his weight on the balls of his booted feet, he bent his hooded head close to the ground and moved a skilled and questing ungloved hand over the snow. "Trickster is at work. He has laid one set of footprints here, and then doubled back, I think, to set another, newer trail. If only I had the eyes of an owl to see by night, I could—"

"But which trail has he taken?" pressed Shateh, intolerant of excuses as he knelt. He wanted to see the tracks with his own eyes. In the darkness, snow had a way of emitting its own feeble light. He bent closer, then frowned. Aside from several small, angular depressions in the snow that were already half-buried by a finger-deep veneer of new snow, there was nothing to see until, like Ranamal, Shateh removed his glove and felt the sign with his hand. "So deeply laid . . . so careless!"

"So like Cha-kwena!" Teikan remarked.

"The fresher sign leads there." Ranamal nodded wearily toward an area of low hills and snow-thickened scrub growth. "Soon snow will be deep, Shateh. In this wind and dark we will lose all sign, and even if we put on our snow walkers we will—"

"My dogs are cold and tired," interrupted Teikan. "Look at them. They have come this far on the scent, but I fear they will soon be of no use to us."

"You worry too much about your dogs, Teikan!" chastised Shateh. "If they were your sons, you would show them less concern!"

Teikan's deep voice was tight with resentment and frustration. "Because of Cha-kwena I have lost two of my best dogs to Bear this day! And the spirits have been with the lawbreakers tonight. If we do not find them soon, we may not find them at all."

Shateh straightened and faced angrily into the wind. "My second woman lies near death in the village while the spirit of the shamed bear roams the night, waiting for the lawbreaker to come to him in fire. If we fail to return with the shaman's woman, my Senohnim will die! Is there a man here who would put his dogs or his comfort above this?"

"We will not fail!" The declaration came from Teikan.

Shateh's eyes narrowed. He looked at the other man thoughtfully, then eyed the others with equal measure from within the deep extension of his hooded winter robe of thick, curly black bison hide. He had selected his fellow searchers carefully and knew that he had chosen well.

Teikan . . . *good friend, as close to an equal as I will ever have in this world, I am sorry about your dogs.*

Zakeh . . . *patient, judicious hunter.*

Ranamal . . . *clever tracker, whose first loyalty is to his people and proving it by looking now for the son of one whom he would take as his woman.*

Xohkantakeh . . . *strong as a bear, and as burly, you carry the burden of three without complaint and make the going easier for all.*

Rek . . . *fleet-footed, accurate with a spear, and as*

quick to mend a broken spearhead or shaft as any man in this world or the world beyond with the exception of Kosar-eh.

Ynau . . . hawk eyed, as lean as a cougar, and as deadly with a lance in your hand.

Shateh's brow furrowed—a handful of men . . . only the best, only the most trusted. He had included none from the Red World—not even Kosar-eh, who had proved his loyalty beyond question this night. A coldness touched the chieftain's spirit. When he had assembled the hunting party, the big warrior from the Land of Lizard Eaters had still been with his blind child in the lodge where the old women kept watch over the babies during times of celebration and mourning. From the piteous wailing of Kosar-eh's woman, Ta-maya, Shateh had known that the blind baby girl had been dead at her father's hands long before the hunters had left the village.

The chieftain closed his eyes. He did not want to think of Ta-maya. He was hunting her sister tonight, and because of his decree against Mah-ree, her mother was dead. He shook his head. There was so much of Ha-xa's caring, giving nature in Ta-maya. The rare beauty and gentle spirit of the young woman touched him, softened his heart, too much, too easily. Had it not been so, the life in her belly would be his life, not Kosar-eh's, for before the long-gone days of war, Ta-maya had been the wife of his son Masau, and at Masau's death, had come to Shateh by right of law. He would have kept her had he not seen her spirit bleeding with need to return to her own tribe and her own ways. He had shocked himself when he had let her go. And now that their people were one, she was Kosar-eh's woman, new mother to the five sons left to the big warrior by Siwi-ni, the wife who had died soon after giving birth to Blind Daughter.

"Shateh! Look there, Shateh!" Xohkantakeh had turned slightly and was bending forward under the weight of his pack load as he peered through snow and wind toward the low hills and scrub.

Shateh was so immersed in his thoughts that he did not

heed the man. The chieftain's eyes were still closed. He was telling himself that the death of Siwi-ni should have been a sign to Kosar-eh. Blind Daughter had never been intended to live. A Land of Grass man would have prevented the child from taking its first breath; an infant whose birth sapped the life from its mother was always denied life. Such a child was the spawn of Spirit Sucker, and Death would follow it to feed upon its people to the end of its days. Only the birth of twins was viewed with more ominous portent. Always, when the beating of two hearts was heard within a mother, she would eat expelling leaves and roots to purge the unnatural contents from her womb or suffer her belly to be kicked by her man lest the dual makers of enmity come into the world alive to bring eternal war and conflict to her band. Land of Grass people understood this. Red World people did not.

Empathy with Kosar-eh moved the chieftain. He, too, had taken life from unfit children. He, too, had abandoned sons—and better sons than One Arm had ever been. It had never been easy. It had never been without a dying of some small part of himself. And tonight a male infant of his had been denied the breath of life and given to the fire. Shateh's mouth tightened. Kosar-eh had other sons; he himself had none.

"Shateh . . ."

The chieftain opened his eyes, stared ahead into the night, and saw his long-dead sons standing before him. "Maliwal! Kalawak! Atonashkeh! Wisak!" With them was Masau, the Mystic Warrior. The name sliced like a dagger across his spirit. "The best of all sons . . ."

"Shateh . . . look . . . a fire burns there! It is far, but I can see it clearly!" Xohkantakeh repeated his declaration, this time with a worried edge to his tone.

The chieftain's eyes focused wearily through the past to the present. His sons were not there. He was staring at his men. And they were staring at him. He could not see their faces, lost as they were in darkness and snow and the protective cover of their winter hoods; but he could sense

tension and concern in them, and with a sinking feeling of
alarm, he knew that he had drifted without warning from
Now into Then like an old man in somnolent reverie
sunning himself on a rock or warming himself before a
winter-lodge fire. Ashamed, he forced himself to follow the
extension of Xohkantakeh's broad arm. The man was right.
There *was* a fire in the distance. "It is far," he observed,
"and burning well away from the trail that the wolves have
left for us."

"Wolves do not make fire! Men make fire! To keep
their women warm on a night of storm!" Teikan's enthusiasm was explosive.

"A little *lawbreaking* woman!" emphasized Ynau.

"Or a deaf, brainless *old* woman being pitied and made
comfortable by the cast-out One Arm?" suggested Shateh.

"No. He is long gone by now. If that scar-headed man
and the old woman want to survive, they will be on their
way back to the Red World of their ancestors." Teikan gave
his opinion freely. "One Arm knows that Cha-kwena and his
woman will be hunted and found! And he has been warned
what will happen to him if he is seen again by Shateh!"

The other men murmured in agreement.

Shateh was not sure. He was thinking that One Arm
had shown a deep concern for the lawbreaker—deeper than
was acceptable for another man's woman. The chieftain had
learned long before that when females were involved, men
could not always be counted on to behave rationally or
predictably. Had it been otherwise, he would never have
given up Ta-maya or taken the treacherous Ban-ya to be his
woman or . . .

"Shateh does not lead his fellow hunters into a storm
unless he is certain of finding his prey!" declared Teikan.
"Now all will see that this is so!"

Shateh was grateful for Teikan's outspoken support—
and for the fact that the man's words had kept him from
drifting into the past again. Nevertheless, he frowned. He
was tired, but he would not let himself show it. His thoughts
were focusing sharply again as he stared into the wind and

snow and saw the dull, distant glimmer of Cha-kwena's fire. The shaman's arrogance ignited his anger. "Does he believe that Shateh will not come for him? Can he be so sure of himself that he risks the life of the lawbreaker by daring to raise fire in the dark and, with its light, taunt Shateh to follow?"

"He mocks us, Shateh," snarled Teikan.

"No more," vowed the chieftain. "Because of him the totem is dead, the sacred stone has no power, and the life spirits of Ishkai and Ha-xa and the son who was almost mine walk the wind forever. I sense these spirits watching us, following us, waiting for us to do what must be done. Come! Let us make an end to what we have set out to do this night!"

5

Cha-kwena could not remember a longer night. It seemed that a lifetime had passed since he and Mah-ree had fled from wolves and into the freezing wind. Exhaustion and a full-blown blizzard had finally forced them to stop and raise a lean-to against a deeply eroded bank. It had been a simple enough procedure—a giant sloth skin taken from Cha-kwena's pack frame was unrolled, then hastily draped over and lashed securely to a brace of sturdy saplings. With the weight of the thickly furred hide laid across the trunks, the young trees arched stiffly forward against the rough stone wall of the embankment to form a small protective space. The weary couple was able to take refuge after weighting the exterior bottom edges of the skin with heavy stones to which sinew lines were attached and then slung across the frame as extra protection from the wind. Of all the work involved, finding those stones and digging them out of the snow had been the most fatiguing.

Now, as Cha-kwena and Mah-ree huddled together beneath the combined warmth of their sleeping furs, a small fire glowed before them in the palm-sized hollow that Mah-ree had scooped out of the frozen earth. They had piled their belongings all around as an added baffle to storm-impelled drafts, which came gusting through small openings at the bottom of the skin.

"We need not let it burn much longer," said Cha-kwena. "Already it has cut the chill of the air. Our breath and the heat of our bodies will be enough to sustain warmth within our shelter while we sleep out the storm."

"I cannot sleep!"

"We have come far since leaving the village, Mah-ree. No one will find us here—not wolves, not men. The storm is too great. It will drive all living things to ground this night. Even if it does not, I promise you that any wolf that tries to penetrate this shelter will have one of my spearheads in its face, and any men passing this way will see the lean-to as part of the cut bank, just another stick mound of a pack rat's nest, covered with snow between the trees. So put out the fire, Shaman's Woman. Its light and scent are the only threat to us in this place."

"First I must raise enough heat to make the coals glow," replied Mah-ree with fixed intensity. She lay on her side, facing Cha-kwena, but she was concentrating on the fire, tending the meager flames, blowing on them in short, gentle puffs, patiently feeding them frayed strips of juniper bark, the dried dung of grazing animals, and small pieces of cured wood that were part of every woman's fire-rousing kit. She did not meet his eyes as she said, "The spirit of fire that lay sleeping within my fire horn died when I fell, Cha-kwena. It is the worst of omens for us."

She shook her head again as she spoke in a tight, half-choked whisper to the flames. "Forgive this woman, Fire. In her fear of wolves and human hunters she has dishonored you. She forgot that you were protected from wind and wet inside your horn, but not from the carelessness of this woman. But now, behold, this woman honors you! Behold, once more she asks you to return to live again within the care of Mah-ree."

Cha-kwena knew that Mah-ree's words had not come easily; acknowledgment of wrongdoing never did. The happenings of the night had humbled her. He was glad to see her yielding to the spirits for a change, instead of challenging them. As he observed her working patiently over the fire, he admired her skill. True, the living coal that she had so meticulously scooped from their well-banked lodge fire and placed within her antelope-horn fire carrier had died from lack of attendance during their flight from the village. But within the lean-to, even with her cold hands, she had roused fire from the small pile of meticulously laid dried grasses and fluffs of downy mountain blue-jay feathers that she had taken from her kindling bag. He had watched her whirl her drill stick back and forth between her palms until it had become almost invisible. Then, when the friction of the stick's spinning had roused sparks and tenuous whorls of smoke from the kindling, she had known just when to blow the breath of life into the tinder. Done a moment too soon or too late, the sparks would have died; but in exactly the right instant, the summoning breath of the fire maker put life into the spirit of fire, and it burst forth hot and crackling and alive, the breath of the fire maker now the breath of its own life.

There was undisputed power and magic in the making of fire. It was a sacred art. As shaman, Cha-kwena should have felt comforted to witness the reverence and dexterity with which his woman applied it. But now, staring into the tiny flames, he remembered the great, flesh-eating pyre in the village and was impelled to look away. He did not want to think of the pyre, the village, or the events of the previous day.

He closed his eyes. Soon enough the storm would abate, and he would have to rise and lead his little Mah-ree on again. Now he needed to rest, to sleep. There would be time enough to think about what lay ahead for them, alone and hunted in this vast and unknown land. The sound of Mah-ree's fire and the smell of its smoke lingered in his nostrils, all at once sweet and acrid with the scent of burned wood and grass, of dung and mountain blue-jay feathers. The latter was a traditional Red World kindling. Its fragrance made him think of home, and gentle memories caused the corners of his lips to tighten with pleasure as he recalled his mother telling him that whenever the blue feathers of a mountain jay were burned, the smoke was a special offering to the spirits of the sky.

But why, Mother?

Cha-kwena's eyelids flickered at the sound of the voice from the past. It was his own voice, high, strong, impatient, and demanding. It was the voice of youth. It was the voice of the boy he had been but would never be again. Yet now, as sleep took Cha-kwena and dreams drew his spirit away from the cold, storm-swept lean-to in which he lay, he was that boy again, and clearly he heard his mother's voice. . . .

"Go to the sacred cave, Cha-kwena, if you would have the best telling of the story of Jay and the blue sky spirits. Go! Ask your grandfather to speak the words of the tale to you. I am not much good with stories."

"I do not want to go to him. He will do more than tell me a tale. He will try to make me a shaman!"

"No one can *make* you a shaman, Cha-kwena! Only the forces of Creation can do that. And your father will be shaman after Hoyeh-tay. It is much too soon for you to be thinking about such things."

"Old Hoyeh-tay always tries to convince me to take the shaman's path."

"Old Hoyeh-tay is a holy man who knows all things! You must respect his wisdom, Cha-kwena! Besides, no one in this world or the world beyond can tell a better story than Hoyeh-tay! He is Tale Teller! He is Spirit Master! Why, some say that he has lived so long that the tales he tells are not stories at all but recollections of his own youth in the magic time beyond beginning, when the animals and people were of one tribe and our totem, Life Giver, Great Ghost Spirit, Grandfather of All, was but a suckling calf drawing the milk of life from the tail of Rainbow, his mother! Go, I say, and stop making such a habit of arguing with your mother!"

Cha-kwena rolled his eyes with strained tolerance, then stood and left his parents' conical, reed-covered little lodge. He blinked in the blindingly bright light of a red-mesa day, then bolted off, all legs, like a young jackrabbit sprinting through the village by the Lake of Many Singing Birds, bounding away through the sage scrub, and sloshing across the creek. He strode up the talus slope and ascended the shallow steps that had been cut into the steep, dun-colored cliff within which his grandfather made his home with a molting old owl inside a sacred hollow in the hill.

And there he was. Old Hoyeh-tay. Great Shaman! He looked like a tortoise out of its shell, small and shrunken into his bones, dry and wrinkle skinned, sitting skinny and bright eyed in cross-legged meditation before his fire.

"Ah, Cha-kwena, so you come again to see your old grandfather Hoyeh-tay! Welcome!"

"Mother *made* me come."

"U-wa is a good woman."

"She would not tell me the story of why the People use the feathers of Blue Jay to rouse fire and make smoke as gifts to the sky spirits. Father is not home, so she told me that I must ask you to tell it."

"U-wa is wise. She recounts a story about as well as she roasts a grub or fries a seed cake! Burns it up! No use eating a meal cooked by your mother, boy, or sitting still for a tale that she will surely twist and lose track of before it is halfway done! Now what is it you wanted me to tell you about? Chickadee, was it? Or Flicker or . . ."

"Blue Jay. Mother would not tell me why the sky spirits want gifts of stinking smoke from the burning feathers of Blue Jay."

"Ah, I see, yes, it is a good and important tale for the young to learn—and for you especially, since you will follow in your father's footsteps and must learn all of the tales in your journey toward becoming Tale Teller, Shaman, Guardian of the Stone and of the Totem and of all the wisdom of the People since time beyond beginning."

"No! I did *not* come to hear that! I simply asked to hear a story! One story! How many times do I have to tell you that I will *not* be a shaman like you and my father! I will be a hunter! I will travel far in search of meat! Beyond the Red

World I will go! Not even Dakan-eh, Bold Man of the Red World, will dare to go farther than I!"

"Have you seen this then, with the inner eye of a shaman's Vision?"

"I have told you! That calling is not for me!"

"Smooth your feathers, boy, and do not run away in a ruffle! Here, sit down close to the fire across from your old grandfather. Yes, that's the way. Make yourself comfortable, Cha-kwena. Take what you will from that little pine-needle basket of smoked ants and pinyon nuts. A gift in gratitude to Shaman from our headman, Tlana-quah himself! Very spicy, very good. And help yourself to one of those spitted lizards on the hearth stones. Another offering . . . I forget from whom. A shaman receives so much in the way of gifts from his grateful people. It is one of the advantages to being a—"

"I do not want to be a shaman, Grandfather! I want to hear the story of Jay and the sky spirits!"

"Hm. Have a lizard then. I roasted them just this afternoon, or was it yesterday morning, or perhaps . . . no matter! Eat! And listen as Hoyeh-tay tells you of how, in time beyond beginning, in the days when the animals and the People were of one tribe, Jay—who was not always blue, you know—woke up one morning and decided to steal the colors of Rainbow and ended up the color of Sky!

"In time beyond beginning Jay was an all-black bird." Old Hoyeh-tay's voice was strong. "Not as black as Raven! Not as black as Crow! Not as black as Blackbird! But as black as pine trees at dusk when the sky and land go gray all around them. As black as mountains seen from far away in that last moment before the sun hides its face behind them. As black as dawn at the sacred salt spring in the depths of the great canyon to which the mammoth come. As black as forest shadows within which a bird can hide himself from hawks and cougars and lynx and great-fanged leaping cats on a hot summer day. But Jay was not happy.

"Now Jay's woman found him beautiful, and all of Jay's children were content to be as the forces of Creation had made them; but Jay has always been a cocky bird, a come-look-at-me bird, and he would say to himself: 'In all of this world and the world beyond, I am only another black bird. Why must I be content to be like others? No one sees me when I fly amid the trees at dusk or through the woods on a hot summer day, or against the mountains before the sun goes down, or in the depths of the great canyon where mammoth come to tusk up salt at the sacred spring. Why can I not be a bird as red as the mesas, or as yellow as the sun, or as green as the pines, or as orange as the oaks when they flame with color at summer's end, or as blue as Sky? Or better yet, why can I not be multicolored like Rainbow? Surely then all birds would look at me and say, 'Come, look at Jay, there are no birds like him in all of this world or the world beyond!'

"And so it was that Jay set himself to hunt Rainbow and steal her colors for himself.

"'You must stop!' warned the forces of Creation. 'The color of Rainbow is the lifeblood of Rainbow, and she will die without it. And if she dies, all of the colors of the world will die, too!'

"But it is the nature of Jay to test all things that come to him, and so he said, 'We will see about that!' And he set out into the blue land of Sky and her children, the sky spirits, with a spear and sling and a great bison paunch in which to carry away the lifeblood of Rainbow's many colors so that he might bathe in it and make the colors his own.

"Now, Sky and the sky spirits saw Jay hunting Rainbow. Cloud and Rain saw him coming. Lightning saw him coming. Snow and Hail saw him coming. Sun, the bright watching eye of Father Above, saw him coming. And Golden Eagle saw him coming.

"'Where are you going, little brother?' asked Eagle, who is brother to Sun and Moon and alone among all birds is welcome in the upper, blue-land reaches of Sky and her children. 'You are a bird of the woodland floor and treetops. You cannot fly with me!'

"'We will see about that!' said Jay, and with a jab of his spear, he sent Eagle on his way.

"'We will fix this Jay!' said Eagle, and together with the sky spirits, conspired to make a great storm that would drive Jay from the blue land of Sky.

"Cloud blinded Jay. Rain soaked him. Lightning stung him. Snow froze him. Hail pummeled him. Then Eagle came swooping after him. Down Jay fell from the blue land of Sky, with his spear and his sling and his bison paunch falling with him.

"Then gentle Rainbow took pity upon Jay. Rainbow caught him up in the great bend of her multicolored arm and sent him sliding gently back onto the skin of Mother Below. 'Be content, cocky bird,' said Rainbow to Jay. 'The forces of Creation have made us both what we are, and they are wise beyond knowing.'

"'We will see about that!' said Jay, and prepared to hunt again.

"'This time he will pay with his life!' declared Eagle and the sky spirits.

"'There is a better way,' said Rainbow, mother of totems and of all that is bright and gentle in this world and the world beyond. 'Let it be like this,' she suggested.

"And so it happened that when Jay flew again into the blue land of Sky with his spear and sling and the bison paunch in which he hoped to spill and catch the multicolored blood of Rainbow so that he might bathe in it and make its wondrous colors his own, nowhere was Rainbow to be seen. On and on Jay flew, peeking behind clouds and around lightning bolts and even going so far as to ask Rain and Hail and Snow and Eagle if they had seen Rainbow.

"'She is gone,' Eagle told Jay. 'From this day Rainbow will hide herself in the blue robe of Sky and will appear above the world only when it suits her. She will do this lest her beauty further tempt Jay to steal her colors and rob the world of all good and wonderful things, thus rousing the sky spirits to make eternal storms on her behalf.'

"'We will see about that!' said Jay. He was angry now. On and on Jay flew, looking for Rainbow, slinging at the blue robe of Sky with his stone-weighted sling, stabbing at the blue robe of Sky with the tip of his spear. Soon the blue robe of Sky was cut and bleeding and beginning to grow pale, as a man will do when the lifeblood runs out of him.

"'Stop!' pleaded Sky.

"Jay did not stop.

"'You are hurting me!' cried Sky.

"Jay did not care.

"'I will make you fall!'

"Jay did not listen.

"'To the ending of your days you will be sorry that you ever chose to leave the forest floor and the treetops!' warned Sky.

"'We will see about that!' said Jay.

"And he did, for in that moment, although he flapped his wings again and again, down Jay went from the blue land of Sky. Down with his sling and his spear. Down and down until he landed with a great thump on the skin of Mother Below, with the bison paunch upside down on top of him and the blood of Sky pouring over him and staining all but his head and shoulder feathers bright blue.

"And so it was that Jay became Blue Jay. No longer was he one of many black birds. No longer did he fly unseen amid the trees at dusk, or through the woods on a hot summer day, or against the mountains before the sun goes down, or within the depths of the great canyon where mammoth come to tusk up salt from the sacred spring. Now he was seen everywhere, a bird as blue as the sky, as brilliant in color as the red mesas, yellow sun, green pines, and the orange oaks of summer's end. Now the color of Jay's wings flashed blue even in the shadow of the forest floor, and in the darkness of treetops, and in the depths of the great canyon where mammoth come to tusk up salt from the sacred spring. Now hawks and cougars and lynxes and great-fanged leaping cats and every other sharp-eyed predator looked at him and said, 'Come, see Jay! There are no birds like him in all of this world or the world beyond! Come! Let us hunt him! He is easy to be seen!'

"'We will see about that!' said Blue Jay.

"And he does to this very day, for from that time to this, Blue Jay pays for his theft and his cockiness with his life and the lives of his children and is forever sorry for flying beyond the treetops into the blue land of Sky with his sling and spear and bison paunch in which he hoped to spill and catch the multicolored blood of Rainbow.

"And so it is that the People collect the feathers of Blue Jay whenever they find them. So it is that when we make fire, we say to the sky spirits, 'Here is a bit of blue, once stolen, but now returned to Sky in sacred smoke! May the color that Jay has stolen return to her robe so that it may someday be as blue as it was in the time beyond beginning. Until that day, the People thank Sky for the color blue, for although Blue Jay has driven Rainbow into hiding and taken for himself some of the color of Sky, we are grateful to that cocky bird. A red mesa without the bright flash of his blue wing would not seem quite so red, nor would the pines seem as green, nor the autumn oaks so gold, nor the winter snows as white. And who can say that in the end this theft of Jay's has not been a good thing? Sky is so blue that she is not diminished by the small loss of color that Jay has cost her, and perhaps gentle Rainbow might not be a source of awe to the People if she walked before us every day . . . and the boy who sits before me now might not often be seen stopping on the hunt to catch his breath in wonder at the rare and beautiful things of this world so that his old grandfather finds himself watching this boy and saying to himself: We will see about that! This boy, this Cha-kwena, will someday be shaman!"

"No!" Cha-kwena awoke with a start to darkness, to the moaning of the wind, to the hiss of snow and the sure and steady sound of the sloth hide straining against the leather thongs that held it fast to the arching, trembling torsos of the trees that formed the bones and bracing of the lean-to.

He closed his eyes again and sought refuge from reality in the dream, even though it was as sharp and bitter to his spirit as the remembered spice of roasted ants. Within its substance he glimpsed a world that he had lost and left behind forever—a drought-stricken world of towering mesas and alkaline lakes and sage flats and pinyon groves, a world in which he, like Blue Jay, had contested with the forces of Creation until old Hoyeh-tay had led him to the heights of the great canyon and he had looked down into eternally shadowed deeps and first set eyes upon Life Giver, the great white mammoth totem, tusking salt from the sacred spring with his cows and little white calf.

Cha-kwena's breath rasped in his throat. He did not like to think of the sacred canyon. It had been there, beneath the bright blue robe of Sky and beneath the watching eyes of the star children of Moon, that he experienced his first vision shortly after his father's unexpected death and reluctantly came to accept the fact that he had been chosen by the Ancient Ones to be Shaman. It had been within the sacred canyon that he mourned when his grandfather was slain by their enemies. It had been there that he first saw mammoth slaughtered and bore witness to the flayed carcass and bones of the little white mammoth calf. It had been there that he had first led men to battle. And it had been there, within the black deeps of that canyon, that the mists of tonight's premonition had placed wolfskin-clad mammoth hunters and a great bear to challenge his progress along a dream path that was littered with tusks and skulls and dismembered bones.

Mammoth bones. His bones. Mah-ree's bones. And the bones of the unborn totem.

Cha-kwena's left hand rose to rest upon his medicine bag. Tonight he had seen that bear staked before the mourning fire that burned in Shateh's village. Tonight he had seen Shateh's warriors transformed into wolves sworn to hunt him, and to slay his woman and the sacred mammoth.

And now, somewhere far beyond the lean-to, mammoth were trumpeting. Cha-kwena tensed, opened his eyes, and stared into darkness. *The mammoth are still out there!*

The spirit of the totem is with them. And despite the terror of his vision, he and Mah-ree were still alive!

"Cha-kwena?"

It was a moment before his thoughts fully emerged from the hurtful tangling of his dreams. He saw that the fire was out. Mah-ree was snuggled against his side with her head resting in the crook of his folded left arm. He assumed that she must have restocked her fire horn before extinguishing the flames, and he was surprised that her movement had not awakened him. Beneath the sloth skin, there was the faintest intrusion of gray light, the first night-thinning promise of dawn. Cha-kwena knew that he must have been lost to his dreams for a long time.

"I hear mammoth, my shaman."

"Yes, Mah-ree, I hear them, too."

"They are still with us, out there in the storm, circling close together. I hear four—no, five, perhaps six, maybe more. And little ones. A band. A family. The matriarch is with them. And with us, my shaman." She drew closer to him, slipped a slender arm around his chest, and gripped him tightly. "*We* are a band. Cha-kwena and Mah-ree. Someday we will be more than two! Someday we will be a family! Until then we will be strong and unafraid as long as we are together in the protective power of the mammoth and of the totem!"

Despite the fervor with which she had spoken, there had been an edge of frightened desperation to her tone. Trembling, she drew even closer to him.

"Oh, my shaman, will my mother not be at my side when I bear our children in this land at the edge of the world? Can it really be true that I will never see Ha-xa or Ta-maya again?"

"Do not think of it," Cha-kwena told her, and with his right hand tightening around the haft of his spear, remembered the woman's scream that had brought him and Mah-ree to pause earlier in the night. Ha-xa was dead. He knew it, felt it, saw it in his shaman's inner eye, but saw no need to share this certainty with Mah-ree. "Your mother is far away," he replied obliquely, and feeling the need to soothe her added, "but Ha-xa's heart is glad to know that you are here, safe with your man, alive instead of . . ." He could not bring himself to complete the supposition or the falsehood.

Suddenly restless, he moved from his prone position to lie, head up, with his back resting against the wall of the cut bank. Water dripped into his face. Still wearing his head-dress, he turned his eyes upward and, in the barely discern-ible predawn light, could just make out water droplets forming at the tips of icicles that still hung from the beak. He removed the headdress and set it aside. A moment passed before he noticed that the mammoth were no longer trumpeting. The wind had dropped. The sound of the snowfall had changed.

"The storm is settling," whispered Mah-ree, moving to share his upright position against the cut bank and pulling her sleeping fur with her. "Snow will fall straight and heavy for a long time, I think. It is good that we are here, safe and warm."

Cha-kwena did not reply. The earth was cold and hard against his back, but thanks to the thick insulation of his traveling robe, he felt no discomfort. It occurred to him that yesterday at this time he would have declared the garment unfit to wear even though Mah-ree had made it for him out of prime rabbit pelts that she had taken in the traditional way of the women of the Red World. Her skills with trip snares, throwing sticks, and rabbit nets were as sharply honed as her skill as a fire maker. He knew that working in secret to surprise him, she had spent much time collecting and fleshing and curing the pelts, twisting them into long, furry ropes, which she then sewed together, side by side, with strong thread corded of milkweed fibers until, at last, she had a full-length robe with a generous hood.

When she had finally presented it to him in front of the assembled band, Cha-kwena had thought it the most beau-tiful and luxurious garment of its kind that he had ever seen. But Shateh and the Land of Grass People had expressed horror and revulsion at the thought of any man, especially their shaman, wearing the pelts of an animal whose flesh was considered unsuitable for human consumption except under a Starving Moon and whose skins were used only to swaddle the bottoms of infants and to absorb the cyclical flow of female moon blood. Since discarding the garment would have been an offense to the spirits of the many wastefully slain rabbits, Cha-kwena had accepted it as a sleeping mattress but would not wear it.

After chastising Mah-ree for being the only Red World woman who refused to learn the ways of her new people, he had hunted and brought her the heavy, thickly haired winter skin of a camel. She had not been grateful. Fleshing and curing the hide of a big grazing animal was a long, tedious chore rarely practiced in the Red World, where large herbivores were few and far between. With her fingers and hands already callused from her earlier effort, his little girl-of-a-woman had eyed the camel skin with disapproval and said that it was far too heavy for a Red World man, even if he was a shaman. Time had proved her right. When complete, the camel-skin robe had been so cumbersome that although he had not admitted it to her or anyone else, Cha-kwena had been hard-pressed to wear it. He had been only too glad to leave it behind, along with the other Land of Grass belongings that he had accumulated since attempting to accommodate himself to the ways of Shateh's people.

"No more," he said to himself and, sleepy again, drew Mah-ree tightly to his side, realizing just how warm and comfortable he was in the lightweight rabbit-skin robe, with its thousands of insulating pockets of weightless air twisted into the spiraling, flawlessly joined ropes of thick fur that his beloved had made for him in the way of their ancestors. "It is a good thing, this robe. I can say it now. I should have said it many moons ago. But I have been like Jay, trying so hard to be other than what I am—a Red World man."

Mah-ree turned her face up to his. Her breath was sweet and warm as she sighed happily, then nestled close, laying her cheek against his throat. "Listen, my shaman," she said drowsily. "Do you hear? The anger has gone out of the storm." Her hand was moving beneath his elk-skin shirt, stroking his chest, slowly, in light circular sweeps that made him sigh with pleasure. She sighed with him. "The Red World is far away, but this woman is not afraid. Her man is Shaman. She is Medicine Woman. Together we have found the mammoth and driven away wolves. Soon, like First Man and First Woman, we will follow the totem eastward over the edge of the world. The forces of Creation are with us, Cha-kwena. I know they are!"

"May it be so, little one," he said.

She made no reply. Her hand was lax and motionless upon his chest. Her breathing was the slow, regular, unperturbed breathing of one who has drifted into deep sleep.

Cha-kwena closed his eyes and, allowing his spear to ease forward across his thigh, joined her. He did not dream.

6

Shateh had the runaways now. He was certain of it.

With the storm settling all around, he hefted his spear in his gloved hand, then paused and signaled the others forward. He had not seen the glimmer of firelight for some time now, but the dogs were on the scent again. The chieftain cast a glance over his shoulder and saw that his men, with benefit of snow walkers, were advancing through sparse woods and high-stepping like cranes around thornbush and through deep drifts. Their heads out, they were hungry for prey and eager for the capture and the kill, whichever came first.

Not a man spoke as the group divided and came to a stop on either side of Shateh. He stared ahead again. It was difficult but not impossible to see; the sun was rising, sending the light of dawn to eat the night and penetrate the storm just enough to turn the world a deep blue-gray. The dogs whined, their behavior confused rather than aggressive. They sniffed and circled a mound of snow that rose amid a bent and broken tangling of young trees. Shateh watched through curtaining snowflakes as big as the tip of his thumb.

Yes! he thought. *We have them at last!*

The chieftain's heartbeat quickened as he waited for the lawbreaker and the shaman to emerge dazed and frightened from their hiding place beneath the snow. But only the dogs moved. Shateh's brows arched speculatively within his hood. And then understanding dawned. He hissed through his teeth in anger and frustration when he saw the decoy raised like a spirit offering atop the mound.

He lowered his spear and, using it as a staff, advanced through the trees, then stopped to stare at the snow-covered, well-made little tent of fur that had been raised over a large stone oil lamp.

"What—?" Teikan choked off the rest of his question as he came with the others to stand around the chieftain.

"Here is what you have had me lead you to pursue instead of wolves and lawbreakers!" growled Shateh, disgusted less with Teikan than with his own judgment; he had allowed himself to be led by the younger man.

"It is her lamp," said Teikan in a tone of self-justification. "She and Totem Slayer must be somewhere near. They—"

"I saw this lamp in Cha-kwena's lodge long after he and Mah-ree had left it!"

Snarling, Shateh reached into the little protective tent and snatched from the hollow of the stone Gah-ti's necklace of lion's claws and teeth. It had been positioned around the twisted moss wick to protect the flame from drafts. The necklace clicked in his hand as he shook it before the stunned Teikan. "One Arm has lured us off the trail of the lawbreaker with the light from this lamp and has left it and his necklace here to prove it! Only the forces of Creation know how long ago! The traces of oil that slick the hollow of the lamp have gone thick and hard with cold!"

"But, Shateh, Cha-kwena and the lawbreaker must be with him," said Ranamal. "Before snow and wind conspired to cover the trail, I followed the tracks of the shaman's moccasins—the same badly made pair he wore upon the hunt this day."

Shateh was aghast. "You did not say that this was what made you so certain of the trail!"

Ranamal shrugged and gave the age-old reply, "You did not ask."

The chieftain shook his head, resigned to his failure to check the tracks himself until late in the journey, when they had been discernible only as the most subtle mark of human passage across the land. "The moccasins of which you speak were on the feet of old Kahm-ree when last I saw them, in the shaman's lodge . . . after Cha-kwena and Mah-ree fled the village."

"But the tracks I followed were made by feet that fully filled the moccasins and stressed the seams . . . a man's feet!" insisted Ranamal.

"Yes," conceded Shateh, "but not Cha-kwena's. Among the Red World people there is more than one Trickster. Gah-ti, even more than Cha-kwena, has tricked us this night!"

The spear came straight up through the sloth skin. Gah-ti leaped aside, knocking Kahm-ree down as the red shaft with blue banding went flying through and past the space where his right arm would have been. The lance made no sound as it disappeared into the snowdrifts through which he and the old woman had just come.

"Cha-kwena!" Gah-ti called the shaman's name a second time and made certain he was out of spear range before he added, "Come out and see whose life you would put an end to before you give reason for men to call you Man Slayer as well as Totem Slayer!"

A moment later a form clad in rabbit skins came rolling sideways beneath the bottom edge of the lean-to, then was quickly on one knee, with a spear pointing straight at Gah-ti.

"Ban-ya!" cried old Kahm-ree. Sagging sideways in the snow she clasped her fur-mittened hands with joy.

"Are you now blind, too, old woman?" Cha-kwena stared in amazement at Kahm-ree and then at Gah-ti. "What are you doing here? How have you found us?"

"I spoke against Shateh's decision to hunt your law-breaking woman. For that I was cast out. Kahm-ree has followed me, and I have followed the trumpeting call of mammoth in hope of catching up with you," replied Gah-ti. "Everyone—including Shateh—knows that where the mammoth walk, there, too, Cha-kwena may be found! But this man and Kahm-ree set him upon another trail last night. He has learned who is fit to live and lead in this far land, for it was a one-armed man and a deaf old woman who lured the chieftain off your trail with the lamp we took from your lodge. Shateh followed the light. By now he must have found it, too late to see the trick or to pick up the trail we took, circling through thornbush that must be deep beneath snow by now. Shateh will not find us." Gah-ti paused in his boastful revelation and, suddenly angry, added, "And it is a good thing for you that I am *not* Shateh! He would have come in silence, and you and your woman would now be on the tips of his spears and he would soon be preparing to hunt sacred mammoth!" Gah-ti frowned. "Where is Mah-ree?"

"I am here," Mah-ree said, lifting a portion of the sloth skin and peeking out at Gah-ti. Then, seeing Kahm-ree, she gave a little cry of joy as she scooted eagerly forward on her knees. Standing and squinting through the thickly falling snow, she looked expectantly for others and called out, "Mother? Ta-maya? Tla-nee? Kosar-eh? U-wa? Oh, somehow I knew that you would all come, and that—"

"There is only us, Daughter of Ha-xa! Only Gah-ti and Kahm-ree and the mammoth!" Kahm-ree stated irritably, huffing and mumbling to herself as she fought to stand upright in the thigh-deep snow. Succeeding, she waded forward and called in a breathy voice, "Ban-ya! Come out, my dear one! Your grandmother knows you are here. Move over, child, and make a warm place beside you for these old bones!" Without another word, she dropped to her knees in front of the lean-to and wedged her way past Mah-ree, burrowing under the snow-covered sloth skin.

Gah-ti saw that neither Cha-kwena nor Mah-ree paid any attention to what the addle-brained woman had done. He turned and followed their gaze. There, straight ahead and barely visible in the falling snow, the herd of mammoth stood in soft gray silhouette against the pale light of dawn, the great tusked cows clustering close, sharing warmth, sheltering the calves and adolescents among them. Gah-ti and Kahm-ree had been following them for some time now; Gah-ti had never doubted where they would lead.

Cha-kwena was looking at Gah-ti again. "I see you have found warmth in my camel-skin robe."

"Yes," Gah-ti grumbled, "but it is heavy, and your moccasins allow the cold to enter."

Cha-kwena did not reply for a moment. Then he said somberly, "It is difficult for me to believe that Kosar-eh would stand by and see you cast out, Gah-ti."

"My father has other sons. He and they are Land of Grass men now." Gah-ti's jaw tightened; pain flared in his bruised jaw and in his heart. He saw no need to tell them about Doh-teyah; it would have hurt too much to have spoken the words.

Mah-ree continued to stare off expectantly, obviously still hopeful that those she loved might come through the snow; but at last her smile faded when she turned her gaze to Gah-ti and said wistfully, "Ta-maya must stay behind with her man Kosar-eh, I know. My sister is so big with his baby! Out of consideration for Ta-maya's *first* baby, Kosar-eh has not challenged Shateh on behalf of Gah-ti. But tell this woman, Gah-ti, why Ha-xa has not come with you? My mother has no man of her own among Shateh's people. And Kosar-eh has so many mouths to hunt for!"

Gah-ti found it impossible to look away from Mah-ree. He loved her so much, his spirit ached. How could he tell her what he had seen in the village? Life would be hard enough for Mah-ree in the long days and nights ahead without his burdening her heart with the truth that Ha-xa had given herself to the spirit of Bear through Fire in Mah-ree's place. He could not tell her. He *would* not tell her. There was no need for her to know. And so Gah-ti drew in a deep, steadying breath and told the first lie that came into his head. "Ha-xa wanted to come, but she has your younger sister, Tla-nee, to think of! Your mother could not bring herself to commit such a little one as Tla-nee to the storm and an unknown land beyond the edge of the world! And Ha-xa has Ta-maya's baby to look forward to. Ta-maya will need her mother when her time comes. Besides, Ha-xa knew you would be safe with Shaman . . . and with me."

Mah-ree looked down, blinking back tears.

"Not long after Mah-ree and I left the village, we heard a woman screaming." Cha-kwena's voice was flat, controlled, yet somehow on edge. "Who screamed, Gah-ti?"

Mah-ree looked up.

"No one," Gah-ti lied. "No one screamed."

7

All morning heavy snow fell. It felt suffocating and seemed endless.

"We cannot continue," said Shateh, acceding to discomfort and fatigue. Despite his multilayered, down-lined winter moccasins and gloves, the extremities of his feet and hands were aching with cold. He knew that the others must be suffering, also. He was certain that they would not speak of it; they had all been so eager to follow Teikan's lead along the wrong trail, now they would go wherever Shateh led them without complaint, even though it had been obvious to everyone for some time now that further travel in any direction was a wasted effort even for men on snow walkers. The snow was simply too wet and heavy to hold their weight. With each step the wide, sinew-webbed, elongated willow frames sank into the drifts to the depth of a man's hand. The wearer would then be forced to lift his knee straight up, and only after slapping hard at the side of the frame to free the webbing of heavy clumps of snow, could forward progress continue, one laborious step at a time.

Shateh cursed the depth and texture of the snow, which had pulled the protective leather coverings from the feet of the dogs. Teikan and the others had hefted the ones that were in the worst condition, carrying the animals slung across their backs, bloodied paws dangling.

The chieftain's mouth turned down. He had gone as far as he was going to go this day. There was no use driving his men on. They had done all they could do in their effort to satisfy the shamed Bear and his righteous rage against the shaman and his woman. Besides, no one had heard wolves or mammoth since dawn. He remembered Teikan's earlier opinion about the spirits being with the lawbreakers and, growling to himself, knew that the man had been right.

He turned now, stared into snow and cloud, and could not see the land beyond the distance of a few strides in any direction.

Where are you, Cha-kwena, you and your brave little lawbreaker? A coldness that had nothing to do with the weather made Shateh shiver as he wondered if the spirit of Bear was still waiting for the lawbreaking woman to come to him, or if he had satisfied himself by summoning the life of Senohnim from her body. The coldness within him intensified. He feared that his woman was dead. *If only I had not listened to Teikan!* Unnerved, he shook his head. "If" was a supposition that wasted a resourceful man's time, and he had already wasted far too much of that.

"We will make a camp here," said Shateh, scanning around, seeing boulders that would break the wind and cold. "We will wait out the storm."

Relieved and grateful, the others nodded and exhaled vigorously, making copious mists before their hooded faces.

The chieftain was still scowling, glaring at Teikan and waiting for him to offer challenge to his stated intent; but the man had said nothing since their discovery of the lamp and the necklace, and he said nothing now. The chieftain was not gratified by his silence; he would have welcomed the opportunity to shame the old friend who had so ably goaded him through flattery into turning from the trail that would have brought him to the ones he sought. But then, he reasoned, through the results of his own bad advice, Teikan had already shamed himself.

"Come! Let us get out of this cold and take some rest!" said Shateh, and slung off his traveling pack and bent to unfasten his snow walkers.

It was no easy task. The thongs were frozen stiff and thick with clots of ice; he had to remove his gloves to undo the noosing, and even then, it was difficult with bare fingers that were as stiff with cold as the leather lacing. At last he kicked off his snow walkers and set to work with the others to make a camp.

No one spoke. While the dogs lay in the snow licking and nipping ice balls from between the pads of their cracked and cold-damaged paws, each man knew what to do and did it well and quickly. In only a few moments Xohkantakeh had unrolled and snapped the hide lean-to covers in the wind and, with assistance from the others, soon had them assembled into a snug, spear-anchored tent close to the lee of the boulders.

Still no one spoke. They crawled into the shelter and huddled inside, shook themselves warm, rubbed their feet and fingers, and listened to the clacking of their teeth as they tried to decide whose dog they would brain to make a meal for them.

Suddenly Ranamal noticed that one of their number was not with them. "Where is Teikan?" he asked.

"Teikan is here," said the man, bending and entering on his knees, dragging the limp body of his favorite hunting dog with him and placing it at the chieftain's feet. Then, still kneeling with head bent and his mouth tight around the words, he said, "The blood of this dog will warm us. The meat of this dog will give us strength. This dog was the best of Teikan's pack. The sacrifice of this dog is Teikan's gift to Shateh."

The chieftain looked long and hard at the man. "You have cost me the capture of the shaman, the sacred stone, and the lawbreaker. Because you failed to kill a bear, I have lost a son and perhaps a woman. Do you truly believe that the offering of a dog is satisfactory repayment for such losses?"

Teikan looked up, stunned.

Ranamal spoke in defense of a hunt brother. "It was Shaman who sent Walks Like a Man to the village!"

"It was Teikan who was entrusted to guard that village!" Shateh countered.

"Along with Ishkai!" reminded Teikan.

"And now Ishkai is dead," stated Shateh.

The silence was palpable. The chieftain allowed Teikan to steep in it.

Several long moments passed before Teikan said stiffly, "I will go into the storm. I will seek the shaman and the lawbreaker. I will bring them to Shateh, or I will offer my own life to the spirit of the shamed bear!"

The chieftain eyed the man. Teikan was worth a full two-handed count of Senohnims, and more. He had never been less than a loyal hunt brother. He was a maker of sons. He was strong and intelligent and brave beyond fault. If it had been possible to prevent the attack of Bear, Teikan would have done so; Shateh had no doubt of that. He also had no doubt that when Teikan had been moved to guide the hunt for Shaman, it had not been out of arrogance or ambition but because his chieftain had, through indecisiveness, invited and allowed him to do so.

Shateh's eyes narrowed as he realized that if he were to heap blame for the current situation upon any man, the full weight of responsibility lay upon his own shoulders. For far too long he had relied upon the power of a dead totem, a useless stone, and a foreign shaman. He was chief! He was a shaman in his own right! And he had proved to all of his hunters last night that without doubt he was a man of sound instincts. In the future—as in the past when he had been chief above all chiefs in the Land of Grass—he would stand or fall by his own decisions.

Now, as Teikan made to turn and leave the confines of the hastily made shelter, the chieftain commanded him to stop. "You will not find the ones we seek in this storm," he said. "And I do not believe that Bear wants your life, old friend."

Teikan knelt back, frowning, unsure. "What then?" he asked, clearly at a loss to imagine a greater penalty than the sacrifice of his life. "More dogs?"

Shateh shook his head. "No," he said, then paused, allowing the importance of the moment to settle upon his listeners so that all would remember what he would say now. "I want your obedience, Teikan. If you cannot yield this to me, then know that I, and not the spirit of the shamed Bear, will have your life and all that you possess. Although I welcome your opinion in council, only one man can be chief on the hunt. Will you concede that this is so?"

The eyes of the two men met and held. All watched, waiting breathlessly to see who would look away first. It was Teikan, but not until after a disconcertingly long count of heartbeats, and only then, staring sullenly into his lap, did he concede to Shateh's words. "This is so," he said.

Shateh nodded, satisfied. "Then I accept the gift of this dog. Take it out. Butcher it. Fling the head and carcass to the other dogs so they may eat of it and be strengthened. If any meat eaters be inspired to come close and make meat of us, the dogs will warn us of their coming. Do this, Teikan. Then let us eat together, and let there be no enmity between us."

And so it was done.

They ate the meat of the dog raw, portioning it and sharing it equally among all seven of their number. When there was not a morsel left—save potentially poisonous spleens and kidneys, which were set aside—they cracked the joints and savored marrow until, weary, they dozed, sitting upright.

And still snow fell.

Shateh, in the role of shaman now, offered ancestral litanies to the spirits of Storm and Sky, praising their power and asking them to take pity upon those of the People who had need of their benevolence. The thin light of day faded into darkness. The night grew very cold. The men whistled the dogs in, and as the hunters spoke together, as men will do to pass time, they welcomed the added warmth of canine bodies. There was no joy or laughter in their talk, for with snow still falling and the wind moaning across the world, they could not forget that it was a time of mourning and that the spirits of the dead and of the shamed Bear roamed the night.

They slept fitfully but deeply, their bellies calm with meat. And still it snowed. They used their spears to brace the tent, and whenever a man went out to urinate and empty his bowels, he also shoveled the drifts back and away from the shelter lest it and those within be smothered. When Shateh went out, he stood for a long time in the freezing wind, arms lifted to the forces of Creation, and raised again the age-old litanies before, half-frozen and numb to his bones, he returned to shiver himself to sleep beside his fellow hunters. Then, sometime just after dawn, they were awakened by the neighing of horses.

The chieftain's head went up. He listened. *Yes!* Clearly he heard horses, far away but as distinct and welcome to his spirit as the absence of wind. His heart was leaping with excitement. Impelled by hope, he crawled from the shelter into the light of the rising sun to stand beneath a clear, windless sky. The storm was over.

"Aiee!" Shateh exalted, raising his arms in gratitude to the forces of Creation and in welcome to the rising sun.

Teikan crawled from the shelter and squinted in the unexpected brightness of the morning. "Sky!" he cried. "It is good to see the sky!"

Ranamal and the others, along with the dogs, were emerging from the shelter and doing their best to find solid, even footing in the drifts.

"Did I hear horses?" asked Xohkantakeh.

"You did!" affirmed Shateh. "Listen!"

As though on command, the whinny of a single horse was heard, and the hunters turned as one toward the sound and away from the sun.

And there they were: a small herd plodding belly deep in snow along the western horizon. Shateh's brow furrowed. Despite the heavily whitened land, he recognized the contours of the boulder-strewn barrens and knew that the horses were headed in the general direction of the village.

He caught his breath, taking their presence as a sign from the forces of Creation.

"We will follow this meat," he said, and thought that with so much snow upon the ground, travel would be difficult. But it was much colder now, and the moisture that had fallen during the height of the storm had come down as powder. Using their snow walkers, the men could be back among their people and within the warmth of their lodges long before sundown, resting and preparing to hunt as soon as the time of mourning was over. Wherever the horses wandered, the mark of their passage across the land would be imbedded in snow for many days . . . unless another storm arose.

"Shateh has led us well," said Ynau, evidently thinking in the same vein.

"It is good that we have not fallen off the edge of the world," agreed Rek.

"But what of Shaman and Lawbreaker and One Arm and the old woman?" asked Teikan. "What of the spirit of the shamed Bear?"

Surprised that the man had had the gall to ask the question, Shateh replied hotly, "If by some chance my woman still lives, then Bear does not want her! If she is dead, then Bear is satisfied!" He eyed Teikan warily and, for the first time in his life, with actual dislike. "Would you continue on beyond the edge of the world even now, Teikan?"

"I will go where Shateh leads," Teikan replied prudently.

Zakeh was staring eastward across the barrens. "We would never be able to pick up the trail of those we hunt. They could be anywhere out there, days and nights ahead of us—if they are still alive."

Shateh, glad to have an excuse to remove his gaze from Teikan, turned and squinted across the distances. "May it be that Lahontay was right when he said that Shaman and Lawbreaker and One Arm and the deaf old woman have followed the mammoth off the edge of the world and have fallen to their death in the burning face of the rising sun!" A new confidence was in him now. "We will not follow them! We will return to the village and see what awaits us there."

He paused, turned again, faced toward the horses and the village, and nodded with supreme satisfaction. "Behold! Now that Cha-kwena is no longer with us, horses run before us. When the time of mourning is over, we will follow these horses. We will ask them once more to be meat for the People. We will hunt. If the forces of Creation allow it, we will return to the land of our ancestors with much meat! Look not to the edge of the world, over which a false shaman would have led us. That man has proved to us all that he has no power."

Cha-kwena gripped the sacred stone with one hand and his spear with the other. Vision had him again. He dreamed of himself standing in a clearing within the depths of the great canyon. The sun was rising above the mile-high rim. He stared up, his eyes fixed on a narrow waterfall—a slender, rainbow river of liquid sunlight—pouring down, down from the heights into the thickly forested canyon floor across which Mah-ree ran, laughing, beckoning him. She was following old Hoyeh-tay and the mammoth along a shallow creek within which the tuskers plodded eastward through morning mists. An owl flew ahead of them. And in the shadowing wings of the ancient bird, a lone coyote trotted on and looked back at him.

Come, Cha-kwena! Come, Yellow Wolf! Come, Trickster, follow me into the face of the rising sun! Why do you wait?

Cha-kwena could smell ice in the air. He found himself looking around for painted men clad in the skins of wolves, for a raven and a bear, for bones and tusks and skulls; but he saw none of these threatening things until he turned and saw them all vanishing into the distance behind him. Relief flooded through him. It was to be short-lived.

"My shaman! You must get up, my shaman! The storm is over, and the mammoth have gone!"

Cha-kwena awoke with a start. Flinching from the unexpected and hurtful onslaught of the full light of morning, he saw that Mah-ree had peeled away the sloth skin and was gesturing to where Gah-ti and Kahm-ree stood outside.

Scowling, Cha-kwena crawled from beneath the bent wood frame of the shelter and scrambled to his feet in heavy drifts. Mah-ree was right: The storm was over, and the mammoth were nowhere to be seen.

"They have gone there . . . circling as is their nature, but clearly putting their backs to the sun," said Gah-ti, pointing off. "I have followed a little way. They have trampled down a wide trail. But it is bad country—no trees, no cover—dangerous for them, and for us if I had not led Shateh and his hunters off your trail."

"You are not Shaman!" reprimanded Mah-ree. "You cannot be sure of that!"

Cha-kwena made no comment. He could not understand what was happening. In his dream, he had seen the mammoth plodding eastward while Shateh and his hunters vanished westward into the land of their ancestors. Yet now, as he followed the extension of Gah-ti's arm, he saw the wide tracks of the mammoth leading across the barrens through which they had come. He did not like the look of the open, snow-swept land. If Shateh and his followers found the tuskers there, wallowing in deep snow, the animals would have no protection; they would be speared to the last cow and calf, and the totem would die with them. And then, if the tales of the Ancient Ones were true tales, Man and all of his children would perish.

"We will follow?" asked Gah-ti without much enthusiasm.

"We must follow!" replied Cha-kwena. "We must turn the herd before it walks straight back into the hunting grounds of Shateh!"

They left Kahm-ree in Mah-ree's care and went hurriedly in the broad trail of the mammoth.

"Tell my Ban-ya that I am waiting for her!" the old woman called after them.

"Yes!" Gah-ti called back. "If we find her, we will tell her!"

"You should not encourage her hope of finding that one alive," chastised Cha-kwena, refusing to speak Ban-ya's name.

"Kahm-ree is old. Hope is all she has," replied Gah-ti.

"Hope is all any of us has if we do not find the herd!" Cha-kwena snapped.

"I know they are sacred animals, Cha-kwena, but the great white mammoth totem is long dead. The others are only mammoth," responded Gah-ti. "We should be leading the women to a hiding place. You do not think enough about Mah-ree! If she were my woman, I—" He bit back his words.

Cha-kwena knew Gah-ti's unspoken thoughts. *What if we fail to turn the herd? What if Shateh finds us? What if he kills us* and *the mammoth, then follows these tracks straight back to the lean-to and to Mah-ree?* "Do not even think it!" he warned, and ran on, lengthening his stride.

Mah-ree stared fixedly across the glinting snow until she could no longer see Cha-kwena and Gah-ti. Aching to follow, she kept her eyes on the tracks of the herd. "Where do the mammoth go, Kahm-ree? *Why* do they go . . . traveling always in their great, broad feeding circles, moving forward and around and back, from one familiar place to another, but in the end always seeking new grazing and drinking pools, eastward, always eastward . . . *why?*"

"It is not for us to know why, Shaman's Woman. Since time beyond beginning, wherever the mammoth kind have walked, there, too, have the People found much meat and drink and all good things. So too will it be for us."

"That is what Cha-kwena always says."

"He is Shaman. He knows all things. Following the mammoth, he has always led our people well." The old woman sucked on the bony stubble of her teeth a moment, then bent and, scooting forward on her elbows and knees, sought the warmth of the lean-to.

Mah-ree felt uneasy. Kahm-ree was wrong. Cha-kwena *was* Shaman, but he did not know all things. He had not foreseen the coming of Gah-ti and Kahm-ree to their little camp. These days, wherever he walked, hardship followed, and people lost faith in him. And now she was hunted and alone with a mindless old woman at the edge of the world, with no hope of ever seeing her family again. Misery weighted her. She wondered if the slurs that Shateh's women had made against Cha-kwena's powers before the coming of Bear might have been well founded. Perhaps he was no longer Shaman? *No!* She would not allow herself to think it. She knew better. After the totem was reborn into the world Cha-kwena's full power would return. The land would grow green, game would come to die upon the spears of the People, the sick and the maimed would become well and whole again if he so willed it, and someday—her heart gave a little leap of hope, for she had not thought of this before—when the great white mammoth was fully grown, Shaman and Shaman's Woman would come walking boldly back into the world of men with all of their many shaman children. They would be a great band, with many young warriors among them. Those who had spurned Shaman and Shaman's Woman would tremble in fear of their power.

The premise brought a smile to Mah-ree's face until she realized that by the time the totem matured, she and Cha-kwena would be old and gray and as withered as staffs of ironwood, and those whom she so yearned to see cringe before her righteous wrath would most likely be dead. And until the great one matured, his full power would not be felt in the world. Her smile faded. If she were to judge by her shaman's many current failures, how would they survive alone beyond the edge of the world—one man, one woman, a cripple, and an addle-brained grandmother? Unhappy again, she reproached herself for lack of faith in her man and conceded that the circumstances in which she found herself could not be blamed upon Cha-kwena; it was she who had broken the laws of the ancestors and put herself and the totem at risk.

"Wake me when my Ban-ya comes," said the old woman from beneath the partial cover of the folded sloth skin.

Mah-ree's eyes narrowed as she continued to stare off after her man. She knew that she could have helped Cha-kwena and Gah-ti with the mammoth. She hated being left behind, but someone had to look after Kahm-ree, who might otherwise wander off. In the land of their ancestors she had often disobeyed her mother and left the other women and girls to berry picking while she sneaked away to the upland meadow, where the great white mammoth totem grazed on tender fern shoots at the edge of the cedar grove. She had known no fear of him or of his kind.

She closed her eyes, allowed herself to remember how it had been to seat herself on the thick, moist, spongy-rooted grasses of the meadow while living garlands of blue damselflies entwined themselves around her brow. She would watch Great Spirit, Life Giver, Grandfather of All, at his feeding. At these moments Mah-ree had experienced a contentment that could only be felt in the presence of the totem.

And because the great white mammoth was totem, she had confided her dreams and secrets, and he had huffed and blown and swayed sympathetically at the sound of her voice, turning his bat-wing ears this way and that, listening, allowing her to know that he understood the way of her youthful heart, for he was older and wiser than the wind and, like the wind, had seen all things in his time. And there, in the shade of the cedar grove, she had observed the movement of his body and the pace of his breathing and had drawn in the scent of his breath and urine and fecal matter and had known that Life Giver was sick and weary of life, aching in his joints and teeth and to the very roots of his massive, timeworn tusks and organs. She had brought him gifts of tender sweet grass and ripe berries and healing roots; the latter she had pounded into a paste, adding oil of willow so that the spirits that lived within that sacred tree would eat his pain. And it had been so. Soon his breath had been sweet again, and his urine and fecal matter that of a healthy animal.

Her people had called her Medicine Girl, and Girl Who Walks with Mammoth. Ha-xa had been proud, and Mah-ree had rejoiced in a happiness so deep that it had moved her to tears of joy, for she had known then that no other girl was worthy to be Shaman's Woman.

Cha-kwena signaled Gah-ti to get down. They went onto their bellies to peer over the top of a dunelike drift. The sun was well up now. Their limbs throbbed after the long lope along the trail of the herd. Twice the tracks had circled back, then broadened and struck off westward again. Now the mammoth were using their tusks to dig up a meal amid a stand of trees just to the east of them. Ahead, coming out of the west, the figures of fur-clad hunters were unmistakable.

A sigh of despair went out of Gah-ti. "I never imagined that they could have come this far after I misled them in the storm."

"It does not matter now." Cha-kwena stared straight ahead, knowing what he must do, counting the distant figures, trying to decide how many he could strike down before he himself was killed.

"They are hunting Mah-ree, not mammoth, Cha-kwena! And they have not seen us. If we turn back now, we can still run ahead with the women. The sight of the herd might tempt them to hunt. There is so much meat, I think they will try to blood their spears before they go on. And look at them! We cannot hope to kill so many! We are two men with but three arms between us! You might as well be alone!"

"Go, then, if you will, but I cannot go back, Gah-ti." Cha-kwena slung off his lightweight traveling pack, then readied his spears and spear hurler. "I am guardian of the sacred stone and of the totem. The sacred stone is around my neck. And the life spirit of the totem lives on in that herd!" It struck him in that moment that he had just broken the sacred trust of the Ancients. It was too late to care. "The forces of Creation are with me. With you or without you, I will not be alone."

Mah-ree had spent most of the day in relocating the lean-to far from its original site along the cut bank. It had taken hours to complete the task of moving their belongings and the little tent within a copse of young trees upon which mammoth had been feeding the previous night.

Kahm-ree complained vigorously until Mah-ree had explained that they must hide themselves in the event that Shateh's hunters came for them. She had not added that if this occurred, then Cha-kwena and Gah-ti would probably be dead. Nor had she explained that even if the worst happened, the totem might still live on within the great cow—the matriarch did not yet show her pregnancy, and if Shateh's hunters pursued the herd, they would kill the youngest, most tender meat. After the hunters' bellies were full of mammoth flesh and the men had much meat to carry back to the village, Mah-ree reasoned that they would probably abandon their search for her. Then it would be her responsibility to drive the surviving mammoth and the great totem-bearing cow beyond the edge of the world, where no hunters would ever find them. Not that she would have much heart to live if her shaman was dead, but live on she would, following the totem as she had once followed the great white mammoth, serene in the knowledge that as long as its life spirit endured within the world, her mother and sisters and all of the never-to-be-seen-again members of her band would also survive.

None of these things had Mah-ree said to Kahm-ree, who, after helping set up the lean-to, promptly crawled into it and went to sleep. Mah-ree had not complained, for the heaviest, most difficult work had just begun, and the old woman had not been physically or mentally up to any of it. After mounding snow over and around the sloth skin so it would resemble a pack rat's nest, Mah-ree had set herself to laying a double trail eastward, one in her own shoes, the other in Kahm-ree's. Meticulous backtracking had brought her back to the shelter, where she obliterated all footprints around the lean-to. It was not a camp she hoped to stay in for very long, for she had arranged mammoth feces and urine-saturated snow to make it seem as if tuskers, not people, were still using the site as feeding and sleeping grounds.

At the end of the arduous labors, Mah-ree sat down and watched the horizon, hopeful that her man would return. Much time had gone by. It was late afternoon, and melancholy set in more deeply with the passing time. She felt shaken by the depth of her unhappiness, in spite of the fact that all of her secret childhood dreams had come true. Never again would she join her mother and the other women and girls of her band at berry picking. Never again would she sit alone in the meadow and watch Grandfather of All at his feeding. Never again would she be lifted in the curl of his great trunk so that she could place root mash into his mouth and rub healing, pain-eating willow oil into his gums. Yes, she was Shaman's Woman. But for how long if Shateh and his warriors came over the edge of the world and found what they were seeking?

Suddenly, the mammoth came over the western horizon and moved toward her. Mah-ree cried aloud in gladness to see the great, high-humped animals in their long, hairy winter coats.

"Mah-ree!"

She thought she recognized Gah-ti's voice, but she was confused, for she also heard the barking of dogs and the high yip-yipping of young boys. Mah-ree's heart skipped a beat. Was Shateh coming for her with his entire tribe?

She frowned into the distance and was so frightened that she was unable to breathe. Many fur-clad, load-bearing people on snow walkers were coming toward her. Dogs plodded along with them, some bearing side packs, others dragging sledges. She counted three men with spears in hand. Mah-ree's heart was beating very fast. Instinct told her to duck between the trees where the lean-to was set up. She cast a glance at it, then stared westward again. The worst had happened.

And then her heart skipped a beat. One man strode aggressively ahead of the others and to one side of the now rapidly advancing herd. With his spear occasionally flashing red and blue in the light of the sun, he was unmistakable in his flowing rabbit-skin cloak and owl-skin headdress.

"Cha-kwena!" Mah-ree gasped his name and stepped from the trees.

The mammoth were very close when they lumbered past her, huffing their way eastward with never a backward glance. The ground shook, but she kept staring forward until, suddenly, her hands flew to tent her exhalation of surprise and disbelief as she realized that it was her own band coming toward her, with the dogs harnessed to sledges upon which the children rode and waved.

"Mah-ree!" called Ta-maya, raising an arm in greeting as she walked ahead of Kosar-eh.

"Ban-ya? Is that my Ban-ya calling?" asked old Kahm-ree, elbowing from the lean-to and looking hopefully around. There was no one to answer her question. Mah-ree was running forward, weeping with joy, stumbling in the deep snow and laughing and weeping as she fell, then regained her footing, only to fall again, until she was at last in her older sister's arms.

"Oh, Ta-maya! My shaman said I would never see you again!"

Kosar-eh stopped beside the hugging twosome.

Mah-ree looked up at him in a daze of delight. "Gah-ti said you had abandoned him forever!"

Gah-ti, standing beside his father with his four young brothers gathered around and little Doh-teyah riding his shoulders, shrugged and looked happily embarrassed. "I was mistaken."

Kosar-eh shook his head. "This man and his woman do not stay among those who feed women and babies to fire. Nor does he abandon his children, even though his eldest does not think enough of him to know the way of his heart in this!"

With her arms around Ta-maya, Mah-ree felt the baby in her sister's belly move and was so happy that she began to cry again. "We are a band once more! Truly now, all that I have ever dreamed of as a child has come to pass! Oh, truly my shaman *is* Shaman to have made this so! Never will I fear for the future or doubt him again."

"Your shaman nearly had a spear in my neck before he realized I was not Shateh!" declared Kosar-eh.

Mah-ree barely heard him. She was too elated, too overjoyed as she ran to Cha-kwena and kissed him hard on the mouth. He looked weary to his spirit and beyond. She kissed him again. Then, euphoric, she went to every newcomer, touching and kissing and speaking the name of each of them, even the dogs, until at last she stopped and asked, "Where is Ha-xa? Why is our mother not with you?"

Ta-maya and U-wa exchanged quick, troubled glances before looking down and away; all of the travelers seemed upset—all but Kahm-ree, who was rapturously hugging her granddaughter's son, Piku-neh, and assuring him that they would soon find his mother, Ban-ya.

Mah-ree tensed. She looked away from Kahm-ree and saw tears well within her sister Ta-maya's eyes. "Where *is* Ha-xa? Why is our mother not with you?"

Somehow, even before Kosar-eh spoke—quietly, smoothly, as though by softening the words with a gentle tone he might ease the pain that they must surely inflict—she knew the truth. She had feared it on the night when she had heard her mother scream. She had suspected it when Gah-ti and Kahm-ree had shown up outside the lean-to without Ha-xa.

Kosar-eh's words struck Mah-ree like projectile points, slicing deep, one after the other, piercing straight to her heart, making her spirit bleed. *Your mother is dead. She has given herself to Fire in your place.* There was no pain; the wounding was too severe. The shock was so cruel that she gasped, suddenly cold, unable to breathe. Light-headed,

120   WILLIAM SARABANDE

she looked at Cha-kwena through a mist of misery and said softly, "My shaman did not foresee this."

How could she ever believe in his powers again? *When the totem is reborn, then you will believe,* she told herself. But Mah-ree was not heartened, for that time was far away, and it would be longer still before the great white mammoth was anything more than a little white calf needing the protection of its herd and of the band sworn to protect it.

Then, with a sigh of remorse, she looked at Gah-ti. "My friend did not tell me the truth." The accusations made, she sank to her knees. "My mother is dead . . . because of me." Mah-ree knew that no matter what happened from this moment on, she would never be fully happy again.

U-wa stepped forward and said firmly, "Ha-xa lives on in you, child, and in Ta-maya, Tla-nee, and in all of us who knew and loved her. Come now, Shaman's Woman. Get up. If Kosar-eh could find his way to you, then Shateh will be able to do the same. Besides, this is not good country. We cannot linger here."

Cha-kwena's hand was around his medicine bag; his eyes were fixed and far away, but he did not speak.

Mah-ree looked up at him and with terrible acquiescence forced herself to her feet. She turned in the direction in which the fate of her people lay. She wondered how it was possible to feel so empty and still live on. "U-wa is right," she said. "The mammoth have gone to the east. We cannot linger here."

8

The time of mourning came to an end in the village of Shateh. The spirit of the shamed Bear, satisfied by Ha-xa's sacrifice, fed no more upon the People after his meat was returned to him in the fire.

In the warming, sunstruck days that followed the storm, with the Red World shaman driven beyond the edge of the world, all saw that White Giant Winter had changed his mind about settling early upon the badlands and instead returned to the cold land of perpetual winter. There he would keep company with his storm children until it was his rightful time to travel once more into the land of the People.

Now, on the morning of the fifth day after Bear had come to the village, Senohnim emerged from the lodge of blood to sit beneath the healing rays of the sun. She was joined by several women who were confined with her for the duration of their menses. Senohnim's movement was graceful and assured, her color high, and her eyes were clear. Now and then she smiled as others came with gifts of healing food and drink and attempted to cheer her.

Shateh, sorting spearheads and choosing lengths of sinew and thong and knapping tools for the horse hunt, looked up from where he knelt on a hide tarpaulin in front of his lodge. As he observed his second woman, the chieftain scowled disapprovingly. Senohnim's smiles were, he thought, inappropriate to her situation. This was not the first son she had seen die. The other male she had birthed had been so puny that it had died soon after taking breath. He would have thought that Senohnim would be prostrate with grief and shame over losing a second son. But there she sat, smiling and chatting, until she caught his eye and looked quickly away.

Bitterness and indignation rose in Shateh. Senohnim, he realized, appeared as well and strong before taking the healing food and drink as after. He found himself wondering if she had ever been near death at all. It occurred to him that she might have feigned a failing condition to win sympathy instead of anger from him because, in her terror of Bear, she had cast his son from her womb before the infant was ready to be born. If this was true and she had not been ready to succumb to Spirit Sucker on the night of the great mourning fire, then Mah-ree's life would not have been asked for, Cha-kwena would still be in the village, and bold Ha-xa would still be alive. The chieftain experienced a wave of anger. It was a troubling assumption, one that he could not prove and therefore would not allow himself to consider.

Shateh drew in a deep breath of the morning to steady his nerves and clear his head. He was glad to be rid of the Red World shaman, his sacred stone that had no power, and his lawbreaking woman. With them gone from the village, Shateh was in control again, the man he was again, and the center of his world again. Things definitely seemed to be improving. Nevertheless, as his eyes remained fixed on Senohnim, the chieftain wondered if he would ever be able to look at his second woman without lamenting the loss of his newest son and Ha-xa. Suddenly disgusted and wearied by the general complexity of human nature and its potential for duplicity, the chieftain gathered up his hunting kit and led the men and youths of his band to hunt horses. Of this, at least, he had a clear understanding.

It was a good hunt.
Young Warakan's eyes glowed with pride when all

praised Shateh as hunt chief and shaman. "My father never needed the power of the Red World man!" the boy declared.

And Lahontay, wan and ravaged by grief, nonetheless stood tall and raised a bloody spear as he brought all to agree through acclamation that they were well rid of Cha-kwena, for without Totem Slayer and Trickster and Enemy to call the spirits of the game for his own treacherous purposes, Shateh had led them to take so much meat that there was talk of bringing the women and children to the killing site and relocating the village.

But the badlands were still the badlands. There was not a man or youth who had any desire to stay in this country into which the Red World shaman had led them. After feasting on hot blood and organ meat, a brief council yielded to Shateh's decision to take their kill back across the snow-covered land to the village, where their hunger-depleted women could work the hides and prepare the meat for the return journey to the land of their ancestors.

The meat, hides, hooves, and usable bones of the horses were loaded onto sledges dragged by the dogs. The men sang as they traveled. The traditional Land of Grass songs were loud, atonal tributes, giving thanks to the forces of Creation and to the spirits of the slain horses. The words recalled the days of their grandfathers in that far country, where bison and mammoth had once been as plentiful as grass and the People who hunted them had been as numerous as the star children of Moon—uncountable, strewn across the great northern plains, one tribe not yet broken by famine into warring factions that had since scattered across the world.

As Shateh walked with the others, he became aware of the fevered, almost desperate intensity of the singing of the hunters from the Red World who had not followed Cha-kwena and Lawbreaker into the storm. The chieftain eyed them warily, as did his fellow hunters. When they did not know the words, they kept the rhythm, shouting and calling and maintaining the resonance of the song. They were trying hard to fit in. And they had hunted well this day. Shateh had to concede that despite their small, stocky bodies, they were muscular and strong and—with the single exception of the young man named Hah-ri, who always tended to be a step behind or a thought too slow—they were quick to learn and brave to the core. He knew that it had taken great courage for them to remain in the village after Kosar-eh's family and the others had fled.

Nevertheless, as the chieftain watched them now, he was not certain he would continue to welcome them among his people. They had proved their allegiance to him, and over the past many moons, two of them had taken Land of Grass women. Both had infants who carried the blood of Shateh's tribe. But what kind of men were disloyal to their own shaman and to their own band?

Given the circumstances, wise men! the chieftain thought, countering his own misgivings. Nodding to himself, he remembered Ysuna and the People of the Watching Star; over the span of his lifetime, for the good of his people, Shateh himself had turned against a more powerful shaman and tribe than Cha-kwena and his little band. He made his decision: The luck of his band in the days to come would determine whether or not he would allow the Red World people a place within his tribe. In the meantime, however, even with such fine warriors as Teikan, Ynau, and Ranamal to strengthen his hunting band, Shateh regretted that Kosar-eh had put the lives of a one-armed cripple and a blind child above his own and those of his woman and sons. The big man from the Red World had always impressed him as being remarkably astute, but by following Cha-kwena into the storm he had proved otherwise. Shateh was certain that Spirit Sucker waited for Kosar-eh and his family beyond the edge of the world.

And now, unexpectedly, the absence of Ta-maya left an empty, aching place within Shateh's heart.

"Look, Shateh! The women come to greet us!" declared Teikan.

Shateh nodded, but when he saw Wehakna and Chee-lapat leading the other women and girls excitedly toward him, they all seemed to be Ta-maya, a small, slender, soft-eyed, incomparable, perfect beauty. He shook his head, knowing that it was just as well that Kosar-eh had left and taken his woman. Ta-maya had brought bad luck to every man who ever wanted her. And yet, Shateh knew that sooner or later he would have been moved to take Kosar-eh's woman, even though he would have had to kill the man to do it. As chieftain, was it not his privilege and his right to have the best?

That night Shateh's people affirmed that this was surely so. Gifts were brought to him from every lodge, for all had seen how the horses that had fled from Totem Slayer had returned to become meat for the People once Shateh reclaimed his former authority as chieftain *and* shaman. Even Ranamal, that good man whom U-wa had left behind to follow her son, enthusiastically joined in the rituals.

That night they thanked the spirits of the horses that had fled from Totem Slayer but had died so easily upon the spears of Shateh and his hunters. Gifts were brought to Shateh from every lodge as he led the People to the feast.

The next day they would work hides, cut fat, boil hooves, extract sinew, and make meat that would be carried on the journey back into the country of their ancestors. But now was time to rejoice in the banishment of the bad-luck shaman and, at long last, sate their bodies upon the nourishment of man-worthy meat. They eased their spirits with a gluttony that drove away the sadness that had come to them with the great bear that Cha-kwena had called to their village.

The skin of the slain bear was still staked above the fire. Shateh officiated as prime cuts of horse meat were offered to the spirit of Walks Like a Man, just in case Great Paws still lingered in the world of the living. The storm had made a ruin of the bulk of the firewood, but shovels made of scapulas and of pelvic bones salvaged from the large grazing animals were taken out and used to clear snow from the area of celebration. The fire was nurtured with fat and the last of their stores of precious dried bones and dung. Hides were spread upon the wet ground, and the People gathered to make offerings to the spirits. Small, vital portions of each of the slain horses were given to the fire—a piece of hoof, a shaving of bone, a shred of hide and flesh and organs, a hair from mane and tail. In this way, those animals that had given up their life for the People would be able to take up vestiges of their old flesh and be born again to run once more before the spears of grateful hunters in the great and never-ending circle of life and death.

Steaks were spitted and seared and eaten while the blood ran hot, as at the moment of the kill. Bones were pounded and cracked, and specially carved scoops probed deep for buttery, iron-rich marrow. Eyes were pierced and passed, and the rich black fluid within was shared and sucked by all. Great ropes of intestines were unfolded and sectioned into manageable portions, then slit lengthwise so that the tangy green pudding within could be fingered out.

At last the revelers could eat no more. The men, sighing and leaning against their backrests, licked their fingers and gnawed on the ends of small bones as the women sang and prepared to dance for them. Meanwhile the children and youths gathered in small clusters to watch while Moon rose full above the earth and a mild west wind moved across the barrens. The sound of melting snow could be heard running away into and across the land.

Shateh did not hear the wind or the melting snow when, in solemn gratitude to the hunters and to their chieftain and shaman, the women danced before him in the traditional steps of the Land of Grass since time beyond beginning. They had not danced in many a long moon. It was a gift to him, and he knew it—a gesture affirming the rightness of his place as a leader of men and the intermediary between this world and the world beyond. The Red World women who had taken Land of Grass men tried to join in, but their dancing was slow, methodical, highly structured, and tedious to his eyes—a reflection of their settled, passive ways, a life of adapting to whatever the forces of Creation sent to them. In contrast, the women of his tribe presented the feast dance of big-game hunting nomads who lived always at the edge of the abyss of life, poised between feast and famine. The whirling, leaping, and twisting were as basic and instinctive as the rhythm of blood beating hot and fast within the veins of predator and prey alike when the hunted runs for its life; it reflected the willingness—no, the wish—to take chances. The women of the Red World did not know such dancing and soon fell back, overwhelmed and intimidated.

The women of the plains mimicked the horses whose flesh and blood had renewed the force of their lives. With their hair loose and their faces oiled with the fat of the kill, they neighed and nickered and bared their breasts and bellies and worked their hips while Shateh and every other man stared and clapped and stomped an ever-faster rhythm.

Young and old, the women danced.

Fair and homely, the women danced.

All danced save virgins and those who carried new life or endured menses and were isolated with Senohnim within the lodge of blood.

They were all beautiful to Shateh, and he felt his loins grow hard and hot and seeking—as big as a stallion's in rut. The chieftain's mouth hungered at the sight of them, and at his own Wehakna, no longer young but leading the others in bold provocations. Secure in her gender, smiling, confident, she pranced close to nip at his shoulder and then, like a mare in heat, turned and bent forward and shook her generous bare bottom, flicking the ends of her long hair as though raising a tail in invitation to be mated. Shateh loosed a loud roar of laughter at her antics. He had not seen Wehakna dance like that since the best days of the great bison kills when the many bands of the Land of Grass had come together into one vast and teeming tribe.

The memory stirred Shateh's blood, as did the woman, for he viewed her now as she had been the first time he had seen her, a young woman, one of three who, with permission of their fathers, had danced and—in the age-old tradition of their ancestors—spread themselves for the man who was chief above all chiefs, inviting him to be the first with them.

Shateh had not refused. Before the watching eyes of the tribe, he had taken Wehakna, and then he had taken the others while the tribe cheered his prowess, seeing with their own eyes that he was like a great bison bull with his herd, most fit to lead his men and to be the first to impregnate the females of his choice.

Later, pleased by Wehakna, he had carried her to his lodge and taken her as one of his all-the-time women. He had put sons into her, but they were dead, and bitterness over the loss touched the chieftain, but only briefly. The old fire was back in Wehakna's eyes. She was ready and eager to be mated again. As was he.

"Shateh is a great chief! See how the women dance for you!"

Startled to hear the voice of Warakan, Shateh raised an eyebrow to the unexpected accolade and looked down to see that his adopted son had insinuated himself through the circle of seated men to come close to his side. The boy's wide face shone with feast grease. His long, dark eyes were filled with firelight and pride in his father . . . and with fear.

"Why are you shaking, Warakan? It is only a dance! They are only women! When you are older, they will dance for you, and believe me, you will have no fear in your eyes then!"

"You will not eat one of them?"

The question would have amazed and amused another man, but Shateh understood the boy's reasoning. "You are no longer a son of the People of the Watching Star, Warakan. You must forget their ways."

Warakan forced a wan smile, seemed to will himself to stand tall and bold, watching the women moving in the firelight. They were circling now, and Wehakna, in the lead and still dancing, was no longer in front of Shateh. She was looking back at her man and scowling at the boy. "Shateh's first woman does not like me," said Warakan.

Shateh laughed. "Not now, she doesn't! You stand in the way of that which she would now have of me. Go back to the other boys. Your place is not here."

Warakan obeyed reluctantly.

Shateh turned his face to the dancers. To his surprise, Lahontay had come to stand before him. The man appeared savaged by fatigue and sadness. He held his daughter Eira by the hand; the girl was naked save for a pale robe of bison calfskin worn lightly over her shoulders and back. Her head was bent. She was trembling.

"At the last moon this girl became a woman," said the old hunter. "She was to be for Teikan in the spring, but now I have put the robe of first mating upon her back and bring her to Shateh . . . a gift from Lahontay to my chief and shaman and Man Who Brings Many Horses. Perhaps she will prove a son maker. No man has been between her thighs. Let Shateh be first. Let it be done in the old way so that all may witness the shedding of first blood and see the true worthiness of the gift! Now, as this band prepares to return to the land of our ancestors, let all see and know the power of Shateh!"

Teikan, seated nearby in the circle of men, jumped to his feet. "I have given gifts for that new woman!"

"I will give them back!" snapped Lahontay. "My son is dead because you were not man enough to keep a shaman's curse from devouring him! You will not have my daughter. She is all that is left for me to give to my chieftain in honor of all that he has done this day, and I will not give her to you."

Shateh's head went up defensively. It occurred to him that grief and fatigue rather than generosity and loyalty were motivating Lahontay's words. Considering the hostility that had only recently been put to rest between himself and Teikan, he thought it might be best to refuse this gift. But Shateh had not seen Eira naked before, or, if he had, he had not looked at her closely. Now, in the light of the feast fire, he saw that she was as young as Wehakna had been in those long-gone days when he could take three women down, put the fire of life into them, and still have enough stamina left to carry one away for further pleasure within his lodge. Eira was as small and slim as Ta-maya, but her breasts were amazingly well grown for one so young, as full and heavy as Ban-ya's had been, with nipples large and dark and peaking in the cold as he knew they would peak beneath the touch of his hand or tongue or . . .

Shateh's heart hardened as he found himself remembering the hated Ban-ya; but even as he thought of her, his eyes burned on the bare breasts of Eira. As he continued to think of that Red World woman, his man bone grew harder and hotter, for in all of his years he had never lain with a partner who knew more ways to please a man. It would be a decided pleasure to instruct a young girl in those ways, he thought, aching with renewed need, eyeing Lahontay's offering, and knowing that it had been many a long moon since he had taken a virgin as young as Eira, and even longer since the taking had been done in the old way, with the tribe looking on.

He raised a speculative brow. Shateh had abandoned the custom of reserving for himself the first piercing of every desirable female in his band. First, jealousy and conflicts occasionally erupted among the other men. Secondly, there were risks involved; the ritual display of power was impressive, but he was no longer a youth with limitless capacity for expending himself. But now, with the success of the hunt behind him and the meat-driven strength of horses running in his blood and throbbing in his loins, Shateh looked at the naked girl before him and knew that his people would marvel at what he would show them now.

"Come," the chieftain said to the girl and, ignoring the audible hiss of frustration that came from between Teikan's clenched teeth, extended both hands to Eira.

She sucked in a little breath—of relief or fright, he could not tell—and eyes still downcast, came to him and laid her fingers lightly, tentatively upon his open palms. Now she raised her eyes to his and, unexpectedly, curled the middle finger of each hand down, probed his palms with quick, light, symbolic jabs.

His reaction to her touch was instantaneous; he caught his breath as his loins caught fire. Shateh felt like a youth again, reckless and proud of the condition that was prerequisite to mating. He doubted if he had ever been as ready to take a woman as he was now. He felt young, powerful, and complete in his maleness.

The chieftain smiled. He rose to his feet and scanned the watching, breathless crowd. He knew that they wanted the old way as much as he did. On their faces were a quivering, animalistic expectancy and an open adoration that he had not seen in all too long.

He nodded. Warakan had been correct when he declared that Shateh had never needed the power of the Red World man! Cha-kwena was gone. The totem was dead. The sacred stone was far away. Tomorrow, while his band prepared for the return trek to the Land of Grass, he would send back to the Red World all those who carried the blood of Cha-kwena's race, for now he was certain that their presence had weakened and allowed him to be seduced by imagined powers outside himself. But in this moment, with Lahontay's gift standing before him naked and willing to be mated, Shateh knew that he was still the man he had always been—chief above all chiefs, shaman above all shamans.

"I will take this woman," he declared. "And for this one night, as we praise the forces of Creation for the gift of many horses and anticipate our return to the land of our ancestors, let it be done in the old way!"

He loosed his loin cover, displaying for all to see that there was no weakness in him now, nor was there inconsideration of the fact that he was about to deprive Teikan of a pleasure that had been promised to him. "In the spring Teikan may take a new woman of his choice. This night he may lie on any woman who pleases him. But now, in the way of the chiefs of the Land of Grass since time beyond beginning, let it be as Lahontay has asked—let all see and know that Eldest Hunter's gift is worthy and that the power of Shateh is the power of one who is chief *and* shaman!"

And so it was decided. Shateh was too intent upon the moment to notice when Teikan turned away, leading Cheelapat.

Ranamal and Ynau and Xohkantakeh had taken up hand drums and were beating a slow, measured rhythm while the women and children pressed close to stare. Lahontay removed the pale robe of first mating from his daughter's shoulders, placed it upon the ground, and stood back.

Eldest Hunter lamented the fact that he had outlived the last of his women and that all of his other daughters had married into other bands many a long summer before. He had little woman wisdom to offer Eira. He had shown her how she must stand, head down and docile, when she was offered to the chieftain. He had instructed her how she must lay her hands upon Shateh's at the moment of initial acceptance, and then how she must invite and excite him with her fingertips. He had shown her the sounds and movements she must make after the initial piercing. He had brought her warmed horse fat and commanded her to slather it between her thighs and deep within her female parts so that the chieftain's penetration would be less painful and she might more easily endure in silence—and, he hoped, pretend to enjoy—that which would in time become pleasurable to her.

As Lahontay watched, his throat constricted, Eira knelt upon the robe, her back to the chieftain, her hands splayed upon the ground. She dutifully spread herself in the way in which her father had instructed—feet well apart, thighs held wide, buttocks held high, and her new-woman parts exposed and open to what must come to all females in time.

A muscle spasmed at Lahontay's clenched jaw. Eira was finding it difficult to keep her backside up, and she was shaking so badly that he feared that her hands would not hold her weight. If she fell forward before the chieftain had achieved penetration or if she cried out in pain at the moment of copulation, the omens would be seen as very bad, and the tribe had had enough of bad omens.

The old hunter chewed his lips with worry. He had warned Eira of this. He had explained to her that many times during the last days he had spoken in opposition of the foreign shaman, and even though he had been proved right in all that he had said against Cha-kwena, he must nevertheless make amends to Shateh for his outspokenness. A man of his years dared not be in disfavor with his chieftain lest one day he find himself named Useless and cast out of the band.

He had explained to Eira that for his sake she must not only be offered to Shateh as a gift but be presented in the old way. A naked young girl standing ready and willing to be mated in the light of a feast fire was not likely to be refused by any man, especially by Shateh, who had savored the pleasure that came with first piercing while others watched and witnessed his virility. Since Shateh was now without sons in a land long without man-worthy meat, Lahontay was hoping that the chieftain would be grateful to him for having offered a daughter for such a time-honored display of masculine power. If the girl were to bear a son as a result of the mating, she would occupy a place of honor within Shateh's lodge, and Lahontay was certain that his own status would be assured.

But now, Lahontay saw his daughter tuck her hips like a frightened dog and pull her heels together. The women were mocking her obvious trepidation and advising her to prepare herself for the advance of the chieftain's "spear." When the assembly sighed in justifiable admiration, Lahontay wondered if he had ever seen a man as big as Shateh was now.

Lahontay stood tall, resolute, and expressionless as the chieftain dropped to his knees. Positioning himself behind the girl, Shateh allowed himself a moment at her breasts before moving his hands beneath her and, mistaking the slickness of applied fat for the readiness of the new woman, placed himself for penetration, gripped her thighs, then pulled her back and rammed deep.

The drums beat loudly. The watching women and men cheered their chieftain on. The children gaped. The youths edged closer. Lahontay grimaced, expecting Eira to scream, then exhaled with relief when she did not. The women nodded and sighed, approving her bravery as, in a fury of release, Shateh pumped the wet heat of life deep into the new woman. Then, in a show of control that awed everyone who saw it, he pulled out of her—leaving Eira slumped forward upon the ground, curled inward like a little mollusk seeking safety within a nonexistent shell—and rose to his feet, displaying himself again, this time blooded. Amazingly, his man bone rose once more, and he asked if there were additional new women who would be honored in the ancient way this night.

Long, hungry days in the badlands had resulted in the blossoming of few new women; but the daughter of Xohkantakeh was nudged forward by her mother, as were the daughter of Zakeh and two girls who were daughters of K-wok and Tleea-neh, Red World men. The latter Shateh rebuffed as unfit vessels for his lineage, and when the Red World People murmured resentfully, the chieftain told them that they were welcome to break down their lodges and return to the land of their ancestors, for he would surely suffer them to live among his people no more after this night.

Without another word, he then took both of the daughters of his warriors, and Lahontay was not the only man to be impressed.

"Behold the power of Shateh now that the Red World shaman is gone!" cried Ynau.

"The power has always been Shateh's!" declared Lahontay. "Now that we have driven the Red World shaman over the edge of the world, we see the truth! We need no other man to lead us or to speak to the spirits of the ancestors or the forces of Creation on our behalf! Shateh is chief *and* shaman!"

* * *

In the darkness of Teikan's lodge, Cheelapat lay sweated and satisfied beneath the man who was not her man as she sneered in contempt of Lahontay's shouting. "Listen to him! That old one is as clever as a pack rat. He stores up favor with Shateh and praises him to our people because he fears that if the people lose faith in Shateh, you will be chief and put Lahontay from the band."

"Then why not give the girl to me in the first place?" asked Teikan, still moving on the chieftain's woman.

"Because Shateh is chief *now,* as he has always been, and over these past days you have become Man Who Fails to Kill Bear, Man Who Throws a Spear to Lawbreaking Woman, and Man Who Follows Wrong Trail and Lets Enemies Escape!"

Teikan was surprised by his reaction to her goading. He was not angered. Sobered by the truth, he drew out of her. He felt weary of her all-too-quickly-sated body and her venomous nature. "In the days of my father, Shateh was chief. And since the death of my father, Shateh has been as a father in my eyes and heart. For many years I have been honored to hunt at his side and proud to be a man in his eyes in days of peace and of war. It is good to know that he has rediscovered what it means to be chief and has cast aside the influence of lesser men."

Teikan got to his feet and went to stand at the entrance to his lodge. He held the door skin back and looked out. "Not since before the great war have I seen a village of our people like this! The blood of the chieftain's life and strength is back inside his followers. It is a good thing! My heart sings at the sight of it."

Cheelapat sat up. The firelight threw her furrowed brow into deep planes and shadows. "Shateh was not man enough to notice me when I danced for him. His eyes were on Wehakna. Did you not see? Only an old man would catch fire at the dancing of a woman who is older and drier than the dead totem! And what is the matter with you, Teikan? Do you no longer yearn to be chief?"

He shook his head. "I am a man of the tribe, Cheelapat, sworn first to the good of my people and then to the honor of my chief. I have yearned for no more and no less than that Shateh be again the chief he once was. In the spring I will show my allegiance to him by taking another new woman. Jheena, I think, if she has come to her time of blood by then, or Vahni, or one of Ranamal's girls. Eira is of no importance to me. Nor are you. Go from my sleeping furs, Cheelapat. I would not have Shateh know that I have been so small a man as to seek to shame him by coming between your thighs this night."

She was indignant. "Are you afraid of him when only old Lahontay has seen more winters than he? With his own mouth he has told you to take any woman that pleases you!"

"You do not please me. I took you only because you are his. I will not take you again. Now that the Red World Trickster is gone from among us and Shateh is chief and shaman once more, this man will not challenge him again."

around him while another... ... ... among the
People of the Waiting... ... ... would trade
glances or whispers with one another, speak the words
Outlander, or peace with... ... ...
boys who would work and live as they did and how he
would solve his... ... ...
tongues of his fellow... ... ...
... ...
... ...
... ...
... ...

9

There was a large oak tree on the bluff. It was not a tall tree, although it was wide of body and broad of crown, with age-toughened bark and outreaching branches as thick as the torsos of reclining men. Warakan, perched between two of these branches, was securely braced in a smooth little notch that afforded comfortable seating from which he could gain an overview of the starlit village.

The boy often came here to be away from others. He would climb the tree and sit hidden within the evergreen foliage from which he could leap strongly, then land lightly on his feet like a young cougar. He imagined that he was just that, an unseen terror of the trees, harassing Namaray and Trop and Oonay and Hranan and the other youths who harassed him behind Shateh's back. Outlander, they called him. Watching-Star boy. Woman eater. Cannibal. Warakan growled to himself and wondered what he would have to do to be accepted by the others, then told himself that it did not matter. Whatever was asked of him, he would do it, but someday he would find a way to get even with the other boys for making him feel the outsider. He scowled, assuring himself that when he was grown he would be chief in his father's place, a man to make Shateh proud of the foundling he had named Son. And then, when Warakan the Brave and Bold and Infinitely Wise was chief, no one would dare remind him of his ancient and despised ancestry among the People of the Watching Star. If they did, he would make them eat the tongues with which they spoke the words.

The thought pleased Warakan. He uttered a deep, slow little chuckle of malevolent satisfaction and, in the way of boys who savor such thoughts as these, debated how he would serve his punishment. Would he first roast the tongues of his offenders? Or would he make them eat them raw? He sighed wistfully and knew that there was plenty of time to decide. Now, chewing on the gristly end of the marrowbone that was all he had barely managed to keep for himself after being forced to wrestle Namaray for his portion of the feast, Warakan was content to sit and swing his legs and stare after Cheelapat as she stalked from Teikan's lodge.

The boy's left eyebrow arched upward across his brow. What was one of Shateh's women doing with Teikan? he wondered. And why was there such anger in her step and defiance in the way she held her head as she entered the chieftain's lodge with an angry slapping away of the door flap?

Frowning, Warakan stared past the great lodge of Shateh with its wonderfully painted hide coverings and bone-beaded banners of eagle feathers and looked toward what was left of the feast fire. Beneath the staked skin and head of Bear, he could see men and women pairing and ferociously coupling on the ground while the chieftain was coming away from the throng. Never had Warakan seen Shateh look so powerful, so infinitely assured—a man as magnificent and ageless as the land or sky. He was carrying the new woman, Eira, gently in his arms. Wehakna proudly followed with the bloodied robe of first mating folded over her arm like a prize hide taken in a great hunt.

Warakan sighed again. Never had he been prouder to have been named Son by Shateh, but he was glad that the fire was dying and that the ritual of first piercing had ended with the new women alive and safe. For a few moments he had feared the worst. The firelit scene had recalled another, in the stronghold of the People of the Watching Star. He had remembered tall, tattooed men and women dancing, laughing, chanting, partaking of the sacred mushroom that made the world glow green while a new woman came forth to be joined symbolically to the tribe, and then . . . devoured.

The marrowbone came down from Warakan's mouth and, held loosely in his greasy left hand, rested upon his bare thigh, then dropped to the ground. "Neea." The boy whispered his cherished sister's name. He had tried to forget her and all that made remembering her so painful, but she had hidden him during the raid that had devastated their village and looked after him like a little mother until they had been found by others of their tribe and cared for until . . .

Warakan shook his head hard, trying to free it of memories. It was no use, because the People of the Land of Grass had been Enemy then. Warriors from the northern plains had raided his village, killed his parents, burned the lodges of his people, raped the daughters of his band, then slain all survivors except the dogs.

But then, the night of his sister's death in the stronghold, Warakan had seen with his own eyes why his people were justly hunted, despised, and slaughtered or enslaved whenever they were found. Now, trembling like a wounded bird within the crotch of the tree, the boy stared straight ahead and saw and heard it all as though it were happening again . . . the vaulted, firelit walls and ceiling of the cavern . . . tattooed men and women summoning the "bride," and the new woman coming forth of her own free will, offering herself to Great Spirit of the People of the Watching Star, to Thunder in the Sky, god of storm and power and the whirling wind and of all that lived and of all that must die.

"Neea." Again Warakan spoke his sister's name. She walked barefooted and smiling through his memories to offer herself to the god, instead of the usual captive given in yearly renewal of a blood covenant too unspeakable to remember but too terrible and grotesque to forget.

He saw the sacred dagger drawn from its casing made of a hollowed human arm. He watched as Neea was stabbed and her heart cut from her still-living body. Then her corpse was flayed and her flesh consumed while the old, hideously tattooed shaman Jhadel looked on and smiled . . . and the high priestess Sheela danced in Neea's skin—

"Warakan?"

The sound of Jheena's voice so startled the boy that he fell from the tree.

"I am sorry," she said, coming to kneel beside him in the light of the moon. "I did not mean to make you fall. Here. You must have dropped this, too."

Warakan sat stunned by his fall and by the unexpected appearance of the girl. She handed the marrowbone to him. Like Warakan, it had landed in an area of bare ground close to the trunk of the tree, where snow had melted away. It was gritty with soil and bits of old, wet oak mast; he took it anyway and realized that he probably would have taken a handful of feces from this girl and still said thank you.

The realization flustered him.

An instant later, he was on his feet, wiping damp earth and oak stubble from his winter leggings and the lower edges of his hip-length buckskin tunic as he stared up at the round-faced, dimpled daughter of Ynau. Warakan felt his face flush. Jheena was so good to look upon! He only wished she were not so tall, but she was older than he by almost two full turnings of the seasons. Staring at her in moonlight, Warakan wished he were older, too.

She smiled.

Warakan, at a loss for words, could not guess why Jheena, who rarely looked his way, had come to him now. He smiled back at her; but his upper lip seemed to stick to his teeth, and somehow the resultant smile was crooked and only half-done. Embarrassed, he looked down at his moccasins, licked his lip free of his teeth, cleared his throat— manfully, he thought—then looked up at her again, stern faced and dignified this time. "What brings you out of the village on a night like this, Daughter of Ynau? A girl

THE EDGE OF THE WORLD

alone—it is not a good thing!" He finished with a masculine flourish that did not quite work out; his voice broke and cracked.

Now Jheena was the one who looked down.

Mortified, Warakan waited for her to laugh at him. He was grateful when she did not.

"A night like this brings me from the village," she answered worriedly. "It frightened me. Truly, this cannot be the way of our ancestors! My mother says that I will be a new woman soon, and if I am fortunate, Shateh will honor me as he has honored Eira and the others. But he is so big, and I am so small. . . . And so I thought that maybe . . . if you could tell your father that his way is not a good way for a new woman, he would listen to you. What was done tonight was more fitting to the harsh and bloody ways of Watching Star People than—" She stopped. "Forgive me! I forgot you are one of them."

Warakan's face flamed with hurt and anger. "I am *not* one of them! When they planned to make war on Shateh's people I ran away to this tribe and warned Shateh of what was to come. Because of my alert, Shateh defeated my tribe in battle and now calls me Son. The People of the Watching Star have been scattered like tattered leaves upon a summer's-end wind! Because of Shateh's victory, you are here, alive, talking to me now and not gutted and skinned and lying dead on the back of some Watching Star shaman! Whatever Shateh does is good for his people. Eira is not dead! The daughters of Xohkantakeh and Zakeh were honored by Shateh tonight! And now that the Red World shaman is gone, *everything* will be good for us. He made Shateh look weak. You will see. Shamans are treacherous liars. *All* of them."

"Shateh is shaman."

Warakan reached out and shoved her, not hard, but sharply enough to rock her on her feet; he was so angry that he did not care. "Shateh is also chief above all chiefs! He is not like other shamans. He does not use tricks and lies or offer the blood of others to the spirits to assure his power. Women need not fear him."

Jheena stuck out her chin stubbornly. "Tell that to Ban-ya of the Red World, who was put from this band to die alone in the Valley of the Dead even though it was said that she carried Shateh's life in her belly!"

"She was a bad-luck woman and a bringer of death, not of life! Shateh gave to her only what she gave to others—a long and painful death. I tell you, no one except his enemies need fear him. And someday, when I am a man, together Shateh and Warakan will hunt and kill them all!"

Jheena was not impressed; she was pouting, moving closer. "If Warakan will promise to talk to his father about his way with new women, this girl will let Warakan feel her breasts. They are not big, but they are growing. This girl will tell no one if Warakan will—"

Warakan was as amazed as he was insulted by her unexpected invitation. "I am not as old as you, Daughter of Ynau, but I am not so young and stupid that I can be tempted by a dishonorable bribe! I am Shateh's son! I will not speak against his will!"

Jheena stamped her foot and hissed at him like a young goose caught in a birding snare. "I hope he has made 'real' sons on Eira and on the others tonight. Then, when he dies, he will have three boys of his own blood to choose from when he gives one of them his name so that his spirit may dwell forever in the world of the living! Then you will be no son to him at all but only what you are and always will be—a foundling of the People of the Watching Star . . . the *real* enemy in this camp!" The declaration made, she whirled around and ran off.

Shaken, humiliated, Warakan watched her go. For a long time he stood very still, thinking that Jheena, who had so captivated his heart, was no better than the boys who taunted him when Shateh's back was turned.

Far beyond the bluffs, wolves were howling. Warakan listened. The lonely sound always reminded him of Neea holding him close in the night, telling him that he was a special boy and precious to her and that he should not be afraid, for as long as his sister was near, she would not let the wolves eat him. Now Neea was dead, and Shateh kept him safe from wolves, but for how long if the chieftain succeeded in siring a son of his own?

"I *am* that son," Warakan declared to the night and the oak tree and the howling wolves. "Not of Shateh's blood but of his spirit. I will never be shaman, as he is, nor do I want to be. But I have saved his life, and he has saved mine. Someday I will be chief and bring meat to him and make a place of honor for him in my lodge, as he has made for me in his. I am Warakan, born to the People of the Watching Star, but Shateh will never have a son who loves him as I do!"

The words had sounded much too loud. Warakan realized with a start that the village was quiet now. The People were settling into sleep beside the dying fire and within their lodges. He knew they were content in the knowledge that Shateh was chief and shaman once more and that with the banishment of the Red World shaman, the bad spirits that had been following for many a long moon had surely left them at last.

Warakan was so glad of this that he smiled, trembling with immense satisfaction as he found himself staring at the staked body of the great bear. He cocked his head, observed the massive head and back and paws, and was suddenly awed by the power of the shaman who had insidiously, treacherously communed with its spirit. And yet the thought occurred to Warakan that when Cha-kwena had turned Walks Like a Man from the path of the hunters and sent it marauding into the village instead, he had turned the forces of Creation also against himself.

Why would he have done this? wondered the boy. *And why would a shaman powerful enough to command the spirit of Walks Like a Man have run away over the edge of the world, following a herd of mammoth into the barrens, instead of facing Shateh on behalf of his lawbreaking woman?*

The questions troubled him. Everyone said that Cha-kwena had lost his powers, but Warakan did not believe it. The man was Trickster, Yellow Wolf, Brother of Animals, Guardian of the Sacred Stone, and Totem Slayer. Warakan's face worked with loathing. Who could say what motivated such a shaman, unless it was hatred of an old enemy whom he had beguiled into friendship with the hope of shaming him and bringing him to his knees before his people.

Now Warakan smiled again, felt better again. It was Shateh who had shamed Cha-kwena and sent him running away in fear of the chieftain's greater power. Trickster's tricks had failed, and not even the reputed forces that were said to live within his sacred stone had been able to help him.

"May you die out there in the dark beyond the edge of the world, Cha-kwena!" willed Warakan, and in that moment the wind rose, shifted to the east, and gave him cause to suspect that even though the Red World shaman was far away, his powers were still at work within the night. Even as he continued to stare at the skin of Walks Like a Man, he could have sworn that the great bear moved upon the posts holding it above the sleeping couples.

Again the marrowbone dropped from Warakan's hand. His eyes widened with disbelief. Walks Like a Man shook himself, arched his great neck and shoulders, and lifted his torn, eviscerated body free of the staking. Warakan caught his breath as he saw the great bear leap toward him across the now burned-out fire and over the sleeping people and the tops of the lodges. Walks Like a Man flew like a huge, dark, and furry cloud over Warakan's head. The boy looked up, turned, and followed Bear's flight over the oak tree and into the barrens beyond. He saw not the badlands stretching away beneath the moon and stars but a vast, abyssal canyon opening wide into the skin of the earth. And within that canyon a woman wailed, and a small band of people walked beneath the shadowing wings of an owl as, pursued by the great bear, a herd of mammoth led by a little white calf plodded on into misted distances toward a river of impossible dimensions.

The boy caught his breath and closed his eyes. He squinted so tightly that colors flared beneath his lids. After he opened his eyes, the colors faded slowly, and his vision returned to normal. The barrens were only the barrens. Bear was gone. There were no canyon, no band, no mammoth, and no owl. The only wailing to be heard was that of a distant wolf singing a solitary song as the star children of Moon shifted ever westward toward tomorrow.

Warakan turned again to look across the remains of the fire. The hide and head of the great bear hung on the stakes that held it high, its paws and the edges of its skin moving gently in the wind. Disappointed, Warakan turned once more and stared past the trunk of the oak and across the badlands over which Cha-kwena and his people had fled.

"I will not fear you, your sacred stone, or your dead totem, Cha-kwena! May it be that the spirit of Walks Like a Man has followed you this night. May he feed upon your people as you once sent him to feed upon mine! I, Warakan, son of Shateh, say this! My father is chief and shaman now!"

PART II

WALKS LIKE
A MAN

"On the steep bank of a river, there exists life. A voice is there, and speaks aloud."

—TEWA ELDER
Seeking Life by V. Laskin

PART II

WALKS LIKE A MAN

1

For many days Cha-kwena and his little band followed the mammoth eastward across the badlands under warming skies. The herd kept a steady pace. Although the travelers took turns climbing to high ground so they could scan across the way they had come, they saw no one in pursuit. Nevertheless, Cha-kwena remembered his dreams, and now and then, when wolves called and coyotes yapped, he looked back and could have sworn that he saw a great bear following far behind, all but invisible within the ever-flowing tide of the wind. He kept this to himself and urged his people onward.

They made no fires and slept in cold camps, fearing that smoke might be carried on the wind and flames seen at night by their enemies. Although the children complained, the adults were content to live off the uncooked meat of whatever their snares brought them, supplementing this meager fare with the pounded fat and season's-end berries and roots that U-wa and Ta-maya had packed with them from the now-distant village.

And when the dark came down, Cha-kwena often remained awake long after the others had succumbed to sleep. Keeping a lonely vigil, he was unable to forget that when he had spoken aloud to Gah-ti of the rebirth of the totem, he had broken the sacred trust of the ancestors.

Although the young man kept Cha-kwena's secret, the shaman was tormented by what he had done, for no one knew better than he that to speak of a much-longed-for thing before it had come to pass was to risk bringing dark spirits against it. And so his dreams remained hauntings, and by day he continued to see the great dark spirit bear in the wind, following his people and the mammoth.

Snow melted rapidly. Soon the snow walkers and sledges that Kosar-eh had brought from the village were no longer necessary. The big man suggested that at least one sledge be cached in a storage pit, to make forward progress easier and a return journey feasible if the land ahead proved too difficult or did, in fact, end beyond the rise of the next hills.

But Cha-kwena would not hear of leaving anything behind. "The land will not end! We will not return into the country of our enemies, and we will need all that we possess and *more* when White Giant Winter returns."

Kosar-eh gave no argument, but when he turned and looked back across the barrens, longing and unhappiness were obvious on his face.

Cha-kwena, watching him, knew that it had not been easy for Kosar-eh to turn his back on the new life he had found among Shateh's big-game hunters and warriors—not even for the sake of a one-armed son and a blind daughter.

"It will be good for us in the days ahead, Man of My Heart," Ta-maya assured Kosar-eh, sensing his concern.

He shook his head. "Who can say what will or will not be!" he snapped. His outburst was not aimed at Ta-maya but at their shared situation as he looked at his beloved woman—serene, confident, her slender fingers laced together as her hands rested upon the mound of her pregnancy. Worry shadowed his brow.

Cha-kwena saw and shared it. Surely the small group remained in jeopardy in the far reaches of this barren and unknown land.

Annoyed, U-wa would have no part of it. "My son *can* say what will be!" she proclaimed. "I, for one, am glad to be

THE EDGE OF THE WORLD 151

away from such people as those who name Shateh chief and shaman!"

Cha-kwena noticed that Mah-ree had not spoken in defense of "her" shaman. He was worried about her. Disconsolate over Ha-xa's death and still blaming herself for it, his girl-of-a-woman remained silent and brooding and often fell behind as the band traveled. She showed no interest in anything except the mammoth, and her appetite was poor. She took no notice when Ta-maya or U-wa spoke to her, when the children fell into step beside her, or when her favorites among the dogs trotted alongside and nuzzled her hand; but at least she carried her share of the load and worked with the other women without complaint, and for this, Cha-kwena told himself, he should be grateful.

Now, as he watched, she unhesitatingly helped Kosar-eh disassemble the sledges. Copying his movements, she separated the wooden side runners, dismantled the top slats, then untied the many meticulously carved sections of rib bone that served as protective shoes for the runners and, after setting them out in perfect order, wrapped them in packets of hide.

"Mah-ree will be herself soon enough, my son," said U-wa softly, coming to stand beside him. "What she needs is new life inside her to give her hope in the days to come. You must see to that, Cha-kwena. It is all any woman really wants . . . children to bring her joy and fulfillment in her youth and comfort in her old age, as you will someday bring to me."

"You are not old, Mother."

"I need the fingers of six hands to count my years."

He was startled. She *was* old.

U-wa smiled wryly at his reaction. "One of these days you will bring me comfort?"

He frowned at the question. Though he was shaman and she had just defended him to the band, he did not know what to say.

They traveled on through pale, sandy hills and crossed snow-fed streams that, when swollen with runoff, became sizable springtime rivers. Their clear, shallow waters ran in broad, highly buttressed beds, and the trees and shrubs growing nearby took root high upon the embankments, so there was much deadwood along the shores.

The mammoth walked in steady progression along these autumn-quieted courses, sucking up water and showering themselves in the heat of the day, then wandering off across broad, scrub-covered beaches to tusk up plants and tender-barked trees before settling down to growl in contentment and sleep in the cool of the day or evening. Sometimes they would rise in the middle of night to feed and converse with one another in the way of the mammoth kind. Usually they returned to sleep, but sometimes they would move on under the waning moon. The People would hear them going on their way, and Cha-kwena, ignoring the whining protests of the children, would insist that everyone gather up the belongings and follow.

"They are not circling. Nor are they walking into the wind as is so often their way when days are warm," observed Kosar-eh with a scowl as he hefted his pack.

"It is as though they *know* where they are going and are eager to return to a favorite place," added Ta-maya, hopeful.

"My Ban-ya is waiting for us there," assured Kahm-ree with a knowing smile.

Mah-ree ignored the old woman. "The mammoth are wise to put distance between them and those who would hunt them."

"As we must be!" Cha-kwena was emphatic as he urged the others on, for his dreams remained blighted by the vision of Death that he had first seen within his lodge on the night that Mah-ree and he had been forced to flee.

Since the day when Gah-ti and he confronted what they had thought to be the advance of Shateh's warriors—and in desperation to win against them, he had broken the ancient taboo against naming and blurted the truth about the impending rebirth of the totem—a new awareness of his people's vulnerability had settled upon him. He slept poorly and always with his back to Mah-ree, which made his mother frown, but his little woman was so overwhelmed by sadness over her mother's death, she did not appear to care. Nor did she seem to notice when her man would be drawn from sleep by the song of wolves.

Unsettled by his dreams and invariably hearing what sounded like Ha-xa's voice wailing on the wind, Cha-kwena would brood over the loss of that brave spirit, then rise and seek a solitary place from which he could stare back across the miles. Listening to the wolves, he recalled the ravens and bear and the painted, faceless, wolfskin-clad men of his nightmares and knew that if Shateh and his warriors ever caught up with the little band, there was no way that two fit adult males, three women—four if he counted Kahm-ree— and a handful of children could fight and win against them all.

Gradually, the land began to change. The hills were broader now, higher, with long, flat summits greened by dry-land pines and devoid of snow except for north-facing slopes where the shadows of ever-shortening days kept sunlight from the drifts. The mammoth kept to their easterly course, and although Red World ways enabled the travelers to eke out enough food to keep them going, soon the trek began to tell on old Kahm-ree. Increasingly she began to look back in the hope of eventual reunion with her grand-daughter.

"Perhaps Ban-ya is following us?" Kahm-ree suggested, and when no one replied to her question, answered it herself. "Yes. It must be so. We should settle for a while and wait for her. She will come."

"I see enough ghosts in my dreams without adding your Ban-ya to their number," said Cha-kwena tersely, and after only a brief rest beside a spring that yielded unpleasantly bitter water, he led his people on.

The women and girls did their best to ease the way for the old woman and were alert to see that she did not wander off when they paused to collect kindling or gather seeds and

frost-puckered berries wherever they found them, grateful to
be able to add to their rapidly diminishing supplies. At night
the women rested with the children out of the wind while
the men took turns keeping watch for any telltale glimmer
that would betray an enemy fire; but if Shateh and his
warriors were still following, they were keeping camps as
cold as Cha-kwena's own. Under the dark of the moon, the
watchmen bundled in their traveling robes yearned for the
warmth of noon, and, feeling the breath of a wind that was
bitterly cold, they knew that winter was not far away.

"If Shateh does not come for us soon, I do not think he
will ever come," said Kosar-eh, rising as Cha-kwena came
to take over his watch. "He will want to settle his people
into a secure winter camp."

"Then ask the forces of Creation to send an early
winter!" responded the younger man. "That should send
him back to the land of his ancestors."

"You are Shaman," reminded Kosar-eh sourly. "*You*
ask them. Maybe they will heed you for a change."

"You must not lose faith in the power of the sacred
stone and of the totem, old friend."

"The totem is dead! And if you or the stone had any
power, you would not have spoiled the horse hunt, Mah-ree
would not have disobeyed the ways of the ancestors, Ha-xa
would not be dead, and we would not be standing here in
this miserable country! What is to happen to us, eh, in this
barren land beyond the edge of the world? How will it be for
the people of Cha-kwena when snow comes to stay and
there is no fit shelter to warm us and no meat set aside to
feed our women and little ones? My Ta-maya is ready to
give birth any day! If anything happens to her, Cha-kwena,
I—"

"I did not invite you to follow me, Kosar-eh," interrupted Cha-kwena, and, for a moment, was certain that the
big man was about to strike him. The moment passed.

"You left me no way by which I could stay behind!"
snapped Kosar-eh, then stalked away, leaving Cha-kwena to
keep his watch alone.

Frustrated, the young shaman ached to call his old friend back and assure him that all would be well once the totem was reborn, but he had already compromised the inevitability of this when he had let the secret slip to Gah-ti. But what choice had he been given? He had knowingly broken the covenant of the Ancient Ones by allowing a one-armed man to take up a spear and, in desperation to have at least one more hand against their enemies, had been forced to tell Gah-ti about the impending rebirth of Life Giver. So far, at least, the forces of Creation seemed to have overlooked his actions. Gah-ti had not repeated the forbidden words, nor had he taken up a spear again. Now, as Cha-kwena watched the thoroughly aggravated Kosar-eh lope off toward camp, he wondered how long it would be before the matriarch of the mammoth herd began to swell visibly with life and the members of his band took note of this. Then, with only a word or two from him to lead their thoughts, they would remember that this was the cow that had often walked with the great white mammoth in the days and nights before Life Giver's death, and they would understand and take heart in the knowledge that the totem was with them still.

"Why have you abandoned me, Owl?" Cha-kwena asked the night wind forlornly. "What lies there, beyond the edge of the world, for me and my people?"

"The mammoth know. Trust them. They will lead you on the way in which you must go," said Hoyeh-tay.

Cha-kwena gasped. His grandfather sat beside him. With his wizened face painted blue in the way of the Red World shamans when they gathered on sacred mesas to commune with the spirits of earth and sky, Hoyeh-tay wore his collar of sacred sage and his towering headdress of sweet grass, festooned with juniper berries, beads of stone, multicolored plumage, and the heads, feet, beaks, and teeth of little birds and animals whose sisters and brothers gave up their lives to be food for the Red World People. "Remember the inner eye, Cha-kwena . . . the eye that lights the way of the shaman's road . . . and remember all that I have taught you. Be wise and wary, and in time the way will be made known."

"Cha-kwena? Are you asleep with your eyes open, Cha-kwena?"

The young shaman blinked. His grandfather was gone, and in his place was Gah-ti. His watch was over. He thanked Gah-ti for coming to relieve him and, rising and stretching, welcomed his relief but did not return to the camp of sleeping women and children, where Kosar-eh and Ta-maya lay in each other's arms and Mah-ree slept alone. Instead Cha-kwena walked beneath the stars, as he did every night, lest he be tempted to return to his sleeping place beside his girl-of-a-woman and turn her toward him so that he might embrace her and kiss away her sadness. Trembling with longing for the warmth of Mah-ree's arms and the return of her affection, he nevertheless walked away from where she lay. The last thing Cha-kwena wanted in this lonely land with enemies on their trail was another woman with child to worry about—especially if the woman was *his* woman, and the child *his* child.

"Not yet! Not now!" he said to the setting moon and shifting stars. *Not until all is once again good and safe within this world! Not until the ancestors and the forces of Creation are smiling once more upon my people! Not until I no longer see my enemies in my dreams or hear the voices of the dead upon the wind!*

A coyote yapped, disconcertingly close by in the darkness. "Fool!" mocked Yellow Wolf. "Wait for a perfect world, and it will never be!"

Startled, Cha-kwena looked around but saw no sign of a coyote and wondered if the words had been real or imagined. In any case, the advice not being what he wanted to hear, it was therefore unwelcome and unheeded. He drew his rabbit-skin cloak more tightly around his shoulders and turned his face upward. As his eyes traced the arching span of the Sky River and followed it across the dome of the night, he saw the cold, glinting eyes of the Twin Brothers, and there—beyond the pale Watcher and the hunting grounds of the Great Snake—the Great Bear looked down at him.

Cha-kwena's hand went to his medicine bag and enclosed the sacred stone. He could feel the pounding of his heart within the curl of his fist as his fingers tightened around the talisman, for he now saw by night that which still pursued him by day, carnivorous and threatening and never quite invisible as it loped along, insidiously hiding itself within the fabric of the wind . . . the spirit of Walks Like a Man . . . the ghost of the great shamed Bear that his woman had slain with Teikan's spear.

"No," Cha-kwena said to the phantom in the stars. "You will not have what you seek. I am Cha-kwena, grandson of Hoyeh-tay, guardian of the sacred stone, of the totem, of my people, and of my Mah-ree! She is mine. No matter what she has done, you will not have her!"

The days passed in a slow, monotonous progression. The band was grateful, for the weather grew warm again. Although Cha-kwena and Kosar-eh and his eldest boys took turns keeping vigil by day and night, there continued to be no sign of Shateh and his warriors—except in Cha-kwena's dreams.

And then, with the rebirth of the moon, Cha-kwena dreamed no dreams at all and awoke refreshed and rested in the morning, troubled by only one question—*Are our enemies no longer in pursuit?*

Two days later he and the others followed the mammoth into a country of towering mesas that reminded them so much of their distant homeland that U-wa and Ta-maya wept to see it. Poor old Kahm-ree kept expecting to see her granddaughter materialize from behind every lichen-clad boulder or rough-needled pine, and Mah-ree actually smiled for the first time since receiving news of Ha-xa's death. In this high, dry country she found many trees and growing things familiar to her as Medicine Woman and was satisfied that, if given time in which to do so, she would be able to gather much that would be of benefit to her people and to her elder sister, for from all signs Ta-maya's birth pains would begin soon.

In consideration of this, Cha-kwena and Kosar-eh left Gah-ti and the boys to guard the women while they ascended the nearest mesa to attain an overview to the north, west, and south. And here, for the first time, Cha-kwena had the answer to his question as he looked down over a vast emptiness of hills and valleys across which nothing moved, save the invisible tide of the wind and a sizable column of dust that was being raised by what seemed to be a large herd of animals moving toward the mountainous horizon.

"Those who were following, follow no more," observed Kosar-eh with finality.

"It is so!" affirmed Cha-kwena, at last exulting in a truth that he had not dared admit to himself before he had seen it with his own eyes. The dust was not being raised by herd animals; it was churned up by a tribe of men and women and children and dogs, dragging their disassembled lodges and belongings toward the distant homeland of their ancestors. "May Shateh's band find much man-worthy meat!" he exclaimed as his spirit soared. "May they come to understand that those whom they have forced to flee before them have never been their enemies! And may the forces of Creation give them cause to look toward the edge of the world no more!"

For a long time Kosar-eh said nothing. He stood motionless in the wind, with his long, black hair blowing back from his strong face and his eyes narrowed from the invasive brightness of the sun as it struck hard upon the vistas below. After a while he turned and stared to the east, across the mesa and unknown land that lay beyond.

"This is what you have always wanted . . . to see with your own eyes what lies beyond the farthest mesa, to hunt where no hunters have ever hunted, to set your feet upon unknown land, and to turn your eyes to Moon and her star children and say, 'I am the first man to see you from this place!' Will you be happy now, Cha-kwena, Slayer of

Totems, now that you have finally led your followers into oblivion?"

Cha-kwena had no chance to protest before the man turned and was gone, moving downslope along the rocky incline. Irritated by Kosar-eh's constant pessimism, the shaman set his eyes across the barrens over which the sun would soon set. With both hands enfolding his medicine bag and the sacred stone within, he smiled at what he saw. Shateh was leading his people back to the Land of Grass. And if the spirit of shamed Bear was moving eastward in the wind, the young shaman could not see it.

Ta-maya's firstborn came into the world with the setting of the sun. Later all would agree that there was great meaning in this, for on this day Cha-kwena and Kosar-eh had seen their enemies vanishing over the far horizon, and the next morning, the sun would rise on a new life for them all in this unfamiliar land.

The baby came so easily and quickly that there was barely time for U-wa and Mah-ree to come to the aid of the mother before Ta-maya—happily amazed by the rapidity of her ordeal—was laughing and crying with joy to see the fat, ruddy little face squinting at her. Held fast in U-wa's hands, the infant shook her tiny fists and, squalling, made her presence known to all.

"Will Kosar-eh accept this child? And will he honor the wishes of this child's mother and consent to name this child Ha-xa-ree, Little Ha-xa, so that the spirit of one lost to her children may now live again in this world through a new generation born of her blood?" asked U-wa formally, in the way of the ancestors since time beyond beginning.

Kosar-eh, still breathless from his angry descent from the mesa top, was only just stalking into the rough little temporary camp that the women and boys had raised within a streamside grove of mixed pines and hardwoods. Having anticipated another night of worrying about Ta-maya and the coming child, he was so shocked to see U-wa coming toward him with a baby in her outstretched hands that he stopped dead.

The mother of Cha-kwena shook her head dubiously at the speechless man. "Have you not enough sons, Kosar-eh? This woman thinks that you can afford to welcome this new daughter into the band, for she is strong and fat and perfect in all her parts and, be it the will of the forces of Creation, will grow to make many babies for the men of this band in future days."

Kosar-eh stared in amazement at his new daughter and then past U-wa and the infant to where Ta-maya lay beneath a hastily raised lean-to amid the fragrant pines. His silence had taken the smile from her face; he spoke quickly so that he would put it back again. "This man accepts this firstborn of Ta-maya and consents to whatever name his woman would have for it . . . daughter or son, a new life is a precious thing—even here in this unknown land into which—"

"*Especially* here!" interrupted Cha-kwena, jogging into the camp and stopping beside Kosar-eh. He felt all at once angry and annoyed and beyond patience with the man's intractability. "Here there is water! Here there is meat! Here are green growing things! Here the mammoth browse in peace! And here our enemies follow us no more!"

Now, for the first time since fleeing the village, the little group allowed themselves to summon Fire, and a great and happy celebration was made to honor the occasion of Ha-xa-ree's birth. There was dancing and singing, and many an old and happy tale was told.

Mah-ree sat beside Ta-maya and held her sister's newborn close, looking into the infant's face and wondering if it could be true that her mother had returned to live among the People once more. "I did not mean to shame Great Paws by killing him," she told the baby. "But I think you would have done the same, Mother, not stopping to think about what was forbidden or what was allowed, but knowing that to save the life of another you must do *something*! As you did for me. Ah, if I had known what you would do, I would never have run away! I would have stayed and answered to Walks Like a Man and tried to explain to him that the forces of Creation had sent Teikan's spear to me and—"

"What is done, is done, dear sister," said Ta-maya. "Let the past rest in the embrace of yesterday. Now, with the life of this new child, let the present begin, so that we all may dare to rejoice once more as we look forward to tomorrow."

The next morning Cha-kwena and Kosar-eh, accompanied by two of Kosar-eh's eldest sons, twelve-year-old Ka-neh and nine-year-old Kiu-neh, picked up a well-used deer trail and successfully stalked and brought down a summer-fat buck. Upon this meat the little band feasted while the mammoth grazed nearby and could be heard trumpeting and growling in contentment at night.

Now, under the watching eye of the benevolent sun, the men and youths followed the deer trail into broken woodland to hunt once again. The younger boys worked with the women and girls to set snares and used their throwing sticks to capture grouse and squirrels. Several surprised hares found themselves leaping ahead of stick-beating, yip-yipping boys and barking dogs into a woven fiber wall of "rabbit" netting meticulously laid and held by Mah-ree, U-wa, Kahm-ree, and the girls. Lizards were noosed, and birds were skillfully netted or stoned when they flew into thickets of skunk cabbage and chokecherry. The women and girls gratefully gathered the bounty of this generous country and rejoiced as they carefully cut long, bladelike leaves from yucca, exposing the tender edible core of the plants, which were shared and relished by all before the roots were dug and pounded, not to be used as food but as a body-soothing lather when they splashed and bathed in the shallows of the stream. Soon the wooden drying frames were sagging with the weight of much "little animal" meat, and the skins of birds, rodents, and even a not-so-wary badger that wandered into one of old Kahm-ree's trip nooses were stretched and staked upon the ground. When the men returned with two deer, their women and children praised them, and that night, with plenty of kindling and deadwood to be found, the boiling bags and spits were laden. The fat of the badger spat and ran, the children licked it up, and the People smeared it over their faces and hands, grateful for its moisturizing properties. In this land the sun still burned hot, even though deer were coming together in the woodlands and the shifting patterns of the star children of Moon told them that soon White Giant Winter would return.

Many days later, in a dawn announced by the distant chattering of quail and the twittering of a woodcock flying overhead, the mammoth moved on. The People were glad, for their hunting had depleted the ready supply of meat in the area.

"It is time," conceded Ta-maya with a serene smile, strong again after days and nights of rest during which good food had allowed her breasts to swell with milk for little Ha-xa-ree. Her hand, pointing skyward, drew the eyes of the others to wedges of flying water birds. "Look! Do you see? The birds fly ahead of us. Soon White Giant Winter will come."

"They fly to the south," observed Kosar-eh. "Always they fly to the south before the wind turns cold. What lies there for them? Perhaps it is a land of endless summer, where grass and seeds and berries are always ripe, and meat comes eternally to the spears and snares of hunters."

"The mammoth walk to the east, as does the wind," countered Cha-kwena. "We will follow."

They broke camp and traveled on.

Always, as in days long gone by, Mah-ree kept as close to the mammoth as she could. Often, under the ever-watchful eyes of Ta-maya and U-wa, the children would join Shaman's Woman as she peered through sage scrub or bare-branched willow thickets, watching the tuskers in silent wonderment—so huge, so caring of one another, shaggy now in their early winter coats and sometimes as fractious and playful as the children themselves.

"Would Shateh's people truly hunt them?" asked Kho-neh, six years old and the fourth eldest of Kosar-eh's boys.

"To the last," affirmed Mah-ree with disgust.

"It was their way in the land of their ancestors, Fourth Son," added Ta-maya, offering neither judgment nor criticism with her answer as her eyes held on the herd. "It is not *our* way. We of the Red World know that the spirit of Life Giver dwells with the mammoth kind and that as long as the great tuskers walk the world, so, too, will the People live forever."

Mah-ree was startled. "Explain what you mean by that!" she demanded, suspecting that Cha-kwena had shared their secret about the impending rebirth of the totem with her sister. Truly, she thought, if he had done this, he had completely forgotten what it meant to be Shaman and the band was more at risk than ever.

"Just as our mother, Ha-xa, is with us now, so is the spirit of our totem with the mammoth," replied Ta-maya. "As long as we cherish our loved ones in our thoughts and hearts and speak their names with love to our children, they are with us always and forever."

"It is so," affirmed U-wa.

Mah-ree was relieved. She smiled wanly and watched her sister gather the children close.

"Look at the mammoth, little ones, and learn from the ways of their kind," urged Ta-maya. "Wherever they go we will always find water and the little food animals that live in the land in which the mammoth find browse."

"Look, Woman of My Father," said Kiu-neh. "The great speckled mammoth—the biggest of them all—she swells with life as you did before Ha-xa-ree was born!"

Mah-ree sensed a sudden excitement in Ta-maya as she leaned forward and, after a moment, caught her breath. "Yes, Third Son of My Man! I believe it *is* so!"

"She is the cow that leads the herd. She was most often with Life Giver in the days before our totem journeyed to the Valley of the Dead," observed Ka-neh. As second eldest of Kosar-eh's boys, at his father's command he was always at Ta-maya's side when Kosar-eh was not with her. Now a look of amazement expanded his handsome features. "Do you think that the great white mammoth and this cow were one together and—"

"Leave it to a boy of your age to notice such things!" teased U-wa.

"But he is right, dear friend!" Ta-maya sucked in her breath with a pleasure that took her to her feet. "Of course, Second Son of My Man! The totem is *not* dead! Life Giver is here with us now, not only in our thoughts, but—"

"Do not speak the words!" cried Mah-ree, aghast. She looked with warning at her sister, then at U-wa and each child. "Who knows what dark spirits may be listening!"

Every pair of eyes went wide with dread, for all except the littlest among them knew and understood the taboo against speaking aloud of a yearned-for thing lest malevolent forces rise to destroy it.

"You and Cha-kwena have known this all along?" Ta-maya asked her sister.

"We have known," Mah-ree replied.

Ka-neh's face tightened with sudden resentment. "You could have whispered it to us, at least, in some quiet, windless place where the spirits would not have heard. If the Land of Grass People had known that—"

"Have you forgotten that there was a time when Shateh sought the totem to slay it?" Ta-maya interrupted sharply. "His people believed that the man who killed and ate the blood and flesh of the great white mammoth would himself become totem, Life Giver to his tribe, Great Spirit, powerful, forever young, a maker of endless sons."

"Cha-kwena killed the great white mammoth," said young Kho-neh. "Why did Shateh not eat *him?*"

"Because Cha-kwena makes no sons," answered Ka-neh in the painfully tolerant, offhanded way of a youth who, feigning much desired maturity, believes he has all the answers. "It is obvious to everyone that the power of the totem cannot be his. If it were, we would not be here now, cast out of Shateh's band to live forever in a land without people beyond the edge of the world."

"I am people!" piped in little Tla-nee.

"And me, I am people, too!" echoed Joh-nee.

"Yes, I suppose you are people . . . or will be someday," conceded Ka-neh. "But thanks to Cha-kwena, I will never be a warrior of Shateh's!"

"Warrior!" Ta-maya spat the word as though it were a foul thing and she could not bear to hold it on her tongue. "What kind of warrior would condemn my sister to death and cause my mother to feed herself to Fire and command your father to kill your little sister and abandon your older brother? That same 'warrior' denied life to his own infants, abandoned two of his sons, and threw the lance that sent his own third son—and my first man, Masau—on his way to the world beyond this world. Have we not all had enough of warriors, and of war and death?"

Ka-neh's head went up and his mouth curled down. "A warrior must do as he must do. And Spirit Sucker must come to us all sooner or later!"

"How 'wise' is the mouth of youth!" sneered U-wa, and gave the boy a flat-palmed strike to the shoulder that sent him reeling.

2

Life Giver was present and growing toward rebirth within
the matriarch of the herd. That unspoken truth lightened the
steps of the band and put newfound hope in everyone's eyes
in the days that followed. Crossing broad sage flats between
the mesas, they soon put the dry and often scabrous land
behind them entirely. There was mixed short-grass prairie
beneath their feet when they at last found themselves upon
a high, windy, undulating plateau that would have made
Shateh and his hunters sick with envy. There, at last, was the
big game the Land of Grass people had been seeking:
long-horned bison in such numbers that the plain was
blackened with great, rivering herds of animals that brought
Cha-kwena's little band to pause and stare in awe.

"So many!" cried Gah-ti, gesturing outward and laughing with pure delight. He did not have to risk offending the
forces of Creation by speaking aloud the names of the
potential prey animals that were there, ahead of him, for all
to see.

Horse.

Elk.

Camel.

Pronghorn.

The assembled members of the little band saw them all
as Cha-kwena lifted both arms to sun and sky and praised

the forces of Creation for bringing them into such wondrous hunting grounds. Meanwhile Kosar-eh raised an eyebrow and nodded in silent approval, conceding without vocalizing a single word that perhaps "oblivion" was not going to be so bad, after all.

They rested out of the wind within a grove of massive cottonwoods close to a broad, shallow river. At noon, when the sun threw no shadows, the men and youths took up their spears and, moving into the wind to hide their scent, went across the land to hunt. They killed only what they needed—a single elk easily flushed from a midafternoon doze in the shade afforded by one of many small, sheltering green woodlands that islanded the plain. To their amazement, they were able to walk into easy spear range of their prey.

"It is as though the great hoofed ones on this far side of the world have never seen human hunters before!" marveled Ka-neh.

Kosar-eh nodded. "Surely they do not seem to associate the sight or smell of us with danger."

Cha-kwena observed thoughtfully, "By their actions perhaps our brothers and sisters among the animal kind are telling us that we are the first of our kind to set foot in this new land."

Again Kosar-eh nodded, and for the first time conceded, "It is a good land, Shaman . . . a land of much meat in which my woman and children will not hunger."

When darkness came down, a fine, hot fire of deadwood burned within a clearing in the cottonwoods by the river, effectively shutting out the sounds of the night—the river, the wind whispering in the trees and grass and moaning across the vast, rolling plain, the intermittent roars and cries of predator and prey, and the mammoth conversing as they fed downstream. The band gorged on the meat of the elk until they grew sleepy and could eat no more of it, and Gah-ti laughed to think of Shateh's trudging toward the land of his ancestors when all the "man-worthy" meat

that he and his people longed for was surrounding Cha-
kwena's band, there for the taking.

"As our shaman promised it would be!" reminded
U-wa proudly, and thanked the forces of Creation for having
chosen such a wise and clever son as her own to lead their
band.

"I only follow the mammoth," said Cha-kwena, embarrassed and discomfited by his mother's flattery.

"Because you have been chosen by the ancestors to do
so! You are their spirit brother, my son . . . Cha-kwena,
Brother of Animals."

"Even so, the bones of the great white mammoth lie in
the Valley of the Dead."

Kahm-ree's statement sobered the gathering.

The old woman was unaware of this as she went on,
speaking with calm, easy assurance, never once looking up
as she picked grass seeds from little Piku-neh's hair while
the greasy-cheeked three-year-old sat as a fidgeting captive
between the grip of her capacious thighs. "The magic power
of Life Giver will have kept my Ban-ya alive in that far
place. Oh, yes, even now she is following us. Any day now
she will catch up!"

"It is time to forget your granddaughter, old woman,"
said Kosar-eh, with an obviously strained patience that he
would not suffer to be stressed any longer. "Without food,
shelter, or cold-weather clothing, Ban-ya could not have
survived winter in the Valley of the Dead. And even if, by
some perverse magic, she had and dared to come in search
of us, any of Shateh's people would have killed her on sight.
And if she had blundered into any of the surviving bands of
the People of the Watching Star, you know as well as I that
she would have been taken captive! Let her spirit go, old
woman! Be grateful that you and her little son were not
banished with her. And be glad that U-wa has brought the
boy to you. Look to Piku-neh for your comfort, Kahm-ree,
not to memories of one whom none of us ever wants to see
again."

Now the old woman looked up and stared at the big

man across the lake of light and heat and glowing wood that lay between them. "*I* want to see her. Listen . . . do you not hear her calling on the wind?"

At that moment a lion roared somewhere far away across the plain, and the dogs, made restless by the sound, looked up from their gnawing.

Ta-maya shuddered and drew her nursing infant close. "No more of such talk of the past, of enemies, and of the dead! Our shaman and our totem have brought us into good country at last. It is time we slept."

That night Cha-kwena dreamed the dream again and saw the spirit of the shamed bear following his people in the wind; but this time the bear was transformed into a woman—emaciated, corpselike, howling his name. Gasping, he awoke to the song of wolves and the low, steady ululation of the west wind. Unable to return to sleep, he went to stand alone at the edge of the grove.

Facing into the wind, he stared back across the plain, thinking that by now Shateh and his people must be across the badlands and passing through the mountains. No doubt they were arming themselves and posting watchmen to guard against attack by the remnant People of the Watching Star. When they trekked past the path that would lead them into the Valley of the Dead, where Ban-ya had been left to die, they would avert their eyes and try not to think of what had happened there.

Cha-kwena shivered. Memories of Ban-ya never failed to unnerve him. Born into his band, she had been given away to Shateh by her own husband, Dakan-eh, the ambitious Bold Man of the Red World. As one of the wives of the great hunt chief and shaman, she might have known a good life had she been satisfied with her lot. Ban-ya had not been satisfied. Her treacherous manipulations against Shateh had resulted in death, including that of the chieftain's only surviving son, and also of Dakan-eh. After her murderous acts had been discovered, she had begged for her life.

Cha-kwena's brow furrowed. Even now he could not

blame Shateh for turning his back to Ban-ya's pleas for mercy. Yet, despite all that she had done, he could not help pitying her and wondering if he should have spoken in her defense. After all, she had claimed to be pregnant, and she had grown up in the same village as he, Ta-maya, Mah-ree, and Kosar-eh. He shook his head, recalling how the malevolent woman had also attempted to poison Ta-maya. To have sided with Ban-ya, he realized, would have been an affront to the forces of Creation.

But now a voice spoke to the young shaman out of the wind. Was it the voice of Owl, or his ghost grandfather, or the phantoms of his nightmare, or only the voice of a fear that he had not experienced until now?

"What if old Kahm-ree is right? What if Ban-ya survived the winter in the Valley of the Dead? What if she sought shelter in the cave? And what if . . ."

Dread raised the hair at the back of Cha-kwena's neck. His hand sought the sacred stone. Deeply troubled, he remembered the deceptively alluring valley, with its sheltering mountains and forests and vast inland lake. His people had prospered there, briefly taking residence within a great sunlit cave that opened deep into the hollow of a high hill. Then Raven had come to the cave, and Spirit Sucker had roamed the valley at will. Cha-kwena had followed the great white mammoth to that hidden place of ancient legend within which all mammoth came to die. Death had been waiting for them both, but Cha-kwena had come away alive.

He caught his breath, reliving days and nights of mourning, when he had retreated alone into the deepest labyrinthine corridors of the inner cave. There, by lamplight, in pigments of clay and ocher and ash, he had painted the story of his people upon the walls of a secret cavern. Only Mah-ree had dared follow him into the depths of the earth to bear witness to what he had done in his grief and hope.

It was all there, everything he had ever been told about the ancestors, and the coming of First Man and First Woman from the spirit world into the world of the living, with Life Giver, the great white mammoth, walking always before them. And then, in a shamanic fury of desperation and inspiration, his painting had transcended what *had* been and dared to depict what he *yearned* to see. He had painted the great white mammoth rising from the lake. He had painted Gah-ti with his arm restored to his body. He had painted his band leaving the Valley of Death, following the mammoth while a tiny white calf that was the resurrected spirit of the totem led the way ever eastward . . . not into oblivion but into a fine, green land of perpetual good hunting.

Cha-kwena gasped to think of it now. Much of it was happening as he had envisioned. And yet he cursed himself for not having struck the pictograph from the cavern walls before leaving it in what he had assumed would be eternal darkness. Now he gripped the sacred stone hard in his fist and wondered if the power of the talisman would be enough to help him keep the totem safe if distant enemies ever discovered the cavern's secret and decided to hunt the totem once more.

Closing his eyes, he spoke to the wind, the night, and the forces of Creation. "Let my enemies not be drawn to the Valley of the Dead. Let the abode of Spirit Sucker and Raven be content to keep its secrets."

"It is far away. You must not think of it."

Startled by the sound of Mah-ree's voice, Cha-kwena looked down to find her standing close at his side, looking up at him, her hair loose and blowing in the wind.

"Surely our enemies have been vanquished and turned from our path, Cha-kwena. Forget the past, my shaman. The future is here beneath these stars, with the mammoth in this new land. Together we will be strong and protect our people and the mammoth until that which we yearn for comes to be."

"Together?" Cha-kwena frowned, suspicious of the way she had used the word, for lions were roaring far across the plain, and he could not help remembering the ease with which his little woman had always resisted her place in the order of male and female life when it came to protecting herself and others against danger. "Have you forgotten that since time beyond beginning, it is up to the men of a band to protect the women and children?" he asked sternly and, even in the starlight, saw her features tighten defensively.

"I have been lying alone and unable to sleep upon our furs, Cha-kwena," she replied. "I have been listening to the wind and to the voices of lions and wolves and leaping cats and coyotes, and I have been thinking that in this land of much meat, we are the only people but not the only hunters. There is much danger to a band as small as ours in this country."

"Where there is prey, there will always be predators, Mah-ree."

"Yes, but I have been thinking that among the tribes of wolf, lion, leaping cat, and coyote, females hunt with their chieftains and guard their little ones against—"

"You are not a lion or a wolf, or a leaping cat or coyote, Mah-ree," he said sharply, and, even as he spoke, tried not to think of her courage and brave heart. Regardless of her good intentions, he would not allow her to incur the wrath of the forces of Creation again. "We are far from the country of the ancestors, but their spirits are still with us, and for the sake of our band and of the mammoth, we will keep the ways that the Ancient Ones have kept since time beyond beginning!"

"Yes, Cha-kwena, I know that this must be so. But as I lie alone, listening to the wind and the four-pawed hunters of the night, I find myself thinking that in the tales that old Hoyeh-tay told about the time beyond beginning, First Woman used a spear as well as a sling when she fought side by side with First Man against their many enemies and—"

"You are not First Woman! No woman can be like her! First Woman is a sacred spirit, Mother of all of the generations of the People!"

Mah-ree made a little snort of hurt derision. "Truly, then, I am *not* like her! Like First Woman, I follow the mammoth into the face of the rising sun and walk in the light of the star children of Moon as they rise and set over unknown country. Like First Woman, I have used sling and spear against the enemies of my people. But unlike First Woman, I have borne no children to the one who is First Man to me. Together we lie down upon the same sleeping mattress, but always my man's back is to me. And so, unless his magic is very great indeed, this woman will be mother of no generations at all!"

Cha-kwena's jaw tightened at her ill-timed words. His mood was already bleak. He stood at the edge of the cottonwood grove and stared across the vast and undulating starlit plain. Then, somehow, he was transported far away, to the depths of the great canyon, and the smell of pinyon and cedar—and the scent of something else—was strong in his nostrils. It was the stench of the butchered and flayed little white mammoth calf. Life Giver had not been with the herd when the hunters of the People of the Watching Star had come into the Red World in search of the totem, so they had slaughtered the little white calf instead. He, Cha-kwena, had been a callow youth so intent upon denying his calling to the shaman's road that he had refused to believe the visions that would have allowed him to save the life of the calf as well as those of his grandfather and all who had died in the war that followed.

"Never again!" Cha-kwena proclaimed, knowing that now, with the bones of the great white mammoth bleaching within the Valley of the Dead, if the calf of Life Giver died, the life spirit of the totem would die forever. If the stories that the Ancient Ones told were true, the People would die, too. "By my life and by whatever power is mine as shaman, it will not happen again!"

"You will never again lie down facing me beneath our sleeping furs and join with me?" asked Mah-ree, bewildered by the ferocity with which he had spoken.

Startled by what he took to be the inanity of her question, Cha-kwena snarled, "How can you come to me with such talk? What do I care about lying down and making new life on you now? I am not First Man, and you are not First Woman! When will you realize this, Mah-ree? Has Ha-xa's death not been lesson enough for you? Do you still fail to realize that had you not disobeyed the laws of the ancestors and picked up Teikan's spear, your mother would have had no need to give herself to the spirit of the shamed bear through Fire, and we would not be standing in this cold wind at the edge of the world and listening to lions growling?"

With a choked cry of misery, she blurted, "And if you still possessed even half the power of the shaman you once had, the bear would not have come to the village, Teikan's spear would not have flown to me, and I . . . I—" She stopped, stared up at him as her hands rose to tent her mouth and tears welled in her eyes.

Cha-kwena was stunned by the realization that she had lost the unquestioning faith in him that had been hers since even before he had become a shaman, and he was assaulted by regret for having spoken to her so harshly. Now, surrounded by darkness, her features defined by the blue light of the stars, and her eyes full of hurt and sadness that had not left them since she had learned of how Ha-xa had died, Mah-ree had never looked more beautiful or more vulnerable. Cha-kwena reached out and pulled her roughly into his arms.

"Forgive me. You are right, little one. We must forget the past. The future is here beneath these stars, with the mammoth in this new land. Together we will be strong. And when that for which we wait at last comes to be, all *will* change. You will see. You must not lose faith in me or in yourself."

And there, at the edge of the grove, Cha-kwena put his mouth on Mah-ree's and took her down. Tangling in their winter robes, he loved her, joined with her, pleasured her until she wept and cried out again and again with the joy he gave her. And then, at the moment just prior to his own release, Cha-kwena turned his face in ecstasy to the sky and saw, through the canopy of nearly bare, wind-whipped branches, the Watcher staring down at him out of the great expanse of the sky.

"What is it, my shaman?"

"The wind . . . it grows cold," Cha-kwena said, his release ruined as he withdrew from Mah-ree without having completed the mating she so desired. Getting to his feet, he lifted her into his arms and returned to the shelter of the grove in which the rest of the band was sleeping.

"Again," she invited as they lay down together upon and beneath their sleeping furs. "This time let it be for you as it was for me . . . so good, as it should be between us always and forever."

And though Cha-kwena loved her once more, he found that the fire of a man's need had grown cold within him. His was a loving of gentle handling and soft stroking that soon had them both relaxed and fast asleep within each other's arms until he dreamed the dream again and awoke to the song of wolves and the low, steady keening of the west wind.

For a long while Cha-kwena lay awake, staring up, glad that he could not see much of the stars through the trees beneath which he lay, yet knowing that they watched him anyway, just as the spirit of the shamed bear followed his people in the wind, while far away, within the Valley of the Dead, a woman—emaciated and corpselike—howled his name and warned that only a fool dared imagine that it was possible to look to tomorrow without realizing that it was composed of all that had gone to create yesterday.

Cha-kwena shuddered. Within his embrace, Mah-ree stirred and sighed and, with soft seeking of her small, soft hands, sought to arouse him again even though she was still fast asleep. "No," he said huskily, and, although he drew his little girl-of-a-woman close within the warmth of their shared sleeping furs, he knew that he could not—*would* not—make love to her again. He did not want to make a child on her until the totem was reborn. Not until order was restored to the world. Not until he could look at the sky and find no threat in it. For even though he had led his little band beyond the edge of the world and into a land of good hunting that was far from their enemies, he could not imagine a bright tomorrow as long as yesterday sang to him in the wind and the spirit of the great shamed bear menaced him from the stars.

Cha-kwena closed his eyes, turned his back to Mah-ree, and pulled his sleeping furs over his head, refusing to look at that which hung above the trees, staring fixed and unblinking at him out of the vast black skin of the night. Yet still he felt it, saw it burning above and behind his closed lids: the Watcher . . . the North Star . . . the one constant star around which all the others turned, and from which all that had been disastrous in his life had ever come.

It was a while before he slept again. When he did, he dreamed of himself as a bird flying high into the blue land of Sky, with a spear and sling and bison paunch in which to catch the blood of the Watching Star after he had killed it. On and on Cha-kwena flew, seeking the Watcher, slinging and stabbing and piercing the blue robe of Sky until he was stained by its blood, and suddenly, day turned to night and a great bear stood before him, blocking his pathway through the stars. He hurled his spear. The great bear hurled it back. Struck, he cried out as he fell bleeding to earth—down through wind-torn treetops, down into the deeps of a great canyon where mammoth came to tusk up salt from a sacred spring, down and down, and then over the very edge of the world itself.

Lions and wolves and every other sharp-eyed predator looked at him while, high above, the Watching Star looked down out of the coil of the Great Snake while, from his own particular hunting grounds within the dome of the night, the Great Bear laughed mockingly as it said, "Come, look at Cha-kwena, grandson of Hoyeh-tay, guardian of the sacred stone and of the totem! He flees with the mammoth beyond the edge of the world, but we see him still. Come! Let us hunt him! He is easy to be seen!"

And so it was that with the first faint banding of dawn on the eastern horizon, Cha-kwena was awake and ready to break camp when the mammoth moved on. The women complained of not having had enough time to prepare the elk skin, but with the wind shifting and growing cold, they rolled the raw hide around the usable bones and remaining meat, then packed it onto a travois contrived of two young debranched cottonwoods and went on.

Geese and ducks and great, long-necked cranes and swans flew overhead in such numbers that they shadowed the sun. Then the first high clouds appeared, wild and upswept like the manes of horses running before White Giant Winter, and the People knew that they must find a place out of the constant wind in which to raise their lodges and store enough meat to see them through the coming months of snow and cold.

"The mammoth will show us the way," Cha-kwena assured them.

In that game-rich country, no one doubted the truth of his words; but then the mammoth veered from the river and moved across sedge-furred dunes, which eventually gave way to stony hills of mixed grass and deep, sheltering, albeit broken woodlands. Cha-kwena could be seen falling back, squinting into the wind, or sitting up alone at night and staring through the treetops at the stars.

"At what do you look, my son?" asked U-wa.

"The future," he replied obliquely.

"But you look across the way we have come . . . over past trails."

"It is the same," he said.

At last the mammoth led them onto the south-facing slopes of a wooded gorge within which a hot spring bubbled into reed-edged pools that promised fresh water even in the hardest freeze. Long after the last lodge was raised and White Giant Winter came over the edge of the world to settle upon the land, Cha-kwena could still be seen sitting on the heights in his winter cloak and owl-skin headdress, staring back across the way they had come.

"My shaman must rest . . . must sleep!" urged Mah-ree.

But Cha-kwena could not rest, nor could he find

comfort in sleep, although his people prospered and grew strong within their new little winter village.

Below, the great herds wintered upon the grassland, and the mammoth dug snow with their tusks from an endless supply of nourishing forage. Nonetheless, the shaman's dreams remained hauntings that moved within his mind both day and night. Even during the time of deepest cold, when his people gathered into a single "great" lodge to conserve firewood by cooking together and sharing the warmth of their bodies, Cha-kwena would seek solitude upon the snowy heights of the gorge. While White Giant Winter howled and spat snow across the world and Moon and her star children marked the slow but inexorable progression of time above the storm clouds, he would stare back across the way he and his people had come and keep vigil lest enemies come against them once more.

Often Mah-ree would seek him out. Sad-eyed, she would bring food to him. She would sit with him in worried silence, and ask him to share his thoughts and concerns, but he would not. One day, when winter was beginning to seem endless even though the position of the sun told Cha-kwena that it was spring, he found himself looking down at old Kahm-ree. She was wandering the peripheries of the village and calling her lost granddaughter's name. Remembering the howling female apparition of his dreams, he shuddered, raised a contemplative brow, and inadvertently admitted to Mah-ree, "I, too, see Ban-ya in my dreams. What if she *is* still alive? What if she has discovered the secret cavern within which I painted the story of our people? If our enemies are ever drawn back into that cursed place and she leads them to see the truth of the impending rebirth of—" He stopped short of naming the totem.

"Is *this* what you have seen with your shaman's inner eye?" Mah-ree asked, appalled.

Cha-kwena shook his head with slow negation and reached to press the talisman that hung at his throat beneath his winter robe. "I see many things, little one, but even with the sacred stone in my hand, I am not sure what is Vision and what is only cautionary fear of that which I would not see come to pass. If only I had struck the painting from the wall of the cavern before leaving the Valley of the Dead or, better yet, never painted it at all, I would have one less thing to worry about!"

Mah-ree's eyes had gone very wide within her winter hood. "Ban-ya could not possibly find her own way through the inner darkness of the cave to discover the entrance to the sacred cavern! She is not a shaman!" Her exclamations had been made in a rush of ferocity that left her breathless. And yet she went on. "Anyway, why would Shateh return to the Valley of the Dead? It is a cursed place! No one would ever venture there twice, for no band that has attempted to dwell there has ever escaped the phantoms of disease and disunity. My shaman's painting will never be seen except by bats and cave-dwelling moles and snakes and spiders! Surely you cannot doubt this, Cha-kwena?"

"When that for which we wait comes to be, my dreams will be clearer to me," he assured her, and, seeing the apprehension in her eyes, felt the need to soothe her. He drew her close. "It will be soon now," he said, and knew that this must be true. The matriarch of the mammoth herd was now huge with new life, and even though Cha-kwena had seen Moon go through her phases twenty times since Grandfather of All had mated with the great cow, he was certain that not even a tusker could be pregnant forever.

Mah-ree understood the way of his thoughts and, always grateful and happy to be in his embrace, snuggled close and offered her own assurances. "My shaman has followed the mammoth to this good place where, all winter long, herds of elk and bison and horse have been ours for the taking! For the first time in many a long moon we dwell in a village that is rich in meat and marrow, in fat and sinew, in horn and many prime hides! Kosar-eh has found much good stone for making into spearheads, awls, gravers, and scrapers! My mother's life spirit has returned to the world to live once more within little Ha-xa-ree. Our enemies have been scattered upon the Four Winds. Shateh has returned to the land of his ancestors. And even if Ban-ya *is* still alive, she has chosen her fate and can be no threat to us now. Surely the forces of Creation are smiling upon our people once more!"

Cha-kwena appreciated Mah-ree's bold declarations, but he was disturbed to hear her guessing at the ways of the spirits again and suspected that her words had been articulated as much to convince herself as to reassure him. He shook his head. A terrible sadness was on him. "The Ancient Ones have taught that in time beyond beginning, the People were one. But now the People are many, and all of the far-flung tribes—friend and foe alike—call upon the forces of Creation to heed and answer their prayers. Can Father Above and Mother Below and the Four Winds grant favor to us all?"

"They will not grant favor to Ban-ya in the Valley of the Dead!"

"You cannot know this!" Cha-kwena shouted, putting her away from him in sudden anger. "Go! Leave me! How can I commune with the spirits with you here to distract me? Return to the warmth of the village. And stop guessing at what the spirits will or will not do!"

Mah-ree's mouth turned down. "I will return to the village. The Valley of the Dead is far away, and I do not want to think of it. Like Shateh and the other enemies of my people, it is of the past and cannot hurt me now!"

Within the Valley of the Dead, a high, savage scream rent the night.

Startled, a giant ground sloth looked up from its foraging amid the reed beds that all but choked one of several thermally heated inlets of a vast, ice-covered lake. Still chewing, with strands of dripping, winter-brown reed hanging from its mouth, the enormous herbivore hefted its two thousand pounds of shaggy girth and stood erect. Hip-deep in evaporating mist and tepid water, it raised its wide, blunt-snouted head and looked up.

The cold, silver light of the rising moon was brilliant; it was this brightness, after many days and nights of cloud and storm, that had drawn the sloth across the snow-covered valley and deep into the reeds, where it had been blissfully glutting itself on tender roots ripped by its massively clawed, black-palmed hands from the muck of the lake bottom. Now, eyeing the moon as though it had been the source of the scream, the sloth's small eyes smarted at the invasiveness of its light. It sniffed for unseen danger while it looked down and away, across the tops of the reeds to the surface of the lake. There, well out from shore, it could see portions of an enormous mammoth skeleton jutting through the ice.

The sloth saw no threat in the bones and tusks of the

great mammoth. And, in fact, there was no peril in them. Danger came from behind, and from another source entirely.

Something moved within the reeds landward of the sloth. There was the sound of sloshing, the unmistakable flurry of wings, and the chittering of a frightened bird. And then—save for the movement of perturbed water—all was silent.

Simultaneously nervous and alert and confused, the sloth made a broad, slogging turn, with the weight of its massive body fixed on the outer edges of enormous, clawed feet. Movement was slow and ungainly, especially because the animal was up to its thighs in an ooze of lake bottom.

"Ai yah!"

Once again the sloth's small, furred ears were pierced by a savage scream. A second later the animal uttered a cry of its own just as the first of Ban-ya's fire-hardened lances pierced its exposed throat.

Her heart was pounding. Her emaciated hands were numb with cold. From the cover of the reeds, she saw the enormous herbivore reach with huge, grotesquely handlike paws for its neck and thorax to snap her thin, hardwood lances. The beast was choking on its own blood. The sounds it made were terrible; Ban-ya laughed with joy to hear them. In moments the beast would collapse and die.

Salivating, her shrunken belly aching and growling from starvation, Ban-ya could not wait. Her mind was afire with images of fresh meat and blood and fat, and of fur and claws and teeth that could be fashioned into tools that would make her life in the cave easier.

Easier?

The word mocked and angered her. Not since the long-gone days of her girlhood in the distant Red World had anything come easily to Ban-ya. Bitterness forced her desiccated lips into a taut, thin line; the cracks in her lips stressed and split, oozing serum from breaks in scabs that would not heal. Pain and resentment of her situation made her snarl as her eyes fixed on the sloth. The fat of the great, stupid beast would soon soothe her mouth, and more.

"Die . . . die . . . die . . ." Over and over the word came in a whispering crescendo like that of a rising war cry as Ban-ya, clad in a patchwork melange of furs and feathers and a crudely woven camouflage cape of reeds and pine boughs, burst from the cover of the reeds. Ankle-deep in the same muck that would not support the weight of the sloth, she was a small woman made gaunt and light by lack of food. Hooting and howling to override her fear of an animal that could easily disembowel, dismember, or decapitate her with the swipe of a paw, Ban-ya brandished the last of her staves. With her sling whirling above her head, she sloshed forward in the full fury of desperation.

"Here, Sloth! Look at me, I say! Expose your throat and belly! Yes! Like that!" She hurled her lance and shrieked with triumph when its sharpened end disappeared into the midsection of the sloth. Before the animal could react to the force and pain of yet another cruel penetration, the first of Ban-ya's slingshot stones struck its face. Confused, the already suffocating creature screamed and swatted ineffectively at the air. Ban-ya laughed at its impotence, reached into the fur pouch that hung at her side, and rearmed her sling again and again with the stones that lay within until the last of her armament was gone. The sloth, blinded, its snout cracked and bleeding, collapsed onto its haunches and clawed open its own throat in a frenzy to breathe until blood spurted and shone black and silver in the moonlight.

Ban-ya was still laughing when the sloth fell sideways, but laughter died in her even before her right hand sought the stone skinning dagger that lay sheathed against her hip. Fear raised hackles on her back and neck. Her eyes went wide. She turned, then turned again and again. A lion-sized leaping cat with fangs nearly the length of a grown man's forearm leaped onto her prey from its own hiding place within the reeds. With a scream that carried as much rage as terror, Ban-ya whirled and fled for her life. If one cat was there, there might be others.

She ran and fell a dozen times before fatigue brought her to her knees. Panting, with head hanging, she gagged on exhaustion, and long moments passed before she was able to rise and stare back across the lake-filled valley. She stood shaking and shrunken inside her ill-fitting furs and sodden foot-coverings, which were no more than strips of mismatched pelts wrapped around her feet. Her eyes, huge and sunken and ringed with gray, watched the leaping cat devour the sloth.

"My sloth! Mine! Mine!" she sobbed with frustration as her hands flexed and unflexed at her sides. She longed to kill the cat and reclaim the meat of the sloth; but her staves were lost, and even if she had not dropped her sling in her mad dash to safety, she had hurled the last of her stones. Tears stung beneath her lids as she realized that she had lost yet another competition for food; she doubted if she possessed enough strength to engage in any more. "By the forces of Creation . . . how can I go on?" She sighed and dropped to her knees again.

Then, from the high hills came the sound of a baby crying. Ban-ya stiffened, listening, as the power of a mother's love for her child surged through her. "Ah, yes. For you I *must* go on." She forced herself to get to her feet just as a sharp, clearly human shout came to her ears. Although it had come from far across the valley, Ban-ya was panic-stricken.

"No!" she cried. "You cannot come back! Not now!"

And once again Ban-ya ran in terror, scrambling madly up and across the icy, scree-covered foothills to a cliff-side cave within which she hurried to see to the welfare of two fretful infants.

"Never will I let them take you from me! Never!" she vowed, freeing her twins from fur bindings that had kept them immobile and safe within their carrying frame while she had been off hunting. Hungry and in need of changing, the fur-swathed babies bawled in unison. "Hush! *Hush!*" cried Ban-ya. She ripped off her cape and opened her upper garments, quieting her tiny sons by placing them to suckle at her shriveled breasts. "Yes," she said, relaxing as she felt them take hold. "The breasts of Ban-ya will satisfy. Always it is so with my babies. Always it was so with men." Leaning against the back wall of the cave, the corners of her mouth moved upward with the pleasure that nursing never failed to bring.

Far below the cave, the valley was silent save for the occasional screech of the feeding leaping cat and the sporadic summoning-to-the-feast calls of wolves. Ban-ya listened for the shouting she had heard earlier, but after a moment, the exhausted woman chastised herself for allowing fear to take possession of her. No men had come to hunt in this cursed valley since they had left her to die in it.

"And I am not dead yet!" Ban-ya snapped, and realized that she was hungry and very cold. Righteous indignation and anger inspired her to rise, and with the babies still at her once-bounteous breasts, she took off her sodden foot coverings and outer garments, then went to squat by her sleeping furs and the circle of stones within which she kept and raised fire. Balancing the infants on her thighs, she prodded the well-banked embers with her fire stick, then added precious bits of dried grass and dung. The last of the feathers had been used many a long moon before. Ban-ya frowned, recalled the Red World story of Blue Jay, and could not help thinking of her happy, carefree youth in the distant mesa country.

"Forgive me, Sky," she said, then blew life into the kindling. "I have no blue-jay feathers left to return to you, for through no fault of my own I am far from the land of my ancestors and must do the best I can." Her frown deepened. One of the babies was fussing, so while she sat back and readjusted the positions of the infants at her breasts, her mood was transformed by worry.

Born at the end of the previous summer, the twins were much too thin and growing thinner every day. Ban-ya cursed the leaping cat that had come to devour the sloth. Soon other carnivores would come to harry it at its feasting; she would not dare venture forth to take a share of the meat until there was nothing left but fragments of bone and tendon. It had been the same all winter; but now Ban-ya's precious stores were nearly gone, and soon she would be reduced to gnawing boiled hides for sustenance. Then her breast milk, which was already waning, would cease to flow. Although she might yet hope to survive, her babies would surely die.

Gazing down at them, Ban-ya found herself wondering, as she often did, if they were Shateh's sons or the get of her first man, Dakan-eh. The time of their coming proved nothing to her; she had opened herself to both men under the same moon, and either man could have sired the babies. Not that it mattered to her. They were hers, and her love and concern for them were the only things that had kept her alive these past many moons.

Ban-ya's face twisted with hatred. She remembered how her firstborn, Piku-neh, had been forcibly taken from her arms and placed at the breasts of a stranger so that Dakan-eh—the boy's father—might further his ambitions to win Shateh's favor. He had given her away to the powerful, aging chieftain who desired to make male infants of his own on her.

"What would Shateh do if he could see these fine sons, eh?" Ban-ya murmured to her babies as she changed their swaddling. "He would try to kill you as I have killed his son Atonashkeh. Yes, I have done that, but only because that man tried to spoil my hope of returning to my first man and Piku-neh."

Sadness nearly overwhelmed Ban-ya as she drew the twins close. "Now Dakan-eh is dead. But the fault of that is not mine. No! It is Ta-maya's for making my Dakan-eh want her instead of me. If she had eaten the baited meat that I had prepared for her, Dakan-eh would not have wolfed it down; instead he would still be alive, and the forces of Creation would not have conspired against poor, maligned Ban-ya. But then, perhaps it is just as well that Shateh imagined he had just cause to put your mother out of the tribe to die."

Ban-ya's arms tightened possessively around her babies. Trembling, she knew that since time beyond beginning—when the twin sons of First Man and First

Woman brought war and divisiveness to the world—twins had been considered bad luck and were never allowed to live. She nodded silent acknowledgment to this truth, then told herself again that it was best that she had been cast out of Shateh's tribe, for if the chieftain had discovered that she carried twins, he would have forced her to ingest baby-expelling leaves and roots; these failing, he would have kicked the offending infants from her womb. Any man from the People of the Land of Grass and of the Red World would have done the same—the law demanded it. And if, by some chance, the infants had come to term and birth, the same law would have commanded their mother to strangle them.

"Never," whispered Ban-ya, shivering within the meager warmth of the sleeping fur. She had pieced it of the pelts of every fur-bearing animal that her snares and throwing sticks and crude lances had won for her. She bent her head to kiss the brows of her sleeping babies. "You are all I have, all I care about, all that gives me strength to live. Ea-nok, Comes Hard, and Ea-ka, Comes Second, you are my life! How could I have denied life to my babies when I have been so alone?" The last word struck her like the stone head of a braining stick. "Alone. Alone. Ah . . . so alone . . ."

The words ran out of Ban-ya's mouth like blood seeping from a heart wound; a sob of despair shook her as she visualized the chieftain as he had been on the day she last set eyes on him—tall, scarred, yet physically magnificent with his collar of golden eagle flight feathers, and as uncompromising as a rock. She remembered begging him for mercy. She cringed as she recalled coming to the man with her neck up like a subservient dog.

The orphaned boy, Warakan—a child of their enemies—had stood at the chieftain's side along with Cha-kwena. Ban-ya's mouth twisted with loathing of the headman and the shaman of her native band. Pain flared in her dry, cracked lips; she sent a finger encroaching past the sucking mouth of one of the twins, touched her nipple, and then moistened her lips with the thin fluid.

"How could Cha-kwena have sided with Shateh

against me?" she asked her sons. "May he be dead along with Shateh and Warakan, that treacherous, spying little whelp of the Watching Star who so cleverly insinuated himself into Shateh's heart by betraying me!"

A sigh of malevolent hatred shook Ban-ya. She knew that it was unlikely that Death had found any of them. The last time she had seen Cha-kwena he was in possession of the sacred stone; the talisman would grant power to him and to Shateh, his new ally. Frustration was bitter in her mouth as she remembered how the war chief had named Warakan Son, and how Warakan had named Shateh Father. "It will do them no good," she informed her twins. "Warakan can never be a true son of Shateh. The blood of the orphan is not the chieftain's blood. Shateh is a fool if he believes that he has any hope of immortality through one who was born to his enemies."

In the valley below the cave, the leaping cat gave a high shriek. Another much deeper cry answered it. It was the roar of a great maned spotted lion. Ban-ya shivered as she imagined the battles that must now ensue for feeding supremacy over the corpse that she had made of the giant sloth. "You should all be thanking me for meat, not driving me from my rightful share of it!" she said, and, balancing the babies again, reached back to pull her ragged sleeping fur around herself and the children. Disturbed by her movement, the babies fussed. She soothed them. "Be at ease, my sons. The lions of the world feed far from this place. Ban-ya will take care of you."

Slowly now, one by one, she fed precious twigs and then larger pieces of wood to the fire. Flames burned high and hot. Comforted by nourishment and warmth, the infants slept. Ban-ya's eyes narrowed. She hummed softly to her sons and would herself have drifted into deep sleep if Spirit Sucker had not come to sit across the fire from her.

Ban-ya glared at Death. It was a female, small and wizened and as shrunken as Kosar-eh's first woman, Siwi-ni. Of late Ban-ya had seen this unwelcome phantom often smiling up at her out of the eyes of her babies, and now she hissed a savage warning at the apparition. "Go away! No one—not even you—will steal my twins from my arms as little Piku-neh was stolen."

"No? We will see," said Spirit Sucker. "Twins are forbidden! You cannot keep them."

"Go!" screamed Ban-ya, and, mindless of her sleeping babes, leaped across the fire at the specter, only to find that there was nothing there. When the leaping cat screeched again, she tightened her grip on her offspring. "Aieee," she moaned, afraid and wearied.

Not wanting to acknowledge fear or weakness, Ban-ya set herself to soothe her babies back to sleep. After she had done this, she scrounged through her meager supplies and came up with a cake of rancid fat into which she had pounded bits of dried mouse and summer's-end berries long before. She ate, sucking rather than chewing, for her teeth had been loose in her swollen, irritated gums for some time. Ban-ya closed her eyes and drew in the warm, comforting scent of nursing infants in fresh swaddling. "Must sleep now, must rest. . . ."

But there was to be no rest for Ban-ya this night.

Once again the loud call of a man came across the valley, and startled out of sleep, she snapped to her feet, hurried to the outer lip of the cave, and stood staring into the moonlit night.

The wind had risen. It was strong and steady and very cold against her face. Panic rose in her breast. Her nostrils caught the scent of smoke that did not come from her own fire, and her brow furrowed when she saw the unmistakable glow of a campfire far below. She stared, then closed her eyes and told herself that when she opened them again, the fire would be gone. But when she opened her eyes, it was still there, brighter than before.

"It cannot be." Ban-ya's heart was pounding. She had almost forgotten what happiness felt like. The long-unexperienced emotion expanded within her malnourished mind and body. After endless moons people had returned to the cursed Valley of the Dead! This time she was not imagining it. She could see the fire of their camp and hear their singing!

Strange thoughts took hold within Ban-ya. She cocked her head and felt confused while memories flashed bright. Although she stood at the edge of her cave, somehow she was far away and looking down. But instead of seeing the Valley of the Dead—where spring failed to loosen winter's grip, where the bones of the great white mammoth lay within the vast, treacherous, ice-covered lake—she saw the distant Red World of her birth. She saw moonlit mesas and sage flats and the conical little woven lodges of her people glowing in the winter night beside the broad, shallow waters of the benign Lake of Many Singing Birds.

"Ah!" Ban-ya exclaimed in pure delight.

All around her, children were laughing and making merry. She recognized the little ones; they were the friends of her youth. Incredulous, she spoke their names, and they spoke hers and called out for her to join them in their games. The aroma of hearth-roasted lizards and basket-scorched pinyon nuts was suddenly strong in her nostrils. And there, just ahead, Kahm-ree sat cross-legged in thin air, smiling at Ban-ya from the far side of a floating fire. A stone-heated boiling bag swollen with cooked meat and roots was steaming and bubbling as it hung from a cross-braced hardwood cooking frame.

"Come to me, my child," invited the old woman. "Come, I say. Bring your babies and have your fill of what I would offer!"

Overwhelmed by her yearning for human companionship, Ban-ya cried out in gladness to see her grandmother. Far below the floating, seated old woman and her fire, she could see her own band trekking toward her across the moonlit valley floor. Unthinking, she shouted a joyous welcome and took a step toward her grandmother. Perhaps if Spirit Sucker had not laughed in that moment, the spell might not have been broken. But in that instant, Ban-ya saw not the beloved face of her grandmother but the jaw-clacking, hollow-eyed skull of Death.

Ban-ya nearly swooned with horror as she found herself on the very edge of the cliff. She screamed and jumped back. Kahm-ree and the bobbing fire were gone; she knew that neither had been there in the first place. Spirit Sucker had lured her forward to what would have been certain death for her and her twins had she not seen the trick in time. Her heart seemed to be pounding in her throat when she realized that the chanting of the newcomers to the valley had stopped. Whoever was down there had heard her cry. They might even be staring up at her while she stood silhouetted in the now meager light of her fire.

Terrified, Ban-ya retreated into the cave. She put the babies down, pulled off her sleeping robe, and threw it over the fire to extinguish its light and smother any telltale scent of smoke.

"Must not see . . . must not scent . . . must not find my babies!" She gasped and, suddenly weak and dizzy and nauseated, was forced to crouch and hang her head lest she faint. If the fire makers were of Shateh's tribe, she knew what would happen to her and to her infants. And if they happened to be men of the People of the Watching Star, only the forces of Creation could say what she would suffer after they slaughtered her babies. Ban-ya retched up the recently ingested cake of fat and mouse meat and pulverized berries. Only after the greatest effort did she fight blind panic and win; then she forced herself to rise and, shaking with terror and exhaustion, did what must be done.

After stomping on her hide-covered fire, she withdrew the fur sleeping robe, scattered the embers, and with several strong sideward kicks of her bare feet destroyed the circular stone embankment. Then, cursing Shateh, Warakan, Chakwena, and all who had contributed to her cruel fate, she gathered her pitiful belongings and piled them onto the scorched sleeping fur. After placing the infants into their carrying frame and securing it to her back, she bent to the task of dragging the ruined blanket across the cave into one of many deep, treacherous tunnels that led into the cold, black, cavernous maw of the hill.

"May those who have brought me to this suffer and die!" she hissed. "And may those who have come into this cursed valley pass through and away with no harm to me or to my babies!"

Led by a stern, battle-hardened warrior named Tsana, the handful of spear-armed, heavily clothed, winter-hungry men and boys of the People of the Watching Star were on their feet and staring toward the hills.

"I tell you, that *was* a woman's scream!"

"Before, it sounded like a baby crying."

"Or a nighthawk keening on the wind."

"Whatever it was, I am sure I saw a light up there . . . and someone standing in it, looking down at us!"

Tsana shook his handsome, tattooed, battle-scarred head and disagreed with them all. "Night and distance and the light of the moon have conspired to make us see things that are not there."

"The light *was* there. *And* the silhouette of a woman," insisted Indeh, a big, broad-faced warrior clad in a robe of heavy, unmatched skins.

"Impossible," said Tsana. "Moonlight glinting on ice and stone—that is what you saw."

"I saw a woman," Indeh insisted again.

"From this distance, how can you be sure of what you saw? And if it was a woman, why did she not answer when you called to her?" asked Hrak, then added with a tone of hopefulness, "Maybe you caught sight of a bear. That would be a sweet sign—to know that the time of Walks Like a Man's long sleep is over, and this cursed winter is finally nearing its end!"

Suddenly, seemingly from out of the face of the moon, a great horned owl swooped to snatch a rabbit from the snowy ground just in front of the hunting party. All save Tsana lurched, startled, as the broad wings of the raptor swept the snow at their feet, and then, in an instant, the squealing rabbit, held fast in the talons of the owl, was on its way to the moon.

"Aiee! A bad omen, that!" exclaimed Indeh.

With the exception of Tsana, every man present raised his right hand and made a sign against evil, for all knew that owls were phantom manifestations of the dark, unseen, potentially malevolent and disruptive forces of the night.

"We must go from this place," said the hunter Unai.

"It is so!" affirmed Indeh.

Tsana eyed them sternly. "Jhadel is not here to interpret the omens for us. Since when have you all become shamans?"

The men were silent. Behind them, the fire made crackling, settling sounds. No one seemed to hear except the dogs, lying close to the warmth of the flames.

"Jhadel has set me to lead you," Tsana reminded his men. "I am not a shaman, but I tell you now what Jhadel would say of this owl that has come before us: Have not the forces of Creation made some creatures to hunt by night and others to hunt by day? Owl is a creature of the night. We have come into his hunting ground. We have seen him take an unwary rabbit. Tonight, somewhere in the far hills, Owl will feast and be grateful to the moon while, in the burrows of the earth, the women and children of Rabbit will mourn and curse the light that took him from them. Now, if the rabbit had flown out of the night to pluck an owl from the ground at our feet, then that would indeed have been a sign to ponder!"

"Make light of it if you will, Tsana," said Indeh, "but I tell you that Jhadel is wrong to send us back into this valley. It is the abode of Spirit Sucker. The coming of Owl reminds us that it is not a good thing for men to return to this cursed place, where the bones of the totem shine white in the light of the moon and where so many of our brave brother warriors have perished in battle."

The men and youths murmured in worried agreement.

Tsana sneered at their trepidation. "Jhadel has sent us here in hope of finding meat for our starving people. Have you lost your courage as well as your pride in the last war?"

The hunters did not react kindly to the query.

"In that war I have lost my father and grandfather and brothers!" snapped Unai.

"And I my sons!" added Xanahay. "This valley ran red with the blood of the warriors of the People of the Watching Star and of those brave men of the northern tribes who allied themselves with us against Shateh and the Red World people!"

"And all because—against the advice of Jhadel—we followed Tsana and the vengeance-driven high priestess Sheela into this valley, to be defeated by totemic powers beyond their control!" reminded Indeh. "If Sheela had heeded Jhadel's warning about the valley's being a perfect site for an ambush, she and most of our warriors would still be alive."

Tsana eyed Indeh out of dangerously lowered lids. "Beware of how you speak of one who was woman to me, Indeh. The young shaman trickster among our enemies used his dark magic to overwhelm Sheela's bold battle plan. It was Cha-kwena who slew our totem. But, in the end, it was Jhadel who saved us by leading us away from our enemies and bringing us to a place of safety, where we could gather our scattered people and grow strong once more. Never again shall I question that old shaman's will. He was right about the ambush. He was right to warn us of the raids that came after. And behold, this, too, is as he foretold: Jhadel said that in this valley we will find much meat. The same lakeside bogs that trapped many of our warriors and the great white mammoth now mire other animals, even as warm springs create open water to which many creatures will come to drink and feed. Too long have we refused to heed him because we feared this place."

Indeh's wide face contorted within his fox-skin ruff. He continued to stare toward the moonlit hills. "I tell you, we have cause to fear it. There was a light in those hills. And something or someone stood there." He paused, then suggested in a lowered voice, "Perhaps it was the spirit of the one you mourn, Tsana. Her body was never found."

Tsana's features tightened. "Sheela's bones lie at the bottom of the lake along with the bones of Life Giver. But if my woman's spirit dwells within this valley, she will welcome and protect us in this land to which our enemies will not come. Cha-kwena and the warriors of Shateh fear this place more than we have feared it, for they, not we, have caused the death of the totem."

Troubled by Tsana's words, Xanahay shook his head. "The legends of the Ancient Ones have told that the man who slays the totem will *become* the totem, brother of the Four Winds, and as powerful as the forces of Creation. How else could such a youthful shaman as Cha-kwena have led Shateh to victory over us? It is Cha-kwena who has sent White Giant Winter to dwell forever upon the land of his enemies. As long as he lives, Cha-kwena will see to it that our people suffer and starve and be forced to hide like rabbits in the rocks lest we be hunted by Shateh and his many allies among the tribes of the People of the Land of Grass."

"They will not hunt us here," assured Tsana. "But someday . . . somehow . . . we will find the strength to hunt them! Until then we must heed the wisdom of our own shaman as we seek meat for our women and little ones."

Xanahay shook his head. "Jhadel is so old that he can no longer accompany us on the hunt. What will happen to our people when his spirit leaves his body to walk the wind? We have no shaman to replace him. Who will speak to the spirits on our behalf when Jhadel can no longer do so?"

"We will capture Cha-kwena. He will be shaman for us."

"Too much do you speak the hated name!" Indeh was openly nervous. Far off across the valley a lion was roaring once again, and Indeh had had enough of sobering talk. He returned to the warmth of the fire, hunkered close, and found consolation by grumbling, "At least I can take comfort in the knowledge that even Shateh must be feeling the lingering bite of White Giant Winter and fearing the power of the young shaman who has willed it to stay so long upon the land."

"Shateh chose to ally himself with Cha-kwena," disagreed Tsana, coming to the fire with the others and taking his place beside it. "The power of Totem Slayer is his power. He fears neither man nor beast nor the cold, chilling breath of White Giant Winter. Now, while we are forced to hide and hunt in the Valley of the Dead, he and Cha-kwena are probably feasting on bison-hump steaks in the Land of Grass."

Indeh's face contorted. "Once, long ago, before I chose to become a warrior of the Watching Star, I was a warrior of Shateh's. I can tell you that there *is* something that Shateh fears: He fears death. He is no longer young. He has outlived all but one of his sons, and that infant was so puny that he would not honor its life with his name. With no male child of his own blood worthy to take his name when he dies, Shateh will die forever, and we will have one less enemy."

Tsana's face worked with bitterness. "Jhadel has been making special magic and incantations to assure that this will be so."

Unimpressed, Indeh retorted in disgust, "And just what has Jhadel's old man's 'magic' done for our people lately?"

Tsana's spear was up and out, with the projectile point pressing Indeh's throat before anyone even saw the man's hand reach for his weapon. "We are still among the living because of that old man's power. Tomorrow we will hunt. Tomorrow we will take much meat. Tomorrow we will seek out the cave that was once the stronghold of the one who has slain our totem. Tomorrow runners will go back to our hidden camp among the dry hills and bring our people here. And here, with Jhadel to guide us and speak to the spirits on our behalf, we will grow strong again. We will be a force to challenge our enemies again! Who is there to stop us? Surely not you, Indeh, if you speak against my will again!"

4

Warakan, growing sleepy, sat apart from the other boys and celebrants who had gathered to praise Moon for having shown herself at last above their winter camp. The skies above his head were clear for the first time in longer than he could remember. The low, threnodic voice of White Giant Winter was singing in the wind, but he could not hear it; the song of the celebrants was far too loud. Led by their chieftain, they had been chanting and dancing and sipping fermented blood and berry juice since moonrise; even though Shateh had never been in better form, the edge of Warakan's pride in his adopted father had long since been dulled by fatigue, and his eyelids were growing heavy with need of sleep.

The next day he would join Lahontay and several youths in a search for the den of a hibernating bear. The old man claimed to have dreamed of a place where one might be sleeping. It was far downriver from the village, in hills above a recent bison kill site. If the boys succeeded in their quest, they would fetch the adult hunters of the band, and after a brief fast beside the place where the bear lay sleeping, they would rouse the animal and kill it. They would bring to their people fresh meat, fat, and an end to winter, for as long as bears remained asleep beneath the protective earth skin of Mother Below, the spirits of spring and summer could not be reborn.

Trembling with anticipation of the adventure, Warakan knew that he would have to be rested if he was going to do his best. He yearned to stretch himself full-length upon his sleeping mattress within the warmth of the chieftain's lodge, but leaving the fire circle would be unthinkable. He yawned, put his head down on his knees again, closed his eyes, and, thinking of the coming bear hunt, soon drifted into sleep.

Not far from the boy, two slightly intoxicated old women sat together, their wizened faces barely discernible within their winter furs as they worriedly eyed the springtime moon and stars. To the sound of song and drums and swan-bone flutes and whistles, the elder revealed to the other in a lowered voice, "I have begun to use the last of my winter provisions. I tell you, Xama, Shateh should never have left the badlands without first slaying the lawbreaking woman and the shaman Cha-kwena or at least taking that holy man's sacred stone. Totem Slayer may have possessed greater powers than we knew, for there is the stink of some dark and potent shaman's magic in this endless winter cold!"

"Always you think the worst, Unal! What need have we of sacred stones or of a Red World shaman who could not even foretell the turning of the wind? We have been strong in the power of our *own* chief and shaman ever since Shateh led our people out of the badlands and sent from among us all who possessed Red World blood. True, we have not found the great herds that we hoped for, and the passes through the mountains to the northern grasslands of our ancestors have been blocked by ice and snow; but hunger is no stranger to us. We have known long winters before. Surely this one will soon end."

"Nothing is sure in this life, Unal. Both of us have lived long enough to know that! So has Shateh. Look at him as he dances. He is powerful, but he is no longer young. You know as well as I that according to the wisdom of the

Ancients, the fortunes of our people are dependent upon the virility of our chieftain. And Shateh has no sons since the last born of your granddaughter, Senohnim, came forth before its time."

Frowning, Xama's face puckered in the shadowed depths of her furs. "You grow sour and full of shadows in your old age, my friend! Or are you only ambitious for your grandson Teikan to be chief in Shateh's place? Hmmph! Senohnim may yet bear a living son. And each of the new women whom Shateh blooded on the night of the great feast fire in our edge-of-the-world village is now big with his life! Not bad for an 'old' man!"

"We will see what comes from between their thighs."

"I think my old friend simply lusts for the chieftain to come between hers!"

"Nah!" Unal waved away the teasing accusation with a bony hand that shone pale and callused, like the claw of a bird, before it disappeared into the protective warmth of her garments. "I am past such longings."

Xama fixed bright eyes upon the chieftain and shaman of her people as he led the other revelers. "Not I," she said, sighing. "Not I. Beside Shateh, most men seem small. And now that the Red World shaman has been driven away, never has Shateh seemed stronger or more pleasing to my eyes. In truth, old friend, I think that Totem Slayer has died out there beyond the edge of the world. I think he and his woman and foolish followers burn in the face of the sun even as we speak. We have nothing to fear. Spring will be here soon."

Unal was not soothed. "There are other magic men, other shamans who have cause to ask the forces of Creation to send White Giant Winter against our chieftain. Among the People of the Watching Star, there was one who even now may be—"

Startled, Xama interrupted with a frightened warning. "Speak not! Surely no one with magic powers enough to turn the spirits against us is left alive among our enemies! They are all vanquished, all slain."

"Not *all* have been vanquished. Not *all* have been

slain," Unal snarled. "There is one among us now . . . one whom Shateh dares to name Son!"

"Unal! You must not even suggest that—"

"I am not the only one to say it! I have overheard old Lahontay tell the other hunters that the spirits stopped smiling upon Shateh when, under Cha-kwena's spell, he named a spawn of our enemies as one of his own. Truly, old friend, I will not sit easy in my skin until that boy is—"

"Is *what?*" demanded Warakan, wide awake now, on his feet, and glowering at the gossiping old twosome.

Unal glared back at him, measuring the risk involved in further offending one who was favored by the chieftain.

"She meant nothing, nothing at all. Just an old woman's talk. No more than that," Xama said, attempting to smooth the situation.

Warakan did not appear interested in her attempt at conciliation. He fixed his eyes on Unal and demanded hotly, "What do I have to do to prove to you that I am no longer one of them? If I could bring the great bears from their dens and by so doing cause the rising of the Warm Moon and the return of the great herds into the land of Shateh, this I would do. But I am only an untested boy, not a hunter or warrior, and *not* a shaman! *Never* a shaman! And no longer am I a 'spawn' of your enemies!"

Unal smirked with contempt. "I know what you are, Warakan," she croaked. "You are Trouble. You are a cold wind in summer. You are darkness upon the face of the sun. You are—"

"I do not care what you think!" interrupted the boy. "Shateh has named me Son. The muttering of useless old women means nothing to me! Your status in this band is less than that of the dogs! Beware of what you say of Warakan lest my father hear of it and decide that the meat that is so generously given to you in hungry times may be put to better purpose among the young!"

Feeling bold and arrogant, Warakan left the two old women to mutter between themselves as he turned and moved closer to the fire around which the celebrants were still dancing. Now, with drums beating a slow and measured rhythm punctuated by the high keening of whistles and flutes, the intricacies of the night's moon rituals shone in his eyes.

They were nothing like the sexual excesses that Warakan had witnessed on the night of the feast fire at the edge of the world; in fact, there was nothing sexual about them. The dance was slow, the singing dulcet. The women and girls had painted their faces white and gray with ash in respectful emulation of the many phases of Moon. The men were arrayed in the plumage and pelage of night-hunting animals and birds; indeed, Warakan had almost forgotten that under his winter cloak he was still wearing his ceremonial tunic of fox skins. Old Lahontay was also dressed as Fox. Teikan was Lion. Ranamal was Wolf. Ynau was Leaping Cat. Shateh wore a cape made of the skin of a golden eagle. The beaked head of the raptor faced forward atop his own, and the wings of the bird were laced to his arms.

Warakan cocked his head, suddenly overwhelmed by the memory of another man wearing such a cape—a visitor to Warakan's father's village, a shaman, Masau, Mystic Warrior of the People of the Watching Star. He had been young, but no youth. He was a man, tattooed around the eyes so that his face appeared masked, like that of a shrike, as he sat condescending and cross-legged in the guest's place of honor in the meager lodge of Warakan's parents. He had appraised Warakan out of black eyes that were as sharp, finely shaped, and dangerous as obsidian projectile points.

Warakan winced. The memory cut him. He could not say why. He knew that Masau had been one of the sons of Shateh's youth, cast out of the Land of Grass tribe to die but raised as a foundling by the People of the Watching Star to become one of Shateh's greatest enemies. Masau was long dead, and from what Warakan knew of him, he doubted if any mourned him, least of all Shateh.

Scowling, the boy willed himself to forget the past. He took in a deep gulp of cold night air and watched the chieftain dance. Pride filled him. As Shateh went through the intricate and ancient choreography, Warakan knew that he was surely a shaman, for he appeared to soar, bank upon unseen clouds, and ride upward on the back of the wind to embrace the moon with his winged arms as he thanked her with his song for returning to the skies.

There was suddenly a deep ache within Warakan's young heart. It was the ache of love and pride and longing to be unequivocally accepted by this magnificent man and his people. He thought of the many tests that he would soon be asked to endure along with the other youths of the band preparatory to the mysterious and frightening rites of passage. These ceremonies would culminate in the boys' eventual full initiation into manhood. Warakan swallowed hard, and although his mouth had gone dry, he knew that he would endure them gladly—starting tomorrow, when Lahontay led Namaray and the other youths from the village to search for the denning site of Bear.

Again Warakan swallowed; his throat had gone dry, too, for he found himself imagining the staked skin and head of Walks Like a Man hanging above the feast fire at the edge of the world. It had been so huge, so threatening. Even in death Bear could be a frightening specter, and Warakan knew all too well that merely scouting out the den of such a beast could be dangerous. Nevertheless, he was confident that, as on past hunts, he would show himself to be as brave as any of the other youths. He had to be! How else could he prove to the tribe that he was worthy of being Shateh's son?

"Warakan! Have you grown tired so early? Join the dance again, Warakan!"

The invitation—or had it been a challenge?—had come from Jheena. Warakan was startled and delighted to see her dancing in front of him. In the now-waning moonlight her smiling face was pretty, even when painted white. Her feather-cloaked young body moved slowly, sidestepping, sliding her feet along the ground. Her small hands reached out to him even as she looked to where Namaray and his brothers and the rest of his young "pack" lounged at the sidelines with other fatigued dancers.

"Come, Warakan!" Jheena invited again.

His heart gave a little leap. How could he refuse? He reached out and would have taken her fingers lightly within his own but was distracted by a high-pitched young male imitation of a female voice.

"Yes, Warakan! Join the dance, Warakan! Oh, do take my hands, Warakan!"

Warakan was startled to see Namaray standing before him. An instant later the older youth gripped him hard by the wrists and swept him off into the thick of the dancing while Hranan and Trop and Oonay and the rest of the boys followed close on their heels, dancing and acting like girls. Warakan, hearing the laughter of the adults, flushed, embarrassed and confused.

"Leave him be, Namaray!" cried Jheena, but there was something in her voice that betrayed pleasure at the antics that she had roused from the boys.

"Come, Warakan! Let us show them how to dance!" exclaimed Namaray.

And for a few moments Warakan's spirit soared with happiness in the unexpected camaraderie between him and the others. But then, suddenly, Namaray's grip on his wrists became painful, and the youth leaned close to declare out of a venomously leering face, "Jheena is not for you, Watching Star Boy! You are not of Shateh's blood. He may call you Son, but you are Cannibal . . . Outlander . . . and he will never honor you with his name. Soon one of Shateh's women *is* going to give the chieftain a son. Have you seen how big both Eira and Cheelapat are with his babies? All the women say that Eira and the two other new women Shateh pierced carry like women ripe with male fruit. What will you do then, eh, Warakan? Will you dance? Will you sing? Will you celebrate when a *true* son of Shateh's takes his rightful place in the chieftain's lodge and you become nothing in his eyes? But maybe you do not have to worry. Maybe tomorrow a bear will devour your flesh and—"

"Do not wish for that!" Warakan interrupted in a rage of indignation. "For if it comes to pass, I will *become* a bear and come for you, Namaray, to grind your bones and flesh between my teeth!" The threat made, he twisted and turned, so ferociously attempting to free his wrists of the older boy's hurtful grip that Namaray was taken off balance and fell. "Ha!" shouted Warakan, and felt inordinately strong when he heard the others laugh at Namaray's expense.

The feeling was not to last. Namaray was not only older, he was taller and broader of back and shoulder. On his feet in less time than it had taken him to fall, he was on Warakan like the bear they would hunt in the morning. Warakan did his best, but he did not fare well in the scuffle that followed. The other boys threw themselves into the fray for the pure fun of it. He felt his fist strike a lip, or a nose, and he heard someone yowl when his knee came up hard into a groin; but he was given a good clouting before they left him behind, furious and frustrated.

Hurting, with blood running from his nose into his mouth, he was too ashamed to check the extent of his injuries. He stood his ground and glowered after them as they returned, self-satisfied, to the celebration. The boys, hooting merrily while they dispersed within the crowd, accepted many an encouraging word and friendly slap upon their backs and shoulders.

Warakan hated them. This was not the first time that Namaray had found an opportunity to instigate the other boys against him. Outnumbered, he always came up short in the melees. Within a brief time one or more of the youths would invariably come with a lighthearted apology, and even Namaray's post-battle teasing was usually offered in a way that opened the way for peace between them. But this time Namaray had dared to challenge and humiliate him in front of Shateh and the entire band. For this Warakan would not forgive him. He swallowed hard; there was the hot, salty taste of blood in his mouth. He barely noticed. Shateh was striding angrily toward him, and the look on his face as he passed through the now stationary dancers to come before his adopted son had nothing to do with pity or concern for the boy's welfare.

"Why do you stand alone?" the chieftain demanded disapprovingly. "Go after them! Show them that you will not tolerate such dishonoring. It is only natural for them to bait you. You must expect this. You must not be intimidated!"

Warakan was overwhelmed by righteous indignation. "I am not intimidated!" he shouted angrily, finding it impossible to blink back the appalling shame of tears even though he knew that the eyes of everyone in the band were upon him. "I fight! I do not run away even when Namaray brings many against me! Again and again this is so! Again and again I do not complain, even though their intent is to make me cower and slink away in fear of them, like a frightened dog unwelcome in their pack! I do not slink! I do not cower! But why does Shateh not make them treat me with the respect due to a chieftain's adopted son?"

Shateh's face tightened angrily. "Respect cannot be portioned out like so much meat at a hunt feast; it can only be earned! What does it matter whether Namaray comes against you alone or with many? This is the way of life! It is a good thing to be tested! You must make the others know that their baiting will only succeed in rousing Lion from your spirit. Do this, and they will be mauled by your courage. Do this, and they will be forced to admit that although you have come to this tribe from a far land and hostile people, you *are* Shateh's son. Fail to do this, and you will bring shame upon my name . . . as you are bringing it now!"

Warakan was deeply shaken. Shateh, openly irked, turned his back and, appraising the gathering and the position of the moon low over the western hills, raised his arms and declared the night's celebration over. A restless murmuring went up from the crowd as the chieftain stalked through the gathering and headed for the sweat lodge.

Zakeh, Xohkantakeh, and several other men broke from the
assembly and, in anticipation of their chieftain's need of
attendants, hurried after him.

Warakan felt sick with shame. His behavior had put an
end to the festivities and driven Shateh to cool his temper in
the sweat lodge, within which he would now seek the path
of understanding and communion with the ancestors. What
would he pray for? the boy wondered. Patience to endure
the shame heaped upon him by his son? Or a new son to be
born of Eira or the other new women—a strong, bold son of
his own blood in whom he could take just pride and whose
life would give him cause to banish the pretender who
named him Father?

Warakan's hands curled into fists. "May it not be so,"
he whispered. Dreading the loss of Shateh's affection more
than anything else in the world, he silently invoked the
forces of Creation to continue to give Shateh only daughters
so that he would always have an uncontested place at the
chieftain's side and in his heart.

The gathering, talking quietly among themselves, was
breaking up. Casting glances of condemnation his way, the
women and girls went to their lodges, and the men followed
the chieftain. Unal muttered against him as she and old
Xama went their way, and from somewhere amid the
dispersing throng, Namaray shouted a contemptuous "Good
night, Warakan!"

He ignored the taunt. Old Lahontay was still fixed in
place and staring at him out of dark, raptorial eyes. Warakan
stared back, wondering if the old man had somehow seen
his thoughts. Guilt stabbed him, and he felt suddenly,
unbearably ashamed. Instead of going to his sleeping furs
within the chieftain's lodge, where he would no doubt be
spitted by the sharp eyes and tongues of Wehakna and
Shateh's other women and daughters, he turned and sought
a quiet place to think and pass the remainder of the night
alone.

As in every village within which he had ever dwelled,

Warakan had his special "spot"; in this encampment, as in the village beyond the edge of the world, it was a fine old tree whose branches invited his ascent into evergreens that muffled his sobs as he stretched upon his belly and cried himself to sleep. . . .

He had not fully yielded to dreams before he was suddenly awakened by two men conversing directly beneath him.

Unaware of Warakan's presence, Teikan's voice was a low, worried rumble in the dark. "I tell you, Ynau, for a time at the edge of the world, the strength and wisdom of the Ancient Ones was again Shateh's when he drove the Red World shaman from among us. But he worries me now—as this winter worries me—and the boy's presence among us weakens the cohesiveness of the People. How can he not see this?"

"You once found cause to encourage Shateh to look upon the youth with favor. The boy is brave. Your Namaray tests Warakan too much, I think. You should tell Lahontay to instruct him to go easy on the boy when they leave the village tomorrow to search for the denning place of Walks Like a Man."

"My Namaray is on to the stink of a Watching Star cub that cannot help being what it is! And when I first set eyes on the boy, how was I to know that Shateh would name him Son? A man cannot take an orphaned cub of wolf or lion or bear into his band to be raised as his own child among his people. A predatory animal will always be an animal, and someday it will turn to savage all who have come to trust it!"

Warakan controlled his need to shout an angry protest. Common sense urged silence and caused him to hold his breath and remain motionless as Ynau said, "Your concerns are valid, Teikan, but last winter you blamed the lack of meat and warmth on the Red World shaman. Now you blame these things on a half-grown boy. I have been in villages where there has been more meat and better weather, but I have also endured much worse. Come. Let us go back to the village and join our chieftain and the others before we are missed. I could use a good sweat this night!"

Teikan snapped sharply, "The sweat of your body will not change what is, Ynau! I have begun to see that old Lahontay was right: It was no accident that the Red World shaman was also called Coyote, Yellow Wolf, Trickster! How cleverly Cha-kwena connived to use the strength of our warriors to defend his own band against our mutual enemies. Then, once our enemies were slain and scattered, he turned his back upon us and has taken our luck away with him. I tell you, somewhere out there across the world, Cha-kwena holds the sacred stone of our ancestors and laughs while he sends dark spirits at us through the bad-luck son of our enemies, whom he has tricked Shateh into keeping among us!"

Warakan was so stunned that he actually sucked in his breath; but in that moment a bird moved in the treetop, and the sound went unheard.

"Cha-kwena lost his power long before he fled beyond the edge of the world," said Ynau.

"Did he? Now there is no way to be sure, is there? If Shateh had listened to me and continued the pursuit of Yellow Wolf until the man himself was dead and the sacred stone was Shateh's, we could have divided the flesh of Cha-kwena among our warriors and women and children. If the power of the great white mammoth lived on in the man who slew the totem, that power would be ours now!"

Ynau snorted with disgust. "You speak as though with the cannibal tongue of a man of the Watching Star, Teikan!"

Teikan exhaled wearily. "Perhaps. And truly it brings pain to my spirit to question the wisdom of my chief and shaman, but these days I do not know Shateh. What kind of a spirit master cannot recognize an enemy standing before him? What kind of a chieftain cannot make sons on his women, or call the great herds to die upon the spears of his hunters, or even summon Warm Moon to rise once more out of winter skies?"

"Moon *has* shown her face to us, Teikan. Time will tell if her light is strong enough to banish White Giant Winter and bring the great bears from their dens to summon the return of summer. It grows late. Let us return to the village and the sweat lodge before our absence is taken for the disrespect it truly is."

The two starlit figures—each still clad in his moon ceremony robes of lion and leaping-cat skins—disappeared into the darkness. Warakan was shaking so badly that he was very nearly sick. Never had he felt more an outsider. What was he going to have to do to win the acceptance of those men? he wondered in silent desperation. He sat up and glared balefully into the night. Something cold touched his brow. He looked up. Between breaks in the canopy of the tree, springtime stars were bright between invisible skeins of cloud out of which snowflakes had begun to fall. He cursed and commanded White Giant Winter to go away.

"The continued presence of White Giant Winter is causing others to speak against you, Warakan, and against Shateh as well. It is not a good thing. Perhaps *you* are not a good thing." The statement came not from the stars and snow but from Lahontay, who had suddenly loomed tall and ominous in the darkness beneath the tree.

Startled, Warakan glared down at the old man whose growing animosity toward him had been evident for some time now. Clenching his fists, the boy vented his resentment. "You are not a shaman, Lahontay. You cannot know this. And how have you found me here?"

Lahontay's face was tight, measuring. "I followed Lion and Leaping Cat into the woods, sensing that somehow— even though they prowled alone and away from my chieftain—they were hunting him." He paused. Then, after a long moment of introspection, he added solemnly, "It seems they are hunting you, too. You must come with me now, Warakan, and do as I say without question."

Distrust sparked within the boy. "Why? What would you have me do? And where would you have me go?"

"If you would be a son of Shateh you must prove your worth to those who name him Chief. You must do battle with White Giant Winter. You must summon Warm Moon by rousing Bear and killing him. But first you must go into the village and, by stealth, take from your lodge your spears and your hunting bag. Let no one see you at this task, lest Namaray and Hranan and the others become aware of what we would do without them."

Warakan's brow furrowed suspiciously. "They will be angry when they learn that they have been left behind."

"The anger of boys is nothing to me, nor should it concern one who names Shateh Father. You must come with me now to the place where Bear is sleeping, Warakan. Or Teikan will soon be chief, and Shateh and the one he has so unwisely named Son will be put out of this band to die forever."

Warakan was appalled. Something in Lahontay's manner caused him to doubt the old man's motivations. "I do not believe you."

"Then stay here if you are afraid to prove yourself and bring honor to 'your father's' name."

Warakan's pride was stung. "I am not afraid!"

"Good. Then do as I say. Before dawn, I will meet you in this place, and we will go together to do what must be done."

After the old man had turned and walked away, Warakan smiled with grim intent. He realized that Lahontay had just given him the opportunity of a lifetime. He would show Namaray and the others what he was made of! He would take up his spears. He would go with the old man to the place where Bear was sleeping. He would rouse Bear. He would do battle with Bear. He would kill Bear. He would bring meat to his people and, by so doing, show them all that he was no longer a child of their enemies but a youth worthy to be a son of Shateh, a hunter to be trusted, and most assuredly *not* the source of bad luck that had brought

White Giant Winter to linger upon the land. In the days and nights ahead, if Teikan had cause to murmur about dark spirits, he would have to look eastward, to where a shaman had taken the sacred stone of their ancestors, and know that Cha-kwena of the Red World, not Warakan of the Watching Star, was their enemy.

5

Mah-ree awoke with a start from a fitful sleep. An owl was *oooo*ing in the dark. She looked up and around, disoriented. For the last few hours she had been tangled within a net of terrifying dreams from which she had been unable to escape before seeing herself overwhelmed and consumed by a great bear. Trees stood tall and close. Stars glinted above. If the moon was still in the sky, she could not see it, for it was low in the west, lost to view behind the massive boulders against which she had passed the night.

Shaking and frightened, Mah-ree sat upright, feeling grateful to the owl for successfully summoning her from her dreams, but also regretful for the impetuous decision that had kept her from returning to the village after Cha-kwena had commanded her to do so. She had intended to obey him. In fact, she had been well on her way to their lodge when she had looked back and seen him climbing higher into the boulder-strewn gorge. The sight of her shaman striding across the misted heights unarmed and alone had caused her to turn and follow, for she had come from the village with her sling and dagger and the new throwing stick that she had sharpened at one end. Even though the use of a lance was forbidden to her, the fire-hardened, pointed end of the hardwood stave could serve as a spear if the need arose.

She had not expected Cha-kwena to go so far. With the

ease and grace of a mountain sheep, he had wandered on and on, ascending the stony, moonlit chasm and leaving her breathless. He followed the call of an owl and soon left the village so far behind that even if she had wanted to return, she would not have dared to go alone. Finally he had paused atop a huge boulder and settled himself, a solitary figure, chanting softly as was his way, seated cross-legged with his back to the moon and his eyes on the eastern stars. Grateful for the opportunity to rest, Mah-ree had dropped to her knees and allowed herself to catch her breath; she had not intended to sleep lest he discover her presence on his return or go on his way and leave her.

Now, berating herself for failing to remain awake and alert, Mah-ree got to her feet. She peered upward through surrounding trees to the top of the great boulder and saw to her dismay that Cha-kwena was gone. And in that very instant something moved in the trees behind her. She whirled, terrified, expecting to see the bear of her dreams, but instead a dark, winged form flew over her head uttering a series of low, sonorous hoots.

"Owl!" Relieved, she exclaimed the name of old Hoyeh-tay's helping animal spirit and, following the flight of the raptor, turned again just as Cha-kwena appeared at the top of the boulder and extended a hand downward to her.

"I did not think you would ever wake up," he said sourly. "Did you not hear me call your name?"

Her face flamed. "I . . ."

"Do not waste my time trying to explain your disobedience, Mah-ree. I have come to expect it from you. As long as you have come this far, there is something you should see."

Ashamed and embarrassed, she obeyed without further question and soon found herself standing beside him, staring down and eastward into a broad, open bowl of snowy grassland surrounded by long, shouldering ranges of forested hills. Just below the gorge, close to the largest of several steaming pools, the herd of mammoth dozed unperturbed. Owl was perched on the head of the pregnant matriarch. Deer and rabbits and pronghorns were browsing contentedly near the water's edge. Mah-ree's heart leaped with pleasure at the tranquillity and beauty of the scene.

"That for which we wait will happen here," Cha-kwena predicted.

Mah-ree looked up at him. How handsome he was to her in the light of the stars, with his owl-skin headdress making him seem half-man, half-bird. It was as though he had only to spread his arms and he would fly away into the night, and she, holding tightly to his hand, would be borne away with him upon the cloak of his magic. She sighed, overcome by love and pride in the fact that she was his woman. Then she frowned. He looked so sad. Her free hand rose to touch his face. "Let me love you," she whispered.

Cha-kwena did not look at her as he pushed her hand away. "Look," he said. "Owl flies to the east."

Mah-ree could not have cared less about owls. She hung her head and did not blame Cha-kwena for not desiring such a disobedient creature as she.

Appraising the stars, Cha-kwena's hand went to his throat and pressed the talisman that lay there beneath his winter robe. "The mammoth are here. Why, then, does the helping animal spirit of my grandfather Hoyeh-tay continue eastward into the sky? And the sky speaks of spring! Why, then, does winter linger upon the land? Somewhere . . . somehow . . . something has unsettled the forces of Creation. If only I could know what it is!"

Mah-ree looked up at him, aghast. "I started to go back to the village as you commanded, Cha-kwena, but when my shaman went on alone and unarmed, I . . ."

Cha-kwena looked down at her and said in a voice dulled by fatigue, "Ah, little one, if I thought it was you—"

"You would throw me from this great rock to my death! I would deserve no more!"

He shook his head, slung a weary arm around her shoulders, and pulled her close. "I am not a shaman of the People of the Watching Star, Mah-ree."

"But I am a lawbreaking woman."

"No more," he said.

"No more!" she echoed, trembling in his embrace. She wrapped her arms ferociously around him, resolved to destroy her new throwing stick lest the forces of Creation view it as a spear. "Mah-ree will not be a threat to her man or her people or the totem again!" she vowed. "This woman will be Obedient Woman! Lawbreaking Woman is now as dead to this world as the People of the Watching Star!"

"Our enemies were not all slain in the last war, little one."

"They are all slain in my heart," she said. "Surely it is the same!"

In the Valley of the Dead, the giant ground sloth breathed no more. Nor did the leaping cat that had driven Ban-ya from her kill. Drawn to the lakeshore by the screeching of the great feline that had prevented them from sleeping, Tsana and his fellow hunters wielded their spears and silenced the cat forever.

"Its skin and teeth and claws will be for Jhadel," said Tsana, looking down at the corpse. "The kill is ours, but the prize would not have been taken had his wisdom not sent us to this place."

The men murmured in agreement—all save Indeh. His favorite spear had overshot its mark and been lost within the reed beds.

"I tell you, it is not a good thing for men to be in this cursed valley! Nothing has been the same for us since our enemies slew the totem," grumbled the man, eyeing the skeleton of the great white mammoth totem where it protruded from the icy lake.

"I am beginning to worry about you, Indeh," Tsana stated with open contempt. "Boldly you came to the People of the Watching Star! Bravely you swore to raise your spear against your own chieftain because he had dishonored his warriors by walking with Red World men. But tonight, as I listen to you whine and worry, I think that you are not so bold and brave. I think that, perhaps, you possess the fearful heart and tremulous belly—not of a warrior . . . but of a *woman* of Shateh's tribe."

Indeh went rigid at the insult and unwelcome reminder of his lineage. "Tsana speaks boldly and bravely, considering that it is *this* tribe—not Shateh's—that is now forced to run and hide from enemies."

The words brought sullen, resentful stares from the other hunters. It was late. They were all tired, in need of sleep. The night was very cold. Loons, unseen on the misted surface of the lake, cried eerily while wolves and lions "talked" together in the darkness, reminding the men that they must stay alert or lose the meat that they had taken this night. Then another kind of ululation striated the wind; it was a disconcertingly familiar sound.

"I swear by the forces of Creation, that sounds like a baby wailing!" exclaimed Hrak.

"A trick of the wind," assured Tsana.

"Or of the spirits," added Indeh ominously.

The men fell to wary silence. Distorted by distance, the humanlike cries continued for a few moments, then stopped.

"I do not like this place!" said Unai. "I think Indeh may be right about it. Too many have died here. There are spirits calling on the wind!"

"And I tell you again that if the spirit of my dead woman, the high priestess Sheela, lingers in this valley, she will protect us. We have nothing to fear!" Tsana gestured toward the kill. "Tomorrow we will make much meat of this. Is there a man here who can disagree when I say that this valley is the best hunting ground that we have seen in many a long, hungry moon? Is there a man here who cannot agree that we must seek a place in which to raise a decent camp so that we may exploit this?"

No one spoke, not even Indeh.

Tsana nodded. "Unless there is one who would go in my place, I will return across the land to bring Jhadel and the rest of the band here."

"Now?" Xanahay was surprised.

"Alone?" Indeh pressed, suspicious.

"Soon it will be dawn. I can sleep no more this night. One man is all that is needed to lead the others. Many may be needed to guard the meat and see to it that wolves and lions do not steal that which will take the ache of hunger from the bellies of our women and children. But if you are afraid to stay, Indeh, by all means come with me. I will keep you safe!"

"Go!" snarled the onetime warrior of Shateh's. "This man is not afraid to stay!"

With the light of the Sky River and the many children of Moon to guide his steps, Tsana left the others, proud of himself for managing to withhold laughter at the easily manipulated Indeh. He wanted to go alone across the land because he had no intention of taking the shortest route out of the valley. Instead Tsana loped toward the hills from which the strange sounds had come. Despite what he had said to the others, he knew that he had heard no tricks of the wind this night. Someone had called. Someone had cried. Someone had stood in silhouette against a transient light. Someone. Or some*thing*. He had to know what or who was out there.

"Sheela!" Tsana spoke the name of his lost beloved with a longing that cut him to his heart. He wondered if any man of his tribe suspected how much of his spirit Sheela had taken with her to the world beyond this world when she had been slain in battle by the insidious Red World shaman during the last war. Warriors did not grieve for their women. Warriors went on with their lives. *Other warriors,* he thought, *not Tsana.* He had been the man of Sheela even before she had become high priestess of the Watching Star, last in the bloodline of the legendary Ysuna, Daughter of the Sun. No man had ever had such a woman . . . unless it had been the Mystic Warrior, the shaman Masau, who had been Ysuna's man before he had degraded himself by betraying her and himself for love of a Red World captive.

Tsana was revolted. Masau was dead. No one in any of the many scattered bands of the tribe grieved for him, even though he had traveled widely among them. In the end he had been what he had been born to be. Not even the Daughter of the Sun had been able to turn a cast-off child of Shateh's into a true and loyal man of the Watching Star.

He wondered what must eventually happen with Indeh. The man had proved a valiant fighter and hunter, but he, too, was what he was; others, including Jhadel, might be willing to overlook his past, but Tsana was not. Someday the man was going to challenge his will once too often, and Tsana would put an end to him once and for all.

Tsana's thoughts made distance seem shorter. He was approaching his destination. The hills loomed ahead. He lengthened his stride until thickening scrub growth caused him to slow his steps even before some sort of night-hunting bird or bat plummeted from the sky on silent wings to rake his head with its talons. He cursed and slapped at the sky. Too late. The creature was gone. Wiping blood from his eyes, Tsana looked up along the soaring, starlit face of a cave-pocked cliff.

"Sheela . . . is your spirit here? Have you called to your man in the night?" he whispered, half in longing, half in dread.

And then he saw her. A woman stood at the edge of the largest cave.

Breathless, Tsana stared, disbelieving, yet wanting to believe. Was she real or a trick of the night? He could not be sure, but he stood his ground, awaiting with trepidation reunion with the one woman he had ever truly loved.

Moments passed. The figure melted away into the shadows of the cave. Disappointed, Tsana stood motionless for a long time before he turned and was about to go his way. But a sound arrested him in midstep. Had he just heard footfalls scurrying along stony ground, or had his ears been misled by the wind blowing through the hollow of the hill? He had to know. With spears at the ready he went forward, picking his way upward to the largest of the caves and, not without apprehension, looking in.

Starlight revealed little of the cavern save hints of

enormous size and suitability as a dwelling site for his people. There was no sign of Sheela; nevertheless, Tsana could not help but wonder if the ghost of his beloved had led him here. Then he caught the sour stink of vomit, the smell of ashes from a cooking fire and of human habitation. Unsure and perplexed, he was about to enter the cave for a better look when he was startled by the sound of a rockfall within the interior of the hill. A moment later a tide of thousands of wings came rushing toward him from the cave.

Tsana was a man who feared little in life, but a sweeping flood of leathery wings was enough to force a quick and instinctive retreat. Stumbling and finally falling, he found himself bruised but unhurt and flat on his back at the base of the cliff. Staring up at the bats as they dispersed seemingly into thin air, he knew that the Ancient Ones taught that bats were the restless manifestations of unhappy spirits. Now Tsana was convinced that the ghost of his deceased woman had indeed called him to this place.

Euphoric, Tsana rose and called to his beloved, "No longer shall you be alone! I will tell the others of my hunting party to come here. They will be afraid, but I will command them to come. They will warm this place with fire and song! Let your spirit sing with them as I seek out Jhadel and return with our people!"

Deep within the cavern, a terrified Ban-ya heard Tsana's promise. She crouched with her babies in complete darkness. Having managed at last to make her way back to the outer cave after fearing herself lost, starlight had given her a good enough look at the man who stood and shouted from the base of the cliff. Recognizing his garments and tattooed face to be those of a warrior of the People of the Watching Star, she had grabbed her belongings and fled into the interior of the hill, to hide until he went his way. Had she not blundered into the bats, all might have been fine. But their sudden flight had frightened her into a mad race deep into the hollow of the hill. Now her way back to the main cave had been blocked by a rockslide.

Ban-ya's heart was pounding. In an effort to silence her infant sons, she had packed their mouths with a wadding of fringes hastily ripped from the bottom edge of her dress. The stronger of the two was fussing again. She pinched the infant's nose, thus silencing him before pressing his face tightly against her breast. She could not risk the sound penetrating the mound of fallen rocks.

"Hush, little son . . . sleep, little son . . . you must be still lest your cries summon our enemies!"

The child squirmed, then relaxed in Ban-ya's embrace. But Rat, Eater of Courage, Father of Fear, was with her now. She heard him moving in the darkness, felt him and his furry, bald-tailed brothers and sisters brush the sides of her bare feet. It was all she could do to stifle a scream. If there was any consolation to be found in her predicament, it lay in the realization that she had her possessions with her—and with them the ability to make fire and create light with her bow drill and kindling. She knew that light would send Rat and his family scurrying for cover. And she was certain that light would banish her rising sense of panic. As soon as she was able to see her surroundings, she would dig her way through the rockslide and make good an escape before the hunters came to the cave.

Ban-ya put her infants down. The smaller baby was making soft sounds of stretching and messing in his swaddling; the other child was quiet, and for that Ban-ya was grateful. She fumbled frantically through her things for her fire makers and the small, crudely fashioned stone tallow lamp. After finding what she needed, she soon had the bow drill spinning between her palms upon a bed of dry grass and lichen; fire making was not easy work, especially since Dakan-eh had broken her wrist in a rage. It had not healed properly, and stress and fatigue made it swell and ache.

The kindling ignited. Gratified, Ban-ya leaned close to nurture flames and light. Moments later, her breath steaming in the frigid air, she had an oil-saturated wick of fiber cord burning within the crooked well of her stone lamp. Curious to see her surroundings, she raised the lamp and was so startled by what she saw that she almost dropped it.

"Ah!" she exclaimed, amazed to find herself in a wide, low-ceilinged cavern that took her breath away. Turning for a broader, more comprehensive view, she gasped in astonishment and awe when she saw glorious, sacred pictographs on the walls of this secret cavern.

At that very moment, a meteor streaked across the skies. Cha-kwena and Mah-ree, coming through the woods on their way back to the village, stopped dead, transfixed. Although shooting stars often flamed across the black sky robe of Father Above, the blue brightness of this meteor was remarkable; as it flew downward out of the constellation that they knew as the Great Bear, it resembled a fiery spear being hurled from the northern ranges toward them and into the first blush of dawn that was now coloring the skies to the east.

Mah-ree caught her breath. "Once before, we saw such a star! Long ago. We were together then, as we are together now. Ah, Cha-kwena, the Ancient Ones have told that flaming stars are omens of good things to come! Surely this is a sign that we will be together always and forever!"

Cha-kwena frowned. He had not forgotten the star of which she had spoken. He had painted it on the wall of his secret cavern. In his mind the star did not mark his joining with Mah-ree, but the beginning of war and of all that had sent his people fleeing from their homeland. Cha-kwena's hand sought and found the sacred stone. With the talisman gripped within the curl of his fist, his eyes turned skyward, and he asked the forces of Creation to lighten his spirit with good omens for a change.

He was about to warn his little girl-of-a-woman to stop predicting the intentions of the spirits, but she was already hurrying forward. Alerted by the sound of her footfall, the village dogs were raising a chorus of barking, yarfing welcomes. Cha-kwena stood his ground while Mah-ree waded into the happy pack. He had not been at ease with the dogs since a handful of their number had run off to join with the coyotes and wolves that attacked the great white mammoth, Life Giver. Were it not for the dogs' usefulness as beasts of burden—and Mah-ree's inexplicable affection for them—he would long since have driven them off.

Night Wind—soft now and dying away in the first tentative light of dawn—sighed, embraced Cha-kwena, then confided in a voice that seemed to come from all around as well as from within the young shaman: *Be wise, Cha-kwena. There is a wounding in the wood. Be wary, Yellow Wolf. The campfires of the dead light the river of the night. There are eyes in the belly of the bear, and the Watching Star sees you now . . . here . . . even though you have led your people beyond the edge of the world.*

"Wounding in the wood? Eyes in the belly of a bear? Fires burning in a river? How can these things be?" Confused and unsure if Night Wind had actually spoken or if he had heard only the voice of his own never-ending fear of the future, Cha-kwena was suddenly annoyed. "I am Shaman! Why must the spirits be always so elusive? Why must the forces of Creation always choose to communicate in riddles and confound me?"

Owl has shown you the way you must go! What more do you need to know of that which will or will not come to be? No man, not even a shaman, may glimpse beyond the curve of the horizon! Though you walk toward it and reach it a thousand times, still it will always loom ahead, ever changing and unknowable, until at last your spirit rises above your earthly form, and you see with spirit eyes what lies ahead for all!

Shaken, Cha-kwena heard and felt Night Wind gust briefly, then drop and disappear. Suddenly tired, hungry, and weary of the emotionally exhausting vagaries of Vision, he stared ahead to where the small, conical lodges of his band were illuminated in the soft light of dawn. Someone had ignited a cooking fire. It would be a long while before the sun rose high enough to show its face above the tall, eastern rim of the gorge, and it was still too dark for

Cha-kwena to see smoke; but he detected the inviting scent of burning wood and dung and knew that soon the fragrance of breakfast would sweeten the air. With Moon down and Morning Star now setting and fading with her brothers and sisters over the snowy western hills, it was a beautiful, welcoming scene to a tired man. He went forward and could hear mammoth trumpeting contentedly far beyond the gorge; he did not look back. Kosar-eh was coming toward him.

"Mah-ree says that you have found good country ahead," said the big man.

"The mammoth have found it."

"Is it your intention to have us move on, then?" Kosar-eh did not appear pleased with the notion. "This is a good place. Our women and little ones have found happiness here. We could stay for many moons and still find much meat on the grassland below."

Cha-kwena looked around and knew that because of his leadership, his people prospered in this new village; he also knew that come spring, the wintering herds would probably disperse to unknown calving and mating grounds. By then, his people would have been at this site so long that they would begin to sap its resources. It was time to move on. Meat and wood and a fresh source of water awaited them on the far side of the gorge. There they would settle and await the imminent rebirth of the totem. And even if—by some odd chance—his enemies were to find his cave painting and discover the truth about the impending rebirth of Life Giver, how could they ever hope to find the mammoth now that Cha-kwena had placed himself and his people so far beyond the edge of the known world?

By a wounding in the wood they shall scent *the way! By the eyes in the belly of the bear they shall* see *the way! You have defied the taboo of the Ancient Ones and broken the trust of the ancestors! By the light of fires that burn in the river of the night your enemies and the enemies of the totem shall* come!

Startled, Cha-kwena tensed, turned, and looked wor-

riedly around for the source of the warning. Night Wind had
not returned. Save for the sound of dogs, voices in the
village, and the rising song of awakening birds, the air was
still. Dawn was fully born now, bathing the earth and sky in
soft pinks and blues. Washed in the soothing glow of
morning, Cha-kwena's hand closed tightly around the sacred stone. He felt its power and knew that he had indeed
been given the gift of Vision as he said, "On the wings of
Owl, the spirits of the ancestors called me to go beyond the
gorge last night. The mammoth were there, waiting. We will
not make our lodges outside the fall of their sacred
shadows."

Kosar-eh was unnerved. "Then we will wander forever? Never knowing a settled village or a land that our
children may call the land of their mothers and fathers,
or—"

"Since time beyond beginning our people have found
food and shelter in the shadow of the mammoth. If they stay
in one place, we will stay in the land they choose, just as our
mothers and fathers remained in the Red World for generations beyond counting. If the forces of Creation urge them
to continue eastward in the path of the rising sun, we will
and *must* follow."

Kosar-eh scowled, turned, and without further comment stalked back to the village.

Cha-kwena was not disheartened. For the first time in
longer than he could remember, he felt relaxed. He knew
that his words could have been no others. As shaman, it was
time for him to put aside his doubts and fears. He must trust
implicitly in the mammoth, and in the sacred stone, and in
the spirits who warned him that since he had broken the
taboo of the Ancient Ones he must always be on his guard
and willing to drive the totem to safety ahead of their
enemies. Besides, the thought of traveling on into unknown
lands was always pleasing to his heart.

"Cha-kwena!"

The children of the band were running to him now,
demanding stories of his most recent journey along the

dream path. Tla-nee and Joh-nee were at his side, taking his hands and eagerly pulling him into the heart of the village, where the women had raised a communal cooking fire. Mah-ree had already brought his lounging mattress and backrest to the shaman's place of honor. U-wa urged him to seat himself. He did not refuse her offer.

Moments later the entire little band was happily assembled, passing woven baskets and boiling bags and sharing the bounty of the new land into which their shaman had led them. For Cha-kwena the gathering of beloved friends and family was as nourishing as the food they shared. Now and then, he would find Mah-ree's eyes adoringly fixed on him as the children pressed him for further stories. He told them all that they would hear. Tales from time beyond beginning when the animals and people were one . . . tales of First Man and First Woman . . . tales of the ever-battling twin Brothers of the Sky.

"Tell the story of how Dog put off the skin of Wolf so that he might walk forever as brother to Man," Ka-neh requested.

Cha-kwena told the story, and afterwards, when the children called the dogs to share more of the food with them, he frowned in disapproval but had no chance to send the animals off, for Kiu-neh was asking to hear the story of how Horn Nose stole his tusk from Mammoth. He started to tell the tale, but then Tla-nee pouted and complained that she had never seen a horn nose. It occurred to Cha-kwena that he had never seen one, either.

"As big as a young mammoth are the horn-nosed kind!" said U-wa, then told of having once seen a herd of rhinoceros when she had been a child not much older than Tla-nee.

"When Horn Nose walks, he and his women and children trot like angry horses," added Kosar-eh. "And the feet of even little horn noses are so big that they make thunder roar within the ground as they pass over it!"

The children *oo*ed and *ahh*ed, and after Cha-kwena told the story of how Horn Nose had stolen his tusk from

Mammoth, they laughed, got to their feet, and worked off their meal by setting themselves to a game of imitating Horn Nose and his trotting, big-footed "children."

While Cha-kwena watched them, it struck him that many animals were rare these days. He thought of Ha-xa and her cloak of jaguar skin and doubted that any of the children of his band had ever seen a living spotted cat. Gone, too, were four-horned pronghorns and fat little hook-nosed pigs with spotted bellies, and dark, hairy oxen with massive horns that seemed to have melted downward to cleave to their foreheads like some sort of strange ceremonial bonnets. Sun Eater rarely shadowed the earth with huge, condorlike wings, and only one kind of horse ran across the grasslands these days. Long-horned bison and his high-shouldered clansmen were less often seen than their shorter, fleeter-footed tribesmen. And whereas old Hoyeh-tay had told tales of his grandfather's time, in which mastodon and mammoth were as plentiful as bison, as far as Cha-kwena knew, the mammoth herd that grazed beyond the gorge might well be the last of its kind.

"Not as long as I live!" he vowed.

"Of what do you speak?" asked a radiant Ta-maya, nursing little Ha-xa-ree.

"I . . . as long as I have lived, I have never seen Horn Nose," Cha-kwena replied, not wishing to shadow her happiness with his thoughts.

Moments later, when a proudly beaming Mah-ree brought more food and drink to him, it occurred to Cha-kwena that his pretty little woman might well have been correct in her assessment of the meaning of the falling star. Surrounded by happy children and doting women, he felt a deep contentment. True, he thought, Kosar-eh could have looked happier. Poor little Doh-teyah was blind; but her eyes had healed from the bad-sickness spirits, and she was a delightful child as full of laughter as any of the others as she sat happily on Gah-ti's knee. Although stump-armed and scarred across the top of his scalp, Gah-ti had matured into a brave, intelligent, and physically powerful young man. Looking at him now with Doh-teyah, Cha-kwena felt his own enthusiasm and confidence strengthened. Perhaps he would soon find the magic power to heal them both.

Cha-kwena smiled as he took Mah-ree's offerings. "Perhaps the omens have been good omens after all," he said.

6

A new day had dawned in the Land of Grass, but images of night and of a falling star burned Lahontay's mind as he led Warakan downriver and across the snowy land toward the place where Bear lay sleeping.

"Soon Shateh will see that I am worthy to be his son!" proclaimed the boy. "Soon they will *all* see!"

"Hmmm," replied the old man, pausing to rest.

"The star that fell last night . . . it *was* a good sign!"

"A sign of ending," said Lahontay.

"So you said last night!" Warakan was breathless with excitement. "An ending to the one we hunt! An ending to my days as an untested boy! Namaray and the others will be angry to have missed this great challenge!"

"This test must be for you alone," replied Lahontay solemnly, hefting again the weight of his traveling pack. "Come, boy. We will go on. And be quiet for a change. You talk too much and ask too many questions."

"There is so much I wish to learn!"

"Hmmm."

"Will you teach me everything you know, Lahontay, so that I will be a great hunter like you someday, and a man to make my father proud?"

The old man regarded the youth from the corner of one eye. "Do not try to grease my pride, Warakan. Watch what

228

I do. Listen when I speak. And stop babbling like a stream at spring flood! Is this behavior what you have learned from your people before you came to my tribe?"

The boy seemed to wilt. "Lahontay's people are Warakan's people!"

"Hmmph!"

"I have known no others whom I have ever respected."

"Hmmph!"

"It is true! And Warakan is grateful to Lahontay for giving this boy the opportunity to prove himself. I will not disappoint you!"

Lahontay made a sour face but neither grunted nor spoke when he impatiently gestured Warakan on.

They walked in silence. In the cold light of morning, the old man's frailty was evident. He stopped often but justified these periods of rest as necessary to his instruction of Warakan in tracking skills. The boy pretended not to see through the deception. His distrust of Lahontay had dissolved, and now and then, when the old man lapsed into talk of hunting and ritual, Warakan found himself spellbound.

"With the love of a brother a man must go forth to the place where Great Paws lies sleeping. With the love of a brother a man must think how he will kill this prey, for the way in which it is done must be an honoring of both hunter and hunted. Only then, after it is done, will the hunter take on the attributes of the one he has killed and thus gain much status in the eyes of the spirits and of his tribe. A man can win more respect only by killing a mammoth."

"Someday I will kill mammoth!" Warakan boasted.

Lahontay stopped dead, then reached sideways and gave the boy a shove. "No man may say that he will kill this animal or that animal. A man must *ask* his prey to give up its life so that it may become food for him. If he does not honor that which he is to kill, it will not consent to die, and the People will go hungry! As our people have gone hungry! Have you learned nothing of our ways and teachings since you have come to live among us? Maybe it is your sloppy, honorless tongue that has deprived us of big meat, Watching

Star Boy! No wonder Namaray and the other youths are pounding you all the time!"

Chastised, Warakan hung his head. He wanted to apologize and explain that when Namaray and the others were around, he rarely had the chance to ask questions of an elder, but he had already said far too much. Clenching his jaws, he waited for Lahontay to walk on again. When he did, Warakan followed without question.

Soon, with the sun well risen but the air still unseasonably cold, the travelers came across an old bison jump. Pausing at the edge of the ravine, they stared down into the killing site at piles of snow-layered bones and skulls and tusks.

"Before you came to live among my people, Warakan, there were many good winter hunts in this place . . . many bison, many horse, many mammoth . . . so much meat, the hunters took only the best and left the rest for carrion. Now that Shateh names you Son, the Warm Moon sleeps in her lodge beyond the edge of the world and White Giant Winter fills the mountain passes with snow that does not melt. How can the herds come through to feed the tribe?"

Warakan looked up at Lahontay. He had not missed the accusation in the old man's words. "The Ancient Ones have taught that in time beyond beginning when the animals and people were of one tribe, White Giant Winter was high chief of the Four Winds. Nothing lived unless he allowed it. But *I* did not live in the land in those days, Lahontay, so you cannot blame me for them!"

The old man took slow, thoughtful measure of the boy before offering a reminder of his own. "Who is to say where the spirits of any of us resided in time beyond beginning? Predator . . . prey . . . men . . . beasts . . . all who live now lived then in different skins."

The premise sobered Warakan and made him inexplicably uneasy, but only for a moment. Sensing the need to secure the trust of the old man, he pressed bravely, "In any life and in any skin, Warakan was and *is* a loyal son of Shateh! With your own mouth, Lahontay, you have said that when I succeed in rousing Bear, Warm Moon will arise and White Giant Winter will ride away on the wings of North Wind. Then snow and ice spirits will become water spirits. Then the skin of Mother Below will become furred with green grass, and the herds will come hungry out of the face of the rising sun to be food for the People. Then will the People of the Land of Grass look upon Warakan and say that it was a good thing for all when Shateh chose to name him Son! Is this not so, Lahontay?"

"We will see," the old hunter replied obliquely. His eyes had narrowed into contemplative slits. "You speak well for one so young, like a shaman I once knew." He frowned, appeared to be attempting to clear a pathway back into time. "So long ago . . . strange . . . I cannot remember the face . . . but the words—"

"It does not matter," interrupted Warakan. "If I sound like a shaman, I will speak no more!"

Disturbed by his failing powers of recollection, Lahontay stared across the land. "We must go on. It is still far to the place of which I have dreamed, and much danger lies ahead for us there."

"I am not afraid!" Warakan insisted.

"No?" queried the old man, then shook his head as he led the boy on once more. "You should be."

Smoke, sweat, and dreams—Shateh was steeped in all three as he continued to fast and commune with the spirits within the sweat lodge. It was a large, low-ceilinged structure of bent willow branches covered with heavy hides. Inside, a small pit had been dug to contain heated rocks; over these, Zakeh, acting as keeper of sacred smoke, tossed water from a bison-horn flask to create steam.

But now as Zakeh, his eyes still heavy with sleep, poured the water upon the stones, it roused nothing but a soft sloshing sound. His gut constricted with dread. It had been awhile since he had crawled to the door flap to ask Xohkantakeh, keeper of sacred flame, to take up the hardwood tongs and bring freshly heated stones from the small fire that had been kept burning outside all night long and into the morning. He castigated himself for dozing off and neglecting his sacred duties. If Shateh awoke to a cold, steamless lodge, there was no saying what the penalty would be for the attendant who betrayed the sacred trust of a dreamer.

Zakeh attempted to alleviate fear with justification. How could he not have slept? It seemed forever since the chieftain had entered the hut, and longer still since Shateh had raised his head from the dreaming position. Breathing deeply and slowly, he sat motionless, wrists resting on bent knees between which his long, sweat-saturated hair hung to the ground.

"Is he still alive?" whispered Xohkantakeh, peering in as he opened the door flap just wide enough to allow himself the narrowest view inside.

Zakeh squinted from the unexpected and hurtful intrusion of light. The intense heat that had filled the lodge when Shateh had begun the sweating-out-the-spirits-of-anger ritual had since abated; but heated stones had been brought to the pit many times since then, and the dark interior remained damp and warm. Zakeh shivered from the chill air of morning and, keeping his voice just loud enough to be heard by Xohkantakeh, hissed, "What is the matter with you? Close the door flap! The dreamer must not be disturbed until he emerges on his own from his trance!"

"Teikan has just come to tell me that Lahontay has left the village with Warakan to seek the denning site of Bear. Namaray and the other youths were left behind. Shateh will want to know this."

"When he comes from the path of dreams I will tell him!"

"But he must be told that the new woman Eira has felt the first of her birth pangs!"

"I will not interrupt the dreaming of a man with talk of women! It is too soon for that one's baby to come from between her thighs. She is a first-time bearer; she does not know what she feels. Bring more stones. I must have heat if there is to be enough steam to sustain the dreamer's thoughts in the world beyond this world!"

Xohkantakeh growled, but he obeyed. The sweat lodge was plunged into blue darkness. Zakeh reached for the single remaining sacred bundle of dried sage and sweet grass. He placed it in the pit atop cooled, palm-sized stones. A moment later Xohkantakeh handed in a leather sack filled with freshly heated stones. The smell of scorched leather was strong in Zakeh's nostrils as he took the bundle. Quickly and quietly, he emptied its red-hot contents on top of the sage and grass, then blew into the pit until a fragrant smoke rose to sweeten the interior with a scent that was sacred and soothing to men and spirits alike. Only when Shateh sighed with obvious pleasure did Zakeh relax. And only when all of the incense had been released from the sacred bundle did he dip the bison horn into the water paunch and begin to raise steam from the stones once more.

Shateh smiled.

He was grateful for the sudden shifting of dreams that had become the hurtful recollections of an aging man longing for youth and for women he had loved and lost. Now he *was* young. He saw himself pursuing big game on the hunting grounds of his youth. He saw himself painted in white clay and ash and ocher. He saw himself ascending the great pole—a debranched cottonwood sunk and braced upright within a ravine—to stand tall, clinging with one arm at its pinnacle, calling the game at the top of his voice, daring the bison to stampede into the ravine and give up their lives to become meat for his people.

"Come!" he shouted.

And the bison came. Driven by the dogs and hunters of his tribe, by the hundreds they came until the earth shook. The flood of black and brown and golden bodies came surging toward the ravine across the Land of Grass. And then they were all around him, shaking the towering pole upon which he stood and called them to their death. Hooves and horns and humps leaped the ravine but failed to clear it.

"Ay yah!" he cried as the bison plunged into the abyss.

No man had ever dared to call the bison as Shateh called the herds—no man save one.

"My son! Come forth! Prove yourself if you dare!" The chieftain saw him now. Masau was ascending the great hunt pole. Masau was daring to accept the challenge of the father who had long since become his enemy. Tattooed and magnificent, what a man that son had become! Never would there be an equal to him. Hunt chief! Mystic Warrior! Shaman! Son of Shateh and favorite of Ysuna, Daughter of the Sun, high priestess of the cannibal People of the Watching Star.

Suddenly Shateh's dream shifted again. Thinking of a son of his body as one of "them" made him cringe. And yet he knew that he and he alone was responsible for Masau's tribal affiliation. Within the fiber of his dream, the chieftain saw the child that the man Masau had been, in many ways much like Warakan: small for his years, as slender as a young reed and as tender. Who could have imagined that he would later grow tall and strong and as dangerous as a bull elk in rut? Wide-eyed and cowering with terror, Masau as a young boy had climbed the pole, then panicked and refused the test of bravery that would have honored him by sending him up the hunt pole with his father.

Everyone had agreed that his cowardice had not been surprising; since infancy the boy had favored the use of his left hand, and this had always been the sign of a potential troublemaker. And yet, with the full face of the Starving Moon staring pitilessly down at the winter world, Masau had stood unflinching before Shateh when the chieftain had explained that when the band trekked on in search of better hunting grounds, it would be necessary to leave him and his sickly older brother behind. In starving times sacrifices were demanded of the few for the good of all. This had been the way of the People since time beyond beginning. Shateh had seen no reason to change it. He had assured himself that he would soon make better sons, stronger, bigger, and braver; besides, no man—especially one who was both chief and shaman—would have been so selfish as to provide meat for those who could not hunt or keep up along the trail to new hunting grounds while others were starving.

Yet now guilt and regret were so strong within Shateh that he moaned as he dreamed of his little boys surrounded by wolves and lions upon the icy plain of the past. Mists closed in around them. The chieftain heard the trumpeting of mammoth and the screams of his children being ravaged by carnivores. Then, through bloodied banks of fog and along a pathway lined with heaped mammoth bones, Masau emerged—not as a child but as a man to curse the father who had abandoned him.

Shateh awoke with a start. He raised his head, stared into the gloom of the sweat lodge, and saw Masau, without doubt the best of all his many deceased sons, standing before him in all of the raiment of Mystic Warrior of the People of the Watching Star. "My son!" he exclaimed, all at once amazed and glad and appalled. "How can you be here? You are a dead man!"

"I am of your blood and flesh and marrow and bone! A man cannot turn his back and cut a son from his life any more than he can cut away an arm or leg and expect it not to bleed."

"My people were starving! There was not enough for you *and* for them!"

"Your enemies were starving, too. But they had enough for me."

"I will not hear it! Too late did you break with those who hunted my people, Masau! Had you returned sooner, as a friend and an ally, I would not have fought you, and you would be alive now!"

"Had you not abandoned me to walk the wind forever, I would never have become your enemy, and there would have been no need for you to raise your spear against me!"

"Aiee!" wailed Shateh, shaken by the pain that his loss of this son still caused him and by memories of the cruel circumstances that brought him to a brief, bitter truce with

Masau only hours before the man had been slain by a spearman of the People of the Watching Star.

The past was more than the chieftain could bear. "Forgive me!" he cried, for he knew all too well that because of him, Masau now suffered the fate that Shateh feared most: Killed before producing a male child to take his name, Masau's life spirit was doomed to walk the wind forever, trapped between earth and sky, never again to be born into the world of the living.

"It is not finished between us!" declared the ghost of Mystic Warrior as he raised his massive spear. "Even now can you not see that? Even now is Shateh still willing to throw away his son?"

"No!" Shateh cut short the ghostly threat. His shout was so loud that, with a start, he came up out of what he suddenly realized had been a continuation of his dream state. He found himself staring into the tired, worried face of Zakeh. The apparition of his son, if it had been there at all, had vanished, leaving Shateh emotionally drained. "Masau . . ." He exhaled the name and shook his head. "Will there ever be another son to equal you?"

"That one's spirit is best lost upon the wind forever. Do not speak his name lest he come forth at your summoning, for great are the powers of Shateh, whose song has called the forces of Creation to awake within the belly of Eira."

"What are you saying?"

"Clearly I heard you speak the words: 'Son! Come forth! Prove yourself if you dare!' May the one that will soon be born out of the new woman be the one to keep alive forever the life spirit of Shateh."

Shateh frowned. He looked around, noted that night had passed and a new day had come and nearly gone. Beyond the walls of the sweat lodge his people could be heard chanting, and the drummers were indeed sounding a familiar rhythm, announcing that once again a woman of the village had entered into labor.

Hope flared in Shateh's heart. Perhaps the spirits of the ancestors had heard his oft-raised prayers, after all? The question brought a smile. He thought of the future now, not of the past. His dream of Masau melted into oblivion as he rose to his feet and went outside.

The sun was down. The frigid evening air assaulted his senses. Suddenly the chieftain was as cold of spirit as he was of body. Had nine moons passed since the night he had pumped the wet heat of his life into the daughter of Lahontay and the other new women? "No. Only six." And still White Giant Winter lingered on the land; it was not natural, not a good thing. Chilled by the inner wind of what could be perceived only as premonitory dread, Shateh tried in vain to recall a newborn that had ever survived such a short carrying term.

"They have left the village, Shateh!" Xohkantakeh's declaration boomed above the sound of drums and singing. "I could not stop them!"

"What?" asked the chieftain, disconcerted as the hunter came close with his winter robe. "Who has left the village?"

"Lahontay has taken Warakan to seek the denning site of Bear!"

"It was his intent." Shateh drew his robe close, grateful for the warmth.

"Yes. But he has gone without the other youths. Namaray was very angry. So Teikan has taken his dogs and his eldest son and gone after Lahontay and Warakan, insisting that Namaray be given his chance at proving his courage. He waited for your permission, Shateh, but Zakeh would not bring the dreamer from—"

"Why do you trouble me with this when a woman of my lodge labors to bring forth new life?" Shateh snapped, and—lest he risk offending the forces of Creation—did not add that the new life might well be male. The last things on his mind now were an intractable old man, an ambitious, headstrong hunter, and a boy named Warakan who was not of Shateh's blood and could never hope to take his name or, at his death, accept the spirit of the chieftain's life into his young body.

7

For Warakan and Lahontay, the journey from the village had
been one of many stops and starts and long periods of rest
for Eldest Hunter. The sun had risen and set, and darkness
had come down once more upon the world. Now the night
was full of shifting wind and stars. The sound of hunting
wolves and lions kept a fasting and much weakened
Warakan alert and on edge.

"Why have we brought no dogs with us, Lahontay?"
asked the boy. "They would have kept watch for us in the
night and spoken out to warn us if meat eaters were coming
too close."

"I do not walk with Dog when I seek the denning site
of Bear," replied Lahontay, and when Warakan asked him
why, he explained, "In time beyond beginning, Dog and
Bear were brothers. Then, in a winter such as this, when
White Giant Winter lingered upon the land and the rivers
slept under ice long after the star children of Moon spoke of
spring, Dog offered himself as a slave to Man in exchange
for meat. It is for this reason that to this day Bear holds Dog
in contempt. If Bear sees Dog he will turn his back and walk
away, refusing to cross his trail or piss on his markings lest
he honor one who is no longer deserving of honor.

"So it is that when Dog sees Bear, he is ashamed and
hates above all the brother who reminds him of how easily

238

he gave away his freedom. Brave is Dog in his shame and hatred. He will leap against the one who holds him in contempt. He attacks Bear as he attacks no other. He will die in his attempt to slay the one whose existence and independence make a mockery of his pride. In his hatred Dog will not obey Man on a hunt for Bear. Dog will try to dig Bear from his den or chase Bear until he finds him. But sometimes, when Bear stands and fights, Dog's valor becomes a thing of mist in sunlight, and Dog remembers that he is a slave. In hope of gaining strength through the spears of his master, Dog runs pissing away, leading to Man the one whom we all have cause to fear."

Warakan's eyes had gone very wide.

Lahontay saw fear and fatigue and awe in them. "Tomorrow's sun will see us at the place of which I have dreamed," he said. "Rest. Sleep. You will need your strength for what is to come. I will keep you safe until then."

Sitting bundled upright in his winter furs, the old man watched as the boy lay down and at last succumbed to sleep. Within his tented robe, Lahontay's grizzled brows arched upward. Warakan was trying so hard to please, to obey in all things; he had worked so diligently at being quiet, he had probably raised ulcers on his lower lip from biting it so often and so hard. He was a brave and stalwart child; Lahontay was finding it difficult not to admire him.

Now the hunter tilted his head windward and listened to the distant, barely audible beat of drums. Again he frowned, understanding their meaning, wondering whose woman was at labor, and then growing heavy eyed as he pondered what would come with the dawn. With his spears at the ready and a small fire burning to keep predators at bay, he allowed himself to doze. The harsh yet lilting song of a shrike filled his dreams. . . .

Sunrise took Lahontay unaware. The old man murmured when Warakan prodded him to wakefulness. The wind had turned; no drumbeat could be heard.

A great excitement was upon the boy. "Now let us find the one we seek! Now let me ask him to give me his flesh to eat and his blood to drink! Now let the power of Great Paws live in me! I *am* the son of Shateh, and I am *not* afraid!"

Lahontay took grim measure of the youth. "We will see," he said, and told the boy to prepare to journey on.

A light snow was falling out of a thin gray cloud cover when Warakan followed the old man to a discolored, ice-encrusted circle in the snow beneath an old root snag. Drifts were high and hard all around. The man and boy, both in snow walkers, both with spears at the ready, knelt. With gestures and signs, Lahontay informed Warakan that the discolored ice marked the breathing hole of Bear. Now, leaning close to the earth, Warakan felt his heart quicken. He heard the sound of breathing deep beneath the snow. Moments later the old man was signing for him to rise and, in absolute silence, follow him once more.

Warakan obeyed without hesitation, dogging the old man across the drifts until the travelers were well away and uphill of the den. When Lahontay took off his snow walkers and shrugged off his pack, Warakan did the same and tried hard not to tremble with relief and fatigue even though he was light-headed and aching in his belly for want of food.

Lahontay nodded in approval of the boy's obvious willpower. "Now it will begin for you," he said, kneeling and speaking softly as he set himself to open his pack. "After the long period of dying beneath the cold, hungry moons of winter, Bear lies waiting to be born again out of the nurturing womb of Mother Below. Dreaming the half-human dreams of Walks Like a Man, Great Paws knows the healing secrets of green growing things, the favorite migratory routes of birds and game, where the roots and berries will be waiting to sweeten the feasting of summer's end, and in what deep rivers and streamside pools the fattest fish may be taken. All this knowledge will Great Paws share with the one who will now go forth to communion with him . . . or her and her bear children."

Warakan frowned. Until this moment he had not

thought of his adversary as a female creature with children, although he realized now that he was just as likely to encounter a sow with cubs as a virile, solitary boar whose male aspects would reflect Warakan's own masculine yearning for power and need to be looked upon as a warrior among the men of his adopted tribe. "I do not want to kill a female thing!"

"Do not spurn what you do not understand, Warakan. Bear Mother has mystic power of her own—a power that pours through her milk into her children, so that both male and female are of the same flesh and spirit. The question is not if she is worthy of you, but if you will be a worthy adversary of her magic."

"I will be worthy!"

"We will know the truth of that soon enough. But enough of words. There are things we must do now to prepare you for what must presently begin. Take off your clothes. All of them. Boots, too."

Warakan found that his mouth had gone suddenly dry, but he offered neither question nor argument as he hurriedly stripped off his garments and footwear. Stark naked, he obeyed without asking why when the old man commanded him to rub himself from head to toe with snow. This he did until his skin was red and aching and it was all he could do to keep from shivering. Lahontay rose and came to him with a palm-sized fleshing dagger. Warakan stiffened and stood defensively tall and straight. When his eyes met Lahontay's, he instinctively knew what the stone blade was for. He caught his breath, gritted his teeth, and held his head defiantly high as with slow, purposeful deliberation the old man slashed him across chest and upper arms. Blood ran hot, but his chilled skin did not allow him to feel much pain; even if he had, he would not have permitted himself to show it.

Lahontay nodded, impressed. From somewhere within the fold of his robe, he withdrew a hardwood-hafted, double-sided stone axe some five man fingers wide and a good twelve man fingers long. "Dig," he commanded, and as the boy took the celt, the old man pointed to the snowy ground and proceeded to stomp out with his feet the dimensions of a space that Warakan was to define with the weapon.

The youth did this and was at first glad for the work; movement warmed his body. But bending over raised pain from the long, deep gashes on his chest and arms, and he could not help but feel sickened when he saw the snow beneath him redden with his own blood.

"Deeper," Lahontay urged.

Warakan dug on.

"Deeper still!" insisted Lahontay.

Believing himself to be preparing a storage pit for bear meat, Warakan made no complaint when his palms grew bloody and sore around the haft of the axe. Sweat began to drip from his brow even as blood continued to stain the snow all around him.

"It is enough," declared Lahontay.

The hollow was long and deep. Warakan wheezed with relief and, reflexively releasing the haft of the blade from his bloodied palm, stood upright to await the old man's next command.

It came. "Into the pit!"

Warakan did as he was told. He landed three feet down on both feet, bent, and retrieved the axe. The jump, combined with exhaustion and hunger, made him dizzy. Warakan bent at the waist and stood with his head down for a moment before feeling steady enough to start to climb out.

"Stay where you are," Lahontay told him. "Lie down. I will bury you now."

Warakan did not like the sound of this. His old distrust of Lahontay was back. "Why?"

"This is the test to which you have been called," explained Lahontay. "If you would dare to take on the power of Walks Like a Man, you must *be* a bear. You must go into the earth. You must fast. You must dream. You must endure the cold embrace of the winter womb of Mother Below before you come forth reborn."

"How will I breathe? And what happens to you if Bear comes from the womb of Mother Below before I do?"

"I will create a breathing hole for you. I will keep vigil. If you are not afraid to hunt this prey we seek, then you must do as I say. Bear will not wait forever for you to prove that you are worthy to be called Son of Shateh."

Warakan was shaken and ashamed. He forced himself to swallow his fear and misgivings. They went down hard. If others had endured this test, then he must endure it, too, and without complaint. Drawing on his courage, he said with a voice that sounded much braver than he felt, "I am sorry that Namaray and Hranan and Trop and Oonay are not here to witness this moment; I do not think that any of them would be as brave as I am now!"

Lahontay's eyes narrowed. Again he reached into the fold of his robe. This time he withdrew a hollow reed and extended it to the boy. "Take this breathing tube. Do not let it bend or break as I heap snow over you. If this happens, you will surely suffocate beneath the snow, and then *I* will have to rouse Bear and, in doing this, banish White Giant Winter and win the gratitude of my people in your place."

Warakan accepted the reed. Again he swallowed fear and misgivings; again they went down hard. "How long must I stay buried and breathing through this?"

"Until the test is done."

Warakan nodded, accepting Lahontay's reply even though he was not satisfied with it. He wanted to press for more specifics about just how long the test would last. How would he be kept from freezing below the snow? And how would he be able to sleep, much less dream, lying like frozen meat in a winter cache pit? He was a small, hungry boy, not a big, fur-covered bear whose skin was layered with cold-defying fat.

"You hesitate!" said Lahontay. "You *are* afraid!"

"No!" cried Warakan, and without further delay lay down on his back, put the breathing tube into his mouth, and, holding it upright with one hand, closed his eyes and tried not to flinch as the old man began to kick snow into the pit.

Now, at last, Lahontay committed himself to the true purpose of his journey. After he had covered Warakan and filled the pit with snow, he was shaking with fatigue. "You are *not* of Shateh's blood," he muttered. "Your presence in my chieftain's camp has been an offense to the forces of Creation and to the ancestors of my tribe. Because of you Shateh's life spirit grows weak and comes into his women only as female life. This is a shameful thing. Because of you my daughter may never bear a son. Because of you, men speak against Shateh. They say that he is no longer worthy to be chief. Soon Teikan will take his place, and in the winter villages and hunting camps of that warrior, there will be no meat or warm spot close to a sheltered hearth for an old man who has outlived his sons and placed his loyalty with one who is no longer chief. For this reason I have brought you to this place, Warakan—not to test your courage but to take your life! I have not foreseen this place in any dream! I found it on the last hunt, through the tracks of the great one herself, who came through the mists to watch the hunters at their work before returning to her winter sleep. I knew in that moment what I must do. Now Bear will accomplish what Shateh should but cannot bring himself to do."

Lahontay walked back and forth upon the bloodied snow, packing it over his victim, but being careful to leave the breathing tube unbroken and unblocked lest the spirits of Warakan's ancestors have cause to accuse him—and not Bear—of killing the boy. Again he reached into his robe, this time taking from his side one of two bladder flasks that he had brought from the village. When excitedly he emptied its contents over the covered pit, blood and bits of meat reddened the snow and spattered his garments. The smell of blood was sweet to Lahontay as he smiled with grim satisfaction, knowing that when Bear awoke, the smell of this final offering would draw her to the pit and to the gullible youth who lay buried within, calmly and trustingly sucking air through a reed, enduring his final test of courage . . . unaware that Bear would soon emerge from her den to dig him up and eat him.

His grisly work complete, Lahontay turned, took up his pack and his spears, and leaving Warakan's garments in the snow, trudged off to a safe distance. On a high swell of land he looked back to the pit and to the denning site of the bear and called at the top of his lungs, "Awake from your long sleep, Walks Like a Man! Come forth from the womb of Mother Below, Great Paws! As you would dig sweet camas root from the meadows, dig now the fresh, tender meat that this man offers! Awake, I say! Come to feed and grow strong upon the nourishment I bring! Then and only then will the Warm Moon rise and White Giant Winter abandon the land! Then and only then will the people of Shateh speak no more against him!"

This said, Lahontay began the high, loud ululating chant that had been used for countless generations to rouse Bear from hibernation. He was tired to his bones and beyond, but he sang strongly and forced himself to dance the dance of the bear caller. His feet were heavy within his winter boots; his limbs rose and fell with difficulty. Only the importance of his intent kept him moving, reaching for the second of the bladder bags that he had brought from the village. From this, one by one, he drew small stones and pitched them as hard as he could toward the den. Soon movement was discernible in the ground beneath the icy spot where Bear lay sleeping, and Lahontay knew that he had succeeded in rousing the animal.

The old man stopped dancing and singing. He stood dead still, suffering a brief pang of remorse over his part in the cruel fate of Warakan. Despite himself, he had come to admire the bravery and brightness of this youth who might well have become as fine a hunter and warrior as any novice he had ever trained—including Shateh or any of the chieftain's deceased sons.

Now, as the old man saw the great bear emerge from the den to scent the air hungrily, he knew that Shateh would kill him if he were ever to discover his part in Warakan's death. The old man's head went high. He knew that he must risk it, for the chieftain's sake as much as for his own. Warakan must die, just as Totem Slayer, the shaman Cha-kwena, should have died before being allowed to take the sacred stone of the ancestors from Shateh and vanish with it into the face of the rising sun.

Lahontay's hands closed into fists. Perhaps, when Warakan was dead, Shateh would once again have the strength and wisdom to recognize his enemies.

Cha-kwena was happy. The sun was peeking through the clouds above the trees, and the children of his band were singing. He held the sacred stone and called upon its power as he observed his people making the final preparations for abandoning the village and journeying eastward beyond the gorge. Already the little lodges had been broken down, the main poles lashed together, then bundled with the rest of the band's belongings onto sledges and back frames and into special side packs that had been fitted to the dogs.

"We are ready," informed Kosar-eh.

Sensing the importance of the moment, Cha-kwena had taken great trouble to dress and paint himself in the ancient ceremonial way of the magic men and chieftains of his tribe. Mah-ree had brushed his robe until each hair in every pelt shone and lay smoothly. She had made him new moccasins in the style of the winter boots of the Red World; and this time the skins fit perfectly. The oiled sinew stitching was not only waterproof but so exquisite as to be nearly invisible to the eye. He wore his owl-skin headdress; the feathers of the bird's wings touched his back, and its talons extended forward over his shoulders. His face was colored blue with a special paint made of pulverized fat mixed with waterfowl secretions gathered along lakeshores. He raised his arms and offered a brief incantation to the Four Winds before leading his people on.

"We come! Be with us. We come! Walk before us and behind us and on all sides of us. We come! We are the children of First Man and First Woman. We come following the sacred mammoth and honoring the ancestors and all that is sacred to the People since time beyond beginning. We ask Father Above and Mother Below to hear our voices upon the winds. We come! Look with favor and kindness upon these children who honor you in this land!"

And now it seemed to Cha-kwena that his prayer had been heard. The wind blew softly. The sun was winking yellow and bright between the clouds and treetops. The air was warm for the first time in many days. As he brought his band forward, the women led the children in song once again, and every now and then he could have sworn that he caught glimpses of old Hoyeh-tay far ahead, walking approvingly between the trees.

Cha-kwena smiled while he walked, imagining great rivers and lakes and abundant hunting grounds in which all of the good and necessary things of life were as plentiful as the stars on a cloudless night. In a wondrous and intoxicating vision, those good lands and the high, stone walls of the gorge suddenly disappeared, and First Man and First Woman, a blue-eyed wolflike dog, and a towering, long-haired white mammoth walked before him. They were surrounded by a sky-high mountain range of pure and glistening ice through which no enemies could possibly ever hope to come. Cha-kwena gripped the sacred stone and cried out in joyful affirmation of all the good things that must surely lie ahead. Then the shaman blinked at the sound of Kosar-eh's voice.

"Listen!"

Vision faded, but the reality of the sunlit day was nearly as sweet, for mammoth were trumpeting beyond the gorge. The sound confirmed the young shaman's hallucination.

"We will reach the new valley soon," Kosar-eh was assuring the little ones.

Cha-kwena looked over at his old friend and was grateful to see Kosar-eh in a good mood for a change. If the man still had misgivings about relocating the village and traveling deeper into unknown country, he was keeping his thoughts to himself. Heartened, Cha-kwena lengthened his stride and soon found himself smiling when U-wa spontaneously lifted her robust, albeit less-than-lovely singing voice in a familiar traveling chant that recalled the ancestral path of the Ancient Ones. Her words told of the many adventures of the children of First Man and First Woman as the People trekked across time out of the far north and ever eastward into the face of the rising sun.

To Cha-kwena's dismay, it was not long before the children were sobered by U-wa's tales of danger and glorious, death-defying deeds done in times when cannibal monsters roamed a cold, terrifying world of ice in which White Giant Winter fed upon the People.

"Will there be cannibal monsters in the new valley?" quavered Joh-nee.

"Maybe we should not go there, after all!" suggested a fearful Tla-nee.

"There are cannibal monsters everywhere!" said Gah-ti. Wishing to dispel the cloud that U-wa's well-intentioned but ill-timed story-song had placed upon the moment, he added, "To Rabbit, you and Joh-nee are cannibal monsters who come stalking them through the shrubs with your snares and throwing sticks and nets and boiling bags! And what must Bird and Fish and Lizard think of you with your stones and nooses?"

"I am a girl, not a monster!" protested Joh-nee.

"Yes, only a girl, and so it is with most 'monsters.' When you look closely, they are only hunters seeking a meal. If you are careful and walk in the favor of the spirits, you will come to no harm."

Tla-nee frowned. "Lion ate your arm and took off your hair forever."

If Gah-ti flinched, no one saw it. "I was not careful," he said tightly. "A man who walks into Lion's cave may expect to be eaten. But you are a cautious girl and will find only good things waiting for you in the new valley. I, for one, look forward to whatever awaits us there. And if there are monsters, Tla-nee, even with one arm I will keep them from you!"

Cha-kwena appreciated the young man's efforts. He also noted that Gah-ti was now looking to see if Mah-ree was impressed by his boast and realized, with a start, that she was. Cha-kwena watched her go to Gah-ti's side and plant a kiss on his cheek. Jealousy flared, to be replaced almost instantly by a surge of pride in his bold, caring little woman. When her eyes found his and she smiled radiantly at him, his love for her was so great that it was all that Cha-kwena could do to maintain the stern, stoic composure befitting his rank while—managing not to smile back at her—he urged his people onward.

"But my Ban-ya will never be able to find us beyond the gorge," old Kahm-ree whimpered pathetically.

U-wa slung an arm around that woman's shoulders. "Be at ease, old friend," she soothed. "If Ban-ya is still alive, she will surely make her way back to her band, no matter how long the distance, how high the gorge, or how thick the woods that separate them."

A sudden fury stopped Cha-kwena dead in his tracks. "No! Your hope is here, old woman! Speak not of the one who is dead by Shateh's command, for if your longings call her spirit from the realm of the Four Winds, I will send her back again. Alive or dead, that one is not welcome to walk among the People of Cha-kwena or among any other tribe!"

Again the trumpeting of mammoth filled the gorge. Soothed by the sound, Cha-kwena urged his people on and was grateful when Ta-maya began a riddle song. Soon everyone but Kahm-ree was happy and laughing. Surly and defiant, the old woman followed along behind, viciously slashing saplings and striking at boulders with her skinning dagger until Kosar-eh took her in hand with a gentle admonition.

"Be at ease, old one," he comforted and soon had her sheathing her dagger and muttering to herself as she consented to ride on one of the sledges.

* * *

A shadow fell upon Kosar-eh's mood when he watched his sons pull the old woman along after the others. Ta-maya came to stand beside him, beautiful in her new winter furs, with little Ha-xa-ree sound asleep and bundled tightly into her pack frame. Seeing his worried expression, Ta-maya asked what could possibly be troubling him on such a fine day as this.

Kosar-eh showed her the dagger marks that old Kahmree had made on stone and trees. "Do you think she has done more of this over the past many days of travel? If she has, she has made a trail by which our enemies could follow."

"They have forgotten us."

A tremor went through him. "I wonder," he said, suddenly and painfully aware of the unseasonable cold and the unfamiliar terrain of the forested gorge. The sun was shining brightly above the trees; but dawn had been frosted by the breath of the White Giant, and Kosar-eh could not believe that it was going to be any warmer in the new hunting grounds that lay ahead. Shivering, he yearned for the sun-burnished mesa country of his distant homeland and for the broad, open plains of the People of the Land of Grass, where his bravery against enemy fighters in two wars had earned him the name Man Who Spits in the Face of Enemies. Because of this, his family—except Gah-ti, of course—had enjoyed great status during his people's brief alliance with Shateh's tribe. Life had been easy for his woman and young ones in the large hunting encampments, where there had been many hands to ease the burdens of life.

Kosar-eh's broad brow furrowed. He had admired Gah-ti's attempt to make light of the fears of the children, but the fact remained that the potential dangers for such a small band as theirs were considerable. Now, eyeing the forested gorge, he experienced an overwhelming urge to turn around and return to the land of his ancestors.

"Kosar-eh, Man of My Heart, you must not look back,"

Ta-maya gently adjured. "There is nothing there for us now."

"I tell you," he confided, "this land beyond the edge of the world seems an alien, hostile realm to a man who has spent his life under the open sky. Cha-kwena invokes the power of the Four Winds and the forces of Creation, but will the helping spirits of our Red World ancestors follow our little band into the dark woods and stony heights? And if they do not, who will protect my woman and children if something happens to me or to Cha-kwena?"

Ta-maya was not upset by the question. With absolute confidence she replied, "All will be well for us as long as we follow the life spirit of the great white mammoth, as our ancestors have done since time beyond beginning. Look, Man of My Heart, see how your fine sons walk boldly ahead. How quickly they are growing toward manhood and learning the ways of weaponry and hunting. Soon they will be men as tall and strong and bold as their father."

Kosar-eh ignored the compliment. He had turned again and now raised a speculative brow as he appraised his boys. Ta-maya was right about them. They were maturing into a strong, rowdy pack, and Gah-ti was no longer a youth but a young man. Despite his mutilations—or perhaps in compensation for them—Gah-ti's limbs and torso and single arm were noticeably muscular; his stride was aggressive as he walked alongside the sledge on which his blind little sister, Doh-teyah, rode high and happy amid the baggage while her brother switched the lead dog to keep the irritable animal moving along. Close at Gah-ti's side, little Tla-nee was babbling happily away and, in an obvious effort to impress him, was doing her best to help him harry the dog.

"Be careful, little one. Brother Dog is in a surly mood again today! Do not put your hand in the way of his teeth!" Gah-ti's warning was stated loudly enough to be heard by all.

Nevertheless, Tla-nee willfully ignored it.

Kosar-eh winced when he saw the animal snap at her hand.

The girl cried, "Ouch!" as she pulled her hand away, then poked an injured finger into her mouth.

The dog turned in its harness and tried for another bite, and Gah-ti attempted to toe the offending animal back into position. A moment later the dog had him hard by the ankle and, as the sledge came to a complete stop, was growling and shaking its head and digging its teeth into and through his moccasin until Kosar-eh raced forward to pull the dog off by the scruff of its neck. By then everyone had gathered round, and the dog was skulking in its traces.

"You cannot trust its kind," observed Cha-kwena with distaste.

U-wa checked Tla-nee's finger and assured everyone that the wound was more to the child's pride than to her flesh, for she could not find even the most minor break in the skin. Mah-ree came close to the dog and knelt beside it. Ignoring the animal's warning growls, she looked into its face, touched the tip of its nose, then shook her head and freed it from its harness.

"This one has a hot nose and angry spirits in his eyes," she informed. "Put another in his place. I saw him chase and catch a squirrel not many dawns ago; since then he has not been himself. Perhaps too much of the spirit of Squirrel is living in him now, and he has forgotten that he is Dog, trained to pull a sledge in return for meat."

"Gah-ti is brave!" Tla-nee said adoringly, ignoring her sister's comments about the dog.

"It is nothing!" he told the little girl as he rubbed his bleeding ankle.

Tla-nee sighed blissfully. "I will be your woman someday, Gah-ti!"

As the boys hooted, the young man blushed, and the little girl dashed in for a quick hug.

Kosar-eh was moved deeply by her display of affection for his son. He had to concede that had Gah-ti been a man of the Land of Grass, he would have had a dismal future among Shateh's hard-living warriors; the mutilated youth would never have been allowed to hunt or to take a woman unless she was old, barren, or as cruelly shaped by life as he. Among his own family band, Gah-ti knew only love and affection. Although the laws of the ancestors would always deny him the use of a spear because of his deformity, someday the lovely little Tla-nee might well become Gah-ti's woman and bring joy to his days and nights. Among Shateh's people such a perfect female would have been only for a hunt chief, warrior, or shaman.

As though reading his thoughts, Ta-maya sighed and nodded and linked her arm through his. "I am grateful to be far from the land of the war chief Shateh."

Again a cloud shadowed Kosar-eh's mood. "Shateh proved himself to be an honorable man. If he were not, he would have hunted us no matter how long it took him; then he would have taken the sacred stone and made slaves of us all! Instead he let us go our way. It is we who have deceived him by not telling him the truth about the—"

"Do not speak the words, Kosar-eh!" warned Cha-kwena.

Kosar-eh clenched his jaw. Ka-neh and Kiu-neh were harnessing another dog to the sledge. A few moments later Cha-kwena, with anger in his eyes toward his old friend, led the band on again.

A haunted expression tightened Ta-maya's features as she saw that her man stood his ground. "Have you forgotten that Shateh asked you to abandon Gah-ti and Doh-teyah? Such a man knows only the false honor of his ancestors, not the true honor of ours! If he had truly believed that Cha-kwena had become totem, he would never have let him out of his sight. He would have slain our shaman and consumed his flesh. I know him, Kosar-eh. Cha-kwena is right to fear and despise him. If Shateh suspected that the great cow mammoth carried the spirit of Life Giver, he would have hunted and slaughtered her so that he might eat of the unborn totem in hope that its meat would make him young again, and man enough to make a son to take his name and grant his spirit eternal life."

"Shateh named Warakan as his own. No man could wish for a better son."

"Yes, but Shateh's people believe that only the son of a man's own blood can take his name and give him immortality. No matter what Warakan may say or do, no matter how much the chieftain may want to keep him at his side, Shateh's people will never accept a child of their ancestral enemies as a true son of their chieftain. They will find a way to be rid of him. He will live no longer among the People of the Land of Grass than we would have lived had we been foolish enough to stay among them. Do not look back. A new life awaits us on the far side of the gorge. We have put our enemies behind us forever. Nothing that happens to them in their land of grass and blood and eternal war can touch us now!"

8

Bear had taken her time emerging from the den. Lahontay had watched in fascination as the snow at the base of the stump moved and writhed, then rose and shook and finally parted explosively. A long, dark snout came questing into the full light of day. A moment later the entire animal was up and out, squinting, growling, then sloppily sagging against the snowbank to take her ease, resting in the sun.

Now, at last, the scent of blood had drawn her to the pit in which Warakan lay buried. The old man rose. The wind was in his face, blowing his scent away from the bear; he doubted very much if the animal would take note of him now when the prospect of a ready meal was waiting just beneath the snow. Anticipation prickled along Lahontay's back and arms and neck while the bear circled the pit, scenting, scenting. . . . The old man's nostrils expanded. He was salivating; it was as though he had become the bear, hungering for prey, for meat, for blood spurting hot from a kill.

Then, with a sudden burst of energy, the bear began to dig ferociously until, bending, she reached deep with one forelimb. Suddenly she backed out in a screaming rage, flapping a lacerated paw.

Lahontay caught his breath with amazement as Warakan jumped out of the side of the pit opposite the bear and brandished the bloodied hand axe with which he had evidently stabbed and hacked at her paw. Blue-faced and grotesquely stiff in his movements, the boy scrambled for footing in the snow and began a mad race for safety . . . straight toward Lahontay.

"No!" cried the old man, seeing all of his plans laid to ruin. "Go back!"

Warakan kept on coming.

Lahontay snatched his spears and ran for his life.

"Wait, Lahontay! Help me!" shrieked Warakan.

"Bear, bring down that boy and eat him," wheezed the old man. He kept on running; but the snow-covered land sloped uphill now, and his feet plunged repeatedly through the crust, slowing his forward progress, bringing him to his knees again and again until, exhausted, he realized that old and frail as he was, he had no chance of outpacing a bear.

But he had not lost his skill with weapons. Lahontay stopped, turned, and stared at Warakan. He saw the look of horror on the boy's half-frozen face and wondered how, after days of fasting and so much time in the pit, he could still move, let alone run with the agility that he was demonstrating now. *By the forces of Creation, what a son Shateh has chosen in this child!* he thought. Hefting a lance, he knew the danger that the boy represented to him now and would have speared him through if Warakan, distracted by distant drums resonating upon the wind, had not tripped and fallen in that very moment.

"Ay yah!" exclaimed Lahontay, watching the small, naked form sprawl in the snow. The old man's face split with a grin of triumph. Now the bear would stop. Now the boy would die. But suddenly Lahontay's grin became a drop-jawed gape of incredulity. The bear was not stopping. She kept on coming, running straight past Warakan and heading up the slope, her eyes fixed on Lahontay.

The old man hurled his lance, hefted another, and threw again. And then once more. His spears found their mark. The bear stumbled, fell, then rose. Her forward momentum had been slowed, but surging adrenaline kept her coming.

"Run, Lahontay! Run!"

The old man blinked, momentarily stunned to see Warakan on his feet and, still brandishing the axe, now running in pursuit of the wounded bear. It was as valiant and selfless an attempt to help a fellow hunter as Lahontay had ever seen. He whirled around and fled for his life, knowing all along that he was not fast enough to win this race.

He did not remember seeing the defile before, but there it was—a deep, dangerous break in the surface of the land that would have made a perfect bison jump; any animal approaching it at a run could not possibly stop in time nor hope to clear the gaping abyss, no matter how desperate its leap. Nevertheless, impelled by images of what another bear had done to his son Ishkai, the old man tried.

Lahontay soared with arms spread wide and torso arching forward while his limbs worked for purchase on thin air. Somewhere behind and high above, he heard the distant sound of drums as Warakan shrieked and the bear scraped along the top of the defile. Then the old man struck the earth. The world went bright, and he heard nothing at all until, through expanding blackness and pain, he opened his eyes to see the bear lying dead beside him with a stone axe buried in her brain.

"Lahontay? Ah! I feared you dead!"

The old hunter grimaced as Warakan's face insinuated itself between him and the head of the bear. Broken by the fall, the old man tried to speak and failed, but he could see from Warakan's expression that the boy was ecstatic and, by the following words, completely unaware of the fact that his mentor had tried to kill him.

"I told you I would kill Bear!" said the boy. "Did you see me as you fell? Ah, Lahontay, you would have been proud of this boy! Truly, I was not afraid! When Bear tried to stop at the top of the ravine, I leaped onto its back, and as we fell together, I buried your axe in its head! And now look, Lahontay . . . the sun stands high, and snow begins to grow soft beneath its warmth! Soon the land will grow green, and the herds will come out of the sun! All this because you have led me to rouse Bear! I have done battle with White Giant Winter and won! Tonight Warm Moon will rise, and my people will have cause to feast with joy! You will see! Not even the great Mystic Warrior, Masau, could have been bolder or braver than I have been this day! I have proved to all that I am worthy to be a son of Shateh!"

The old man's face expanded—not only with pain but with a sudden insight and recognition that was so startling and appalling that he managed to raise a bony hand and grasp the boy by the hair, pull him close to stare, and stare until he realized who the whelp reminded him of and wept with incredulity. *No!* he thought. *It cannot be! Not you . . . how could it be?* A shudder went through him. Somehow, deep within his body and mind, a river was running cold and black, and as it ran, his spirit followed, to be washed away in the deeps. The world grew dark even though his eyes were open and . . .

"Lahontay? . . ." Warakan watched helplessly. The old man's body went lax, and his eyes fixed and glazed with a look in them that made all of the boy's pride shrivel and grow cold. "Are you dead, Lahontay?"

"He did not have the body of a bear to break his fall."

Startled by Teikan's voice, Warakan looked up to see the man, his son Namaray, and several dogs standing above him at the edge of the ravine. He got to his feet. "How long have you been following us?"

"Long enough to see that if you had not run from Bear like a frightened rabbit, Lahontay would be alive," said Namaray with a sneer.

Warakan felt confused, then angry. "So you were close enough to help, at least to loose your dogs to distract—" He stopped. Teikan was coming down into the ravine and raising a small avalanche of loose snow and stones as he descended in long strides on the sides of his feet, with Namaray and the dogs close on his heels. In a few moments he was kneeling beside the body of the old man, shaking his head and clucking his tongue.

"This is not a good thing," said Teikan of Lahontay's death. "You will regret talking the old one into leaving the village without Shateh's permission so that you might come alone on a quest for an animal that you are not worthy to hunt."

Warakan rose hotly to the insult. "It was Lahontay who talked me into coming! Together we have roused Bear! And I have killed Bear! I have proved that I am worthy to be called a son of Shateh!"

Namaray was smirking. "Do you not hear the drums? In your absence from the village the spirits of the ancestors have once again smiled upon Shateh. His youngest woman, Eira, has given him a great gift. The drums say that she has given him a male child. Even now the chieftain will be praising the forces of Creation as he honors the Four Winds by waiting the necessary four days before giving the child his name to accept its life into the tribe. Even now the People will be preparing for the naming ceremony. No longer will Shateh find need to name a spawn of our enemies Son."

A terrible hollow opened within Warakan as he listened to the distant beat of drums. "Shateh may give another child his name, but he will always call me Son. And I will always call him Father."

"Because of you Lahontay is dead," observed Teikan dispassionately.

Despite his best effort to maintain control, Warakan was shaking. "I tried to save him."

"And failed," reminded Namaray with malicious emphasis.

Teikan informed Warakan coldly, "Now, because of you, the People no longer have cause to rejoice. Now we must mourn the death of Lahontay and of Shateh's newborn son. When life comes forth in a time of mourning, it cannot be allowed to continue lest it offend the spirits of the dead and cause the forces of Creation to turn their wrath upon the

People . . . as they have seen fit to do ever since our chieftain welcomed you among us."

"I first heard the drums before Lahontay's spirit left his body!" Warakan told them.

"So you say," answered Teikan. "We will say otherwise."

Appalled, Warakan could not find his tongue for a moment, and when he did, his words came in a rush of righteous indignation. "You would speak falsely? Shateh will not believe you!"

"No?" Teikan lifted a telling brow. "Because of Warakan, an old man is dead. Because of Warakan, Shateh will be forced again by the laws of the ancestors to deny life to a newborn son. Cha-kwena and his people are long gone from this land. Warakan is the only enemy remaining among us."

Namaray added, gloating, "I will see you driven from the tribe, Cannibal Boy of the Watching Star!"

"My father will never drive me out!"

"If he refuses, he will be banished, and my father will be chief. Either way, the newborn will be killed, and our people will be rid of you."

Teikan's eyes were fixed on Warakan and solemnly affirmed his son's words. "Shateh will not hesitate to do what must be done. And at the moment that he stills the breath of his newborn son he—and every man, woman, and child among the People of the Land of Grass—will know that Warakan has, by his actions this day, proved beyond doubt that he is the source of the dark spirits that have come against us!"

"It is not true!" cried Warakan.

Teikan sneered. "Who else would turn the winds against us?"

It was dark within the cavern now. A trapped, frightened Ban-ya whispered curses against Shateh for having condemned her to her terrible, lonely fate. "May he suffer in this life as I suffer!" she moaned, longing for light and warmth, lamenting the necessity of allowing her lamp to gutter and go out lest its meager light penetrate hair-thin breaks in the rockfall, or the telltale smell of burning oil be detected by those who had taken over the outer cavern.

Ban-ya closed her eyes. She leaned back against the farthest wall of the cave and would not let herself think of them. She would not hear their masculine voices or their occasional laughter or arguing as they came to her through the stone. Beneath the press of her eyelids, she conjured images of the sacred painting that she had seen upon the wall; they seared her mind.

"The totem is not dead!" Ban-ya whispered, rocking her babies in a darkness that was so profound she feared it would smother her; even the smallest sighs helped lessen the weight of it. "The totem lives within the great mammoth cow. It will be reborn! Perhaps all is not lost for us, my little ones! We are Red World people, you and I, and as long as the totem lives we—" She stopped and opened her eyes to stare wildly ahead and around.

Something was moving in the darkness—rats. Ban-ya pressed her back against the wall and drew her knees up as she tensed with terror of the small, adventuresome marauders that had brought her near to screaming several times. "Must not scream. Must whisper only! Must tell the rats that this woman is not afraid . . . not of them . . . not of the dark . . . not of anything. *No!* Ban-ya is not afraid! Will not be afraid. Cannot be afraid."

But as her smaller son began to draw fitfully at her breast, she knew that she was afraid. Her milk was waning. A terror much greater than her fear of rats made her catch her breath. How would she feed her babies in this cursed place if her milk failed? "The totem lives!" she told herself. "Draw nourishment and strength from its spirit, Red World woman!"

Seemingly in response to her own command, inspiration sparked within Ban-ya, and she reached for her belongings. With her nooses and trip snares she might well be able to capture at least a few of the rats that menaced her.

Their flesh might be enough to energize her and restore the flow of her milk.

"Ah, rats that move unseen around me within the dark, you should not have been so unwise as to make yourselves known! This woman has dispatched bigger, meaner, more dangerous carnivores in her time." She thought of Atonash-keh, son of Shateh, and smiled as she remembered the way he had died screaming. "Yes," she promised the rats in a sibilant sigh. "Now you will be meat for me and for my babies!" But to her chagrin, she was so enervated from the effects of starvation that she could not will herself to rise, much less seek out her belongings or set snare lines for food.

"Soon," she promised. "Soon Ban-ya will hunt rats." She closed her eyes and allowed herself to think of how it would be to eat again, even of an uncooked rodent. "Soon Ban-ya will eat. *Must* eat! Then her milk will flow again. *Must* flow!" Already one of her infants was too weak to nurse at all; it lay as limp as an understuffed buckskin doll in the fold of her arm. She opened her eyes, looked down into darkness, and forced a nipple into the gaping little mouth, unsuccessfully urging it to suck, refusing to believe that in her earlier attempt to silence the child she had broken his neck or suffocated him. "No! Did not happen! Baby is fine. Sleeps. Only sleeps."

Ban-ya closed her eyes again and rested the back of her head against the wall. She would not allow herself to think of poor little Ea-nok lying dead in her arms. She would not believe that the child who had come so hard into this world, wrenching her body with a pain that had seemed to tear her in two, could have left it so easily! She would not acknowledge his death, for she knew that she would not be able to bear it in silence. She would scream . . . she would howl . . . she would lose what little was left of her sanity and self-control, and these things she must possess if the other child was to live and not leave her utterly alone.

Ea-ka began to fuss. Panic stirred within Ban-ya. "Hush, my little one. As long as the spirit of the totem still lives within the great mammoth, all is not lost for us. You will see. You must trust in Ban-ya of the Red World. You must—" She cut off her words in midflow.

The sounds of men and the scent of roasting meat were coming to her through the rockfall from the main cave. Ban-ya's need for food was overwhelming. Saliva welled in her mouth. Hunger became a beast that prowled her body and spirit until, feeling the imperative, impatient tugging of Ea-ka at her drying breast, a strange numbness expanded within her mind. She sighed, conceding to a realization that she had not considered until now.

"Yes," she crooned softly to her little son. "Suck and be still, my little one. My *only* little one. They must not hear you. If they do, they will come for us. My milk will nourish you. Soon it will flow rich and thick and sweet again. Yes! You will see. Now I will eat. *Must* eat. Smell the good scent of meat? Yes. It is a gift from the totem, through your brother who has given himself to be food for us. Yes. Twins are forbidden. No woman has a right to more than one son. I see that now. So we will eat the meat your brother offers. His spirit and the spirit of the totem speak to me in the dark. They say that it will be a good thing."

Tsana paused beside the mammoth-bone sledge of the shaman Jhadel and gestured to the cave in which his fellow hunters were waiting. The rest of his remnant tribe, hungry and ragged, trailed behind and sniffed the air. It brought the scent of roasting meat.

"It is as I have foretold!" exclaimed Jhadel, his voice scraping over a timeworn larynx, the words pouring thick and slow over a cleft, tattooed tongue and through seamless black lips. "There is life for the People of the Watching Star in this Valley of the Dead."

"There are many kinds of game," affirmed Tsana. "Our men have hunted. Our women will have flesh and bone, fat and hides and sinew. Our little ones will not go hungry or shiver from the cold. The life spirit of Sheela has called to us out of the night, Jhadel. Her spirit dwells within the cave. I have seen her!"

The weary travelers were made uneasy by the man's reference to a ghost. Mothers drew their daughters close. Boys and men stood taller, wanting to appear bold and unintimidated.

Jhadel raised a jaundiced brow at the comment. In his tawny, moldering bearskin robe, the last surviving shaman of the People of the Watching Star was an extraordinary figure. A browband of raven's feathers encircled his greasy gray hair. His small, squinting round eyes, placed close on either side of a huge, thrusting beak of a nose, were like those of a condor. His prominent skull, set on a long neck that seemed far too thin to support its burden of skin and bone and muscle and brain, oscillated constantly as though sighting for prey. And his entire face—including his ears and eyelids—had been tattooed with ashes and fat so that it seemed as though someone had charred his head black in a smoldering fire pit.

Physically frail, Jhadel was nevertheless a commanding presence after he forced himself to rise and stand breathlessly beside Tsana. Leaning on his sacred cottonwood staff with its streamers of pounded mammoth hide, tufts of woven mammoth hair, and many tiny beads of bird bones, he eyed the cave with recognition. "I know this place. It was *his*. Before the last great battle *he* stood here . . . Cha-kwena . . . slayer of warriors, the totem, and the sacred dreams of the wise ones among our people. He is totem now—and our enemy. Often I dream of him and of the sacred stone. I see them in blood—dark blood, hot blood, heart blood surging in the veins of the father of the night, womb blood gushing between the thighs of the mother of the world."

Tsana frowned. "I do not understand, Wise One."

A growl resonated at the back of the shaman's throat. "My dreams feed my spirit with the blood of my need for vengeance against the one who, by slaying the totem, became the totem and brought my people to destruction. If we were strong enough to hunt him, to consume him, then the blood of his power would be ours and—"

"With his own hand Cha-kwena slew my Sheela in battle," interrupted Tsana defensively. "I, too, dream of vengeance in the night, Jhadel."

The shaman was openly irked by the interruption, which, by his expression of annoyance, he took as a sign of disrespect. "Your woman is dead, Tsana. It is time for you to take a new woman."

Tsana was stung by the suggestion. "I tell you, she is here in spirit . . . in the cave . . . summoning us to this valley of much meat! You will see!"

"*I* am the one who has foretold what you would find in this valley! *I* am the single unifying source of whatever spiritual strength has been left to my tribe. Ah, had you listened to me, Warrior, it would not have been so. But what has been done cannot be undone. Now I am an old man who wonders what will happen to my people after my spirit leaves this body to walk with my ancestors. Who will be shaman for them, then? You, Tsana? No. The power of the vision seeker is not yours. But without a shaman, how will my people find the will to survive when their mortal enemy has become a totem who sends curses against them upon the wind?"

A disheveled, scar-faced woman came close, and bowing respectfully before the shaman, she asked, "If this cave to which Tsana has brought us was the cave of Cha-kwena, dare we presume to live in it, Wise One? If the Red World shaman still lives, will he not—"

"He lives." Jhadel's face tightened. "On the wind of my dreams I hear his chanting. But Cha-kwena is far from this valley, Oan. Now the power that was his in this place will be ours. Remember this in the days to come. Hatred of an enemy can be as nurturing as meat to a vanquished people. The one who has led Shateh to victory over us has slain the totem and *become* the totem. Someday he will be hunted, as the totem was hunted. Someday he will be slain, as the totem was slain. Those who dare to eat of his flesh and drink of his blood will take his power into themselves. On that day a new shaman will arise from among them. And that shaman will be totem, invincible before the powers of the Four Winds."

The words were heady stuff. The travelers murmured appreciatively and purposefully.

Oan's cruelly disfigured face twisted. "And the boy who was placed into my care before he ran away and for whose behavior I was punished and maimed . . . does Warakan also live when so many of our people have died because of him?"

Now it was the old man's face that twisted. "He lives," answered Jhadel bitterly. "How else could it be for him? With Cha-kwena as shaman of the combined tribes, he is cared for and nurtured as if he were a cub of Shateh's and will live long among the enemies to whom he betrayed us."

The woman's hand moved to her ruined face. "I, too, dream of vengeance in the night, Jhadel."

Jhadel nodded. "It is good," he told her just as Indeh called from the cave, summoning the others to join his companions at the feast of leaping cat and sloth steaks that they had prepared. Weary, Jhadel sought the comfort of his sledge and urged Tsana and his fellow travelers on. "Come! We will eat! We will warm ourselves! We will talk of how it will be when we grow strong again and vengeance is no longer only a thing of our dreams but is in our grasp at last."

9

The drums had stopped. Rain was falling now. Warakan went to his knees in a slosh of melting snow and looked up into the sodden gray bellies of the clouds. How he wished they would go away!

"Get up, Cannibal!" demanded Teikan, standing over the boy and poking him with the end of a stone spearhead. Lahontay's body, slung over Teikan's shoulders, was dangling head down, like a deer taken on the hunt. "You cannot delay our return to the village by pretending fatigue."

"I *am* tired," wheezed the boy. "I need to rest and eat!"

"Soon you will 'rest' forever, Watching Star Boy!" portended Namaray, leering down at Warakan out of the circular extension of a sodden hood of dripping wolf tails.

Until this moment Warakan had known that he disliked Namaray; now he hated him. Since being forced to abandon the body of the bear, Warakan had been prodded and kicked and driven across the land. And all the while Namaray had taken open pleasure in his misery. Teikan, at least, had been circumspect in his treatment, handing the boy a cake of fat and pulverized dried meat to end his fast and allowing him to put on his clothes and boots before they set out for Shateh's village in the broken sunlight of yesterday.

They had run most of the way, loping into the night like a pack of wolves, stopping only long enough to see that the dogs were fed and rested. Warakan had unsuccessfully attempted to slow their progress in hope of delaying their return until after Shateh had named the newborn whose birth was boldly proclaimed by the drums; once given the gift of a name and, with it, a spirit, the baby could not be denied life unless starving times demanded such a sacrifice.

But now the drums had stopped. A pounding rain had been falling since dawn. Combined with runoff from the melting snowpack, the downpour was causing the river to rise, and streams were swelling and running in fast confusion in every gully and depression—even beneath the snow. Warakan was soaked through to his skin and cold to his spirit and beyond. He knew all too well that the sudden silence of the drums could mean only one thing: The new life that had come into the village had left it before it had a chance to be named.

Namaray smirked. "He will blame you."

Warakan was battered by mixed emotions. He had not wanted a competitor for Shateh's affection, but he would never have wished death to the infant lest this bring pain to Shateh. Nevertheless, he was glad that the chieftain's newborn son was dead.

Feeling sick with apprehension and guilt, Warakan slogged to his feet and attempted to appear bold. "It is you and Teikan who will be blamed," he warned, "for you have forced me to leave the body of the great bear that I have slain to lie in the cold rain without honor and may well have created an angry spirit that has gone out across the world to feed upon the life of the six-moon baby!"

"You killed no bear." Teikan's voice was untroubled as he embellished his lie. "Ask Namaray. He will tell you what he saw—you, running for your life and bringing Death to Lahontay before my spears and those of my son brought down Walks Like a Man. But you did rouse Great Paws and, by your summoning, bring Rain. A bad omen for you, Outlander. Shateh will not be pleased, but both he and the tribe will be well rid of you when this is done."

"Shateh will never believe you. May the forces of Creation strike down the man or boy who tells such lies!"

"Don't you curse me!" Namaray punched Warakan so hard in the belly that the boy went down with a *woof* of surprise.

Namaray laughed, but Teikan, annoyed, shook his head, then bent to pull the stunned boy up by his hair. "We will go on now." Shifting the weight of Lahontay's corpse, he eyed the sky. "There will be a flood if the rain does not stop soon."

"Are you going to blame me for that, too?" snapped Warakan.

A tremulous hope swelled in his bruised belly that if he told his side of the story first, Shateh would surely believe him. So he ran. In intensifying rain, across the melting snowpack, stumbling and falling and rising again and again, Warakan raced for the village. He waded across one raging stream and then another until, at last, the dogs of Teikan brought him down.

He landed with a splat, facedown and sprawled, stunned and breathless, in the mud and snow of an exposed bison wallow. The dogs were at his boots and the sleeves of his winter tunic until Teikan called them off and uttered a high, keening cry that was meant to alert the village that he was returning.

Warakan looked up. The village lay ahead. And the chieftain was coming toward them, with many of the villagers and dogs following close behind.

"Shateh!" He spoke his father's name and, spitting mud from his mouth, tried to rise, only to find that the heel of Namaray's foot was planted squarely on the small of his back. In a fury of outrage, Warakan twisted hard to his right, grabbed Namaray's ankle, and jerked the youth off balance. Then Warakan rolled sideways and clambered to his feet, leaving Namaray sputtering in the muck.

"What is this?" asked Shateh, his voice deep and dulled by grief.

Before Warakan could say a word, Teikan stated his

twisted version of what had happened. Stunned by the extent of the man's infamy, Warakan started to stutter in his own defense, but Namaray spoke first.

"It is all true!" insisted the youth, rising and shaking himself like a wet dog. He affirmed Teikan's lies, then compounded them. "I overheard Warakan goad old Lahontay into taking him from the village to search for bear without me and the other youths. I warned him that he must ask the chieftain's permission, but he laughed and said that he was a son of the Watching Star and would do as he wished, with or without Shateh's permission! My father came to tell the chieftain this, but by then Shateh was walking the path of dreams, and Zakeh would not disturb him. Now Lahontay is dead, and the new woman Eira has lost a father and a son because of the arrogance of an outlander."

"The new woman has given up her spirit birthing the six-moon son," informed Shateh flatly.

Warakan winced at the news. He ached to tell the chieftain that he shared his grief and bled for the sadness that he saw in Shateh's eyes; but a deep murmur of anger had risen from the assembled people, and by the time the boy found his voice and attempted to form the words, everyone was clamoring against him and Shateh had heard more than he could bear. Like a gut-wounded wolf the chieftain threw up his head and howled in anguish.

A terrible cry rose from the villagers who stood with the chieftain in the rain. Warakan found himself standing like a wet, befuddled pup, shaken to his spirit by Shateh's pain, wanting so desperately to lessen it that he had no fear for himself as he proclaimed in righteous indignation, "I, Warakan, son of Shateh, have roused Bear and driven White Giant Winter from the land. Teikan's tongue twists truth like a woman's hands twist sinew into rope. I will not be snared by the rope of Teikan's lies! I, Warakan, son of Shateh, say that—"

"I . . . have no . . . son!" The words ripped from the chieftain's throat.

The blow that dropped Warakan came from Shateh's hand. It was a brutal, backhanded strike that sent the boy spinning backward. For a moment the world went white, then black, then colors swam and eventually came together as Warakan found himself crumpled on his side in the mud, his head reeling and a terrible hot, thick pain in the middle of his face. He fought to sit up, and then to stand; his limbs would not serve his will, and he could draw no breath through his nostrils. His questing hand reached up and encountered pain and thin air where the bridge of his nose used to be.

Shocked, he sucked air through his mouth and looked up at Shateh through the falling rain. To his horror, he saw his own impending death in the chieftain's eyes and in the blade that Shateh had drawn from its sheath at his side and now held in one hand. Their eyes met and held. Warakan looked for compassion but found none. Shateh had accepted Teikan's lies over his pronouncements of truth.

A sob shook him. An overwhelming wave of excruciating hurt and betrayal rent him to his spirit as he realized that he was about to be gutted by the man whom he trusted and loved more than anyone else in the world.

"You have brought Death to my people," accused Shateh.

"No!" Warakan sobbed in outrage and, terrified, forced himself to rise and run toward the river for his life.

It was Teikan who cried out for the warriors of Shateh with their dogs to pursue the boy. They obeyed, and Warakan looked back over his shoulder as he ran and stumbled and fell while attempting to cross the river.

"Aieee!" cried young Jheena, and clasped her hands before her face when the boy disappeared beneath the rushing, tumultuous waters.

Shateh called Teikan and the others back. "The forces of Creation have taken him," he said, his voice hard. "It is a good thing." He did not add that he was grateful to the spirits of the river for having done what he had no stomach to do.

The chieftain's mouth tightened. It had hurt him to speak the words. Bitterness nearly staggered him as he stood staring toward the river. Not since the death of Masau had the loss of a single life hurt him more. And yet he knew that he had done what had to be done. His people's unexpectedly volatile display of hatred toward Warakan had left him no choice. Nothing had gone well for him since he opened his heart to this child of his enemies and then—in a moment of unparalleled weakness and bad judgment—gave up the hunt for Cha-kwena and the sacred stone. *Is it any wonder that the Four Winds have mocked the will of Shateh?* he thought, and found the answer sobering.

Standing tall in the pounding rain, the chieftain stared at the cold, compassionless sweep of the river and felt old and weary. Yet he allowed himself to show no trace of his inner devastation. He was certain that Teikan and Namaray had lied, but he was also certain that since Warakan had become the focus of his people's hatred and insecurity, no one among them would have been willing to believe him. Shateh felt them watching him now and knew that in this moment they were no longer men and women, no longer hunt brothers and sisters of his tribe; they were wolves, and he was the aging leader of their pack who had led them well, but not flawlessly, for moons beyond counting.

Somewhere deep within Shateh something seemed to be bleeding, dying with the drowned boy. The cold, snow-covered land and the rain and wind were combining to raise mists above the river. While he continued to stare into the falling rain—grateful to it for washing away the hot tears that stung his eyes—with a start, he could have sworn that his many dead sons had materialized along the far shore. Wisak. Maliwal. Kalawak. Atonashkeh. And, standing fore-most among them, his tattooed face set and glaring like a ceremonial mask carved of stone, Masau.

Shateh's heart was racing. His long, heavy lids came down to shield his eyes as he strained to see the ghost of

Warakan standing with his brothers; then, realizing that the figures he had construed to be his sons were only trees looming in the mists, he mocked himself as a fool; even if the ghost of Warakan did roam the far shore, the boy was not of his blood, and his spirit would not be welcome to walk the world beyond this world in company with Shateh's true sons. As an orphan and outcast, the boy was condemned by his premature death to roam the wind and sky alone forever. But Shateh would not let himself think of this now.

"For too long has Shateh forgotten that in the eyes of a chief the value of one life can be held as nothing when the life of the tribe may be at stake!" he proclaimed. "To this end Shateh has sacrificed sons before, and on this day has sent the spirit of Warakan to walk the wind forever. Now may the forces of Creation smile once more upon Shateh and his people!"

"May it be so," agreed Teikan. "But Warakan, Son of the Watching Star, may still be alive, for behold the river. The waters are rising fast and may soon come to drown the People in their lodges if we do not relocate the village! Shateh cannot put his back to an enemy until the People see with their own eyes that the bringer of bad-luck spirits is dead!"

Shateh stiffened. Apparently it had not been enough for Teikan to maneuver him into a position from which he had been forced to drive Warakan to certain death. The man was of a mind to challenge his ability to make good decisions for his band. The chieftain felt cornered by one whose ambition, though fed by genuine concern for their people, had made of him a treacherous rival. Slowly Shateh turned and stared at Teikan, whose lies and easy recourse to deception would be an offense to the forces of Creation if ever he were to become chieftain.

"Never!" said Shateh, and vowed that until he found a man—or made a son—worthy of taking his place, no one, least of all Teikan, must ever again be given cause to believe that he lacked courage or acted for any reason other than that which served the will of the ancestors and the good of the tribe.

Now, with his head held high, the chieftain spitted Teikan with eyes full of controlled fury. "Go to the river then!" he commanded, and barely managed to choke back, "and drown yourself in it as you have no doubt hoped to drown me!" Coolly, he added, "Hunt the runaway. Bring him or his body to the People so that Shateh may offer with his own hands whatever is left of his life spirit to the Four Winds!"

Teikan appeared stunned; obviously he had not expected this turnabout. "B-but the river has taken him! How can I hope to find him? I am one man . . . not a shaman and—"

"As shaman I will lead my people to high ground and see to it that the new site is one that will please the spirits of the ancestors."

"But—"

"You have said with your own mouth that the People must see that Warakan is dead and no longer a threat to us. Find him, Teikan. I would send no other in your place! You of all men know that Shateh's obligation is to his people, not to the boy Warakan! The blood of my body flows not in him. He was not my son. You found him once. Find him again. And do not come back unless you do!"

10

"Warakan!"

The spirits of the river called his name. Exhausted, numb with cold, and so badly battered by the tumultuous race of the river that he could no longer fight against it, a drowning Warakan heard and felt the spirits all around him, invading his body, taking him down, and then bearing him up again and again—strong, hard hands and whispering, imperative voices combining in a strange, otherworldly, singing embrace that carried him away into dark depths from which he knew there could be no return.

And still the river raced onward in thunderous tumult. Unconscious, Warakan knew nothing of his journey.

He would never know how long the rushing water held him in its grip or in what moment the uprooted tree came rising from the deep to catch him within its branches and bear him up and away to eventual beaching; but consciousness slowly returned through a black void of raging sound, and Warakan was aware of something pricking hurtfully at the back of his left hand. He winced and tried to move but was instantly overwhelmed by a terrible wave of nausea. Water gushed explosively from his lungs and belly. It took him only a moment to puke up what he had swallowed. Exhaustion followed. So overwhelming was it that he lost consciousness again until the sharp *chack chack* of a scolding shrike woke him.

Warakan's eyes batted open. He lay sprawled on his stomach atop the uprooted tree in a pounding rain. A gray, thoroughly soaked, black-masked shrike was perched on his left hand, its delicately taloned feet inadvertently pricking his skin as it peered at him out of black eyes. Its handsome head was cocked and its hooked beak ajar, as though the bird were expressing surprise to see the boy alive. Startled by the closeness of the shrike and eager to have its hurtful talons gone from his hand, Warakan raised his arm and flicked his wrist. Shrike stayed with him a moment before it spread its wings and flew off into the rain, leaving the boy to sit upright and look around.

Cold, shivering, and disoriented, Warakan did not recognize the river as the same one into which he had fallen on his mad dash from the villagers. Swollen by continuing rain and the rapidly melting snowpack, it was engorged and roaring and monstrous to his eyes. It ran wild and brown and thick with ice, tearing at its own embankments and sending spume-topped, debris-laden waves hissing at the clouded sky. Hugging himself in a vain attempt to draw warmth from his own body, Warakan felt the deep ache of countless bruises and wondered how he had survived the pounding race of such a waterway. Blinking against rain, he eventually recognized the contours of the mist-shrouded, rain-pummeled hills and realized that he had been carried so far downriver that he was not far from the denning site of Bear.

Suddenly frightened, Warakan looked around for the ghost of the dead bear whose spirit would no doubt hunger for the flesh, bones, and blood of the boy who had put an end to its life and left its body to lie without honor in the rain. Breathless with dread, he scanned upriver, desperately longing to see Shateh coming for him with forgiveness in his eyes and spears in his hand with which to drive off the ghost of Great Paws. But even as Warakan yearned for protection from the spirit of the dead bear and a reunion with the man who named him Son, he remembered the expression of betrayal and killing madness on Shateh's face and knew that he had lost his place within the chieftain's heart and lodge and tribe forever.

"Father!" he sobbed, overwhelmed by the desire to set out for the village and beg Shateh to hear and believe the truth of what had happened on the hunt for bear. He rose to his feet, shaken by thoughts of Teikan's lies and broken-hearted that Shateh could have taken that man's word over the word of his son.

Because you are not his son, not of his blood, not of his tribe! You are Cannibal Boy of the Watching Star! You are Outlander! Warakan choked on the acknowledgment; it hurt more than he could stand. "No!" Alone and miserable, he cried like a baby until, ashamed, he snuffled up his tears.

Soaking wet and cold to his skin and the marrow of his bones and spirit, he stared at the rising river and told himself that he had to be wrong. "Shateh has named Warakan Son. Shateh has said that there will always be a place for Warakan in his lodge. Shateh does not say one thing and do another; he is not a man without honor, nor will he long be tricked by the lies of Teikan! When anger has left his heart he will know who has told the truth in the matter of the killing of Bear. Then he will come for Warakan! *Soon* he will come!" This said, he sat down upon the sodden tree and waited.

But Shateh did not come.

With darkness falling and the river still rising, Warakan knew that he lingered in vain. Weary, cold, and hurting, he felt a part of his spirit die until, suddenly, he decided that he was being foolish and unfair to Shateh. "My father is the chief! He cannot leave his people and look for this boy until the time of mourning is finished for Lahontay and Eira and the six-moon baby! Then he will search for Warakan! He *will* come!"

But how was he to stay alive until then? The question was sobering. It occurred to Warakan that he should try to make his way back to the village; but beneath his sodden garments his skin was blue and stiff with cold—and he was now so tired and in so much pain—that he doubted if he could walk even half the distance before collapsing. He eyed the sky. Continuing rain and intensifying cold mocked him. Shivering, he realized that he must soon find warmth and shelter or die.

"But how?" Warakan asked, and when the answer came from within himself, he shivered with fear but knew that it was the only way that he was going to survive. Swallowing hard, he sought the killing site of the bear.

With a chill wind rising, Warakan put the river behind him and soon breasted the hills and stopped at the brink of the ravine. He was so exhausted and feverish that his surprise at seeing two cubs nuzzling the corpse of the great bear barely moved him. He clambered down the slope, slipping and sliding most of the way, frightening off the cubs when he arrived shivering to their mother's side. He curled up close to the dead bear's body and pulled one massive, stiffening forelimb over himself as a barrier against the wind and rain.

For a long moment Warakan lay perfectly still, waiting for the ghost of Great Paws to materialize and devour him; but the moment passed, and with clattering teeth, he apologized for having been forced to leave the body of Walks Like a Man dishonored by death in the cold rain. "After I have rested and grown warm and the rain has stopped, I will honor the one who now grants to this boy its body's remaining warmth and shelter."

Warakan closed his eyes and whispered his regret over having frightened off the cubs. Exhaustion claimed him, as did hunger when he picked up the scent of the milk that the cubs had been extracting from their dead mother before he drove them away. Hunger drew him to a nipple from which he greedily took suck until, at last, sleep, deep and dreamless, took him. . . .

The cubs cautiously returned. Smelling their mother's milk and body scent upon the sleeping intruder, they no longer perceived him as a threat. Hungry and in need of comfort, they came sniffing and sidling close, joining the newcomer in their mother's bloodied embrace, rooting at rigid nipples for what was left of the milk of life. Soon they, too, were asleep. Their new brother folded his arms around them and, sighing and drifting deeper into sleep, nestled into their furry warmth.

Teikan and Namaray had traveled far and hard in their search for Warakan. Although darkness was falling with the continuing rain and the dogs were sodden and miserable, Teikan was in no mood to allow them, himself, or his son to rest.

"We cannot go on, my father!" Namaray, crouching, resting his forearms on his knees, stared belligerently up at Teikan. "If you do not care about us, then think of the dogs!"

Teikan was not unaware of the boy's sarcasm; he chose to ignore it.

"If we have found no sign of the bad-luck bringer by now, we are not likely to do so in the dark!" snapped Namaray.

"It is not dark yet!" Teikan was disgusted with his son, but as he stood footsore and weary of back and thigh beneath the endless rain, he was tired enough to believe that Namaray was right. Spear in hand, he stared off. Recognizing the surrounding hills, Teikan was amazed to see that they had come so far from the village. Beyond the next fold of land lay the ravine and, within it, the body of the dead bear. He scowled. Close as that place was, he knew that he, his son, and the dogs had no hope of reaching it before dark; besides, if Warakan had survived his fall into the river, it was unlikely that he would have dared to come alone and unarmed into country where the ghost of a shamed bear was probably lurking.

Teikan's gut constricted unpleasantly; he knew all too well that he, more than Warakan, was responsible for abandoning the body of Great Paws. If the spirit of Walks Like a Man was lingering around the body from which it had been rent, it would not welcome him or his son. Nevertheless, having found no sign of Warakan along the ever-expanding river, frustration made Teikan face into the storm and shout the boy's name once more.

"You waste your voice!" Disgusted, Namaray sneered. "Warakan is dead. Drowned. Washed away. And even if he lived, do you really believe that he would answer you?"

Teikan did not reply. Sick of his son's complaints, he saw no need to explain again his intent to lure Warakan from hiding by assuring him that he had been forgiven by Shateh and was welcome to return to the village. Instead he called out to the boy once more, his voice hoarse from repeating the lie, "All is forgiven you, Warakan! I come to bring you back to your father and your people and beg your understanding of my part in—"

"I tell you he is dead! The spirits of the river have swallowed his body. We will never find him!"

Teikan grimaced. Namaray's voice had become an accusing whine. The man knew Shateh had sent him on a fool's errand. Even if Warakan had somehow come out of the river alive, the rising water had obliterated his tracks; not even the dogs had picked up any scent of him. And if he had been washed out of the river dead, his body tossed onto some far embankment, his corpse must have been carried away, for the water had long since flowed over the confines of the old shoreline to run wide and wild, in many places filling the lowlands to assume the dimensions of lakes. Disgusted by his failure, Teikan eyed the still-rising river and knew that Shateh must have already moved the band to higher ground. If Namaray and he did not return to their people soon, they might well be cut off from them until the river dropped in summer, many a long moon from now. But how could they return without Warakan? Shateh had forbidden it.

"It is all your fault," whined Namaray. "If you had not tried to goad Shateh into going after Warakan, we would be with our people, warm and dry on some high hill—"

Teikan could stand no more of his son's complaints. He kicked out and sent Namaray falling backward, then kicked him again and again until his anger at last began to cool. "I did not ask you to follow me!"

"You are my father!" protested Namaray from a protective tuck. "I would not have let you go alone or—"

"Or missed another chance to go at a boy half your size in order to win favor in my eyes and the eyes of Jheena! Bah! Do you think I do not know why you came? You heard her cry out when the whelp of the Watching Star went into the river! You wanted to take his body back and make her cry and know that you, and not Warakan, would have her!" Teikan kicked Namaray again. "As though I would ever let a girl like that go to you! Get back to the village! I am sick to my belly of your whining. You find no favor in my eyes this day, Namaray!"

The boy, gripping his ribs, was on his feet, knees bent to keep him steady as he glared hatefully at his father. "Nor do you find favor in mine . . . you with your man bone always seeking to find a place between the thighs of young girls, taking even one of Shateh's women when he was not looking, and leaving no virgins for me or—"

Teikan's next kick took the boy hard in the face.

Namaray flew backward. Hands to his head, he lay still for a long moment before he managed to get to his knees, spitting teeth and blubbering through a smashed and bloodied nose. His father's dogs, curious and unnerved by the violence and the smell of blood, came near to sniff his face.

Teikan shook his head; until this day he had been so proud of this son. Now a strange, expanding feeling of disconnection with the youth focused his thoughts and took them along a path that quite astounded him. "You saw me with Cheelapat? This is not a good thing."

"Not for you!" threatened Namaray. In blind, misdirected anger, he struck viciously out at the dogs. When they yipped and backed away, he looked up at his father and knew that he had made the last mistake that he would ever make in dealing with this man.

"I have younger, better sons back in the village," Teikan said, and before the boy had a chance to react defensively, he drove the long, lanceolate, rain-slick projectile point downward through the youth's throat and deep into his body before the stone jammed in the torso. "Unlike Shateh, Teikan has no trouble making sons on his women. Even now Cheelapat may carry one of mine! But you will not tell the chieftain of this, Namaray. Of only one thing will you assure him."

Kneeling, Teikan impassively watched the death throes of Namaray, then frowned when he realized that they would take longer than he had patience to endure. The boy's eyes were huge, and the garbled sounds he made were hideous and pathetic; but Teikan was not moved as he drew his skinning knife, knelt behind his son, and took Namaray's scalp. Smiling with grim satisfaction, Teikan reached beneath his traveling robe and secured the scalp to his waistband.

While the dogs looked on, he put his right foot between Namaray's neck and shoulder, and ignoring the youth's convulsions, jerked his spearhead free. Teikan frowned when he saw the stone projectile point emerge from bone and muscle and flesh with a damaged tip. Sighing with acquiescence to the unavoidable, he lifted the still-living boy in his arms, carried him to the river, and threw him in. Satisfied, he watched his son disappear into the roaring flow before he turned away and, confident that Namaray would be dead soon enough, headed back for the village, calling the dogs to follow.

He alternately walked and ran until dark came down, then found a place within a grouping of large boulders and spread a tarpaulin of oiled hide beneath which to shelter himself and his animals. "Soon we will be back among our people," Teikan assured the dogs, sharing his traveling rations with them and allowing them to sniff at the scalp of Namaray when he took it from his belt and admired it. "We will present this to Shateh so that he will have something of Warakan to offer to the Four Winds. It is what he asked of me—some evidence of the boy . . . his body or whatever is left of his life spirit. I will tell him that wolves were at the body of the runaway, and after I bravely drove them off, all that could be returned to Shateh is what you see. The People will be relieved to have their uncertainty about the death of Warakan put to rest. And which one of you, my friends, will inform the chieftain that the scalp belongs not to Warakan but to my unfortunate son who has lost his life to the river? I will tell them that. It is not untrue." Teikan smiled, amused by his own cleverness and duplicity. The dogs were licking the scalp; he let them, watched them, then folded it and tucked it away beneath his robe. "And if Vral should, in mourning for Namaray, accuse me of not watching out for her eldest son's safety while seeking Warakan, I will have to say that his death must, when all is said and done, be blamed not upon the father who bravely obeyed his chieftain when he was commanded to go in search of the runaway but upon Shateh's bad judgment in adopting the enemy child in the first place."

Warakan stirred and murmured in his sleep. In his dream he flew with the great bear across the starlit sky. Incredulous, he moaned. Bears did not fly! Yet, as on the evening of the feast fire, Walks Like a Man leaped across the night, a huge dark cloud of fur and claws and teeth. And everywhere the great one flew, Warakan flew also, tucked safely within the fold of its massive arm.

"Aiee!" the boy cried as the great bear plunged and swam through the vast sweep of the Sky River, forcing Warakan to blow stardust from his face.

Walks Like a Man caught hold of a comet and was swept across the infinite folds of the black robe of Father Above. The cold eyes of the Watcher glinted; the ever-battling Twin Brothers of the Sky stared in amazement; and the bright little multicolored cluster of Many Old Women murmured resentfully at their passing.

"Behold, that boy has brought the great bear from its den as he promised!"

"And now the Warm Moon will rise!"

"But he is not one of ours, that boy! He is Trouble. He

is a cold wind in summer. He is darkness upon the face of the sun. He is—"

"He is mine!" declared the Watching Star.

"No!" countered the boy. "I am Warakan. Shateh names me Son!"

"No more!" mocked the Twin Brothers of the Sky.

And now the great bear banked and flew down, down through the glimmering Sky River, and somehow the comet was grasped in Warakan's hand. No longer a boy, he had become the bear, huge and powerful and furred. He flew eastward over the curve of the earth, into the rising sun, and over the edge of the world. As his left hand tightened around the tail of the comet, he frowned, remembering his mother warning him never to use that hand, although he could not remember why.

He was startled to discover that the comet had turned to stone—the fang-shaped, thumb-sized sacred stone of his ancestors, which Cha-kwena had stolen when he had fled into the storm with the lawbreaking woman. Warakan growled. He saw Trickster walking far below, leading his band through the depths of a great gorge. Mammoth walked ahead of him, with a little white calf leading the way. Then, suddenly, Warakan sensed that he was not alone within the sky. He heard footfalls behind him. Wondering how this was possible, he turned and looked to see who dared follow him across the night. But the Sky River was so bright and the sound it made was such a terrible roaring, Warakan growled again, recalling the raging river that had nearly drowned him. In that moment reality flooded his mind.

The dream expanded, then collapsed as he awoke with a start. He tried to sit up but was smothered by the weight of something big and warm and smelling of blood and milk; it lay over and all around him, and whatever it was, it was breathing.

Panic clutched at Warakan. He could hear the river running wild beyond the ravine, and in a fever of desperation, he pushed up with his hands and attempted to be free of the suffocating cave of living flesh and fur. Then, immediately, he relaxed and felt foolish when he remembered seeking shelter beneath the body of the slain bear. He sighed, actually chuckled at himself . . . until something alive gripped him so tightly around his waist that he could feel the tips of its claws press inward against his belly through the still-sodden layering of his hip-length winter shirt. When he felt hot breath against the back of his neck, panic took him again. Certain that he was caught in some sort of grotesque snare laid by the ghost of the slain bear, he screamed, expended every bit of his strength, and shoved up on the forelimb of the bear. Warakan lifted it just high enough to allow him to sit up before its weight pushed him down again.

A wet tongue slurped across his face.

With yet another scream and burst of energy, Warakan went into a tuck and, in a passion to be free, propelled himself sideways and backward until, at last, he was able to scramble to his feet in the cold light of dawn. So weakened by the ordeal was the boy that he fell to his knees the moment he tried to walk.

And in the next moment the cubs of the slain bear came peeking from beneath their mother's massive forelimb to stare at him.

He stared back, startled into remembering Teikan's words: *A man cannot take an orphaned cub of wolf or lion or bear into his band to be raised as his own child among his people. A predatory animal will always be an animal, and someday it will turn to savage all who have come to trust it!*

"No!" cried Warakan so loudly that he frightened the already worried cubs.

When the little orphaned bears scampered off in fear of him, Warakan got to his feet and looked upon the dawn. The sun was rising through long, thin striations of purple and blue clouds; above these the sky appeared bruised, drained of all color and moisture. He was glad that it was no longer raining, but he did not like the sound of the river. It was so loud, so vicious, and although he knew it was far from where he stood, he could have sworn that he could feel it moving within the ground beneath his feet. Troubled and curious, he ascended to the top of the ravine for a look back at the land across which he had come.

And now for the second time since falling into the river, Warakan knew that he was drowning, but this time it was in bewilderment. He looked around and wondered how this could possibly be the same country across which he and Lahontay had come in search of bear. He did not recognize it or the river into which he had fallen while attempting his reckless run from the village. It had risen up and over the far hills, overpouring its banks, swollen to a magnitude that dwarfed its earlier considerable dimensions, and all but consumed the land. Only the hilltops showed; they were now islands in a hideous brown lake within which the tops of trees extended like the fingers of upreaching hands, and bloated animal corpses could be seen floating belly up amid uprooted trees and other flood debris.

Warakan closed his eyes. "It is not real," he told himself. "When I look again, the forces of Creation will have put the world back into the order in which it should be!" But when Warakan opened his eyes, all was as it had been, and with a cry of despair, he knew that there was no way he could cross the river or lake of devastation to reach the village that lay on the other side.

He sat down. He reminded himself that his father, a shaman as well as a chief, would find a way to come for him. *Yes!* "When the time of mourning for Lahontay and Eira and her six-moon baby is over and my father has had time to sort out Teikan's lies, then he will come!" A wan smile turned the corners of Warakan's lips upward; then pain flared in his broken nose, and he remembered the chieftain's blow and repudiation. A lump the size of a fist formed in his throat. It took him more than a moment to swallow it down. "He *will* come!"

He sat very still now, staring across the distances and wanting to see Shateh striding magically and majestically across the water. Once, he thought he saw Shateh coming over the horizon and snapped to his feet, only to sit again when he realized that what he had seen had been merely a raven flying toward him from the west. Soon he saw many ravens, but no Shateh. He wondered how long the carrion eaters had been coming to scan the new lake and settle amid the tops of drowned trees so that they might feed upon the easily taken meat that floated in the newly gathered water.

At some point it occurred to him that he had no idea how long it had been since he had fled the village. It could have been a day and a night, or two or three, or . . . Then other thoughts came to him, and shivering in his cold, wet clothes, he felt as though he had been punched in the belly.

What if there is no more village? What if Shateh and Teikan and Namaray and all of the women and children and warriors and dogs are dead and floating in the lake?

It was then that he rose again and ran. He went feverish and sway legged from weariness across the hills and down into the drowned lowland to search along the shore of the lake for his father and his people and their dogs. Ravens watched him as he went, but of all the carcasses that he found, there were no people and no dogs. At last he rested awhile and watched a raven pecking on something floating well out in the lake. It was a strange body of water; tranquil at first glance, but actually moving with unseen currents as the arm of the river ran through its depths. Warakan, staring at it, calmed himself with the certainty that at the first sign of a flood Shateh would have commanded his people to break down their lodges and prepare to leave for higher ground. It was a comforting thought until he wondered how far they would have traveled to find a suitable site and, in his absence, if Teikan would have found a way to blame Shateh for their people's continuing bad luck.

It was in that moment that Warakan knew what he must do. He thought of his dream and suddenly felt reborn. He could not return to the village. Nor was it likely that Shateh would come for him now. But in the ravine lay the body of the slain bear whose life he would now honor in the way of his ancestors, for in death and dreams Great Paws had shown Warakan the path that lay ahead for one small child.

"The meat of Walks Like a Man will nourish this boy! The skin of Great Paws will warm me. The teeth and claws and sharpened long bones of Walks Like a Man will give courage to my spirit! Transformed and strengthened by Bear, Warakan will go forth under the sun and stars to prove to Shateh once and for all that this boy is not the source of the bad luck of his adopted tribe. Warakan will hunt and find Cha-kwena! Warakan will convince that shaman to return the sacred stone of the ancestors to Shateh, or Warakan will steal it and bring it with his own hand to the chieftain!"

The statement made him tremble with resolve. Drawing a deep breath, Warakan started back toward the ravine. He knew that what he proposed was dangerous, but he also knew that only after he had done these things would good fortune smile once more upon the band of the great war chief Shateh! And only then would a runaway son of the People of the Watching Star be able to prove to his new tribe that his loyalty to Shateh had been as absolute as the love that he continued to feel for the chieftain whom—despite all that had happened— he still thought of as his father.

Again he trembled, knowing all too well that he was only a small boy who had little likelihood of success in the days and nights ahead. But what had he to lose? Only his life. And as far as Warakan was concerned, when Shateh had struck him down and driven him from the tribe, he had already lost all that had ever made his life worthwhile.

PART III

THE EDGE OF THE WORLD

"It is like this: As long as you stay within the realm of the great Cloudbeings, you may indeed walk at the very edge of the Deep Canyon and not be harmed. You will be protected by the rainbow and the Great Ones. . . . You may fight the witches, and if you can meet them with a heart which does not tremble, the fight will make you stronger."

—Tewa elder
Seeking Life by V. Laskin

1

Far away beyond the edge of the world, Cha-kwena and his band raised new lodges above the hot springs on the eastern side of the gorge. As they worked to put the finishing touches on the conical little structures of wood, hide, and thatching, Mah-ree was distracted by the sound of something moving in the nearby forest. She looked up to see a small, dark, bright-eyed bear staring at her through the shadows of the snowy woods.

"Aiee!" she exclaimed in surprise, and even before she could alert the band, the dogs were off after the creature, driving it away and into the forest.

"If Bear has come from its denning place, then surely it will soon be spring!" said a rapturous old Kahm-ree after Mah-ree told her and the others what she had seen. "My Ban-ya will be able to find us now!"

Cha-kwena rolled his eyes and gave the old woman's longings up to the spirits. He had learned that nothing he could say would turn her from her dearest hope. Besides, he was troubled by the sighting of the bear and called upon Kosar-eh, Gah-ti, and the boys to help him hunt it down.

Although the group went deep into the forest on the trail of the dogs, they could find no sign of bear, nor was the animal seen again.

Later that day, rain came. It fell sporadically for many

days, so the band settled into their new little encampment and watched by day as the mammoth grazed. When the wind and rain allowed, the great tuskers rooted up tender new grass shoots and rhizomes from under the snow. In the worst of weather the herd sheltered within the forest. By night the People were comforted by the creatures' "talk"; as long as the mammoth were nearby, the band knew that it was doubtful that large predators would venture close enough to endanger them.

And so, warm and dry within their well-made circular shelters at the edge of snow-covered woodland meadows, they rested and recovered from their long overland trek and listened to the tumultuous passage of winter from the land. In uncountable, riotous rivulets and streams, White Giant made his departure, roaring through the gorge and raging in distant rivers, where his transformed substance raced away in endless protest across the world.

And then one morning the People awoke, emerged from their lodges, and saw that the rain had stopped and the last vestiges of the cold, white skin of White Giant Winter had gone from the earth.

"He will return soon enough," Kosar-eh told his sons with a droll sigh and a slow shaking of his head.

"By speaking so, you have just affirmed that!" Tamaya scolded him.

"But he must return," said Cha-kwena. "Since time beyond beginning it is the way of the world and of the great circle of all living things. White Giant Winter covers the earth with his white skin, and all living things go to ground in their own way as they seek to escape the freezing wind of his breath. Then Rain comes, and even as White Giant Winter flees on the back of North Wind, his melting skin awakens the spirits of River and nourishes the seedlings that have hidden from him within the flesh of Mother Below. Soon Grass grows tall, offering her long, sweet hair to be food for grazing animals that, in turn, are food for hunters such as we. And when the last of the meat is sliced and dried, the People are weary of hunting, and Grass has grown brown and withered after birthing many seed children, again White Giant Winter comes, and again all go to ground, to rest."

Mah-ree smiled with delight at the well-remembered tale. "It is as though old Hoyeh-tay is still with us when my shaman speaks so!" she declared proudly.

Now U-wa smiled and nodded, well pleased by Mah-ree's words. "That is a true thing! My man's father's shaman spirit was a gift to our son even before Hoyeh-tay left this world to walk the world of the spirits."

Cha-kwena was not soothed by his mother's words. He had strongly believed that Hoyeh-tay and Owl would be waiting for his people in the new valley where the mammoth browsed. But since bringing his band beyond the gorge, he had seen no sign of his grandfather's ghostly spirit nor caught a single glimpse of a molting, golden-eyed phantom owl winging through the trees. Nevertheless, with the country of his enemies on the far side of the gorge and no trace of the bear that Mah-ree had seen when the band first raised their lodges, Cha-kwena was forced to admit that he was sleeping soundly and dreamlessly for the first time in longer than he could remember. Yet, although grateful to be free of troubled dreams, he was puzzled as to why he dreamed no dreams at all . . . unless, perhaps, his lack of Vision was in and of itself a portent. He caught his breath and reasoned that perhaps all was going to be well with his people at last.

Later that very day, although hardwoods were not yet budding within the predominantly evergreen forest, the first geese came flying out of the south. After circling the grassy little prairie and open marshy areas between the long, dark fingerings of the trees, they came settling onto open water wherever they found it and sent up nasal, raucous, honking invitations to all their kind that continued to fly overhead. Soon the women's birding slings were whistling in the cold, misted air of morning, and when the dark came down, the fragrance of roasted geese enriched the scent of the spring night.

The next day dawned clear and warm. While U-wa and Kahm-ree stayed behind with the younger children and babies, the rest of the band took the best-trained dogs and ventured well out from their new village to hunt geese, check the snares, and lay new ones. Cattails were showing the first signs of new growth in the shallows of numerous small lakes and ponds, and the women rejoiced at finding the promise of many familiar "green growing things" en route to and all around their new hunting and gathering sites. The mammoth browsed contentedly on the marshy central grassland and at the edge of the forest. From the appearance of the herd's matriarch, the trekkers knew that it would not be long before her calf, and the totem, would be born.

"May it be so!" Cha-kwena invoked the forces of Creation.

And Gah-ti, walking beside him, asked with his voice lowered, "It is said that when this comes to be, even such wounds as I have suffered will be healed by the breath of the living totem."

"It *is* said," affirmed Cha-kwena.

"And will the eyes of my little sister widen with joy as they see all that is before them in this world?"

"This, too, is said," the shaman verified.

Gah-ti, walking with Cha-kwena, was silent for a long while. The young man's eyes were fixed on Mah-ree and Ta-maya, who were well ahead and guarded by Kosar-eh, Ka-neh, and Kiu-neh. The sisters armed their slings, and the geese—not recognizing the human threat—took flight only after Kosar-eh and the boys called out. Everyone yowled with pleasure when slain birds began to rain from the sky. "Doh-teyah would smile at the sight of so much falling meat!" said Gah-ti.

"More so at the sight of the brother whom she loves above all others," Cha-kwena told him.

Gah-ti stopped short. "I would not have her see me as I am!"

Cha-kwena paused. "She loves you as you are."

The young man's face tightened. "If she could see me, she would not!"

"She would!" countered Mah-ree, coming close with two dead geese in hand. One of these she thrust at Gah-ti. "Here. For you! And surely you must know that Tla-nee sees you as you are! And I think she is wise beyond her years to boast that she will someday be Gah-ti's woman!" This said, she stood on her tiptoes to place a kiss upon Gah-ti's cheek.

"What does Tla-nee know?" he shouted, taking a step back. "Tla-nee is a baby!"

Mah-ree was openly amazed and hurt. "She is four!" she reminded, yelling back at him. "In another five winters, perhaps six, she will be a woman . . . *your* woman!"

"In a land beyond the edge of the world with no people in it, what choice has she?" he blurted hotly, and brazened on, "Surely not the same choice you once had, when you turned your back on a scar-headed, one-armed man and chose another over me!" He stopped, stared at her and at Cha-kwena, and realized with a start that he had spoken words that he had never intended to speak aloud. Ashamed, he thrust the dead goose back at Mah-ree, then turned and was quickly off.

Her face flushed as she shouted after him, "Tla-nee could choose any of your younger brothers over you, Gah-ti! And maybe she will! Ka-neh and Kiu-neh, at least, are not so short-tempered as you have always been! Or so stubborn! You know that I have never wanted any man but my shaman—*never,* not even when you possessed both your arms and all of your hair!"

"Mah-ree!" Cha-kwena's tone was pure reprimand.

She pouted and, holding the geese by their necks, slung one over each shoulder. "I am Cha-kwena's woman. Always Cha-kwena's woman. *Forever* Cha-kwena's woman. Gah-ti is wrong to say that it might ever have been otherwise."

"He has always wanted you."

Mah-ree's head went high. "We cannot always have what we want," she told him snippily, and, with an

impertinent toss of her head, started back toward the
encampment.

Cha-kwena frowned as he watched her; he knew only
too well that Mah-ree's statement had been meant to sting
him with the reminder that although she wanted a baby, he
had not coupled with her since they had been together on the
far side of the gorge. Now, as he watched her stalking
angrily off, he was stirred by the provocative roll of her slim
hips and by the way she held her head and shoulders high,
despite the considerable weight of the geese that swung at
her back.

A moment later, she turned her head and looked to see
if he was watching; their eyes met and held, and something
sparked within him. How warm and inviting were the
bright, black eyes of his little girl-of-a-woman! Suddenly
remembering how much of a woman Mah-ree could be
when lying warm and inviting within his arms, Cha-kwena's
loins flamed, and his face did the same. Seeing his expression, Mah-ree dimpled, then turned and went her way at an
impudent trot that made his man bone ache and rise.

"She needs a man as well as a shaman," said Kosar-eh.

Cha-kwena was startled to see that the older man had
left his woman and sons to their birding and had come to
investigate what had caused the hot words between Mah-ree
and Gah-ti. Now Kosar-eh was smiling with drolly amused
speculation as he stared off after Mah-ree and offered his
opinion that she was in need of mating, and soon.

Embarrassed, Cha-kwena informed him sharply, "I do
not tell you when to join with your woman!"

"There is no need; my Ta-maya is content."

"So will my Mah-ree be in time, when that for which
we wait has come to pass and I do not need to concentrate
all of my powers upon a shaman's dreams and visions!"

The big man's brow furrowed. "And what do you
dream these days and nights in the way of Vision in this far
land beyond the edge of the world, Grandson of Hoyeh-
tay?"

Cha-kwena almost blurted the word *nothing* but was

disconcerted by the realization that this would not be a good admission for a shaman to make; besides, he was annoyed by Kosar-eh's presumptuousness. "Have things not been going well enough for you in this new land to which my dreams and visions have brought you?"

Kosar-eh shook his head. "In my opinion it is strange country—half bog, half woodland, with little grass, trees I do not know, and in the forest a feeling of cold rot beneath branches that shut off the sky."

"The mammoth are happy in this land. And when the Warm Moon is fully risen and the spring rains have stopped, the earth will dry and the grass will grow green and tall. That which is now strange to us will become familiar."

Kosar-eh's brows expanded upward across his forehead. He looked around, then shrugged and shook his head again. "Does it not trouble you that there are no other people in this land, Cha-kwena?"

"And no enemies!" Even as he spoke, Cha-kwena regretted the audacity of his quick retort. He found himself waiting, expecting a spirit voice to speak with an inner warning that enemies might yet come to make a mockery of all of his hopes; but there was no spirit voice and no inner warning.

Then, hearing Ta-maya laughing with Kiu-neh and Ka-neh as they worked with the dogs to gather the geese that her sling had slain, Cha-kwena felt gladdened. Life was good for his band at last, and after the long winter and seemingly endless rain, he was sick of shadows. The sun was warm in his face. The sight of it pleased him. The heat of it summoned a deep, all-pervasive languor that made him stretch and yawn with contentment. He was pleasantly relaxed and surprisingly drowsy, considering that he had enjoyed another night of sound sleep; it was such a satisfying feeling after so many moons of restlessness and fatigue.

"He is not following?" U-wa appeared surprised as she looked up at Mah-ree from where she sat with the babies and enjoyed the morning sun. Old Kahm-ree followed the children, keeping a rheumy eye on them while they went about the edge of the wood, setting little snares, practicing pebble pitching, and generally enjoying themselves in happy squabbling.

"No, he's not," Mah-ree conceded unhappily. "For a moment I thought he would, but as always, he has forgotten all about me!" She dropped the geese onto the ground at the older woman's feet. "These are for you."

U-wa beamed at the gift.

Mah-ree went to her knees and confided in a lowered voice, "Our secret plan is not working, Mother of My Man! I have pounded and mixed together the roots and fungi that you have given to me and put them into my shaman's meat to make him sleepy and take away his bad dreams. But they do not cause him to turn toward me in the night or look at me with a man's eye of interest by day."

"You must be patient," advised U-wa, handling the geese and admiring them. "The spirits that reside within my medicine sometimes take a while to work their magic; but I assure you they have been taken from those growing things that, at maturity, are long or hard, things of spore and milky juices and many seeds. In time they will make my Cha-kwena hard for you again and put the magic of new life in your belly! I have never known them to fail."

Mah-ree sighed. U-wa was right, of course; she knew that she should be more patient with her man. As shaman his responsibilities were great. Perhaps after the totem was reborn and Life Giver, the great white mammoth, walked once more among the People, Cha-kwena would remember that his woman *was* a woman! But it seemed to Mah-ree as though the mammoth was never going to birth the sacred calf, and she longed for the embrace of her man, yearned for the warm loving wind of his breath on her face, and hungered for the joy that the press and penetration of his body gave to her. And now, as she looked down at little Ha-xa-ree lying fast asleep and bundled within a cradle-board at U-wa's side, Mah-ree longed for a baby of her own—Cha-kwena's baby, a child to make her shaman proud!

Seeing the expression of longing on Mah-ree's face, U-wa offered motherly encouragement. "It will happen for you, dear one. I have been certain of this since the day you saw the little bear in the woods when we first came into this country. Old Hoyeh-tay used to say that wherever Bear walks, there will also always be food for the People, for our wants are much the same in the way of nourishment. And when seen by females, Bear represents powerful baby-making magic, for Bear is life itself coming in the spring from the womb of Mother Below!"

Mah-ree shook her head. "But Bear is also a fearful, dangerous creature! And, in truth, I often wonder if there is simply not enough of me to turn a man's head beneath the sun or cause him to become hard and seeking beneath the bed furs. Indeed, Mother of My Man, the fault that underlies my shaman's disinterest in this woman may be in me, not in your medicine."

U-wa frowned. Seeing the young woman's unhappiness, she assured her with concern and affection, "There is enough of Mah-ree to stir the best of men! Can you have forgotten Teikan?"

Mah-ree blushed. "That man was *not* the best of men!"

"He *thought* he was!" teased U-wa.

Mah-ree could not keep from smiling. "He was mistaken."

"Yes," agreed U-wa, and further attempted to cheer Mah-ree. "Perhaps we are going to need some special kind of magic to get a baby for you out of 'our' shaman. As his mother, I will tell you now that he has always shown more interest in what lies beyond the slope of an unknown hill than in the pleasures to be found between the thighs of even such a fair woman as you, dear one!"

Mah-ree's blush deepened, but her eyes widened with hope. "What kind of magic, U-wa?"

The older woman chewed her lower lip thoughtfully for a moment, then apologized, "Ah, if only I knew more.

The women of the Land of Grass once spoke of an old man who was of the People of the Watching Star . . . a teacher and healer and spirit master whose knowledge of magic was such that he once made a woman young and beautiful and irresistible to all men even when she was older than the land upon which she trod."

"You must not talk of our enemies!" Mah-ree was appalled and might well have said more to admonish U-wa for her carelessness, but in that moment Kahm-ree let out a great shout of anger and Piku-neh began to bawl.

Mah-ree and U-wa looked off just in time to see a dog running toward the forest. The little boy, meanwhile, sobbing and holding up a bleeding hand to Kahm-ree, sat flat on his buttocks, his pudgy limbs splayed.

The old woman took one look at the injured child and was suddenly energized into a fury. "Bite my Piku-neh, will you?" Kahm-ree raged, and sent her braining stick flying with deadly accuracy.

The dog gave a yip of pain. Its front legs collapsed. It fell forward, then staggered to its feet and turned to stand staring back at Kahm-ree as though inviting her to do further injury if she dared.

With a whoop of anger, Kahm-ree obliged. She hefted the little rabbit-skin sack that slung from her wrist and began to throw pebbles at the offending animal. The dog yelped and ran off again.

Mah-ree, dismayed, recognized the animal as the same dog that had been snappish on the trail through the gorge. It had been skulking and slobbering around the village for several days; when she had attempted to offer solace, it had raised a quivering snout, shown its teeth, and growled her away. Now, watching the dog disappear into the trees, Mah-ree felt pity for it and regretted not having been more aggressive in her attempts to help the creature.

"Stop!" she cried to Kahm-ree as the old woman hurled the last of her stones. In an instant Mah-ree was on her feet and racing after the animal. "Dog! Dog!" she called. "Come back, and this Medicine Woman will try to make you well!"

"Mah-ree!" U-wa cried out in protest of the young woman's run for the woods.

Mah-ree did not respond. She was soon deep into the trees, maneuvering lightly over, around, and through ever-thickening scrub growth and downed, lichen-covered branches. The ground was moist and strangely pithy beneath her feet. Again and again she called to the dog until, suddenly, she stopped and stiffened. Gooseflesh rose on her arms as she realized that she was being watched. Somehow she was certain that the eyes of a creature other than a dog were fixed upon her.

Breathless with fear, Mah-ree turned and stared to her right and left into a surrounding wall of tree trunks beyond which distances of conifers massed like green-robed spirit giants. *Kosar-eh is right to distrust this forest!* she thought. The bear she had seen when the band first entered into this strange new country came to mind, and she imagined the animal lurking behind every tree. Her hands flexed at her sides. With no armament for the sling looped to her waistband, Mah-ree yearned for the long, sharp-ended throwing stick that lay hidden beneath her side of the sleeping mattress back in the village; but it was too late to think of weapons now. A branch snapped in the woods behind her.

Mah-ree whirled around. Something flew at her from the evergreens, and she dropped instinctively into a protective crouch just as Cha-kwena's blue and red spear came slicing through the trees to impale the dog that had leaped at her from the cover of the trees. The animal was dead before it hit the ground at her feet. Stunned, Mah-ree stared at it. With Cha-kwena's lance through its mouth and protruding from its haunch, it twitched its last.

"By the forces of Creation, Mah-ree, did you not hear my mother call you back? Did you not see that little Piku-neh was hurt? If I had not followed you, this dog would have had your throat!"

She cringed at his rebuke; he was right, and she knew it. She waited for his permission to rise, and only after it had been given did she get shakily to her feet. "This dog was sick, my shaman. I wanted to help it. I only wanted to—"

"Your medicine is not for dogs!"

Mah-ree nodded, truly penitent. "I meant no harm, Cha-kwena."

"So you say, and yet somehow you invariably find ways to bring it!"

Hurt, she blinked back tears as old Kahm-ree came through the green with Piku-neh clinging to her side. When the little boy saw Mah-ree, he held his injured hand out to her.

"Make better, Medicine Woman!" Piku-neh demanded in the hopeful, chin-quivering way of a hurting child. "This boy will be brave!" Then he saw the dog. He screamed and burrowed his head into the hollow of the old woman's neck.

"That dog will bite no one ever again, my little one!" assured Kahm-ree. She came to stand between Mah-ree and Cha-kwena. Looking down at the dead animal, an expression of hateful satisfaction twisted the old woman's time-ruined face. She kicked the dog so hard that the force of the blow made her wince. Blood ran from the dog's mouth, and its hindquarters gushed foul-smelling fluids; but Kahm-ree smiled. "Look and do not be afraid!" she demanded of Piku-neh. "This is what happens to enemies of Red World People! Even when those enemies are dogs!"

The boy looked. He whimpered at the ugliness of what he saw. Then he extended his hand once more for Mah-ree to see. His little chin was quivering again, but his tone was one of pure command as he said, "Give me spirit things to make pain go away! Now!"

Mah-ree's eyes widened, not at the boy's impertinence—for Kahm-ree spoiled Piku-neh badly, and Mah-ree doubted that any offspring of bold, brazen Ban-ya and arrogant, self-serving Dakan-eh could ever have been anything less than audacious—but at the extent of the boy's injury; the dog had thoroughly savaged his little hand. "This will need sewing," she said as gently as she could.

"The son of my Ban-ya will not be afraid!" Kahm-ree gave the boy an encouraging hug.

Cha-kwena exhaled a sigh of ill-disguised impatience with the old woman, but when he spoke it was to the child. "When we return to the village, Piku-neh, Medicine Woman will give you spirit things to lessen the pain of the stitching." Then he said out of the side of his mouth to his woman, "Unless she has forgotten or ceased to care about the healing ways for people and would rather stay here to mourn for this dead dog!"

Mah-ree flinched, despairing of ever winning his affection, then shook her head. "Shaman's Woman has not forgotten the healing ways for people. Medicine Maker will be honored to tend the wound of Piku-neh."

Cha-kwena nodded, satisfied but not mollified. He bent and went to work at drawing his spear from the dog; in the end, grimacing, he was forced to break the shaft.

Mah-ree looked at the careful incising and coloring of the hardwood and cringed, knowing that it had been his favorite.

They returned to the village in silence.

"Now all will see how brave is the son of my Ban-ya!" proclaimed Kahm-ree, and told the boy, "Your mother Ban-ya will be watching you. She will know if you cry!"

"He will be brave," assured Mah-ree.

But when she entered the shaman's lodge in search of her medicine things, Mah-ree clearly heard Cha-kwena say, "Do not listen to that old woman on all things, Piku-neh. You may howl like a wolf if it will ease the pain for you. Your mother Ban-ya is dead. She cannot hear you!"

2

A child was crying.

"Piku-neh!" Ban-ya came up out of deep sleep and was calling the name of her long-lost son. She stared ahead. Darkness surrounded her. She realized where she was and what she had just risked by speaking aloud. "Stupid . . . stupid . . . stupid woman!" The self-recrimination had been less than a whisper.

A foul odor assailed her. It was the stench of body waste—her own and her baby's. The child was making sounds of discomfort at her breast; her milk was drying again. Ban-ya, fighting an upwelling of desperation, began to rock the child. Already the last of the gift meat was gone; she knew that she would soon have to set snares for less palatable flesh.

Startled, Ban-ya heard the sounds of male voices and stones being moved. For days now she had listened to the men coming ever closer through the rock heap. She pressed the infant to her bosom with one hand and, with the other, reached into the protective circle that lay between her legs and crossed ankles to touch the skull and bones of its sibling. The little pile comforted Ban-ya; as long as she kept it close, that child was still alive to her. She lay her hand upon the skull, caressed the soft skin that remained as a gradually shrinking cap upon the cranium, then allowed her fingers to drift to the other bones.

The pile was growing smaller. She snarled. Often she would be awakened by the sound of bones being dragged away, and she would become aware of warm, furry bodies moving around her. Gasping, she would slap at them in the dark. Once she had actually caught one, and though it had bitten her, the bites she had returned had been much more severe as she had consumed the thief on the spot, all save its hair and tail. She had shuddered not in revulsion at what she had done but at the small sound she heard over her own breath and heartbeat—consistent gnawing and scraping.

"Be still, my babies, be still. Mother will protect you from rats!"

Now, suddenly, a single stone fell in the darkness. The sound was explosive. Ban-ya tensed and pushed her back tightly against the inner wall of the cave. Another stone fell and then another and another. Finally, the smell of dust invaded Ban-ya's nostrils, and the rockslide was fully breached. The light of an oil lamp invaded the blackness. Stones of all sizes came cascading into the cavern, and a large male figure loomed in the aperture.

Ban-ya saw feathers and fur and black-tattooed skin. In the yellow glow of the stone lamp that the apparition held gripped in one extended hand, the time-eroded face that peered in at her was not human. Ban-ya knew that Death had come for her at last. When the apparition gagged and spat from the stench of her hiding place, she saw only the raven feathers that encircled its hideous face. Her heart seemed to stop.

"Spirit Sucker!" Ban-ya screamed in mindless horror at the demon. "No! I will not welcome you!" With her infant gripped so tightly that he began to wail, she rose and ran screeching into the greater blackness within the depths of the cave.

Tsana followed Jhadel into the cavern. "What was it?" he queried, revolted by the stench of the place.

"A woman . . . I think," said the old man, moving forward and holding the lamp high.

"And something else . . . something dead from the stink of it," suggested Indeh, walking close at Tsana's back.

"Sheela?" Incredulity turned Tsana's question; he was not sure if it was hope or dread that tightened his gut.

"If what crouches ahead of us in the filth of its leavings is the spirit of your lost woman, Tsana, I would not seek her farther. You will not like what you find," warned Jhadel.

Tsana stared ahead. The creature, possibly concealing something under its furs, had stopped. It was standing on shaking limbs no thicker than his wrists. Its equally thin arms were crossed over its chest, and its hands, which looked like those of a long-dead corpse, clutched its bony shoulders. Gaunt, filthy, with hair as dry and wild and bleached of color and life as sedge grass at the end of winter, it was staring at him out of enormous eyes so filled with terror that he knew at once that the creature was alive. After another moment he realized that it was a woman. "Sheela?"

She flinched at the name, moved, and began to make her way one slow, sidling step at a time back into the cave, pressing against the stone wall of the cavern, her eyes still on his face. Tsana followed, moving ahead of Jhadel, drawn on by a mix of awe, fascination, and revulsion as he wondered if this hideous, foul-smelling apparition could possibly be all that remained of his beloved Sheela. Doubt shadowed hope. The woman before him was a small, shrunken, foul thing. Sheela had been tall, proud, and glorious to behold even after enslavement among their enemies had scarred her face.

Tsana looked for signs of his deceased lover's spirit in the torchlit eyes of the retreating woman, but he found only the madness of a cornered animal in her fixed, ferocious stare. He was shaken by it; in the days and nights before Sheela's death, his woman's eyes had also been fixed and filled with an intense resolve that bordered on madness. Was it possible that she had returned to live within the body of this emaciated creature?

At this moment Indeh gave a contemptuous snort. "I know this 'thing.' Yes! She is much changed, but before I left the People of the Land of Grass to make alliance with the People of the Watching Star, Shateh took this one from a Red World man who was living as a warrior among his tribe. What a body she had! Yes, it *is* she. I recognize the face. She was trouble from the start. I knew Shateh would tire of you in time, Lizard Eating Woman, but why are you alone? How have you survived winter in the Valley of the Dead?"

A moan tore out of the woman.

Indeh sneered in open contempt of her misery and obvious terror. "Ban-ya . . . yes . . . that was the name you answered to." He shook his head, smirked, and informed Tsana, "It would do your Sheela's spirit good to know that this woman has ended her days here . . . like this."

"Ban-ya?" Tsana tested the syllables upon his tongue; bitterness and hatred filled his mouth. "Woman of Dakan-eh?"

The woman, seeing the change in him, moaned again and pressed against the cavern wall as though she wished to dissolve through it; an odd mewling was coming from her now, not from her mouth or throat but from the ragged furs that covered her breasts.

Rage filled Tsana. "Ban-ya!" He knew the name; his beloved had spoken it often enough. The woman of Dakan-eh had been merciless toward her man's war captive; indeed, Sheela had told him that Ban-ya had been pleased and empowered by Dakan-eh's continuous degradation of a woman of the Watching Star and had mocked her when she was beaten and offered for the pleasuring of as many men as Dakan-eh had sought favor from. It was Dakan-eh who had scarred Sheela's face, but it was Ban-ya who had come close to breaking Sheela's spirit in the days before she had at last escaped her captors and returned to her war-devastated people. "My Sheela wanted you dead," he told the specter.

"It was something she yearned for . . . and will now have at my hand!"

But at this moment an exhalation of amazement came from Jhadel, who had gone slightly ahead of the others. Now, raising the source of light above the woman who slumped to her knees, the old shaman gasped in shock and swayed on his feet.

Tsana looked up. His heart lurched when he heard Indeh's quick, startled suck of breath. There, above the cowering woman, and all across the cavern wall—colors . . . forms . . . and revelation! "The totem lives!" he cried, his eyes taking in the meaning of the pictographs. "It lives! Not in the flesh of the shaman Cha-kwena, as Jhadel has told us, but in the herd of mammoth that we saw at the lake on the day of the war's last battle! Behold! The truth is here for us to see!"

Livid, Tsana strode forward, put a strong, hard hand on Jhadel's shoulder, turned the old man toward him, and glared at him with eyes bulging with accusation. "After that battle, you advised us to flee before the wrath of Shateh's warriors. If just a handful of us had doubled back to pursue the mammoth, the tusker that carries the spirit of Life Giver might have been taken. The totem itself might have been taken! If we had been able to consume its flesh and blood, we would have been strong again, invincible before Shateh. All those who perished and now walk the wind would be here among the living!"

Jhadel was so stunned that the few tattooed teeth he had left were clacking, and it was all he could do to hold the lamp steady. Indeh looked around, disconcerted.

"You did *not* foresee this, old man!" roared Tsana, and from the many labyrinthine tunnels within the hollow hill, his voice echoed back to him a thousand times.

After the echo died away, Jhadel, staring at the painted wall, managed a defensive reply to Tsana's accusation. "Behold! The Red World shaman walks in the power of the sacred stone! He blinds all who—"

"Have no sight to see?" snapped Tsana.

Indeh was now staring at Ban-ya. The mewling at her breast was louder now; she seemed to be attempting to stifle the sound by rocking herself. He raised both hands in an open-palmed sign against evil. "The wailing of this woman has led us to the truth! Perhaps the spirit of Sheela *does* dwell within her. How else could she have survived two winters alone in the Valley of the Dead?"

The woman stiffened, cocked her head; her breathing quickened. "Not alone," she whispered. "*She* is here. . . . Yes . . . Tsana speaks true words. The spirit of Sheela lives and answers through the mouth of this woman, who was forcibly separated from her people to become the woman of Shateh and who was his enemy as you are his enemies."

"She lies!" accused Jhadel. "Kill her, Tsana. Her life is a foul thing."

"No!" cried the cowering woman. The look of madness had gone from her eyes; there was clarity in them now and more ferociousness than before. "The forces of Creation have sent you here . . . to me . . . for if you let me live, you will have among you one whom Shateh desires above all living things!"

"You?" mocked Indeh, then barked a laugh.

"His only son." She opened the furs at her breast and revealed the infant that she had hidden there until now.

Indeh frowned. "When last I saw Shateh, he had recently lost his only son."

"Atonashkeh," confirmed the woman.

"With the Red World shaman and the power of the sacred stone at his command, Shateh may have other sons by now!" said Jhadel.

"Can you be sure, old one?" Desperation tightened the woman's features; her wild eyes were unnaturally bright in the lamplight. Slowly she rose to her feet and held out her baby. "Kill him then, and me with him. I am not afraid. I am already dead. A spirit speaks through me and has kept these bones and this flesh alive for you and for this child. But when I am truly dead and Shateh comes against you once more, the People of the Watching Star will not have a hostage in this child. They will be forced to run and flee before their enemies, as they have run and fled before. But this time they will die because you do not see the truth when it stands before you."

With the exception of the fussing infant, the woman's statement brought dead silence to the cave. The three men stared at her in amazement, hope, hesitancy, and distrust.

"Shateh will not seek us in the Valley of the Dead!" proclaimed Jhadel.

A strange calm seemed to wash through the woman, transforming her stance and expression. Looking at Tsana, she smiled gently and spoke in a lover's tone. "I have called you here. I have led you to see with your own eyes the truth about the totem. I have kept this woman alive for you and suckled this son of Shateh for you. If his warriors should find you and attack you, they will see Ban-ya, not Sheela, and they will know that a true son of Shateh dwells among you. They will not attack. Shateh is old. He is weary of war."

Tsana was stunned, enraptured, and bewildered all at once until the movement of a rat across the floor of the cave drew all the men's eyes to the scattered bones and skull of another infant.

"Twins!" shouted Jhadel, and now it was the old man who made the sign against evil. "Cannibal Mother of the ever-warring Brothers of the Sky!" he called her. "To what have we come? To what would you lead us?"

She stared at the bones of the dead baby. Again her stance changed. Again she cocked her head. Something cold and cloudlike seemed to be expanding within her eyes. Then she sighed, smiled gently once more, and moved forward. The three men stepped aside to let her pass.

Kneeling, she reached with one hand to caress the skull as she spoke tenderly to the remains of the dead infant. "His flesh was made by the forces of Creation to be food for the other. His death assured the life of his brother. And the brother's life is a gift to the People of the Watching Star from the spirit of the Valley of the Dead. Shateh will not name Enemy those who have raised a son of his to be strong in his name. But with this son they may someday break him. With this son they may rise again . . . strong and invincible as they—"

"I have heard enough!" Jhadel angrily shook his head. "I do not believe it. She lies. She is not what she seems. She is . . ." He stopped. Others were coming through the break in the rockslide; Xanahay carried a torch, illuminating their way.

"Behold the living spirit of Sheela and the truth to which she has led us!" Tsana commanded them, gesturing to the painting upon the wall. "The totem lives! Jhadel has not seen this! Or he has known it all along and has deliberately misled his people in order to assure a soft life for himself in his old age."

The shaman went as stiff as a heron about to spear a frog with its beak. "Beware, Tsana, of what you say!"

"Because of your misjudgment," shouted the younger man, "we are here, outcast, weak when we might have been strong!"

Jhadel was appalled. "I am Jhadel, spirit master, teacher of the shaman's way since time beyond beginning. The Daughter of the Sun, Ysuna, came forth to learn from me, and the one you named Beloved knew nothing of the ways of magic until she took the knowledge from my mouth and was foolish enough to twist it to serve her own ambition! If she had not insisted upon leading my people to war, the tribe would be strong now—and it will be strong again in the wisdom of Jhadel, who has led his tribe to good hunting in a valley where their enemies will not hunt them."

"I will hear no more 'wisdom' from your mouth!" retorted Tsana. "Ysuna and Sheela both turned their backs upon you in the end, as I do now!"

"And perished for their disobedience!" cried the old man.

"No," Tsana seethed. "They died because they did not see you soon enough for what you are! But now the spirit of my Sheela has returned from the world beyond this world. She has led us here so that we might know that soon our totem, the great white mammoth, will live again! In the meantime we will hunt. We will grow strong in this Valley of the Dead. Then we will return to the land of our enemies to hunt the power of the totem and claim it as our own."

Jhadel was aghast. "And if Shateh and the Red World shaman try to stop you?"

"The Red World shaman is not totem. We no longer need fear him. On the day the true totem falls beneath our spears, we will take the sacred stone from Cha-kwena and drive him from the land of the ancestors. Shateh will no longer have power or the will to stop us—not as long as we hold his only son hostage."

Warakan was tired as he trudged on in the skin of the great bear. Despite his efforts to drive off the cubs, they were still following him. Warakan felt sorry for these orphans he had made. He had honored the bones and skull of their mother to the best of his ability, but rising floodwaters had forced him to hurry on. Now he stopped, sighed, and turned around. How small the cubs were and how much like dog pups in their look and manner and persistence. Encumbered by the warm weight of the bear-skin and by the meat he had packed into its intestines, which he wore looped over one shoulder and bound around his waist, he could not afford to hold himself responsible for them.

"Go away," Warakan told them. "Return to the country of your bear family. Surely there is some sow somewhere that will take you in!" He continued on his way, bent double under his load but thankful to possess warmth and nourishment, and the tool kit that old Lahontay had abandoned when he had fled from the charging bear.

Plodding along, Warakan set himself in the way he thought the Red World shaman Cha-kwena must have gone when he had traveled toward the edge of the world. Now and then he heard the *chack* of the shrike and saw the bird winging ahead. He wondered why that strange, black-masked bird of carnivorous habits had chosen to keep company with him and, soon after, noted ravens and blackbirds and crows gathering in the shrubs to his left and right. At first he attributed their presence to the carnage that lay in the drowned land behind him, but soon the boy began to suspect that they were attracted to the scent of the uncured bearskin as well as to the smell of meat and fat softening and aging within the intestine carrying roll. Warakan swallowed hard and resolved to keep on going, certain that carrion-eating birds would not be the only predators to see him as prey.

The cawing of ravens and bawling of cubs caused him to look back. The little bears were swatting in great confusion and dismay at a great gang of savagely harassing ravens. Warakan saw blood on the snout and back of one of the cubs. Something in the pack manner of the birds roused instant anger. It was in that moment that a bond was made between the orphaned son of the People and the orphaned children of Bear.

With arms outstretched and voice roaring, Warakan charged the birds. "So Namaray and his friends have brothers among the winged kind! Get away from those cubs! They will not be meat for you! This boy will not stand by and allow so many to attack only two!"

They flew off and away in a panic, and the cubs, not recognizing a savior when they saw one, ran for cover, too. The boy watched them disappear behind a range of lodge-sized boulders. "Be watchful and wary, little brothers," he advised. "You cannot depend on this boy to look after you when he is also among the hunted of this world!"

Warakan walked on and on. Often he looked back. When he saw that the cubs were following, he smiled, not really sure why he was glad to see them; but they were company of a sort in the lonely land across which he trod, and the boy's spirit rested easier within his skin knowing that they were near.

Then the lions appeared. Big, tawny, their bellies

spotted, they drove Warakan back to the river. And still they came, the manes of the males black and bristling with intent. In desperation, with the bear cubs gamboling nearby in blissful ignorance of danger, the boy attempted to contrive an air-filled raft of the bearskin. When it was done, he called to the children of Bear and invited them to join him in what he was optimistic enough to believe would be an escape and not a drowning. But they would not come to him. He shook his head, despairing of being able to help them, and— begging the forces of Creation and the spirits of the river to be with him once more—risked the deeps, hoping that the advancing lions would not be as brave as he.

Swept downstream, Warakan tried to hold on to the heavy bearskin, but the current tore it out of his hands. And yet he managed to ride the rapids and keep his head held high. He clung with all his might to the meat-filled intestine, and his body was borne up by the buoyancy of the many air pockets he had inadvertently trapped within the carrying roll. At last the river hurled him up on the far shore, where he found the bearskin lying spread upon the gravel bar as though patiently waiting for him. He stared at it and thanked the spirits of the river and the ghost of the slain bear for being so kind as to consider his needs. Then, wrapping himself in the sodden bearskin, Warakan looked around for the cubs; but if they had followed him into the water, there was no sign of them now.

Saddened, thinking of the threatening lions and the defenseless cubs, he plodded on again, only to be startled and overcome with pure joy when he saw the pair down-river, alive and rooting at something dead along the shore. Nearly covered by flood debris and insects, it seemed to be a haunch of some pale and hairless animal.

"Children of Bear!" he called, and found himself running forward.

The wet little cubs eyed him and backed away.

"You must not be afraid of me!" Warakan told them, and knelt beside whatever it was that had drawn their interest.

Warakan raised an eyebrow; he had never before seen a beast like this drowned thing. The insects, unlike the cubs, were not so quick to abandon a potential meal. Curious, he swept them away and poked at the flesh, then gouged the first three fingers of his left hand into one of several breaks in the bluish skin and pulled out a few thin, bloodless shreds of pinkish flesh. He held them up and wondered if perhaps scent and flavor would identify the kind of animal or scaleless fish that lay dead before him. Brought to his nostrils, the flesh had the vague smell of spoilage. Nevertheless, Warakan was curious enough to touch it to his tongue and then to chew a bit. It had little flavor; but decay was breaking down the tissue, and it would probably be tender and not totally unpalatable if cooked.

The boy's brows arched as he realized that this strange meat might be a gift to him from the spirits of the river. If so, he knew that such a gift could not be wasted.

"I will share this meat with the children of Bear," said Warakan, looking back over his shoulder at the cubs, who kept their distance from him. "You have found this meat, little brothers, but you are so small and fresh from the teat, I wonder if you can eat of it? We will soon see!"

And so it was that Warakan began to remove stones and sand and good-sized pieces of driftwood from the haunch and discovered not the identity of some unknown animal but the body of Namaray.

He cried out and leaped to his feet. Remembering a night of fire and drumbeat and anger, he heard Namaray wish him death in the jaws of Bear, and then heard his own threat: *Do not wish for that! For if it comes to pass, I will* become *a bear and come for you, Namaray, to grind your bones and flesh between my teeth!*

With the taste of the fulfilled threat in his mouth and the weight of the slain bear upon his back, the hated names pounded in his head: *Cannibal! Watching Star Boy! Enemy!* Warakan was suddenly gut-wrenchingly sick. He went to his knees, vomited until he was weak and shaking, then stared at the remains of Namaray and wondered if, perhaps, he *was* a shaman, after all? No, he thought, if he were that, he would have known what had lain beneath the debris.

Now, confused and dismayed, Warakan pulled the body of Namaray onto higher ground. The river had battered the drowned youth. The body was badly gashed, pierced, and cruelly stripped of skin, especially across the top of the head, almost as though deliberately scalped. Warakan covered the remains with stones, piling them high and deep until his fingers were raw from the effort, and wondered what had happened to cause Namaray's death. Had Shateh's village been flooded? Were others also dead? And if so, would the survivors—if there were survivors—blame him for their fate? The question was more hurtful than Warakan could stand.

A cold wind made the boy shiver. He knew that he could not pass the night in the open. He looked around. Dusk had turned the world and sky to a dull gray. The river raced on. A shrike was sounding in the eastern hills. Emotionally drained and physically exhausted, he resolved to go his way in pursuit of the sacred stone and to think no dark thoughts about the fate of Shateh and his people. Surely the great hunt chief would have led most of them to safety, and when Warakan at last returned to them with the talisman of their ancestors, he was certain that there would be many surprised faces to make apology to the one they had so severely wronged.

The boy's thoughts of eventual vindication kept him warm as he traveled on. Later, with the river still rising and nightfall imminent, he found shelter in high hills and settled in to rest. It was a while before he thought of the cubs and found himself looking for them, thinking that since he had killed their mother, there was no one else to watch over them.

"Children of Bear . . . Warakan welcomes you to his camp. Come. We will rest together as we once rested and fed in the embrace of your mother!"

But the cubs did not come.

Loneliness settled more heavily upon Warakan than did

the skin of the slain bear. He slept fitfully, dreamed of terrible things, and awoke hopeful that the cubs would be there beside him. But they were not. He lay back, stared up at the stars, and followed the path of the Sky River northward into that part of the sky where the Watcher seemed to be eternally menaced by the ever-circling star body of the Great Snake. He frowned. The Watching Star was so pale, so tiny, sometimes it was difficult for him to see it. But there it was, staring down, observing him, mocking him. Warakan's frown deepened. He did not like that star. Glaring up at it, he realized that it must surely possess powers beyond knowing. How else could such a puny thing keep the Great Snake from devouring it? He closed his eyes, refusing to look at it. He would not be influenced by its malevolent stare. He was Warakan, son of Shateh, and soon he would prove beyond all doubt the extent of his loyalty to his adopted tribe. His thoughts drifted into sleep. This time he did not dream. . . .

When he awoke it was morning, and the little bears were nestled close to either side of his chest, each sucking on one of his thumbs as though at a teat. Amazed and delighted, Warakan smiled, accepting them as his children as he tried very hard not to laugh and conceded, "Perhaps I am a shaman, after all! How else could this boy be your mother?"

A strange and troubling realization had come over Shateh as he led his tribe from the rising floodwaters. He knew that although he had vowed to return to the land of his ancestors, there would be no going back for him yet. The high passes into the heartland of the country of his ancestors would still be blocked with snow. Spring flooding would soon make them equally impassable for many a long moon. His mouth was set as he turned and stared eastward into the rising sun and downward across the drowned lowlands in which Warakan, the six-moon baby, Lahontay, Eira, and young Namaray had died.

"It is a true thing that the luck of this tribe has vanished with Cha-kwena and the sacred stone," said Teikan.

The words poured over Shateh coldly, like yesterday's rain. Teikan was right, and he knew it; he was tired of arguing with the truth, no matter how uneasy concession made him feel. "We will seek him. We will travel around the drowned land and across the wasteland, then over the edge of the world. The sacred stone will be ours."

Teikan caught his breath. "And what will you do with Cha-kwena?"

The weariness in Shateh was almost painful. "My people blame him for all. If we find him, he will die."

"As he should have died on the night of the feast fire! It is what the People yearn for. It is what they need. What else do we live for if not to make war upon our enemies? Shateh will not regret committing the tribe to vengeance *at last*."

Shateh felt the barb of the last two words and with open dislike looked the man up and down. "A son of your blood is dead, Teikan. Why are you not still in mourning?"

Teikan's face tightened defensively. "The time of mourning has come and gone. I have set the life spirit of Namaray free upon the wind. Unlike Shateh, this man has other sons."

3

Within the distant forest it seemed that overnight spring had turned to summer. The air was heavy, warm, and loud with the drone of swarming insects and the hectic calling of nesting birds.

Mah-ree awoke with a start. Once again Bear had been prowling her dreams, charging at her, devouring her. It was not the little black bear that she had sighted when the band first set up camp beyond the gorge, but the towering, short-faced, yellow bear she had killed to save Senohnim's life on that long-gone, much-regretted day when she had dared to take up the spear of a man. She wondered how Senohnim was now, then realized that she did not really care.

Upset by her dream, Mah-ree sat up within the little hut of blood that had been raised for the women of the band to occupy during times of menstruation lest their passage of moon blood offend or unduly arouse the forces of Creation. She sighed; it was stifling within the hut. She did not want to be there. Four days of confinement were almost too much to endure, but still her moon blood flowed. Given past patterns, she knew that it was likely to continue for another two days and nights.

She closed her eyes and imagined herself outside, sitting close to the edge of the meadow, where a faint wind would be stirring the grasses and the slender bodies and wings of damselflies would be forming transparent blue mists as they hovered over the grazing mammoths. Again she sighed, wondering if the herd was out there now, belly deep in grass, sunstruck, and scooping up water from any of many little boggy lakes. She had not heard them for some time, so perhaps the matriarch had led them into the shade of the forest. Wherever the mammoth browsed, they did so in silence.

Mah-ree drew in a little breath and imagined the great cow, huge now with calf, then exhaled in envious longing. She wanted to be pregnant, as full of promise as the season, swelling with new life for herself and her man. But it was beginning to seem as though this would never be; since their sharp words in the forest over the slain dog, Cha-kwena had dragged his sleeping mattress apart from hers. Although they continued to share the same lodge, when night came down upon the world, they did not lie together under the same bed furs.

Nonetheless, she secretly continued to treat his meat with woman-wanting potion. Instead of having the desired effect, the pulverized roots and fungi accomplished little but stealing her man's dreams and giving him long nights of deep and undisturbed rest. Mah-ree shrugged, grateful that her shaman was no longer tormented by his dreams.

She opened her eyes. Daylight was filtering through the woven walls. Someone had drawn back the outer hut covering of elk hide to allow light and the wan breezes of the ripening day to enter; of the latter there were nearly none. Mah-ree wiped her sweated brow with the back of her hand. Outside, U-wa, Ta-maya, and Kahm-ree were chanting. Listening to the troubling ululation that was being offered to the spirits for the sick, she wondered why Cha-kwena was not leading it. Little Piku-neh had come down with a fever, and although his meticulously sutured hand was healing, he had been fractious, unnaturally thirsty, and salivating like a little camel in rut. No one had ever seen anything like it; Mah-ree suspected the boy of sucking salt-encrusted rocks taken from the lower spring, but Kahm-ree swore that he had been nowhere near them. Whatever the case, Mah-ree regretted not being free to be with him and to minister healing herbs.

Suddenly bright light invaded the confines of the hut as U-wa swept aside the woven entry door and, on her knees, peered in to place a fresh supply of clean furs and a basket of water inside. Looking at her, Mah-ree frowned. "You appear worried, Mother of My Man."

"The little one burns. We have given him those healing things that usually calm the fever spirits, plus those special things that you have told us of. But still bad fever spirits eat at his insides."

"Cha-kwena will make special smokes and songs for him!" assured Mah-ree.

"And how will my son do that when he has gone to seek the mammoth? They have not been to the pools in many days."

Wide-eyed, Mah-ree caught her breath, suddenly exultant. She knew in her heart that the totem was about to be reborn; this would be the only reason that her shaman would have left his people when one of them was sick. The expanding feeling of joy was so great within Mah-ree that she clapped her hands and cried out with pure exaltation, "Ah, Mother of My Man, the totem is about to be born again into this world! Soon the fever spirits will cease to burn within Piku-neh, and Gah-ti will grow a new arm, and Doh-teyah will no longer be blind, and this woman will grow a baby in her belly. You will see, U-wa!"

But U-wa's face had collapsed into an expression of horror.

"Why do you stare at me like that? It *will* be so! Cha-kwena and the forces of Creation have promised it!" In an instant of awareness that actually stopped the beat of her heart, Mah-ree realized what she had just done and nearly swooned with dread and sorrow.

U-wa was backing away on her knees, staring at her son's woman with an expression of fear and recrimination.

"Lawbreaking woman . . ." The words bled out of U-wa, low and tremulous, and she shook her head with grim admonishment and infinite regret. "Would that Shateh had found you and offered your spirit to the slain bear! Would that my son had never taken you to be his woman! Would that my poor, dear, beloved band sister Ha-xa had never birthed you! May the forces of Creation and the spirits of the ancestors have mercy upon your people now, for if the Four Winds have overheard your reckless words, all that for which we yearn will never come to pass!"

Cha-kwena tracked the mammoth through the ever-thickening forest. He could not understand why the herd had left the clearing by the hot springs and the good grazing of the meadows for this troubling woodland. Puzzled, he followed deeper and deeper into dusk and darkness until, at last, he found himself gripping the sacred stone and asking for the gift of fortitude as well as Vision.

Both came to him. He was grateful for one, but not at all sure if he welcomed the other when courage braced his body and spirit against the specters of phantom predators that came from within the trees to surround him in the night.

Eyes . . . golden eyes . . . green eyes . . . red eyes . . . the eyes of unseen carnivores. Round and elliptical, unblinking, all staring, all drawing color and light from only the forces of Creation knew what, for few stars showed above the canopy of the forest, and if there was a moon, Cha-kwena could not see it as he found the closest tree and put his back to it.

"I am not afraid," he stated, coolly, he thought, and wondered if the spirits of the night knew him for the liar he was. Within his hand, the sacred stone was hard and hot and inflexible against the press of his palm; its shape defined itself to his flesh and bones and tendons until he saw the ancestors moving before him in the dark.

"First Man! First Woman! You are with me!" Cha-kwena exclaimed, heartened until he realized that the sound of his voice had gone forth like wind-roused waves of water upon a pool; the gentle specters of the Ancient Ones rippled and bent into grotesque distortions, then dissolved into invisibility. In their place emerged another phantom. The great bear of Cha-kwena's erstwhile nightmares rose out of the darkness.

The young shaman's knees went weak; he locked them as the watching eyes of carnivores, glinting like stars, moved toward him through the trees and around the phantom bear. The creatures materialized into the predatory beasts that stalked the resolve of any man who dared to spend the night alone within such a forest as this one.

Cha-kwena spoke their names. "Lion. Wolf. Coyote. Leaping Cat. Cougar."

They purred and growled in reply.

"Do you not know me?" he asked. "I am Cha-kwena, grandson of Hoyeh-tay, Brother of Animals, Yellow Wolf, the kinsman of Coyote, and guardian of the sacred stone and totem. Will you not let me pass this night among you in peace?"

A soft, restless wind whispered and stirred among the trees, and suddenly the phantoms of the forest were gone.

Cha-kwena breathed a tremulous sigh of relief and lowered himself to his knees. "Be with me, spirits of my ancestors and of all that my people have held sacred since time beyond beginning, for though I am Shaman, I am only a man. If I am to follow where you would lead me, I must have my rest."

He lay down and closed his eyes. And soon it was dawn.

For four days and three nights Cha-kwena trailed the mammoth. The languor that had been on his spirit within the village left him as their spoor led him on and on. Although he heard their trumpeting, he began to despair of ever catching up to them. On the fourth night, after having fallen asleep with his back to one of the many oddly shaped lichen-and-moss-covered boulders that he found lying like great stone eggs laid and abandoned by an indiscriminate giant, he awoke to a strange, unnatural stillness.

Cha-kwena looked up, stared into darkness. He waited and listened, but for what, he could not say. Somewhere beneath the earth something moved, trembled; beneath his hands the ground shivered like the skin of an animal after a fly has bitten it. Startled, he jumped to his feet. The earth could not move! And yet it just had, unless he imagined it.

Breathless, Cha-kwena looked up. Wind was stirring in the trees, a warm, sighing wind that was more strange than the silence had been, for somehow the young shaman could see this wind as it blew from the world beyond this world to envelop him and urge him forward through the darkness.

"Come!" said the wind.

And Cha-kwena obeyed, unafraid, for now old Hoyeh-tay walked before him, with Lion and Leaping Cat and Dire Wolf at his side, while Owl flew ahead, parting the way through the darkness and leaving a trail of stars dripping from his wings to light the path for those who followed.

As in a dream, the young shaman was impelled onward through the forest until, just before dawn, he came to a clearing. The tuskers were there, waiting.

Cha-kwena stopped and stared. Tears filled his eyes, and a smile broke upon his face. In the light of the rising sun, a little white mammoth looked back at him from amid the protective circle of its family.

The totem had been reborn.

Cha-kwena raised his arms to the wind and sky and thanked the forces of Creation for leading him to this place. "Life Giver! Great Spirit! Little Grandfather of All Mammoth! Cha-kwena, the grandson of Hoyeh-tay, Brother of Animals, guardian of the sacred stone and of, of . . . *you,* Totem . . . I welcome you into this world! I thank the great mother mammoth who took your spirit and nourished it within herself for all of these long, long moons so that she might give birth and renewed life to you! For this moment Cha-kwena has waited! For this moment this shaman has fought the dark spirits and phantoms of his dreams! Now the People will live forever and rejoice and be healed and—"

A great and sudden roaring in the forest silenced Cha-kwena. He froze, listening, realizing that the roaring was not the voice of the rising wind. It was something else; something indefinable and infinitely threatening. In an instant the ghosts of old Hoyeh-tay and Owl and the spirit animals disappeared.

The ears of the tuskers were pivoting. The herd was huffing and growling and closing protectively around the calf. The great matriarch raised her trunk and trumpeted to the sky. And to Cha-kwena's amazement, the roaring in the forest had become so loud that even the cry of the mammoth went unheard.

In that moment the earth moved—not in a gentle rippling as on the previous night, but violently, in a great, lurching spasm that rocked Cha-kwena on his feet. Birds exploded in frenzied flight from the treetops, and the entire forest swayed madly. It seemed as though Mother Below was howling. Startled, frightened, and appalled by the horrendous sound and sight of whiplashed trees being shaken by their roots rather than their crowns, Cha-kwena grasped the sacred stone and cried out while the ground beneath him wrenched straight up and then moved forward. A heartbeat later it plunged down fast and hard, jarring him so badly that he screamed. He was lifted forward and up again. The next time the earth fell, Cha-kwena fell with it, dizzy and deafened while the ground shivered so ferociously that he felt as though he were a child being shaken unto death by a murderous parent. And then, when he was certain that the earth was about to explode and hurl him away into the world beyond this world, the sound and shaking subsided, and he lay sprawled on his belly, afraid to move or breathe lest it all begin again.

The world was still. Cha-kwena listened to the unnatural silence, welcomed it, and gradually became aware of the pounding of his own heart and the rush of blood in his veins. Choking, he looked up into clouds of brown dust.

Light-headed, he forced himself to rise. It took him a moment to steady himself, and when he did, he squinted through settling dust to see that a long, deep, irregular gash had opened in the earth behind him. Ahead of him the mammoth had vanished into the forest.

His right hand reached for the sacred stone; relief flooded through him when the familiar contact was made. Whatever had unsettled the forces of Creation seemed to have passed, and Mother Below was relaxed and motionless again; he felt more soothed by that than he would have believed possible. Slowly, cautiously, he advanced to the clearing where the mammoth had stood. And then the earth moved again.

"Aiee!" Cha-kwena wailed like a woman. With the sacred stone clutched in his hand, he expected to be pitched into the sky or down onto the ground, but the movement was not as severe as before. The ground continued to quake, settling beneath his feet. He trembled with it and gasped when he looked down. At his feet where the great tuskers had stood only moments before, he saw steam venting from a ragged rift in the ground. Water was seeping through. His eyes widened as he realized that there, in the clearing, a new spring had been born! When the mammoth trumpeted somewhere ahead, although he was badly shaken and confused, Cha-kwena reasoned to himself that this portentous omen could mean only one thing.

"I will bring the People to this place in which the totem has been reborn," he said, and knew without the slightest doubt that "The forces of Creation have spoken!"

He ran back to the village and held the hope that Mother Below and the forces of Creation had spared the People. But the smell of smoke and the songs of mourning alerted Cha-kwena to disaster long before he came through a tangled wall of fallen trees and stood before the ruined settlement. The lodges were down. There was no sign of the dogs. Mah-ree sat alone, well apart from the frightened women and children who were gathered in a little cluster outside a single hide lean-to. And Kosar-eh was waiting for him.

"You have been long gone from this place, Shaman," said the big man, his face haggard and set hard with accusation.

Stunned, Cha-kwena looked with disbelief while the others rose and stared toward him across the desolation of what had once been a happy encampment. Kahm-ree looked aged unto death, and Ta-maya, whose arm was bent and bound, appeared so ravaged by grief that she seemed barely able to stand. Only Mah-ree remained where she was, looking at him with such longing and misery that his spirit went numb when he saw the depth of the pain that welled in her eyes.

"You did not foresee this, Shaman!" stated Kosar-eh.

"I . . ."

"You offered no warning when you led us to this place, where Piku-neh has been unable to fight the fever spirits that have taken his life . . . where Spirit Sucker shakes the skin of Mother Below until trees fall to crush my infant daughter, Ha-xa-ree, while she slept in her mother's embrace . . . where the bones of my Ta-maya's arm have been sundered, as has my woman's spirit."

Cha-kwena's hand went to the sacred stone; there was no comfort to be found in it as he heard himself protest, "It cannot be! The totem has been reborn! Little Grandfather of All walks in the forest but four days from this place! Surely now that Life Giver is among us once more, all will be well for our people and—"

Kosar-eh's blow came so unexpectedly and with such speed that Cha-kwena had no chance to avoid the back-handed strike that caught him hard across the mouth.

A gasp went out of all who saw their shaman staggered.

Kosar-eh was so livid that he was unaware of the reaction his unprecedented behavior toward a holy man had elicited in the others. "Do not speak to me of Life Giver when two children of this band are dead and a woman has been injured!" he raged at Cha-kwena. "Even the dogs have run away, and animals and birds have vanished from the forest. Springs and pools have disappeared into the earth that still shakes and growls!"

"But the spring has been born anew in the place where I saw the mammoth and the totem!" informed Cha-kwena, one hand working his jaw as he tried not to wince against pain. "It is a sign! A great omen! A calling to the People to follow the mammoth into the forest and—"

"I will not hear it!" interrupted Kosar-eh. "Now that you have returned, I will take what is left of my family and return into the land of living things! Old Kahm-ree and your mother and sister are welcome to come with me, or they may stay behind with you and your lawbreaking woman. The choice is up to them."

Cha-kwena was aware of Mah-ree looking at him. She had not moved; he doubted if he had ever seen her appear so dejected. Suspicion prompted him to ask, "What have you done in my absence, Mah-ree? Why does Kosar-eh call you Lawbreaker?"

Mah-ree hung her head.

It was U-wa who spoke. "When Shaman's Woman learned that my son had gone from the village to look for the mammoth, she broke the ancient taboo against naming. She spoke aloud of that which we have all yearned to see happen and of all the good that would happen afterward. Before the setting of that day's sun, Piku-neh breathed his last. And now, on the fourth day after his death, the spirit of Ha-xa-ree walks the wind forever!"

A sob came from Mah-ree. "I have caused my mother to die twice!" Bereft, she shook her head and buried her face in her hands as she mourned the realization that now Ha-xa's life spirit—born into the world again through Ta-maya's baby—was surely lost forever.

Gah-ti, standing back from his brothers and close to the young woman, was visibly angry. "Piku-neh was sick before Mah-ree spoke forbidden words! And long before we came to this far land that shakes, Cha-kwena broke the taboo against naming!"

Once again a gasp came from the assembled band.

Mah-ree looked up. She appeared dazed as she whispered with obvious disbelief, "Can this be true, my shaman?"

Cha-kwena's face had gone as tight as the skin covering of an overstretched drum.

"On the day we thought we were to die under attack from Shateh's men, Cha-kwena told me why we must protect the mammoth with our lives," informed Gah-ti. "So if dark spirits come against us, it cannot be your fault, Shaman's Woman. With his own mouth it was Cha-kwena who first spoke the forbidden words."

Cha-kwena's head had gone high; although his mouth was bloodied, his lips whitened with strain as he said, "But Shateh did not follow us. We did not die. We trekked over the edge of the world and away from enemies who would have slain some of us and enslaved the rest. To good hunting we have come. And now I tell you that the totem has at last been reborn."

Kosar-eh was not impressed. His tone was one of pure contempt as he said, "And you alone have *seen* this?"

"I *have* seen it!" Cha-kwena fought down his rising fury. "Moments before Mother Below rose to shake the roots of all living things, I saw it—a white calf, as I have seen it in my dreams before ever I left the country of our enemies."

"Then Mah-ree's words have not killed it!" proclaimed Gah-ti, glaring at his father. "The totem lives! And now, despite all that has happened, who among you will dare say to me that the Ancient Ones have lied? They promised that when Life Giver has grown to power again within this world, the sick will be healed, the blind will be given sight, and even the spirits of the dead will be born once more into the country of the living."

"The promise was made only to those who follow the sacred path of the mammoth," reminded Cha-kwena.

No one spoke . . . until an owl was heard *ooo*oing in the forest out of which Cha-kwena had just emerged.

"When Owl calls by day, it is an omen of death," Kosar-eh intoned.

"It is *dusk*," said Gah-ti sharply. "And since when has my father become a shaman?"

Cha-kwena felt the weight of the tension between them and knew that he must ease it. "I tell you that Life Giver walks in the dark woods. I tell you that there is a newborn spring in that place. Surely this is an omen of life! And so it is that Owl calls to us and invites us to follow him in the way of the totem and of the ancestors since time beyond beginning. In that place where his wings come to rest, there will this band find a new and better life."

"And if you and this owl are wrong?" Kosar-eh's voice was as deep and full of troubled portent as thunder rumbling restlessly within a storm cloud. "How many more of my children will I see maimed and dead?"

"We will not live forever, any of us, Kosar-eh. But as long as we keep the ways of First Man and First Woman and walk always in the path of the rising sun, our spirits will be born again and again into this world. We have been honored above all tribes when chosen by the forces of Creation to be guardians of the sacred stone and the totem of the Ancient Ones."

"Here. We will take this with us to the sun."

Cha-kwena was distracted by old Kahm-ree's command. He had not noticed her come forward. Now she stood before him and shoved a tightly bound rawhide parfleche into his midsection. "What is this, old woman?" he asked.

Kahm-ree was surprised by the question. "Let the magic of the shaman be with these ashes as we travel to a new camp. We will water these ashes in the spring within the forest. We will lay these ashes on the sacred ground upon which the totem has been reborn. Little Grandfather of All will see what we do. Life Giver will make baby and boy grow again! Ha-xa-ree! Piku-neh! Ah, yes! It will be so! Then, when my Ban-ya comes, she will not be angry with her old grandmother for letting the fever spirits eat the life of her only son. And when Shateh finds this band at last, my

Ban-ya will be his woman again, and we will have enemies in this world no longer."

"There will always be enemies, old woman," said Kosar-eh.

"Perhaps," conceded Gah-ti. "But it will not be Shateh. He would have no reason to follow us into this shaking land of many trees beyond the edge of the world. That man is no longer following us."

4

The drowned land lay behind them. Shateh led his people back across familiar country. On a clear night, with a full moon rising, they saw a fire glimmering in not-too-distant hills, and the chieftain led a war party from their encampment with spears and braining clubs at the ready.

The smell of smoke brought them to pause, hunkering low, hidden in the night.

"I do not smell the stink of boiling rodents and grubs that are often mixed into the meat of lizard eaters!" whispered Xohkantakeh.

"That is camel being roasted!" exclaimed Ynau, his voice a controlled scrape of sound as he raised his head, the better to scent the seared meat and dripping hump fat.

"With the sacred stone in their possession, they must be making many good kills and enjoying many a feast fire," sneered Teikan.

"Wait . . . listen. . . ." Shateh's tone and gesture commanded silence.

The wind had risen slightly. It was bringing to their ears the low, easy talk of men and women relaxing around a campfire and the occasional laugh of a child. Then the wind turned.

Shateh hissed a wordless curse through his teeth. With the others, he instinctively lowered himself against the earth. It was too late. A dog barked, and a man called from the fire circle in a voice Shateh and the others knew but did not expect to hear.

"Who is there in the dark, lurking in the way of a stalking beast?" the voice demanded with an arrogance that did not quite mask underlying trepidation. "Rise and show yourselves and speak to us as men, if you *are* men and not frightened old women! We know you are here. Our dogs have scented you!"

"Axwahtal?" Shateh was incredulous; the man was well-known to him, a chieftain of a northern band of his tribe. During the great autumn hunt gatherings in the far reaches of the Land of Grass, they had often tracked bison and mammoth together as hunt brothers. Although the hardships and stresses of the last great hunt had seen their bands go their separate ways, they had not parted as enemies. *What is the man doing here?* Shateh wondered. Weapons poised, he rose to his feet, determined to find out.

"You!" Axwahtal exclaimed, and, with a laugh of sincere gladness to see an old friend, welcomed Shateh and his men to his camp and sent runners off to bring the rest of the chieftain's people to share in the night's feast.

They ate together in silence, for this was the etiquette of the big-game hunters of the Land of Grass upon meeting old friends; to partake of meat in trust and gratitude and without question, then to share news and whatever fellowship the night would bring. For this reason Shateh took his portion of hump steak and, as he ate, did not speak to the young man and woman among Axwahtal's people who served the feast—their eyes downcast, their hair clipped, thong nooses dangling about their necks. Slaves. And yet he knew them: Hah-ri and Ili-na, both Red World People whom he had sent from his band. He looked around and saw no others of their band.

"I have thought of you often during the past moons of endless bad winter," said Axwahtal at last, wiping grease from his long mouth with the back of a broad hand. "Many of my brothers from the far north joined with Indeh against you and traveled to make war upon your people as allies of our enemies, the People of the Watching Star. I have not seen them since that time. Did they win or lose against you, Shateh? And is it true that you walked in company of lizard eaters?"

"I am here," replied the chieftain. "My enemies are dead or hiding in distant country from my many raids against them. You will find no lizard eaters among my people. I cannot say the same for yours."

"Slaves! They are not men, not women, only 'things' to be used. And these slaves claim to have come from your encampment, where they lived as equals among your people. When last I saw you, under a black moon, you had a lizard eater hunting among your warriors."

"No more. Never again. A shaman of their race used his powers to blind me to the wisdom of the Ancient Ones. That shaman has stolen the sacred stone of our ancestors and fled with it beyond the edge of the world. Now I hunt him and his kind, to kill him and his kind. Have you killed the others who were with these slaves when you took them?"

Axwahtal nodded. "It is not good to have too many slaves; the use of them softens the will, and in numbers they can form a pack and become as dogs, dangerous if they are not kept well fed. In times such as these, who has enough meat to waste on slaves?"

"And the children?"

"I would not bring baby lizards into my camp to grow up among the young lions and wolves that are the sons and daughters of my blood and the blood of my warriors!"

"As Shateh once brought a cub of our enemies to live among us and came to regret it!" said Teikan.

Shateh gave the man a withering glance that warned not to intrude again into the conversation of chiefs, then turned his attention back to his old hunt brother. "What brings you so far south, Axwahtal?"

"As I have said: endless bad winters, much snow, ice in

the high passes. Never have I seen the like. It has been similar to the stories of First Man and First Woman, when ice spirits ruled the world. Cold sun. Cold moon. Voracious wind. White Giant Winter oppressing the People until Spirit Sucker was much among my hungry band. Again and again I have brought them to river crossings where we have always waited for the herds to come in spring, but the herds have not come. And the rivers have mocked us . . . one moment as dry and frozen as old women to the needs of men, the next swollen and rising to drown everything in their path. So we have called council. We have come south, seeking the totem, hoping to find better luck in land where the great white mammoth was said to graze. But it has been much the same in this new country. And the omens have been bad this spring—falling stars and great floods and an earth that trembles while a talking bear has been seen crossing the far hills with a pair of cubs. You are a shaman, Shateh. You must tell Axwahtal the meaning of these signs and if there is something more than chance to our meeting this night in a land that is strange to both of us."

Shateh's head went high. Every eye around the feast fire was upon him. "I know only this: Once, the forces of Creation smiled upon my people. Once, I led my band to the river crossings and to the great lakes of summer grass, and the herds were there to greet them. The waters did not rise to drown the land, nor did the earth tremble beneath my feet. I have thought much about this. And now I say that the totem is dead, and the man who has killed it has stolen the sacred stone and taken it away with him beyond the edge of the world. The forces of Creation will not smile upon my people until I have . . ." He paused. A terrible hush had fallen over the gathering.

Axwahtal exhaled as though in pain. "The great white mammoth is dead?"

"Its bones lie in a lake within a place called the Valley of the Dead," confirmed Shateh. "I have seen this with my own eyes."

"Then, truly, dark spirits walk the world," whispered

Axwahtal, "and the omens could not be other than they have been for us."

Shateh nodded. "The ancestors have told that the man who slays the totem will become the totem, invincible and all powerful, until he himself is slain and his power taken by the one who eats of his heart and drinks of his blood."

"Yes, so it has been said. The People of the Watching Star hunted Great Spirit. There was war over that. But tell me, Shateh, when this totem-slaying enemy lived among your people, why did you not kill him for the good of us all and become totem yourself?"

The question should not have taken the chieftain off guard, but somehow it did. He drew in a breath and held it. And when he exhaled, the truth came with it. "I thought Cha-kwena was my friend." The admission made, he felt the sting and the shame of it.

"He was a lizard-eating trickster, a coyote-chasing shaman from the Red World who brought us nothing but trouble from the moment he came among us!" informed Teikan in a rush of venom. "But Shateh's loyalty has always been great! Even to lizard eaters!"

Shateh eyed Teikan with eyes that would have crushed him where he sat had they possessed the power to do so. "Yes," he affirmed evenly, coldly, straining for control. "My loyalty is great, but you must remember that it is not without bound, Teikan. Do not again force me to remind you that your place at this feast fire is beside your chieftain, with your mouth shut until your opinions are asked for!"

Teikan stiffened; even in the firelight the flush of his face was evident. Axwahtal harrumphed with satisfaction.

Shateh was gratified. "Now, as to the Red World shaman—Cha-kwena fought beside me in war against our enemies. Together we were victorious. The sacred stone was his. I had no cause to suspect that he would use its power to harm me or mine, and so I agreed to let him be shaman, guardian of the sacred stone, totem, to my people. I am chief; I thought that what I did regarding him would make us all strong in the favor of the Four Winds. But I concede now that the Red World shaman was Trickster, Yellow Wolf, Brother of Coyote. After the war was done and our enemies were slain and scattered, he robed himself in a skin that showed him to be a man of little power. Although this Red World man had slain the totem and been brave in battle, I came to know that the power of the totem could not have passed to him. His magic could not heal the sick, command the wind upon a hunt, put life into his woman, or even make her obey him and the laws of the band. Even the sacred stone had no power in his hand. And so I let him leave my people, believing that the stone no longer possessed the power of the Ancient Ones and that the presence of such a weak and ineffectual shaman was an offense to the forces of Creation."

The gathering murmured in understanding.

Shateh nodded; he had spoken at enough gatherings to know that he had his listeners now.

"Perhaps he did not do these things because he was afraid you would sneak up on him and brain him while he slept, then eat him and take the stone for yourself," suggested Axwahtal.

Shateh frowned; it occurred to him that he did not understand why Cha-kwena had betrayed him. "I know only that he has sent Spirit Sucker for my sons and my new woman and for others of my band. I will not rest until he pays for this with his life and the sacred stone is mine." He paused, scanned the assembled people slowly, meaningfully, and then continued with great emphasis. "Since time beyond beginning, the Ancient Ones have told us through our storytellers that the sacred stone is more than stone—it is all that remains of the bones of First Man and First Woman; within it the spirits of the ancestors live and speak to empower the People. How can we hope to live a good life when that which is most sacred to us hangs around the neck of Totem Slayer and he uses its powers to set the forces of Creation against us?"

"Ah, it is so," agreed Axwahtal, sighing.

Shateh raised both hands, fingers up and spread wide.

"Like this are the warriors of our two bands. Like the fingers on the hand of this man, when separated these fingers are vulnerable, easily bent or broken or cut away. But when these fingers come together like this—" he curled his hands into fists "—then together these warrior bands could take the sacred stone. Cha-kwena has slain the totem. Now Cha-kwena *is* the totem. He has betrayed and abandoned those who have trusted him. Now he is hunted. And now Axwahtal has asked Shateh if there is something more than chance to our meeting in this land that is strange to us both. Shateh says *yes* to Axwahtal. Shateh says that together our combined bands would be a great warrior tribe! Together, as in time beyond beginning, these two people could become one and take back from the lizard eater that which will make the forces of Creation smile upon us all."

Axwahtal was so overwhelmed that he was on his feet. "And which one of us will eat the flesh and drink the blood of the totem when he is slain?"

"All!" declared Shateh, and rose, arms extended, eyes fixed upon the crowd. "All of us. Every man, woman, child, and even dog of us! Together the people of Shateh and Axwahtal will be totem, invincible before the Four Winds and the forces of Creation!"

A great shout of approval went up from the combined tribes.

"Let it be so, then!" agreed Axwahtal, and suddenly men were reaching for drums and whistles and flutes.

Teikan stared at his chieftain through the firelight and knew it was possible to love and loathe one man at the same time.

Ah, Shateh, he thought, *when you shamed this man you made an enemy. But even so there is none to equal you—not a warrior or chieftain or shaman in this world or the world beyond. But surely even you must know that no one, not even the totem, can stand invincible before the Four Winds and the forces of Creation. Always there will be another*

*seeker of blood and flesh and "invincibility" to renew the
eternal circle of life and death.*

A terrible sadness and a sense of destiny touched
Teikan in that moment. He wondered if he was the only one
who saw the weariness and undying grief that underlay
Shateh's powerful stance. Since the death of Warakan, the
chieftain had not been the same. He kept to himself. He
fasted. He prayed. It was common knowledge, thanks to the
wagging tongue of Cheelapat, that Shateh did not take a
man's release upon her or even the youngest and most
appealing of the women of his band. Teikan would have
found this strange under any circumstances; but it was
especially upsetting because Shateh had not impregnated
any females since the night of the feast fire, and the
new-woman daughters of Xohkantakeh and Zakeh had both
recently failed to bring forth male life. Disappointed and
committed to his quest for the sacred stone, Shateh had
declared that he had enough daughters to feed and denied
life to the newborn females lest their mothers be unduly
weakened in the days and nights of travel that lay ahead.

Teikan's face tightened. Three days after the abandonment of those infants, Cheelapat had given birth. And only
the night before, she had sought him out, smirking as she
had displayed her huge belly and boasted in a whisper,
"Behold this life that you put into me on the night of the
feast fire, Teikan. Do you see how I carry it? Wide and all
out front. Xama and Unal both say that it is male life. Soon
it will come from between my thighs—a son for Shateh!
Heh! It will be the child of an old man's longings put into
his woman by a dishonoring hunt brother! And Shateh will
give his name to one who will never bear his spirit because
that child's blood is not his blood. It is your blood, Teikan,
the blood of one who could have been chieftain in Shateh's
place! But no matter. Soon I will displace Wehakna as first
woman at his fire. I will be Mother of Shateh's son and have
the place of honor in that man's lodge, thanks to you."

Teikan's breath snagged in his throat. Only yesterday
the vindictive Cheelapat had birthed a daughter and, failing

to displace Wehakna as first woman of Shateh's lodge, had not been allowed to put the child to her breast. It pleased him now to see her grieving along with the other women who had failed to please their chieftain by giving him a son. But as Teikan looked at the man now, he knew that Shateh was grieving, too.

The warrior's eyes narrowed when he saw Shateh's gauntness and the lines of sorrow that were as deep as any of his scars of lamentation. Teikan was certain that Shateh could not live much longer if he went on like this. What did it matter if he found Cha-kwena and, with the sacred stone in his hand, danced in the betrayer's skin like a priest of the Watching Star? Be he chieftain or totem, without a son to take his name, Shateh, the finest of all men, would die forever.

And then Teikan would be chief.

5

The men were journeying to the lake again. Ban-ya, Spirit Woman, watched them go. From the outer edge of the cave, with the rising wind of morning warm in her face, she looked down and across the Valley of the Dead to observe a good-sized hunting party heading toward that part of the lake within which lay the skeletal remains of the great white mammoth. Each day, before they went forth to hunt, the men of the People of the Watching Star made a pilgrimage to the carcass of Life Giver. They would wade into the shallows to grasp the tips of the massive tusks, then swing themselves up and climb along the tusks onto the half-mired skeleton in order to take and consume small scrapings of bone and cuttings of desiccated hide, certain that whatever totemic power lingered within the remains would make them strong on the hunt.

And it was so, for each night since Ban-ya had been brought from the interior of the cavern, the People feasted on the rich, red meat of deer and horse and antelope.

Ban-ya's head went high. For the first time since entering the Valley of the Dead, she felt well, strong, and at equilibrium with life. Her teeth were settling firmly into her gums. Her hair had ceased to fall out in matted clumps. The lesions in her skin were healing, and her breasts were swollen with milk for "the son of Shateh."

A smile moved at the corners of her mouth as the slow, steady, aggressive pull of little Ea-ka at her nipple roused the deep, sensual satisfaction unique to nursing women. Each day the baby fattened, grew more demanding and impatient, and, by his disposition, caused others to say that he was surely a chieftain's son. But whose? *You must be Shateh's if you are to live.*

Ban-ya's eyes narrowed with thoughtful speculation while she continued to observe the hunting party. Today they were hunting more than meat. Today they set themselves to extract the tusks from the massive, half-sunken head of the totem; if they were successful they would bring the tusks to the cave. Already hoists had been fashioned from tree trunks, and strong ropes of twisted thong had been made ready to support the weight of the tusks as they were hefted up the sheer wall of the cliff and maneuvered into the cavern. For what purpose? Ban-ya dared not ask. Sheela, high priestess of the People of the Watching Star, would have known. Ban-ya, pretender to Sheela's rank and spirit, did not. So she watched. She listened. She tried to learn.

For days the men of the Watching Star had no longer been content to journey to the skeleton of the great white mammoth. For days they had done more than consume scrapings of bone and dried flesh; they had been dissecting the skeleton of Life Giver and returning to the cave with vertebrae and sections of ribs and long bones and even a huge grinding tooth. And for days—ever since Tsana had sent runners across the land to bring news of the rebirth of the totem to the war-dispersed remnants of the tribe—small, pathetic bands of Watching Star People had been finding their way to the Valley of the Dead. Ensconced within the cave, the men and boys worked on their weapons by night and hunted and retrained themselves to be warriors by day; and all the while the women and girls seemed to be waiting with almost breathless anticipation for something of great ritual importance to transpire.

Suddenly aware of being watched, Ban-ya turned, stared into the crowded interior, then cringed when she saw

THE EDGE OF THE WORLD   343

Jhadel glaring at her from the little space he had made his own close to the entrance leading into the sacred cavern. Ban-ya glared back at him. The man had no power. He spent most of his time within the inner cavern communing with the spirit of the totem, or so he said—but she knew better. In truth he hid his ugliness from Tsana's censorious eyes and tongue, for since emerging from the cavern with Spirit Woman, Tsana was undisputed headman of the assembled bands; he suffered Jhadel to live, not out of deference to his shaman's rank but in prudent acknowledgment of the fact that there were those among his people who still feared the old man's reputation and because, in days and nights to come, the warriors would have need of a magic man to propitiate the spirits on their behalf as they prepared for battle.

"You must eat, Spirit Woman!"

Ban-ya was happy to see the scar-faced woman Oan step forward between her and the old man.

Eyes downcast, Oan proffered a hardwood spit upon which was a well-seared waterfowl. "Tsana has said that the spirit of his beloved must be strong when the thunder comes again . . . perhaps tonight, if we are to judge from the clouds that passed before last night's moon. But this duck is—"

Ban-ya took Ea-ka from her breast and, handing the baby to Oan before the woman could complete her statement, eagerly accepted the spit in both hands. Without a word of gratitude, she began to eat greedily. Ban-ya wondered if her appetite would ever be sated. Surely her need to be cleansed of her ordeal within the inner cave was still an overriding concern. "Bring the paunches of warm water if they are ready!" she commanded, eager for what had become a morning ritual.

"Bring the paunches!" Oan called to others.

In moments, several women and girls hurried forward. While Ban-ya was seated in the sunlight on the floor of the cave and continued gorging, the females of Tsana's band sloshed heated water over her back and shoulders. The feeling was exquisite; Ban-ya sighed with pleasure. She could not be clean enough. "Bring soap root!" she ordered. "And heat more water!"

The women complied. A moment later two young girls knelt and began to lather her back. Ban-ya closed her eyes and, still gnawing on the spitted meat, smiled while she ate; as in all things, the people of Tsana saw to it that the woman within whom the spirit of Sheela had taken residence was granted her every wish.

"The one long dead has much appetite, especially for meat that Sheela disdained in life," observed Jhadel with open cynicism.

Ban-ya tensed and opened her eyes. Realizing that the old man had tricked her by ordering Oan to serve the duck, she hurled the spit at him. "This body lives only to sustain Shateh's son!"

Jhadel easily sidestepped the missile of gnawed bones and shredded duck flesh. "And affirm the People's need to make war upon their enemies," he snarled.

"It was the way of Sheela and of Ysuna before her," said Oan sharply, appearing both embarrassed and vexed as she came forward with nourishment again, this time contained in a bladder flask. "Here, Spirit Woman. This *was* one of Sheela's favorites." Oan's emphasis had been an unspoken confirmation that although she had cooked and offered the waterfowl, it had been at Jhadel's command. "Drink deeply of this blood that was drawn from yesterday's kills. Would that it were taken from mammoth! But it is, at least, big meat. Deer. Horse. I have heated it myself. It will make you strong and steady for the offering that is to come."

Ban-ya knew that she dared not hesitate. She accepted the flask and consoled herself with the reminder that she had consumed far more revolting nourishment during the past many moons. Gulping thick, clotted blood, she felt the eyes of others upon her and was gratified when she saw Jhadel frown when she handed the flask back to Oan, who took it and, finding the contents nearly drained, nodded with approval.

"A true woman of the Watching Star!" declared Oan.

"We shall see what she is," hissed Jhadel. "Soon. When thunder comes. Perhaps tonight. Yes. We shall see."

And it was so.

That night the tusks of the great white mammoth were brought to the cave, then raised upright and secured into a pale arch. Beneath it, flames burned within a circle of mammoth vertebrae. When dark clouds gathered and thunder rolled within the Valley of the Dead, Spirit Woman was called forth to make an offering.

The dagger that Tsana held out to Ban-ya was newly made of mammoth bone. She stared at it as she sat in the position of infinite honor upon a seat fashioned from the massive grinding tooth of the great white mammoth. The dagger was carved into the shape of a half-human female raven. The breasted body of the bird formed the haft, the head and beak of the bird the blade, double edged, deadly sharp.

"For your hand, Sheela, to replace that which was lost when your body was slain and consumed by the waters of the lake," explained Tsana. "The blade will have a name after it has tasted that for which it has been made. And that name will be—"

"Spirit Sucker." Ban-ya continued to stare at the dagger. She knew its name all too well, from stories she had heard of the cannibalistic terrors practiced by the tribe with whom she was now forced to dwell. The blade was Death. Suddenly she realized what was to be asked of her. She swallowed; there was no saliva in her mouth. She had expected to witness such deeds. She had not expected to perform them.

You have killed before, Ban-ya reminded herself. *You can kill again. For the sake of your son, to save your own life, and to assure vengeance against those who have brought you to this moment, you can do anything!*

Ban-ya rose to her feet, took the dagger from Tsana,

and looked straight into his eyes. "I *am* Sheela," she told him.

"Yes," Tsana replied, his eyes filled with love and pride. "I know."

"We will see what she is," said Jhadel, smiling vindictively. Dressed in all his ceremonial finery, he now began to walk a slow and deliberate circuit of the assembled people.

Ban-ya watched him. She knew what was to come.

"A bride! We seek a bride to come consenting to Thunder in the Sky, Great Spirit of the Watching Star, Maker of Power, Restorer of Strength!" cried the old shaman. "Let the blood of this union with Maker of All be the offering that will render this people strong once more, so that our enemies will tremble as they fall before us in days and nights to come!"

"Come forth, Bride!" called Tsana.

The people echoed his summons.

And from among the gathering several young girls stepped forward. Jhadel came close to appraise them, to touch them, to scent their hair and breath, and reach between their thighs. The girls stood bravely as the old man fingered deep, testing for virginity. The crowd sighed in approval when he drew his fingers from each and nodded, satisfied, then slowly circled the girls until at last, for reasons known only to a shaman's mind, he gently brought one forward.

Ban-ya found herself puzzled by his choice. The girl was shorter than the others and no true beauty. But she was pretty enough in a sturdy, strong-limbed, meaty-bottomed, bosomy-for-her-age way that suddenly caused Ban-ya to catch her breath. If she had not hated Jhadel before, she hated him now; he had chosen the girl who most closely resembled how she herself had looked as an adolescent. And now, as the man saw understanding of his motivation flare within her eyes, he actually laughed at her.

Breathless, Ban-ya tore her eyes from his. The People were singing now a song of solemn joy. She watched the mother and father of the girl come forward to kiss their child upon the mouth.

"You will go bravely to the Watching Star!" declared the father, pride shining in his eyes.

"I will go bravely!" replied the girl, her child's voice high and tight with an odd mixture of excitement, hesitation, and fear.

"You will wait for us in the world beyond this world?" The mother's query was tremulous.

"I will wait! And make the way easy for you when it is time for you to come!" The girl smiled, albeit wanly.

Ban-ya felt sick; unlike the adults, the girl was not quite sure of what was about to happen.

Now, suddenly, came the beat of drums, the high shriek of whistles, and the wailing cadence of flutes. The children and adolescents were sent away to pass the remainder of the night in the care of elders behind woven screens, and the sacred mushroom was passed among the adults. All ate of it. Ban-ya did not find the taste unpleasant. . . .

She was not sure just when the world began to pulse and glow green. She stared ahead, saw the Chosen disrobed and rubbed with red ocher by the old shaman; the color appeared strange, as green as the world. Ban-ya saw Tsana hand the girl a branch of sacred sage, and then somehow the bride was standing before her, with Tsana towering to her right and Jhadel leering close at her left. The girl's eyes appeared strange, the pupils enormous as she looked trustingly up at Ban-ya.

Ban-ya is not here, the Red World woman told herself as she reached out to stroke the girl's hair. *Ban-ya is far away! It is Sheela, in the guise of Spirit Woman, who stands in this place with Death in her hand.*

And so it was Sheela, not Ban-ya, who curled the fingers of her left hand into the bride's hair and pulled the girl's head back as she raised the raven-woman dagger and sent Spirit Sucker to slash the girl's throat from point of jaw to point of jaw. Blood spurted and gushed before the victim knew the cut was made—green blood, it seemed to the woman who had brought it forth. Held by Tsana and Jhadel,

the bride stiffened but could not flee while the second cut
was made. Ugly sounds came from the girl's mouth when
the raven-woman dagger stabbed upward under her ribs,
easily piercing soft, young flesh and muscle as it sought and
found its way deep into the heart of its victim.

The girl slumped, then crumpled onto the ground as the
men let go of her.

Spirit Woman, blinking through a pulsating green
miasma, dropped the dagger and nearly went to her knees
when she saw Tsana doing strange things to the body. As
Jhadel stared at her with penetrating eyes, daring her to
faint, she used the power of her hatred of him to make
herself strong. Suddenly, something warm and wet and
heavy was upon her back, and Tsana had her by the hands.

"Sheela!" He proclaimed the name of his beloved.

Others proclaimed the name back to him.

Spirit Woman heard it through a green haze. The smell
of blood was strong in her nostrils as Jhadel handed her
something dark and pulsing. His eyes made her understand
that she was to eat of the heart of her victim. She obliged,
and the People cheered. It tasted sweet, as raw meat always
tasted, and yet it was all she could do to keep from retching
as she passed it back to the old man. Jhadel took his share,
tearing into it, his eyes never leaving hers when he passed
the heart to Tsana. The headman half buried his face in the
organ, then, bloodied from chin to cheekbones, he gave it to
Indeh and turned his full attention to his reborn woman.

"Come!" he invited, and led her in a dance she feared
she would not know.

The gathering roared.

Jhadel glowered.

With the flayed corpse of the victim at her feet, Spirit
Woman danced in the skin of the bride. She did know this
dance. It was the dance of triumph, the dance of rebirth. It
was a savage, instinctive rhythm; her response to it was
driven by the heart blood she had partaken of, and the man
who danced before her guided her in the way her steps must
lead.

"Now!" urged Tsana.

The celebrants roared again.

The tempo of the dance quickened and intensified. Spirit Woman saw that Tsana had thrown off his garments to dance naked before her, ready to respond to a rhythm even more instinctive than the first. And this dance she knew well. Holding up her milk-laden breasts and offering them to her partner, she then joined with him for all to see, reveling in the feel of him deep inside her, wrapping herself and the man in the skin of the bride until, slipping in gore, they went to their knees and, still joined, moved together in a frenzied mating while thunder rolled over the Valley of the Dead.

Now men and women of the People of the Watching Star joined the savage dance while Jhadel took the raven-woman dagger and portioned the flesh of the bride so that it could be shared by all. But of all this green-blooded cannibalistic madness, Ban-ya knew nothing. She was not there. Sheela, Spirit Woman, had done it all.

In the days and nights that followed, the consciousness of the Red World woman gradually emerged through the mists of Spirit Woman's mind. Ban-ya trembled from memories that she would not acknowledge to be anything other than grotesque nightmares, and she would often become cold with fear as she observed her surroundings and circumstances.

Jhadel kept mainly to the inner cavern now, and the enemies with whom Ban-ya was forced to share her cave were growing stronger and more committed to their purpose of abandoning the Valley of the Dead and journeying forth to hunt the totem. While she watched them and listened to their endless talk of power, confusion swarmed in her head like insects winging over a bog on a windless summer day. She stared at the altar that had been made of the bones of the great white mammoth, and she wondered why the People of the Watching Star sought that which was dead. Then she remembered the painting upon the inner wall of the sacred cavern.

The totem has been reborn! Somewhere far from this place, a little white mammoth calf walks strong in the power of the forces of Creation. Cha-kwena and Shateh guard this child of Life Giver. But with Shateh's son held hostage by their enemy, the warriors from the Land of Grass will be ordered by their chieftain to stand aside while Tsana's men slay and take into themselves the living power of Life Giver.

Her feelings of regret for the newborn totem's fate vanished as bitterness about her own predicament caused a shift in Ban-ya's perspective. *Because of Shateh and Cha-kwena I am alone with my baby among cannibals who will slay me and my child if I ever give them cause to suspect that my son is not Shateh's or if they come to believe that I am anything other than a corpse animated by the spirit of a dead woman!*

Ban-ya moaned, sickened by misery and apprehension. Tsana had been working every day with the youths of the band, teaching them to perfect their skills both at hand-to-hand combat and with their newly made spears. Soon they would be prepared for war in the eventuality that Shateh refused to allow them to have their way with the totem. The thought nearly drove her mad with fright, for she had no doubt that if it came to that, Tsana would slay her little hostage of a son as easily as he had skinned the corpse of the bride.

It would be so good to see all of them die, she thought, *Cha-kwena and the People of the Red World, Shateh and the People of the Land of Grass, and Jhadel and Tsana and all of the People of the Watching Star! With them dead, I would—*

The small pleasure that Ban-ya had taken in her thoughts bled out of her as she realized that her little boy Piku-neh and beloved grandmother Kahm-ree still lived among those who had abandoned her, and with all of those hated tribes dead, she and little Ea-ka would be alone again.

Now, with the baby asleep at her breast, she sat in her

favorite place—in full sunlight at the edge of the cave. Nevertheless Ban-ya shivered as she looked at the child and wondered what the future would bring him. She could not be sure of anything these days, except of the fact that this infant was not Shateh's son. The boy was plump, healthy, and resembled his true father, Dakan-eh, more and more every day in disposition as well as appearance. The realization was disturbing. Would Shateh see the truth? And even if he was duped into accepting this son of her body, what would become of her? Surely he would never forgive her for what she had done to Atonashkeh. Ban-ya cringed from the memories of Shateh's killing his own son to end the young man's agony.

And what of Tsana? Confrontation with Shateh would eventually reveal the nature of the crimes for which she had been found guilty and left to die by the chieftain. Would Tsana continue to be beguiled by her then? But it was Sheela whom Tsana loved, not Ban-ya.

With a start, she saw that he was ascending the narrow, rough-cut stairs to the cave. Watching him, Ban-ya felt her heart pounding. She knew what must happen now. She was clutching Ea-ka so tightly that the baby woke and began to fuss.

"Hush, my little one!" she whispered in a fever of desperation. "Remember, as long as Tsana believes that you are Shateh's son and that Sheela lives within me, we are both safe! And if he comes to love this woman and not the other, then all will be well for us both and—" She cut short her words. Tsana was standing before her.

"Sheela . . ." The man's need growled out of him as he loosed his loin covering.

Ban-ya tensed at the sight of him. Rumor had whispered its way to her that since Sheela's death, he had not taken a man's release upon a woman until his first coupling with Spirit Woman. Now that he believed that his beloved had returned to him, it was not enough for him to have her every night. He also came to her every day. And every day the ever-watchful Oan hurried from her solitary fire to take Ea-ka from his mother's arms.

Among the People of the Red World and of the Land of Grass, the traditions of the Ancient Ones forbade a man to copulate with a nursing mother; but here in the Valley of the Dead, the surviving People of the Watching Star and their headman, Tsana, mated wherever and however the mood took them. Now Ban-ya saw the hunger in Tsana's eyes and enlarged, upright condition of his exposed man bone; she knew that he would be in no mood for the extensive foreplay that pleased him in the night.

Without protest, Ban-ya yielded the baby to the scar-faced woman, then lay back, spread herself, and accepted from him that which soon made him weak in her arms while he gasped the name that was not her name.

Ban-ya's mouth twisted. *It is Sheela he wants. And if Ban-ya would live, it is Sheela he must have.* "Yes!" she cried in mimicry of expended passion. "Yes! Come again and again. Fill Sheela with your life, as you have yearned to do for so long. She cannot have enough of you!"

Tsana levered up and, while his people gathered to appreciate yet another of his many displays of masculine prowess, he worked his woman until release was his once more. All the while she moved and groaned with simulated pleasure until, sated at last, Tsana withdrew and left her.

Ban-ya sat up and watched him go to the main fire. Other women would offer food and water to him now; after coupling, Tsana preferred not to look at her. Ban-ya understood and feared the reason why: His mind was filled with memories of the one he truly loved.

Dangerous. Dangerous. You must please him always, or he will see through your deception.

"Here, Spirit Woman. The son of Shateh hungers," informed Oan, holding the baby to its mother.

Ban-ya took the child and suckled it until she was aware of Tsana's watching her out of dark, steady, speculative eyes. Startled, she was chilled, then burned by fear. She felt her face flush. Why was he looking at her? What did he see now that he so seldom wished to see after he had taken a man's release on her? No longer the foul, emaciated thing that he had found near death within the cave, she had sleek skin, smooth flesh, and breasts nearly what they had been before the starvation. But she was still and would always be Ban-ya—not Sheela. *Never* Sheela.

Suddenly unbearably hot in the light of the sun, Ban-ya rose to her feet and sought the place within the cave where she kept the many fine, newly made bed furs and garments that Tsana had ordered prepared for his beloved. She sat down, pulled a meticulously stitched robe of matched wolf skins around herself, and leaned against the cool stone wall; a draft of air cooled her cheek, wafting from one of many narrow, almost invisible fissures that led into the interior of the hill. She closed her eyes, felt Ea-ka at her breast, and tried to calm the pounding of her heart.

She was not sure just when the old woman from one of the newly arrived bands came close to look at the baby. "Hmmm . . . there is no look of Shateh about this one."

"What know you of Shateh?" demanded Ban-ya, annoyed and disturbed. She strained to affect her best Spirit Woman voice as she claimed, "His spirit is here in this child, in his son."

"Hmmm," the woman repeated, cocking her head this way and that as she admired the baby. "I saw a son of Shateh's once," she mused, mainly to herself. "It was long ago. At the time I thought he was a man of our own tribe. Later I learned he was one of those sons whom Shateh threw away upon the wind. Ysuna, Daughter of the Sun, found him in the storms and raised him to be one of us." She shook her head in remembrance. "A beautiful boy. His mother must have wept for the loss of such a son. Some have said he was the best of us. From what I saw, I would agree. But then you must already know all about that, Spirit Woman."

For a moment Ban-ya thought that the old woman had finished speaking and was about to go her way. Instead she closed her eyes and, drifting happily in her memories, continued.

"A blizzard kept him a day and a night within our village. He made a son upon a daughter of mine while her man was away. My daughter never told him. She shared the secret only with me, for her man was a jealous sort, and although he would have considered it an honor to have his woman chosen to entertain Masau, the great and powerful Mystic Warrior, he would never have allowed her to carry the life of another man's child. Many seasons later Mystic Warrior passed through our hunting ground again; my daughter and I greeted him as a stranger. He eyed the child. Hmmm. I wonder if he knew? . . . If he did, out of respect for my daughter's man, he said nothing. But I knew what he had made." She opened her eyes and appeared to be staring into yesterday. "What a fine child he was—a lean, quick, and clever boy with eyes as black as obsidian, not like this small, plump scrap you suckle. No, your babe has the look of the People of the Red World." She paused and turned her eyes thoughtfully and kindly at Ban-ya. "It is good to have sons. All of my boys are gone, killed in the great war. And my daughters. And my band. I left before the massacre, to live in the village of the son of my long-dead brother. He is a good man to keep me and—"

Ban-ya cut short the old woman's rambling. "And this so-called son of Masau—Shateh's grandson—he is dead, too?"

The old woman sighed wistfully. "I have been told that he and his sister survived the war and came as orphans to live with Tsana's band. When Neea was honored by Great Spirit and given as a bride and sacrifice to Thunder in the Sky, Warakan ran away. It is not likely that he survived the storms of winter."

A stunned, disbelieving Ban-ya was grateful to be seated apart from the others in a place at the back of the cave, where a cool draft of air kept her from swooning. "Warakan? You are sure of the name?"

"It was the name given him by the man of my

daughter," affirmed the old one. "It was meant to honor his own father's life spirit; but of course it could not, for his blood and the blood of his father were not in that boy. The blood of the chieftain of the Land of Grass was in him, and I tell you now that Warakan was the best of boys, a brave son worthy to take the name of the strongest man of his line—of Shateh himself! Had Warakan lived, he would have grown up to be a great hunter, warrior, and shaman, a man deserving of that chieftain's name and life spirit. But it was not to be. For you, at least, this is a good thing, eh? For if Warakan still lived and Shateh were to know of him, this plump little bundle you suckle would not be a valuable hostage. But as I have said, it was long ago, and I have told no one of it. And I know that I can trust Sheela, Spirit Woman, to keep my secret."

6

Warakan was not at all sure of his new role in life, but he did know that being Boy Mother of Bears was no easy thing.

"It is true what they say about twins!" Warakan declared. "You are trouble, Little Bear Brothers! But since I have made myself your mother, what am I to do? I must take care of my cubs."

Boy Mother of Bears hunted for his "children" with snares and lances fashioned from the long bones and sinew of their true mother. He worried that he had no milk to give them and, not knowing what else to do, gave them the blood of his kills instead, mashing the meat of birds and small rodents and an occasional deer in it and encouraging them to suck this "baby bear food" from his fingers.

By day Warakan kept moving. The cubs gamboled along at his heels, slowing his forward progress with endless explorations and side trackings that often drove him to shouting distraction.

"Where are you off to now? Come back, I say! We will never reach the edge of the world or find Cha-kwena and the sacred stone if you do not obey and keep up with your mother!"

Toward dusk of each day, Boy Mother of Bears would seek protected places where he and his cubs could pass the night in safety. Sometimes he would be lucky enough to

356

find a small cave that offered no scent or sign to warn of occupation by other predators. More often he would secrete himself and his children within large hollows beneath the exposed roots of trees that grew along cut banks or find a little space of safety within encircling boulders. Once the place of sleep was chosen, he would set snares and little deadfall traps or, if a stream was nearby, raise fishing weirs of sticks before retiring, so when dawn began to eat of the night, he and his cubs would also have food, fresh meat with which to strengthen them for the long journey that lay ahead.

Always, no matter how secure his evening retreat, Warakan kept his lances at the ready, for he knew that he led his children across a land in which they were not the only hunters. On a cold, wind-driven day not long after turning his back to the drowned land, the boy, bundled against the weather in the skin of the slain bear, had seen a good-sized band of hunters moving across the curve of the western hills. He had been shouting at the cubs at the time but was immediately startled into silence. He stared westward in hope of seeing Shateh coming for him, but the only thing that had come his way was a well-hurled lance. The spear had struck so near that he could still hear it slicing the air near his ear as it sped on its way to graze one cub's shoulder.

"Killers of little bears! What kind of hunters are you?" Warakan had roared in outrage while the wounded cub scampered away in pain and fright. The men hurried off beyond the curve of the western horizon. "Come back! I will return your lance, straight through the belly of the one who has thrown it at my cubs!"

The men had not come back, and Warakan had been glad. The lance was of a color and with markings that were completely unfamiliar to the boy, and although it had occurred to him that the strangers might have known the way in which Cha-kwena had gone, the injured cub was in need of his attention. He had taken up the lance, picked up his unwounded child, and spent the rest of the afternoon convincing the injured orphan to come to him.

That night the little bear had sucked the boy's thumb and whimpered itself to sleep while Warakan licked its shallow shoulder wound. And on many a night that followed, the boy and the bear cubs huddled together, listening to the songs of dire wolves and lions and, sometimes, even to the curious huffing of a passing bear.

Breathless with apprehension, Warakan would whisper to the cubs, "Be still, Little Bear Brothers, we have many enemies, you and I. And the scent of Man is on you now. The bear kind will eat you if they find you. Lion and Wolf and all of the toothed and fanged hunters of night will see us only as meat. So stay close to Warakan! Boy Mother of Bears has lances and stones and, thanks to the warrior cowards who ran away from us, a great, man-sized spear! This boy will keep you safe if he can."

And so the days and nights passed for Boy Mother of Bears and his cubs as Warakan strode boldly across familiar country toward the very edge of the world and beyond. All that he had learned from the great war chief Shateh, from the old hunter Lahontay, and from his original band came to the fore. His skills and effortless adaptation to new situations sometimes surprised him, and since he had passed this way before, his recollection of the landscape eased the way ever eastward into and across the badlands. He knew where to find water. He knew where to find the best camps. When he began to find piles of stones and an occasional scratched rock and notched sapling, he felt puzzled, for surely this was a trail of some kind. He followed it and soon came to an old campsite.

"Is the Red World shaman Cha-kwena deliberately marking the way he has gone, or is Trickster attempting to lead me off his path into the rising sun?" Warakan asked the cubs.

They did not reply, nor did they seem interested; they were wrestling and grunting and rolling on the ground like a pair of young boys testing each other's mettle. Warakan frowned, remembering many such past skirmishes with Namaray.

THE EDGE OF THE WORLD

The *chack* of a shrike proved a welcome diversion. When the black-masked bird appeared out of a tangle of thornbush, Warakan followed its flight and could not keep himself from taking the appearance of the bird as a sign. "You have led me well in the past, Brother Shrike. Where would you have me set my footsteps now?"

The bird led him into nearby low hills. The cubs followed, then took the lead, happily chasing ground squirrels and lizards. Following his children when they scrambled upward across stony scree under the shadowing wings of the shrike, Warakan was soon brought to pause by large crystals of some of the finest white quartz he had ever seen. Hunkering down, he shook his head and examined them.

When the cubs came sniffing close, he told them, "This white stone is among the most difficult to work; but in the hands of a master knapper, it could be fashioned into projectile points fit for the greatest chief or shaman! I have heard it said that the Mystic Warrior, Masau, made great spearheads . . . magic spearheads . . . weapons of great power . . . from such stone. They were lost in the war but found by Cha-kwena, who used one, it is said, to take the life of the totem in the Valley of the Dead. After that they were lost once more and—"

Warakan caught his breath, stunned by sudden inspiration. "If I were to bring such fine white stone to the Red World shaman as gifts from my hands to his, perhaps he would accept them as an offering of goodwill between us and agree to return with the sacred stone to Shateh's land?"

The question hung in the air.

The shrike made low, chortling noises in its gray throat. The cubs lost interest in the white rocks and took off after a blue-tailed skink.

"With the sacred stone in his hand, Cha-kwena could bring the greatest gifts of all to Shateh—good weather and much game and the confidence of his people! Then Shateh will not be angry at this boy."

Warakan looked across the land and decided that Cha-kwena might have traveled over the edge of the world by way of the Valley of the Dead. "Yes. The great white mammoth died in that place. Its bones lie within a sacred lake. We will go there. Perhaps if I touch those bones, they will allow me to see in which direction the new totem has gone."

Night settled upon the earth. The stars made Warakan think of the many cooking fires of Shateh's village and caused him to long for the day when he would return to his adopted tribe. Snuggling close to the cubs, he again confided his greatest hope of all—that with the return of Cha-kwena and the sacred stone, Shateh would look upon him once again with favor. "I will never receive the gift of his name or be the one honored to take his life spirit on the day he leaves this world to walk the wind forever. But if I bring him the sacred stone, perhaps I can hope to be at least his friend. With Cha-kwena at my side, it is possible. You will see. Cha-kwena has great power. He is totem. Those who walk in his favor also walk in the favor of the Four Winds and the forces of Creation."

Again the shrike, perched nearby on a weather-stunted tree, made low, chortling noises. Warakan found himself staring at the bird, confiding his thoughts to it as though to an old friend. "What is it *you* would say to me, Shrike? Do you mock me for suggesting the possibility of bringing gifts to one who has made himself an enemy of Shateh's? Perhaps you are right. Even if I do manage to convince Cha-kwena to welcome me among his runaway band, there is no way I will be able to convince him to return to my people. We both know that Shateh would kill him. And yet I must make Cha-kwena believe that I am a friend! How else am I to steal the sacred stone?"

The question was disturbing, as was the realization that he had not considered it before. Warakan frowned down at the pale, sun-warmed quartz crystal that he held within the cup of his hands, absently smoothing its glistening surface with his thumbs. "Just how *am* I going to get the stone away from Cha-kwena when I discover the place to which he has taken it?" he asked, and looked again at the bird. "I cannot just walk up to him and ask for it, nor will it be an easy thing to steal; he wears it always around his neck."

More disturbed than ever, the boy shook his head. "I suppose I could sneak up on him when he is alone. The big spear of the would-be little-bear killers is mine, and the fire-hardened bone lances that the great bear mother yielded to me for the protection of her cubs fly straight upon the wind. Even though I am only a boy and Cha-kwena is a man and a shaman, I would not be afraid to take his life!"

The statement brought Warakan to pause. The veracity of his boast was open to question, and he knew it. "Cha-kwena is not only a shaman, you know," he informed the shrike. "He is Totem Slayer! And he is Trickster, too, clever enough to have gained Shateh's trust in order to secure the alliance of Land of Grass warriors in war against his enemies."

Now the boy's frown became a scowl; he did not want to acknowledge the identity of those enemies. With an indignant huff, he dismissed all thought of his native tribe. "Cha-kwena was brave in war. You should have seen him, Shrike! All who fought beside him saw that the power of the slain totem was in him. How else could a Red World man who had grown up eating lizards, ant eggs, and boiled grubs have been so brave and strong? Shateh named him Brother and Totem and Shaman when the fighting was done. The trust of People of the Land of Grass was his. But Shateh is a shaman as well as chief. He needed no lizard eater to call the spirits! I knew this! And somehow, all along, I knew that Cha-kwena was Enemy."

Warakan shook his head again, puzzling over past events. "Why? When the war was over, why did he turn upon those who named him Friend? Why did he pretend that he had no power, even as he was calling upon the Four Winds and the forces of Creation to work his will against Shateh? *Why*, Shrike? And how am I, a small and insignificant boy, going to trick Trickster himself? Cha-kwena will never allow me to come into his band. I am afraid that it will take a shaman to trick a shaman or to kill one, and I have none of the blood of their kind in me!"

The shrike chortled for a third time, cocked its black-masked head, and moved aggressively forward among the branches. Warakan cocked his own head as, appraising the bird, he thought of a man—of Masau, Mystic Warrior. Handsome, arrogant, sitting straight backed and cross-legged in the guest's place of honor in the meager lodge of Warakan's parents, the man would appraise him out of long, black eyes that had been as sharp and finely shaped and somehow as dangerous as obsidian projectile points . . . eyes set in a mask of black bands of tattooing . . . just like the eyes of the shrike.

A wave of revulsion swept through Warakan. He had heard men say that Shrike had been the helping animal spirit of the shaman Masau; if true, the alliance would have been fitting, for despite the beauty of the man and of the bird, both were dangerous, treacherous carnivores who took their prey unaware before impaling it—the bird upon thorns, the man upon projectile points flaked from chalcedony.

Warakan stared at the stone in his hand. "Chalcedony. Rare white quartz. It is the same!"

The boy snapped to his feet and threw the chunk of pale, glistening rock at the bird. "Go away! Why do you follow me? I want no part of your kind! Masau may have made peace with Shateh before his life spirit went to walk the wind forever, but before that day he was a cannibal priest of the Watching Star, an impaler of women captives, and slayer of many brave warriors. If his shaman spirit lives in you, he has no cause to follow one who is glad that he is dead forever! I am Warakan, Boy Mother of Bears, and if an animal spirit has chosen to help me in this life, it is not you, Shrike! It is the great she-bear whose skin I wear and whose blood and flesh now lives on in me and my little bear children!"

His tirade done, Warakan stood angrily on the hillside and surveyed the vast distances of empty land into which his long trek had brought him. The shrike disappeared into low, thick, tangled woodland, and the boy's words echoed back to him, mocking him, from the walls of some distant canyon that he could not see. Somewhere to the east, a blue jay was scolding. Even though the sun was hot upon his back, Warakan shivered and drew the bearskin close around his shoulders.

Drawn by the noise of the cubs bounding recklessly through a thick gray thicket of artemisia, Warakan looked downslope. Although the wind was cool and carried the scent of distant glacier-clad mountains, the light of the sun was intense upon the scree-covered hill. The pale rocks radiated heat and a glare that forced him to squint. He saw his charges running in happy pursuit of the stone that he had thrown and causing a small, dusty avalanche of loose pebbles to go clattering down the hill.

Warakan smiled despite himself at the antics of his children. He was amused by their boundless enthusiasm and curiosity and pleased by the rich, oily scent of sagebrush that rose from the many leaves that their paws had crushed. Sage was sacred. The scent of it in his nostrils seemed a benediction as the boy was suddenly struck by the extraordinary beauty of the day. Observing the surrounding majesty of wild hills, distant mountains, and cloudless, eye-burning blue sky, Warakan regretted his display of anger toward the shrike. The race of the river had carried him into the hunting grounds of the bird's kind; simply because its appearance reminded him of one whose memory stirred hatred within him was no reason to transfer his feelings of animosity to the creature. After all, the shrike had done him no wrong; if anything, it had led him to the one possible chance he had of finding a way to win the confidence of the Red World shaman Cha-kwena when at last he found him.

Warakan knelt and picked up another chunk of quartz. "I have not the skill to strike from this chalcedony projectile points such as those lying at the bottom of the lake in the Valley of the Dead, but even a shaman and trickster such as Cha-kwena cannot fail to be dazzled by such fine stone! He can knap them himself or let the man Kosar-eh do it for him! Surely he will welcome me and never guess my intent when I come before him with such a wondrous gift!"

An invisible cloud of doubt drifted across Warakan's mood. In this moment neither the cool wind, sunstruck vistas, nor scent of sage pleased him. Indeed, he was unaware and unsure of anything except the extent of his foolishness. Across the long miles he had been so preoccupied with his own survival and care of the cubs that he had not thought past the singular need that drove him on—his hope of someday returning to his beloved Shateh with the sacred stone in his hand.

For Warakan the future seemed less bright until his doleful gaze fixed across the all-too-empty world and, with a start, recognized the distant pass that led into the Valley of the Dead. Now hope flared as brightly within him as inspiration. When the cubs came charging upslope to flop and roll into his lap in search of hugs and scratches, he gave them exactly what they desired as he spoke to them in great excitement.

"Our friend Shrike has led us well!" he declared. "We must thank him when next we see him. Do you see that pass into the mountains? The great white mammoth totem gave up its life spirit to Cha-kwena in the valley beyond. Its bones lie there within the shallows of a sacred lake. Maybe there is still some magic left there in those bones, just enough for one small boy and his little bear children. We will go there and find out."

The possibility left the boy breathless and teary-eyed. Curious about the shining wet streaks upon his cheeks, the bears slurped kisses across his face. Warakan slurped them back, as a good mother bear would do, and then he laughed, remembering the long, hard way he had come and the many times he had done battle with the forces of Creation in order to reach this particular place alive.

Suddenly his task did not seem so impossible. It did not seem so unlikely that he might walk once more at the chieftain's side and know that Shateh looked upon him again with favor.

"The Four Winds have been with us, Little Bear Brothers!" Warakan told his cubs. "In the Valley of the Dead, we will touch the bones of the once-living totem, then go forth together to take the sacred stone from Cha-kwena. We will find a way. I know we will! That Red World trickster of a shaman has walked strong in the favor of the forces of Creation far too long!"

7

Nothing was the same; everything was changing. The Four Winds were scourging Cha-kwena's life, and he could not understand why. Ever since he had returned to his people, the old, mind-stultifying languor was on him by day and kept him dreamless by night. He could not understand it; with the rebirth of the totem, then the herd's disappearance after the earthquake and the misery suffered by his band, his sleep should have been charged with dreams and omens, warnings or hope. With no dreams to interpret, he could not be a shaman for his people. He was powerless, directionless.

Although unpredictable, shivering lurches and occasional hard, sudden jolts that had followed the shaking of the earth were rare, now and then the ground still moved, and despite his best efforts at calling upon the spirits of the ancestors to intercede on behalf of his people with the forces of Creation, his sense of Vision was more elusive than ever before. And everything continued to go wrong for his band.

Sitting glumly outside his lodge, the young shaman scanned upward across the canopy of hardwoods and dying evergreens. He was a stranger in this forest; he could find no beauty in it. Summer was hot and oppressively humid within the dark woods. Animals and birds that he did not know called and sang and moved both night and day within screens of unfamiliar trees and thick matting of undergrowth. Insects swarmed everywhere around the encampment and newly born sacred spring. The children complained of bites and rashes, and everyone, including the usually calm and imperturbable Ta-maya, was irritable. Gah-ti was down with a fever. And, after an intensive search for the mammoth, Cha-kwena had yet to locate the herd or the little white calf that was totem.

"We must go deeper into the forest," he said. "We must follow the totem. Owl will show us the way. I have heard him calling my name in the night." He frowned, knowing that he was not altogether sure of this; his dreams had been turgid rivers of mud that granted him insight into nothing save confusion. "The totem is there, waiting for us." Of this much he was sure—or was he?

"Where?" demanded Kosar-eh, looking up from his work; with no source of good, malleable stone nearby, he had set himself to reknap much-used spearheads and tools that might otherwise have been discarded. "Not even the dogs have returned to us from out of that dark and cursed woodland! No doubt they have formed their own band and returned to the land of sun and sky! And now you would lead us deeper into the darkness of those trees? Where are the mammoth, Cha-kwena? I have heard no trumpeting from them in days."

"They are there. The totem is with them. Ahead . . . *somewhere*." Cha-kwena knew that his vagueness would not be appreciated, but Kosar-eh's constant challenges were rattling him—and abrading what little was left of his people's faith in their shaman . . . and his faith in himself.

"I will go nowhere until Gah-ti is well," replied the big man, his tone acerbic. "And when he is strong enough to travel, the last thing I will consider is venturing deeper into this—"

"There is nothing wrong with me!" protested Gah-ti with a surly snap. He lounged against the moss-thick trunk of a downed tree well away from the nearest lodge. "The water in this place makes a strange thirst in me, that is all."

"Then why will you not drink to satisfy that thirst?" Kosar-eh responded in an equally surly manner that did not quite manage to hide his deep concern. "The women bring water to you, and you shout them away as though you wished to bite them! Not since witnessing the behavior of that bad-tempered dog that Cha-kwena killed have I seen such nastiness as you have been showing to—"

"I cannot drink!" Gah-ti interrupted. His hand went to his throat. "I am thirsty. So thirsty! But it hurts to drink. My throat makes war on all that would pass through it, even my own spit!" This said, he made a convulsive effort to swallow and was suddenly overcome by paroxysms that shook him as viciously as Mother Below had once shaken the land.

Mah-ree was at his side in an instant. Bending to touch him, she attempted to soothe him with soft words and stroking of her gentle, healing hands. He screamed, back-handing her away so ferociously that she fell. Both Kosar-eh and Cha-kwena leaped to their feet and went to him, but his brothers hung back, staring as grimly as the women and girls who had come from their lodges. Seeing the young man screeching and twitching and slobbering upon the ground, little Tla-nee began to cry.

"Others drink from the spring and do not grow ill!" Cha-kwena shouted in frustration and anger to the spirits of the forest. "Why, then, does this man suffer?"

Mah-ree was on her feet. Visibly shaken, she stared down at Gah-ti and made no attempt to hide her unhappiness. "Medicine Woman does not know what to do for this Cannot Drink sickness. Gah-ti will not swallow the medicines I make. He has said that his skin hurts. Now that the totem has been reborn, maybe Gah-ti's arm has begun to grow back, and this suffering that he endures will soon end. But in the meantime you must use special shaman magic, Cha-kwena, so that he will swallow the healing drinks and oils!"

"What do you think I *have* been doing!" demanded Cha-kwena, resenting her implication that he had not been doing enough. He was in no mood to be pressured by her.

Mah-ree had changed toward him since he had re-turned to the village after the earthquake. Indeed, every-one's attitude toward him had become noticeably guarded. U-wa had been cool toward him and had not said so much as a word to Mah-ree since his little girl-of-a-woman had spoken aloud of the rebirth of the totem. Well aware of her guilt in this, Mah-ree was greatly sobered and contrite; nevertheless, she was not the only one who had been unable to forget Gah-ti's revelation about "her shaman's" breaking of the taboo against naming. Sometimes Cha-kwena would find her looking at him with such a sad expression of hurt and disappointment that he would wince, ashamed, and often he would look up during a meal and see such aching earnestness and love in her eyes that he would be distracted to the point of anger. He would not love her, could not love her, until he managed to refocus his powers and bring his people to find the totem once again.

At last, under the strong, sure restraint from his hands and Kosar-eh's, Gah-ti was relaxing, staring upward in drooling, gasping confusion. Cha-kwena's heart ached to see him like this. Suddenly aware of Kosar-eh's gaze, he turned his head to see that the big man was looking at him with an expression that the young shaman had never before seen in his eyes: contempt. And hatred.

"I think maybe you have lied to us, Cha-kwena," Kosar-eh accused in a low voice.

"It will not be the first time," Mah-ree said, sighing.

Cha-kwena glared at her.

"I think maybe there is no power in this place," Kosar-eh continued. "I think maybe there is no totem, no mammoth, only Death . . . as there was for Shateh when he called you Shaman."

Cha-kwena felt his face flame. "What are you imply-ing?"

"I imply nothing. I ask, and I accuse. If Life Giver has been reborn, then when are things going to get better for our people, and when will someone other than you set eyes on the totem—if there *is* a totem?"

A wan, almost reluctant response came from Mah-ree as she spoke out. "Little Doh-teyah has told me that she has seen it."

"In her dreams!" Kosar-eh was furious. "In images conjured from a shaman's empty promises! Do not try to twist my hopes with words, Shaman's Woman! You and your man both broke the taboo against naming. What am I to think when Cha-kwena has vowed that my little one would regain her sight and that my Gah-ti's arm would grow again when the totem was reborn and—"

"I will be all right, my father," Gah-ti interrupted Kosar-eh again, looking worriedly at Mah-ree. "Let me rest here awhile. The pain is passing. I—"

"All right is *not* enough!" Now the father interrupted the son. "If the totem has been reborn, then you should be well and strong, and all should be good for this people! This is what Shaman has promised!"

"The *ancestors* have promised!" reminded Cha-kwena. "I have only repeated their vow!"

Kosar-eh's face convulsed with anger. "Then let me repeat this: I say that you have seen no little white calf in the dark woods. No totem! No mammoth! No omens of power! I say that you have led us here to hide from enemies of whom you are afraid! I say that you have used the name of the totem to lure us on with false hope in wondrous things that can never be."

"The totem *has* been reborn!" Cha-kwena was emphatic.

"Even though you and your woman broke the taboo against naming?" Kosar-eh pressed.

Mah-ree appeared pale enough to faint.

Cha-kwena either did not notice or did not care. "Life Giver walks in the dark woods in the skin of the little white calf. I *have* seen it!"

"Then what of its powers?" queried Kosar-eh with disbelief. "And what good is the sacred stone? We have risked all to guard them both. As reward, the world trembles beneath us while we mourn our dead, springs become sour or vanish into the earth, my daughter remains blind, and my one-armed son is driven by pain to be dangerous to himself and all who come near. Is this how we are compensated by the forces of Creation for obeying their will and turning our back upon the land of our ancestors and all that we have known and loved? While my woman grieves and my heart bleeds for my dead infant, my blind daughter, and my suffering son, I say to you, Cha-kwena, that we would have been better off to remain in the country of Shateh and take our chances with his tribe than to live as we live now."

"Impossible! After all that has happened, how can you say this? We are bound to follow the totem!"

"Ah, Cha-kwena, I have come to think that you care more about the mammoth than you do about your own people. The herd was content in the country of Shateh. It is you who took it upon yourself to drive the mammoth to the east."

"Because Shateh is our enemy! He would have forced you to abandon two of your children, and he would have slain Mah-ree and—"

"It was you who drove him to this. It was you who betrayed his trust. The totem could have been born under the eyes of the People of the Land of Grass."

"Then Shateh's hunters would have slain the great cow and eaten of the sacred calf and—"

"So you say."

Cha-kwena was staggered by the man's challenge and loss of faith in him. "This I have foreseen in my dreams. If the mammoth walk ahead of us, it is because they are leading us to better country. I will go into the forest again. I will find the totem and prove to you that this is so."

Kosar-eh's head swung back and forth. "Again and again since making this new camp you have sought the mammoth. With your own mouth you have told us that there is no fresh sign of the herd—no new droppings, no scent or trace of recently released urine, no newly tusked-up earth or torn bark upon trees." He clucked his tongue with droll admonition. "But then, it is a spirit mammoth we seek . . .

a totem calf . . . and perhaps it has no need to eat or defecate. Indeed, then, it will be difficult for mere mortal men to track it."

"My shaman *is* Shaman!" proclaimed Mah-ree; but the defense of her man had not put the color back in her cheeks. "He *must* be!"

"Prove it," responded Kosar-eh.

"Yes," echoed Gah-ti with an earnestness that twisted his exhausted features with yearning. "Prove it . . . please, Cha-kwena . . . please prove it!"

Cha-kwena was shaken. His hand sought his medicine bag; he clutched the sacred stone. "I will go into the forest now. I will find the totem and prove to you that my words have been true words."

"No." Kosar-eh shook his head again. "The only remarkable spoor that I have seen around the encampment has been the leavings of a sickly bear on the path that leads to the springs."

"Ah!" exclaimed Mah-ree. "Perhaps it is the same bear that I saw when we first entered the forest!"

"Perhaps," he conceded, in no mood for distraction. "But I would imagine that this black woods is home to many of its kind. It would not be a good thing for Cha-kwena to go far from the village now, with only this one man and his boys to guarantee the safety of the women and children. Shaman must use his magic to heal you here, Gah-ti, in this place." He paused and turned his face from his son to Cha-kwena. "If you are a shaman, Cha-kwena, then use your power to call forth the totem so that we all may see it with our own eyes. Let the white mammoth know and understand that your people are weak with sickness and grief and in need of faith and hope in the future. Do this, Cha-kwena. Convince me that I have not been a fool to trust the lives of my woman and children to one who has led them over the edge of the world to . . . *this*."

For all of the remainder of that day Cha-kwena kept to himself. He fasted now, neither eating nor drinking as he sat alone at the edge of the village in the little circular sanctuary that he had built. U-wa had shown the children how to leave "shaman offerings" of feathers and kindling for their spirit master so that he would be assured of keeping alive the sacred fire and smokes that would take his prayers to the spirit world as he remained withdrawn into his "place of dreams." In absolute silence the children came, like small, venturesome little drafts of wind, for even the smallest among them knew better than to intrude on the sanctity of Cha-kwena's self-imposed solitude. The circle that he had hollowed in the earth and roofed with open boughs was the equivalent of a sacred cave and as close as he could come to such a traditional refuge in this land of trees.

He fasted. He prayed. He sought the visionary path of a shaman's power that would enable him to call forth the totem and bring the mammoth back to the place where he had last seen the herd. Slowly, with neither food nor liquid to distract his thoughts from spirit needs to functions of the flesh, his mind began to clear. But no matter how hard he attempted to will his spirit outside himself, it drifted in a vast, inner emptiness of body that chilled him long before the first cooling breeze of evening moved through the forest and trespassed through the boughs of the sanctuary.

Cha-kwena clutched the sacred stone. Frustrated, he knew that it would take days and nights of endless fasting to accomplish the state of mind he so desperately sought. But now he could not wait! His people needed his shaman power now! And so he implored the spirits of the Ancient Ones and forces of Creation to grant clarity to his thoughts. *The totem has been reborn. The spirit of Life Giver walks once more in the world. I have seen it! Why, then, has it vanished? And why does Spirit Sucker feed upon my band? Since coming into this dark wood I have been so careful to abide by every tradition and to break no taboo that might possibly offend the spirits of the ancestors. Yet I fear that something has upset the forces of Creation and turned the tide of luck against my people. But* what?

And then, when the sound of someone advancing

toward the sanctuary from the heart of the village drew his thoughts and glance outward through open spaces between the boughs, his heart sank as he realized that perhaps he already knew the answer.

Mah-ree was coming toward him.

Cha-kwena stiffened and stared at his beautiful little lawbreaking girl-of-a-woman. She was carrying his winter robe. How lovely she was as she approached through the deepening shadows of impending night, how circumspect in her manner, walking with her head bowed in deference to his rank and gender. Yet, watching her, he frowned and wondered if she had forgotten that it was forbidden to disturb a shaman in his place of dreams. Then he assured himself that Mah-ree had certainly learned from past mistakes as well as he. She would not speak to him as she placed his robe upon the ground. She would leave him, and the taboos of their people, intact.

Perhaps if their eyes had not met through breaks in the boughs it might have been so. Cha-kwena would never know.

Their gaze held. He could not look away. For the first time since he had returned from the forest her eyes did not sting him with reproach. He felt their spirits reach out to each other and experienced such love and wanting for her that he was stunned, completely unaware of speaking her name until it left his lips and he heard it whispering with the wind. "Mah-ree . . ."

What could only have been described as a startled sob of joy came from her throat, and a quick, shy, eager-to-please smile dimpled her face. She knelt and laid the robe before the sanctuary. "The night grows unexpectedly cold. The chill is sweet after the heat of the day. But I have brought my shaman's robe to keep him warm as he summons the totem from his dreams. You must call it forth to us, Cha-kwena! You must! If you can."

" 'If'?" The sound of her voice had been no more than a whisper; nevertheless, its underlying lack of confidence shattered the moment for him. "You dare to break the silence of a shaman's meditations!"

"I . . . n-no! I saw you looking out at me. There was welcome in my shaman's eyes and in his voice. And . . . I thought . . . love. I would not have spoken otherwise. I thought it would be all right to—"

"By the forces of Creation, Mah-ree! You must *stop* thinking! It should be forbidden to you! No wonder the totem has vanished into the forest! Why should it wish to stay close to a village when a lawbreaking woman like you dwells within it? Go!"

Her eyes were enormous. "B-but . . . my shaman was not on the dream path. You *did* call my name and look at me!"

"I do not want to look at you now, Lawbreaker!"

With suddenly quivering chin and brimming eyes, she snapped to her feet. "This woman is not the only lawbreaker in this camp!" Her voice broke as she retreated in hurt confusion.

Cha-kwena watched her go. His conscience flexed. She was right; he had also broken the taboo against naming. And he *had* looked at her. He *had* spoken her name. He had *not* been on the dream path. She had broken no law. *This* time.

The rising wind of evening touched him and chilled him. He reached for the robe, pulled it into the sanctuary, put it on, closed his eyes, took a grip on the sacred stone, and with his owl-skin headdress firmly in place upon his head, called for Vision once more.

It was a long while before it came, a dream of mists and darkness through which he walked alone, without the sacred stone of the ancestors, while the mammoth plodded ahead toward . . .

Cha-kwena woke with a start. Something in the substance of the night told him that great hanks of time had passed since he had closed his eyes. And the distant *oo-ooh*ing of an owl in the woods called him forth to what he must do. He listened. Deeply shaken, he understood.

Despite Kosar-eh's understandable wish for him to remain with the band, he knew that he could not do so. He was impelled to seek the mammoth again. This time he would not return until he had found the totem and driven it and the rest of the herd before him, back to the sacred spring, back to the village, back to the doubting eyes of Kosar-eh.

But before he went his way into the night, there was one additional thing Cha-kwena knew that he must do. For a long moment he remained motionless in the dark. At last, he took the sacred stone from around his neck and set the talisman in the center of the sanctuary, where its power would remain for Kosar-eh and his people if they had need of it.

"Be with them, Spirits of First Man and First Woman, and keep them safe. Now I must follow the totem. May the Four Winds and the forces of Creation grant that I be strong in the power of Life Giver until I return to guard you and be shaman for my people once again!"

Mah-ree could not sleep. Alone in the lodge that Cha-kwena rarely shared with her these days, she lay awake on their sleeping mattress and felt deeply troubled, wanting him to come to her but knowing in her heart that he would not.

"This time I will not say that I was wrong!" Mah-ree whispered to herself as guilt vied with righteous indignation. She closed her eyes and tried hard to relax and will herself into dreams. It was no use. Cha-kwena filled her thoughts.

Mah-ree sat up, pulled her sleeping robe around her shoulders, and stared into darkness, speaking as though her man were before her. "I have been a foolish, loose-tongued, lawbreaking woman many times, but not this time!"

She sighed, longing for her man. She sighed again, found herself unworthy of his love, and nevertheless ached to have him come to her and offer apology for his unwarranted hostility. But Mah-ree knew him well enough to be sure he would not come. Since leading the band to the new encampment he was preoccupied, brooding; he rarely spoke to her these days; but she had to admit that this was her fault even more than his, for she had been so shocked and dismayed by Gah-ti's revelation about her shaman having broken the taboo against naming that for a very long time she had not wanted to talk to him. After all of his warnings! After having struck her and called her Lawbreaker when, nearly all along, he had been Lawbreaker, too! Still again Mah-ree sighed, realizing that to save the totem, he had simultaneously been forced to put the totem at risk; as shaman and guardian of the band, he had been given no choice.

Now, in spite of the woman-wanting potion she had secretly put in his food, nearly all of his nights were spent at the sanctuary; this night would be no different. She felt hurt, wounded by his disinterest in her and unfairness to her, and worried about him, too. Her arms went around her bent knees; she hugged herself, seeking inner warmth and courage to face the thoughts that were running wildly through her mind.

What if Kosar-eh's accusations were true? What if there was no little white mammoth, no totem to lead the People and keep them safe and strong against the Four Winds? What if her shaman had lost his power? He had certainly possessed it when he had led the band away from Shateh and into good hunting grounds beyond the gorge. So, if he was suffering from a lack of it now, it could only be because—on that dreadful day when she had inadvertently broken the taboo against naming—the great matriarch had cast off its sacred calf unborn.

Mah-ree's skin prickled with dread while the ancient warning ran through her consciousness. *On the day the totem dies, the People will begin to die forever.* "And it would be my fault. But no! Cha-kwena has seen the totem! My shaman does not lie! The totem will come! Kosar-eh will see! We *all* will see!"

Beyond the woven walls of the lodge, a strong wind was moving in the trees. Mah-ree raised her head, listening.

And then, suddenly, she was reaching for her moccasins. "I will go to him. Yes! I will wait outside the sanctuary. At dawn the totem will come through the forest in response to my shaman's spirit calling, and I will be there. I will be the one to call the others! And my shaman will know how strong is the faith of Mah-ree in his power!"

And so she went into the night, moving soundlessly away from the sleeping lodges, disturbed by the low, tortured moanings of Gah-ti. Mah-ree's heart bled for him. Just before dark he had dragged his sleeping robe and mattress from the lodge he shared with his brothers. Foaming at the mouth, he shrieked that he could not bear to have anyone near him, then sat down beneath the lichen-clad tree where he had been resting earlier in the day. Young Kiu-neh, nursing a bloody nose, had emerged from the lodge to stare at Gah-ti. Mah-ree could still see the look of bewilderment upon Kiu-neh's face and hear the boy's words as he warned Gah-ti that if he hit his younger brother again or made another aggressive move against any of their siblings, Kiu-neh would kill Gah-ti.

Mah-ree sighed with acute distress and whispered to herself as she tiptoed past, "Ah, my dear friend Gah-ti, I do not know what dark spirits eat away at you these days. But when the totem comes you will be well again. Surely it must be so!"

The sanctuary lay just ahead. She approached, knelt before it, and prepared to wait for the dawn. After a time she realized that no one was inside. Slowly, still on her knees, she advanced, peered through the boughs and into the interior's darkness. There she saw something small and pale lying on a medicine bag at the center of the circular retreat and knew, even before she held it in her hand, that it was the sacred stone.

8

Warakan stood in the high pass that was the entrance to the Valley of the Dead. It was very late or very early; he was not sure which. He and the cubs had come far and traveled many days since leaving the hills to which Shrike had led them. He had risen with the first light of false dawn and now stood staring eastward.

"Come, Little Bear Brothers, you have slept enough," he told the cubs, toeing them gently. "We will go on now. If the spirits of the ancestors are still smiling upon Warakan, perhaps there will be some small power left in the bones of the great white mammoth—just enough to let this boy know if the path of piled stones and notched trees is the true way in which the Red World shaman has gone or only a trick of Trickster to lead us astray."

The words raised his hopes and made him tremble with longing and trepidation. He added softly, "And perhaps when this boy lays his hands upon the sacred bones of the great mammoth, he will find wisdom and courage, not only for the journey ahead but for what he must do if he is ever to return to Shateh."

Steal the sacred stone however you can, even if you have to kill the shaman who possesses it.

Warakan did not speak these words aloud; the closer he came to the Valley of the Dead, the more he felt the presence of potentially hostile spirits and heard their thoughts. Suddenly dry-mouthed, the boy attempted to swallow a wave of rising apprehension. Once, the Red World shaman and his band had resided within a cave in the Valley of the Dead. For all Warakan knew, Cha-kwena had left behind vestiges of his power in that valley, to confound anyone brazen enough to enter it with the intention of seeking the bones of the great white mammoth.

Try to stop me! Boy Mother of Bears will not be afraid! This boy will find you, Cha-kwena, and have the sacred stone for Shateh!

Again words, albeit unspoken, lifted Warakan's hope. The boy assured himself that his prospects for success were good. He tried to swallow; his mouth was dryer than before.

With several selections of unusually fine chalcedony in a bag fashioned from the gutted body of a fox—that animal had made the fatal error of going for the dead mouse in one of Warakan's trip snares—the boy was eager to look again upon the place where the great white mammoth died. The idea of bringing the rare white rock to Cha-kwena as a gift still seemed a good one. Whether the shaman would accept it and be taken in by the one who brought it, that was another thing entirely.

"Whatever happens will happen; but by the power that may or may not lie in the slain totem, this boy has no choice but to go forward and risk whatever awaits him."

Warakan sighed. This time, instead of hope, his words had brought a disquieting sense of fatalism that made him feel bereft. *Find Cha-kwena and take the sacred stone to Shateh or be Outlander forever, alone in this world, unwelcome in the hunting villages of men, named Enemy by all save these two Little Bear Brothers. And in time even these two will go from your side, forgetting Boy Mother of Bears as they go their separate ways to seek bear women and warm dens and the long sleep of bear winter.*

At his feet, the cubs were yawning and stretching sleepily. Warakan looked down at them and noticed that they had grown considerably over the past moon. He wondered if he had changed. He still wore the bearskin robe; it did not seem to be as heavy as it once had.

He turned his face up to the dying night. The stars above his head were as bright as campfires strewn across a vast black plain. Suddenly Warakan smelled the smoke of distant cooking fires. He started, turned, and stared back and down across the way he had come. He could see the morning fires of a sizable encampment of people. His gut constricted. Who was out there? What tribe? What chief?

"Shateh?" Warakan spoke the beloved name with such yearning to be at the chieftain's side that tears of frustration smarted in his eyes. He was momentarily overcome by the same hope that had given him the determination to live after he had come half-drowned from the river. "My father has *not* forgotten me!"

Breathless with excitement, the boy bent, scooped the cubs into his embrace, and lifted them high; they were an armful now, so much so that the heftier of the two dangled over Warakan's back and nibbled at the long strands of his unplaited hair while the other sniffed at his face and earlobe.

"Look, Little Bear Brothers! Shateh comes for Warakan!" he exclaimed.

And then he wondered whether he should be rejoicing or trembling in his crudely fashioned moccasins. There were so many fires—too many for Shateh's band, he realized. Warakan's arms tightened around his cubs. "Could this be the tribe of the would-be little-bear killers?"

The boy's heartbeat quickening, he continued to stare across the distances. Unless he waited until dawn, there was no way to tell who was out there. Even that would not be sufficient; the travelers were simply too far away. He would have to remain at the neck of the pass until well into daylight and perhaps even until dusk before the band came close enough to be identified by the color and adornment of their spears and garments and body paint.

"And if I am wrong about there being too many fires, why would Shateh take the entire band out of the land of the ancestors to help him search for the one he has called Son?

The bison grounds are far away. There is nothing for the chieftain's people here in this country through which we once journeyed toward the edge of the world." Warakan felt as though dashed by cold water when a possibility made itself known. "Unless he also hunts Cha-kwena and the sacred stone."

That was a frightening thought until the boy turned around and stared across the valley. He saw distant firelight flickering in what had to be a hillside cave. Warakan caught his breath, knelt, and released the cubs. "*We* will find them first!" the boy declared. "It is to this place that the Red World shaman has come! He has doubled back from the edge of the world beyond which he and his lawbreaking woman fled during the storm! Ah, Little Bear Brothers, he is indeed Trickster! Who would have thought that he would bring his people into the Valley of the Dead? If that *is* Shateh, he would have passed this place without suspecting what that Yellow Wolf Cha-kwena has done! But we will go in stealth to the lake in which the bones of the slain totem lie. We will touch them and find power in them. We will find a way to steal the sacred stone! We will take it to Shateh. Then, despite Teikan's lies, the chieftain will have cause to trust Warakan and name him Son again!"

Dawn found Cha-kwena far from the sad little village in the dark woods beyond the edge of the world. The strong night wind had died with the coming of morning, and now—his head much clearer and his thoughts more focused than they had been in days—he stopped, disconcerted yet again by the sensation of being watched and followed by something even more elusive than the mammoth herd.

Cha-kwena's brow furrowed beneath the projecting beak of his owl-skin headdress. Since leaving the woods just beyond the village, he had not picked up sign of the bear that had been prowling close to the spring, but now and again he had crossed the scent line of dire wolves and detected the occasional strong stink of feline urine; the latter put him on guard against lions and great, fanged, leaping cats. He regretted his decision to go unarmed into the night.

And now—overriding the threat of predators—something else raised the hair along the back of his neck. Somehow, somewhere, the forces of Creation were disturbed, moving, pooling, expanding invisibly outward toward him, like ripples on a wind-stirred lake. Chilled, he shivered, pulled his robe closer around his shoulders, and reached for the sacred stone. It was not there. He grimaced. Without the talisman, he felt powerless and all too vulnerable in this strange, unknown part of the forest.

"Grandson of Hoyeh-tay!"

Cha-kwena winced, startled by the summons.

It came again. "Guardian of the Sacred Stone, many have fought and died to take the talisman from you and turn its powers to their own gain. All have failed. And now you have left it behind in the care of others who do not share your power."

Cha-kwena turned and stared in all directions. Who had spoken? He executed another full circle before a chortling in the branches above his head and to his left drew his eyes to the gray form of an old, molting owl. "You!" he cried in recognition.

"Did you imagine that you had come alone into the dark wood?" The bird ruffled its feathers. The nictitating membranes of its eyes slid slowly over the golden orbs, then slid back again. The owl stared down at him, moved lightly on its horny feet, spread its broad, gap-feathered wings, and was gone.

Cha-kwena stared after it, snarling in resentment. "Go ahead! Fly off! It seems to be what you are best at these days. Surely, Owl, of late you have not been the helping animal spirit to me that you were to my grandfather! Where are you leading me? And why do you speak against my leaving the sacred stone behind when I did so only in obedience to the spirits of my dreams? What else could I do? Am I not also guardian of the totem and of my band? I must find the little white mammoth calf. With sickness and despair in the village, my people have lost faith in its existence and in me. Until I return to them with Life Giver, the presence of the sacred stone will give them courage! They will keep it safe!"

"Will they? Willtheywilltheywillthey . . . will . . . will . . . will willlll? . . ."

Cha-kwena listened to the owl's questioning shrill as it faded into the distances of woodland. After a few moments, the sound seemed no more than the screeching of any other bird. He scowled, wondering if his conjuring of the all-too-vocal raptor had been less a shaman's Vision than an imagining born of his second thoughts about leaving the sacred stone behind.

Annoyed and frustrated, as he always was by the vagaries that so often confounded him whenever he set himself upon the shaman's path of Vision, Cha-kwena drew in a deep, steadying breath and went on his way. Time would tell if the exasperating but nonetheless comforting communication with Owl was reestablishing itself. In the meantime, his mind and body no longer felt quite as webbed by fatigue as they had over the past many days. He followed the familiar trail of old mammoth sign that he had explored before to no avail until, at last, he came to a place where the tuskers had circled and then broken off onto a new trail entirely. Heartened, he paused and stared ahead into unexplored woodland. He had no doubt now that the herd was out there somewhere, and the totem was with them. He had only to go far enough, and he would find them. In the meantime, he was certain that the little white mammoth was safe within the protection of its own kind. He wished that he could say the same about himself. Without his spears or his talisman, he felt too much like prey—until, shrouded in the muted color of the deep-forest morning, a diaphanous mist appeared ahead of him, wisped through the trees, and formed itself into the figure of a man—blue faced, bright eyed, and as wrinkled as an ancient tortoise.

"Come, Cha-kwena, Grandson, Little Brother of Animals, Guardian of the Totem, Yellow Wolf, Kindred of Coyote, and Trickster! Come! The animals of this world are the brothers and sisters of our kind. You have no need to fear them. Come, I say! Why do you hesitate? Surely you remember the way through the dark woods?"

Cha-kwena's breath caught in his throat. His eyes narrowed. Was the misted form of his grandfather real or imagined? Had the voice come from the trees or from within himself? He could not tell. His mind expanded, then seemed to narrow and collapse backward into time until he found himself a boy again, lost in a dark forest while Owl led the way across a world that gleamed silver, not in the light of morning, but of Moon, Mother of Stars. Night Wind whispered all around while Owl, beckoning, disappeared into thick woodlands. Without hesitation, Hoyeh-tay walked ahead, his pale, skinny legs lifting and falling into and over thick scrub brush. And then, at last, the old shaman also disappeared between the trees.

"Wait!" Cha-kwena called out to his grandfather. "I do not know these woods. It is too dark to go on!"

"Owl and I know the way. Come. Use your third eye—the inner eye that is a gift of Seeing into and beyond a shaman's soul. Hurry. Follow! Or Great Ghost Spirit may not be within the sacred canyon at the salt spring when we arrive!"

"Salt spring?" Cha-kwena cocked his head, remembering and supposing, "Is this where the mammoth are leading me and my band? To salt? It is a need in them and in most of the grazing kind—and in people, too, when we can find it."

Cha-kwena!

He blinked at the sound of his name; there was a different quality, something imperative, about the summons. He came up out of what had surely been a trance. Scanning the forest for the ghostly presence of old Hoyeh-tay, he stood and waited for the voice to call again. Ground mists surrounded the trees up ahead, but if his grandfather had materialized within any of them, Cha-kwena could not see him. Instead he heard the *oo-ooh*ing of an owl. Although this time the sound was clearly the call of a bird and not of a spirit creature, Cha-kwena nevertheless changed direction slightly and set himself in the way that the voice of Owl would lead him. Spirit bird or living creature of flesh and bone and feathers, wherever that old raptor flew, sooner or later he invariably found mammoth grazing beneath the shadow of its wings.

It was not to be different this day. Soon, just beyond the next stand of hardwoods, Cha-kwena found more mammoth sign, but this not even two days old, a place of much digging with tusks and much fecal matter, with broken shrubbery and tree bark and leaves ripped and shredded to the height of a mammoth's reach. In that moment, relief was as sweet as food would have been to him—had he thought to bring anything to eat.

"Would that I were a mammoth and could eat trees!" he said, and went on again. He foraged for food in the unfamiliar landscape, which yielded only a few grubs and insects, hardly enough to take the edge off his appetite.

At last, growing tired, Cha-kwena paused within a mossy copse of ancient conifers and sought a place in which he could rest in relative safety. A broad, gnarled, outreaching branch drew his eyes. He did not recognize the type of evergreen from which it grew, yet he smiled nonetheless, remembering a similar tree from the distant Red World of his childhood. The spirit of that massive father of all junipers had called him into the forest from his ancestral village by the Lake of Many Singing Birds. With the wind combing through its pungent, scaly leaves, the soul of the ancient tree had invited him to climb high amid the musculature of its enormous arms, to stretch himself like a young lynx beneath the stars and seek the dream that all youthful, would-be hunters of the Red World sought—the special reverie to identify his helping animal hunting spirit and ultimately lead him to discover the name that would be his throughout his adulthood. Old Hoyeh-tay had found him perched within the branches of the great tree at the center of the ancient juniper grove and had told him that only shamans were drawn to the power of such places. Although the boy had sullenly fought his destiny, in the end he had dreamed the dreams of a shaman, not of a hunter.

Now, eyeing the massive, wind-and-weather-formed trees, Cha-kwena knew that his old grandfather had been right. He had yet to find any affection for this strange, dark wetland forest, but there was magic in groves such as this one: a sacred and undefinable silence broken only by the occasional, brazen coming and going of blue jays and the trespass of the wind. But the jays did not linger. And once within the sanctuary of the trees, even the strongest wind was somehow gentled, moved to whisper with hushed reverence among the soaring trunks of silent sentinels that reached for the sun and stars, bearing mute, compassionless witness to the passage of all things that lived and died within their province.

Cha-kwena stared up. In his distant homeland, he would have been able to see the sun through the broad, broken canopy of junipers and pines and wide, open crowns of oak trees. In this place the forest was closed, vaulted like a great dark and ancient lodge of perpetual somnolence, roofed with layer upon layer of evergreens and hardwoods that, in their upward reach for the sun, denied all but transient rays of its light to that which grew below. Cha-kwena sighed, wondered how far he would have to travel before he came to a break in the forest, then decided that however near or far it was, he would need rest if he was to accomplish the journey.

Because of the young man's agility, he needed to exert no real effort to climb to the rough, lichen-furred branch of the great tree before which he had paused. Toe- and finger-holds were easy to find in the deeply reticulated bark. In moments he seated himself, with his back to the trunk. Safe from predators, he was soon asleep. . . . .

Cha-kwena would never be sure how long he drifted in deep, soothing darkness before the dream came to him. It was the old nightmare, more intense and violent than he had ever experienced it before.

He was in the shadowed depths of the sacred canyon. The black walls of the abyss towered above him, veined by waterfalls pouring from the heights—red waterfalls that spurted over the rim, then streamed in thick, reeking vertical rivers of blood to the canyon floor.

Cha-kwena gasped. Trapped within the dream, he looked down and saw that he was ankle-deep in blood and bones: mammoth bones and tusks, human bones and skulls. Death, in the guise of Raven, swooped toward him on black wings, nicking his scalp with its beak as it summoned him onward. Under the hot wind raised by its wings, the shaman walked deeper into the canyon, wiped blood from his eyes, then looked ahead to see painted men running wild in the skins of wolves as they hunted the sacred mammoth beneath a flaming sky.

He screamed at them to stop. They looked back at him and laughed: Shateh and Teikan, Ynau and Ranamal, Xohkantakeh and all of the warriors of the Land of Grass, and others—warriors of the Watching Star, men he had seen and battled in the distant Valley of the Dead. Cha-kwena was stunned. How could these two forces have melded into one?

It did not matter.

Cha-kwena saw the warriors hurl spears of lightning, encircle the herd, and slaughter every mammoth until only the little white calf was left alive. Alone and confused, it raised its trunk and cried like a frightened child.

"Run!" Cha-kwena screamed, but it was he who ran, toward the totem, slipping and falling in an ever-widening river of blood, then rising and running again. The marauders were closing on their prey. Beyond the narrows of the black canyon, an owl flew toward blue sky and a great white mountain range that glistened like ice. The sun rose behind it and sent its light pouring forward across the world.

"Run into the face of the rising sun!" cried Cha-kwena.

The little white mammoth, still bewildered, was moving now and looking back toward the howling ranks of wolf-skin-clad men who followed. Cha-kwena gained on his enemies. By the driving power of his shaman's will, he empowered the totem to put greater distance between itself and the warriors, too . . . until the ghost of the great shamed bear rose from the river of blood to block his passage forward upon the path of Vision.

Cha-kwena stopped dead in his tracks.

The great bear stood before him.

He stared, appalled, as the animal stood upright on its hind limbs like a towering, fur-clad man with its neck arched and its small, bright eyes glaring down at him from either side of its massive snout. The jaws of the animal clacked in warning. The lips pulled back to show teeth that would have put dread into a corpse. And there, standing close to the animal and safe within the shadow of its extended forelimbs, was a spear-carrying woman who spoke his name.

"Cha-kwena! Awake, my shaman! Help me!"

Cha-kwena emerged from his nightmare in a daze of horror. Mah-ree was standing below him within the grove. Wolves were closing on her. He stared, wondering if this was still a portion of his dream, for surely he had lived this scene before, long before, on the night when he and his woman had fled from the wrath of Shateh. Now, as then, like First Woman in the ancient tales, Mah-ree faced the threat of wolves with a trithonged birding sling whirling above her head.

Despite her call for assistance, she needed no help from him. Yipping and yelling, she whirled her bola until the long arms of the sling screamed for release. Frightened by the sound of the weapon and the sight of the bold, shrieking woman, the wolves scattered and ran for the cover of the surrounding forest long before Mah-ree loosed her weapon.

"Ay yah!" she cried, triumphant, as a wolf yipped in pain and was heard no more.

Cha-kwena leaped to the ground.

Mah-ree, beaming with pride in herself, hurried to retrieve a pack roll that she had evidently set aside just prior to the advance of the wolves. Hefting it, a handful of short staves, and three red spears with blue banding, she came to her man and laid these things at his feet. "I have been following close on your heels, my shaman! I would have called out, but I feared that you would send me back. Now—like First Man and First Woman—together we will seek the totem for the good of our band! Guardian of the Totem must have his spears. And this . . ." She reached to her throat and removed the thong from around her neck. "The sacred stone! When I saw it, I knew why you had left it behind. You must not lose faith in your power, my shaman. As the little white mammoth totem grows toward maturity, so, too, will your power return and—"

Rage overwhelmed Cha-kwena. "The stone was left to protect the band in my absence!" he roared.

Her face fell. "But the powers of the stone speak through my shaman, who is sworn to guard the talisman with his life. How can my shaman leave it? How can—"

"I am sworn to guard the totem. I must find it. I must see why the mammoth have left the forest around the newly born spring."

She nodded. "Yes. This I understand. And so I have come to—"

"And you have dared to touch and carry the weapons of a man!"

"Your spears! I have not used them. And the staves are merely sharpened throwing sticks. Surely the forces of Creation will not be angered by—"

"Enough!" Cha-kwena interrupted her flow of words with a coldness of heart and tone that shook him to his spirit. He was beyond anger. Beneath his feet another aftershock went through the earth. It was a short jolt of a tremor that passed almost as quickly as it had begun, but not quickly enough to go unnoticed or to fail to define a terrible truth to Cha-kwena as he stared at his woman. "Shateh was right

about you, Mah-ree. You *are* the cause of all the trouble that
has befallen our people. Again and again I have warned you
about defying the laws of the ancestors! Again and again
you defy me! And now I see you for what you are—the
spear-carrying dream woman who walks with Bear and
blocks my way along the path of Vision!"

"Never!" she protested.

"Always!" he insisted. "You are incapable of obeying
my will or the laws of the Ancient Ones. You have offended
the spirits of the ancestors and turned the forces of Creation
against our band. Because of you the children of our people
sicken and die! Because of you the earth shakes, water
becomes poison, and the totem has vanished from the
country into which the mammoth have brought us!"

Stricken, Mah-ree shook her head. "No, my shaman!
This cannot be! I have been trying so hard to be obedient!
And even when I sometimes forget, surely I have behaved
no differently from the way First Woman behaved on behalf
of First Man." She stepped forward, her expression desperate. "My shaman must know that this woman would die
before standing in his way of Vision!"

"Then do it and leave me alone!" he told her. "You are
not First Woman! Take your cursed spears and be gone from
my sight!" Although he regretted the words the moment
they left his lips, he did not take them back. He repulsed her
so violently that she cried out, covered her head, and
dropped to her knees before him.

Mah-ree remained motionless. "I cannot leave my
shaman here," she whispered in a hurt and broken voice.
"Not alone and unarmed in the dark wood without the—"

"Stay here, then! I will leave *you!*" he declared, and,
eyeing his spears, conceded the point that they might yet
prove useful to him. Without a word he snatched them up.
Her own little lances made small clattering sounds when the
larger, longer, stone-headed hafts were withdrawn from
among them. "Take your weapons and return the sacred
stone to the village!"

"But it is far! It will be dark soon. This woman is afraid for herself and for her man! Let my shaman allow me to walk at his side."

Cha-kwena shook his head. "I do not believe that you have ever been afraid of anything in all of your life, Mah-ree! Go back to the village. Gah-ti has need of Medicine Woman. Cha-kwena does not. I must seek the mammoth! I must know that they are safe. I cannot and will not let you stand in my way!"

She looked up at him. Hope was shining in her eyes. "This woman is Cha-kwena's woman. My shaman cannot leave Mah-ree behind."

The tremor that went through Cha-kwena had nothing to do with earthquakes. It was a deep, upwelling shiver of resolve that ripped through his heart until he felt it torn in two. Until this moment he had been a man and a shaman. In this moment he knew that he must choose between the two. And from this moment he knew that he would never again have a choice to make. His dream had shown him that the totem was in danger; if the totem died, the People would die, and for reasons that he did not understand, this little girl-of-a-woman was a threat to them all. Somehow, even as a boy he knew that the shaman's path would demand more of him than he would be willing to give. Perhaps this was the sacrifice he had been dreading all along.

He shook his head. The way of the shaman's path lay before him. He could not turn back.

"I *can* leave you behind," he told Mah-ree. "I *must* leave you behind. Now, in this moment, let the Four Winds, the forces of Creation, and the spirits of the ancestors hear this man's words! Always and forever, this woman Mah-ree is no longer Cha-kwena's woman!"

The statement made, he turned and went his way. Even when she cried his name, he kept on walking. He dared not look back. The woman Cha-kwena loved was waiting for him in the grove, but he was Shaman now.

* * *

For a very long time Mah-ree remained kneeling, waiting, certain that Cha-kwena would return for her. With the sacred stone a calming presence in her hand, she smiled, remembering the many times she had followed her man and been scolded. She had always been forgiven and taken along in the end.

"He did not mean what he said. He will come back for me," Mah-ree said to the talisman. "And for you, too, Sacred Stone! Surely he knows that he is wrong to leave you behind, Spirits of First Man and First Woman, for you must always be in the care of a shaman through whose spirit you may speak your thoughts and through whose mouth you may form your words. And my shaman is the best of shamans! The bravest! The boldest! You must not be angry with him for leaving you behind, Sacred Stone. He fears for our people more than for himself. He seeks the mammoth and the totem for the good of all!"

She sighed then. *Surely,* she thought, *he will not go far. His anger will cool toward me. He will come back for me. He always does.*

Soon the wan light of day ebbed toward evening, and still Mah-ree sat alone. She looked around, listened to the growing sounds of night, and trembled. "He will come!" she quavered to the trees and to the animals that she sensed moving in the deepening shadows of the forest beyond the grove. She thought of the wolves that she had driven off and of the bear that she had seen lurking in the woods beyond the village. "My shaman will not leave me alone. Not when there are predators in the forest!"

It was not until darkness filled the grove that Mah-ree took her lances and pack roll and climbed high into the great tree. "I will wait for him here," she said to the sacred stone. "It will be safer for me, until he comes."

With the sacred stone clutched tightly in her hands and held against her breasts, Mah-ree remembered Cha-kwena's command to return to the village with the talisman. Unhappiness washed through her. *Again this woman has disobeyed her man!* Her mood became as dark as the night.

"How was I to know that this time he would not return?" Mah-ree asked the stone. "I am not a shaman. I am only Medicine Woman. And in this far land beyond the edge of the world, I am a stranger to the healing spirits of the trees and grasses and all green growing things! They will not share their secrets with me, and so, although I can stitch a wound, I am not much of a Medicine Woman, after all!"

Thinking of her inability to help the suffering Gah-ti, Mah-ree shuddered with feelings of utter worthlessness as she sat dejected and alone within the sheltering heights of the great tree. She acknowledged that Cha-kwena had been right to accuse her of standing in his way of Vision. Her selfishness and desire to bear a child had prompted her to steal his dreams with U-wa's woman-wanting potion. Her despondency grew.

"My presence is not needed in the village. I am good for nothing. Not woman, not daughter, not mother, not healer. Even if I were, there are wolves in the forest, and it is now too dark for me to return alone to my people."

The justification was comforting until it occurred to her that darkness had been no hindrance to her the previous night; but on that night she had followed close on Cha-kwena's heels. It would be different now. "I will wait here for my shaman. It is what Cha-kwena really wants of me. I am sure of that!"

She sighed with the knowledge that she was not sure at all and, fighting misery, rested the back of her head against the trunk of the tree and closed her eyes. "This woman is tired!" she declared, using the formal order of speech that, with luck, would be favorably received by any spirits that might be listening. "This woman thanks the spirits of this tree for offering her a safe place in which she will be able to find rest. This woman will think more clearly after she has slept. And by then, surely, this woman's shaman will have come back for her."

Again Mah-ree sighed. The last sentence had been spoken with extra emphasis. *May it be so! May it be so! May it be so!* Her yearning was an unspoken litany that took her into deep sleep. . . .

With the sacred stone warm in the press of her palms, Mah-ree dreamed of her mother and father and of little Piku-neh and Ha-xa-ree. The dream brought no sadness, for they were all together in the warm, welcoming distances of the Red World. She was home again, a happy child again, blissfully ignoring the taboos of the Ancient Ones as she defied the proscriptions against her gender by clambering up the creek-side bluff to old Hoyeh-tay's sacred cave. Cha-kwena was there. Mah-ree, smiling in her sleep, reached out to her shaman, but he flew at her like a riled hawk.

And now she fell, tumbled down the face of the bluff, fell and fell through the night sky. A shooting star flamed bright, and a small black bear ambled across the great sparkling sweep of the Sky River. When the animal paused and turned and reached out with a helping paw to her, she reached back until, suddenly, the little bear became the great shamed bear of her nightmares.

She screamed and awoke with a start. Gasping with fright, expecting to see a bear prowling in the grove at the base of the tree, she looked down and trembled with relief. Nothing was there.

But with a new dawn a predator came from the forest—not to the young woman who waited for her shaman in the wood, but to the old woman who wandered from the village in mindless search of a little boy she had no hope of finding.

"Piku-neh!" Old Kahm-ree called the name of her dead grandson. "Where have you gone, you troublesome boy? Do you not hear your grandmother calling? Your mother will be angry if I tell her that you have run off again."

The woman paused. Beneath the canopy of the trees, the morning air was heavy, motionless, and thick with mist that congealed and fell in droplets from the tips of needles and leaves. She did not hear the gentle "rain," but she felt it and pulled her moldering old squirrel-skin robe around her bony shoulders.

U-wa had made her a new robe of prime river otter and beaver pelts. Kosar-eh's boys had caught the animals and skinned them just for her, and Ta-maya had done a fine job of fleshing and curing the pelts until the furs were as shiny and supple as newly melted tallow. Kahm-ree wrinkled up her already wrinkled face. Maybe someday she would condescend to wear the new robe. Maybe . . . They had all worked so hard to please her with it. But she was not pleased. Because the old robe of red squirrel fur reminded her of home, she was loath to part with it.

"My Ban-ya helped me to fashion this robe! I do not need another!" she declared to thin air and dripping mists. "Back in the Red World we sat together by the Lake of Many Singing Birds and sewed and talked, and my little Ban-ya learned to make her stitches. Ah, what a fine time we had!"

Kahm-ree's eyes widened. Something was moving in the bushes ahead of her. "Ban-ya? Is that you, sweet child?" Confusion momentarily clouded her thinking. Where was Piku-neh? she wondered. *Dead. Burned up with the baby Ha-xa-ree.* "No!" She gasped and reoriented her thinking. "Piku-neh! Are you out there with your mother, little boy? Ban-ya? Have you finally found the trail I have left for you? Wait! Do not run away! Grandmother is coming!"

Kahm-ree waded forward into the green. She heard Kosar-eh's and U-wa's worried calls, but she would not return to the village until she had found her dear boy and his mother.

A feverish Gah-ti rose from where he had been sleeping nearby, beneath a pine, well away from the lodge he shared with his brothers. She paid him no heed, for he was too old to be her Piku-neh.

She did pay attention to a snort of annoyance that came from the center of a thicket. A bear stood and glared at her, its black snout and paws bloodred from the juice of berries it had been carding from the shrubs.

Kahm-ree stopped. She cocked her head. It had been many a long moon since she had set eyes on her grand-daughter. In long-gone days many had accused her beloved girl of being as brazen and easily riled as a bear. But surely, Kahm-ree thought, her beloved Ban-ya could not have been so transformed. Or could she?

"Ban-ya, dear granddaughter, is that you?"

Perhaps, had the old woman been content with the question, the bear might have gone its way. But Kahm-ree's eyes were as misted by age as the morning air; she needed a closer look to be sure.

A moment later the animal charged.

Kahm-ree screamed, dropped, rolled into a ball, and felt herself struck again and again.

Suddenly the pummeling stopped. Stunned, Kahm-ree ventured a look up and through the bright light of her own fear and saw that the beast, grazed by one of Kosar-eh's spears, had turned and run. She heard Kosar-eh's voice through the pounding of her heart.

"Gah-ti! Catch!" The big man tossed a second spear to his eldest son, who—although forbidden the use of such a weapon—was closer to the bear and therefore had a better chance of bringing it down than did the other boys, standing beside their father.

The one-armed young man reached out reflexively, then looked horrified to see the spear in his hand. Loosing a high-pitched howl from his drooling, saliva-encrusted mouth, he cast the weapon away as though it hurt him to hold it, then ran unarmed and screaming into the forest.

The danger now passed, Kahm-ree felt gentle hands upon her back as U-wa and Ta-maya bent close and helped her to her feet. Shaken, she was aware of warm wetness and dull pain across her upper back; but when she cried out, it was not at the news she had received that a wound would need stitching. It was when she saw what the mauling had done to her robe. "We can mend it!" she insisted.

"We must mend you first," said U-wa.

Ta-maya said nothing. She was staring off toward the forest into which Kosar-eh and Ka-neh and Kiu-neh had just disappeared. They had spears with them, but she knew that they were not only hunting the injured bear. They were pursuing Gah-ti.

He ran, stumbled, and cried out in pain. Not since the long days and nights of healing after the lion had taken his arm had Gah-ti known such pain. Fire lived beneath his skin and at the back of his throat—from the top of his head to the palms of his hands and the bottoms of his feet, it was a dry, predaceous beast, kindred to the fever consuming and weakening him. Pain prowled his body, waiting to be roused by the slightest touch; even the dim light of the forest seared his eyes and made them burn and swell and tear. And when he swallowed, much less tried to eat or drink, the fire burst to life within his throat, convulsing his entire body in spasms of agony.

And yet now, thinking of Mah-ree out there somewhere in the forest with a wounded bear, Gah-ti knew that for her sake he must now fight and win against the beast of his pain. Too long had he lain exhausted by his illness, afraid to move lest the simplest activity intensify his anguish. From the lonely place that he had made his own after abandoning his brothers' lodge, he had seen Mah-ree follow Cha-kwena from the village. He had watched her and hated her for following the shaman into the dark woods rather than remaining behind and caring for the sick, moaning man who was in desperate need of her.

And so he had not said a word to anyone about her leaving but had lain still and alone, alternately cursing her and brooding over his love for her, wanting her to die along with her shaman out there in the dark wood, and then wanting her to come to him, kneel close, and assure him again that he would soon be well, even though he was beginning to know in his heart that he would not.

Whatever was eating him alive with pain and fever was

killing him; when he slept, he dreamed of Spirit Sucker, then woke, sobbing, because in his thirst and hunger and growing misery, he knew that it would not be long before he welcomed death. Besides, he had been unfair to Mah-ree and knew it; why should she feel obliged to be solicitous of his needs, when he struck out at her and was jolted by pain every time she attempted to soothe him with her healing hands?

And now she and Cha-kwena were unaware of the danger presented to them both by a wounded predator. He would warn her. He would warn them both, for despite his yearning to believe in the power of the shaman, Gah-ti had lost faith in everyone and everything except the depth of his love for Mah-ree.

Gah-ti actually felt glad when he came upon the bear. He halted and raged, "Stop! Now you will die and trouble my people no more!"

Pain flared in his throat as he shouted; he felt the agonizing, all-too-familiar constriction of muscle that threatened to throw his entire body into mindless tumult; but somehow he found the strength of will to override this betrayal by his physical self and run forward, levering back with his one good arm, preparing to make the final, close-in thrust that would surely finish the bear. And then he laughed. He had no spear. He had thrown it away. His father had overlooked his deformity and honored him by tossing him the weapon of a man, and he had thrown it away! *What matter?* thought Gah-ti, and kept on running.

They found him floating facedown in an algae-choked pond. It was the color of the water that told Kosar-eh what he would find when he drew his firstborn son from the shallows.

"We will find and kill the bear that has killed our brother!" declared Kiu-neh.

Kosar-eh, hefting Gah-ti in his arms, made no reply. He was surprised to find him so light, so easy to lift; the long days and nights of illness had stripped the young man of much of his former musculature as well as his dignity. Kosar-eh looked down at the beloved face. "Come," the big man said to his surviving sons. "We will take Gah-ti home."

"But the bear!" protested Ka-neh. "We must hunt it and finish it. Cha-kwena and Mah-ree are out here. And it could come back to the village and—"

"We will not be there to greet it," informed Kosar-eh. Drained and knowing that he could stand no more grief, he turned and—followed by his stunned boys—carried Gah-ti's body back to the village.

"Behold my oldest son!" Kosar-eh cried as Ta-maya, U-wa, old Kahm-ree, and the children gathered around him. Little Tla-nee wept to see her future man hanging limp and bloodied and spiritless in his father's arms. "Now listen to this man: From this moment Kosar-eh is no longer of Cha-kwena's band! Our shaman has taken his woman and the sacred stone and gone into the unknown. I will not wait for his return, nor will I follow him! Let Cha-kwena walk in the path of the totem if, in fact, there *is* a totem. I will not stay in this land that consumes my children! I will go back into the land of my ancestors!"

"But to do this we would have to pass through hunting grounds that Shateh has claimed as his own!" reminded U-wa.

Ta-maya paled. "The totem does not lead us there, Kosar-eh!"

"I have done with totems! This man will rely upon his own judgment and skills, not upon faith in forces that may not exist at all or, if they do exist, are set against me!"

"We cannot leave without Mah-ree!" Ta-maya was shaking.

"Your sister Mah-ree has gone to be with her man," Kosar-eh told his woman coldly. "The two of them walk strong in the power of the totem and of the sacred stone. We do not. I will not allow my people to stay another day in this cursed land." He paused and fixed his gaze hard upon U-wa.

"Mother of Cha-kwena, you are also the mother of Joh-nee. For the sake of that child, will you come with us?"

U-wa did not hesitate. "I will come. This woman will be mother of Cha-kwena and his lawbreaking woman no more!"

9

The sun had not yet risen over the eastern ranges, but as Warakan stood within the Valley of the Dead on the misted shore of the great lake, he felt that he was being reborn with the growing light of the new day.

"Soon we will know if there is any power left for us in this place!" he said, watching the cubs cavort through the reed beds and make great whopping splashes as they plunged in and out of the water in search of fish. He envied them their careless contentment but wished that they would not be so noisy; everywhere was sign that people had been through these reeds, often and not long before.

Warakan stared ahead at the bones of the great white mammoth. The great one had come to its final rest upon some sort of underwater hillock or a gravel bar. The boy's heart quickened at the sight; nevertheless he frowned. From what he could see protruding through the wraithlike mists of morning, not much was left of the skeleton. Although a man might easily wade out to it, Warakan would have to swim. His throat constricted as memories of nearly drowning intimidated him. A moment later he reminded himself that he had survived the race of the river not once but twice, and with a deep intake of breath to steady his resolve, the boy stripped to bare skin. With his spears and belongings laid aside, he went forward into the reeds.

And soon he was there.

Clambering onto the half-submerged skull of the great white mammoth, the boy embraced the totem and closed his eyes. He felt the shock of its power surge through him. Was the jolt real or imagined? Warakan was sensible enough to realize that it was best not to press for an answer. What mattered was that just as he lay with his flesh in contact with the bones of the great white mammoth, so, too, must he open his spirit if he was to receive whatever lingering vestiges of totemic power remained.

"Life Giver . . . Great Ghost Spirit . . . Grandfather of All . . . if you can hear this boy, know that he has come far in his need to ask you to be with him now. Warakan seeks the sacred stone of the ancestors. Warakan must find a way to take it from one who uses it to send curses upon the Four Winds against the people of Shateh. Warakan must take the sacred stone to Shateh, for only then will Shateh be strong again . . . chief above all chiefs and shaman above all shamans again . . . and only then will he name this boy Son again!"

The words spoken, Warakan pressed himself even more tightly against the skull of the great white mammoth. Unsure of what to expect, he waited for an answer. Would the voice of the totem rise clear and resonant out of the skull to inform him that he was now gifted with wisdom and powers beyond those of a mere boy, and he could go forward on his quest? Or would the totem warn him away from his intent and name him Fool, or Presumptuous? Or would there be a voice at all? Might some heightened awareness within him assure him that his wish was to be fulfilled or denied? Or perhaps there would be some wondrous sign of magic in the sky?

Having heard no totemic voice either outside or inside himself, Warakan opened his eyes and looked up. The sky was gradually gaining color as the sun rose higher behind the eastern ranges. Soon the full light of morning would be upon the world, and the warmth of the newly risen sun would spread across the Valley of the Dead—soon, but not now.

Moments passed. Warakan remained motionless, waiting, cold now, shivering under the chilling touch of the dank mists of early morning that fingered over his wet, bare skin. He wished that the cubs would stop their splashing; the sound was intrusive. Somewhere in the reeds he heard the *chack-chack* of a shrike. He exhaled impatiently. Although it was comforting to know that his old "friend" was back with him, Warakan felt annoyed to hear the voice now; it was as distracting to him as the splashing of the cubs and surely, Warakan thought, was not the sign he was waiting for.

He closed his eyes again and waited. Tense with cold, he tried to keep his teeth from clicking while he listened for the sacred voice of the totem. Instead he heard the occasional call of the shrike, the splashing of the cubs, the rising drone of insects, the rippling of fish, and the sounds of other small water creatures moving amid the reed beds. Somewhere far across the valley a lion roared. But no voice emanated from the skull of the great white mammoth.

Now Warakan shivered with frustration as well as with cold. And then he heard the sound of a drum coming across the valley. Recognition was instantaneous. His eyes flew open, and he gasped. Only one thing in all of this world and the world beyond made such a deep and menacing rhythm.

"A thunder drum of the People of the Watching Star!" Appalled, Warakan swung himself upright upon the mammoth skull and stood staring toward the hills that were the source of the sound. "Has there ever been a more stupid boy than this boy?" he asked himself, shaking now with fear. "There are people in that hillside cave all right, but they do not belong to Cha-kwena's band!"

With the realization that he had unwittingly entered the new hunting grounds of whatever the war had left of his native tribe, Warakan leaped into the water. Desperate for the cover of the reeds, he swam like a frog beneath the surface, half choking on terror.

Ah, Life Giver, Great Ghost Spirit, Grandfather of All, if you are ever going to be with this boy, you had better be with him now! Warakan sent the unspoken plea bubbling to the surface as he swam for shore and, he hoped, out of sight of those whose cannibal ways he once fled to become a loyal son of Shateh. He knew all too well that if they caught him and recognized him as a traitor, they would kill him—slowly. If they caught him and did not recognize him, he would be enslaved—forever. Either way, his life would be over. Either way, he would be unable to win the sacred stone for Shateh. And if the faraway tribe camped beyond the pass *was* of the Land of Grass, he would be unable to warn them that they were venturing into the country of their worst enemies. And what would happen to the cubs?

Now, desperately afraid for his children as well as for himself, Boy Mother of Bears clambered onto solid ground. The shrike was making sounds of great restlessness. Warakan ignored the bird. He could see the cubs clearly. They were well out from shore, belly deep in shallows within a section of broken reeds and old, scattered sloth bones. He could see that they were scuffling and nipping at each other in rough but brotherly enough warfare over what was left of a fish. He clucked his tongue to summon them and did not expect them to respond at once, taken as they were with their minor but earnest conflict; besides, they always ignored a first summons from Mother. He clucked his tongue again and took advantage of their continued disobedience by taking the time to rub himself dry as best he could, pull on his ragged garments, stuff his feet hurriedly into his foot coverings, and don the welcome warmth of the bearskin.

"Little Bear Brothers, we cannot stay in this place!" he whispered to his cubs while he picked up his belongings and spear.

They did not appear to have heard him.

"Little Bear Brothers, you must come now!" Warakan commanded in an imperative whisper.

The cubs did not come.

But suddenly the shrike took wing and flew so aggressively over Warakan's head that, startled, he dropped to his knees and looked up at a flurry of gray, white, and black underwings just as a dark spear hurled from afar sang overhead and arced toward the lake. A moment later Warakan heard one of the cubs bawl, and then he heard footfalls coming through the reeds at his back. He positioned his spear. It was too late.

In the sacred cave, no one heard the cry of a boy above the constant repetitious sounding of the drum. Ban-ya listened and watched as the People of the Watching Star offered a mourning ceremony for the old woman who had succumbed in the night to a stomach ailment. The illness had come on suddenly; the end had been violent and unpleasant, but no one was unduly concerned by it. Ban-ya, in her position of honor within the configuration of mammoth bones that formed the sacred circle within which her new people observed their rituals, fought the impulse to smile; she had known that the members of the band would react in this way. The woman had been old and of no importance. A recent arrival to the Valley of the Dead, she had outlived all of her family except the son of a long-dead brother.

Now, she watched that man as he stood with Tsana and Jhadel before the great drum that spoke with the voice of thunder. With the padded mammoth-skin beater that he had taken from the hand of the shaman, he struck the solemn cadence alerting the spirits of the ancestors that one among the People was now coming to join the Ancient Ones in the world beyond this world. The sound was not as rich and full as it would have been had he taken the time to tighten the drum skin by slowly heating it over a low, scrupulously maintained fire; but to do that, he would have had to take time from hunting and weapon making as well as find others to assist him—the massive, bone-framed drum was spanned by an old and much cherished mammoth hide, and to tune it to exactly the right-sounding pitch was no easy task.

Besides, it was not as though he or anyone else was actually grieving over the old woman.

Again Ban-ya fought the impulse to smile. With little Ea-ka hefted on one hip, she stood resplendent in fine new garments sewn for her by the women of the Watching Star. Her hair was combed and plaited into innumerable feathered braids that shone with sage-scented oils extracted from the female glands of her new band's many recent kills. She wore a collar fashioned of the finger bones and intricately woven hair of the sacrifice. A quilled cape made of the symbolically patterned, tattooed skin of the slain girl fell down her back. At first the grotesque raiment had revolted Ban-ya to the point of nausea, but gradually she had grown used to it; in fact, the weight and scent of the collar and cape somehow brought a strange, soothing sense of power to her. Sometimes, as now, when she wore them and little Ea-ka entertained himself by handling the collar and sucking on the finger bones, she wondered if the spirit of the slain Sheela *had* come to reside within her, to give her courage to face her new role in life and understanding of the ways of the band who had made her their own.

At last the mourning cadence was finished. The last living relative of the old woman handed the beater back to Jhadel and stepped aside. Ban-ya watched as, one by one, the People of the Watching Star filed by the drum. Each, in turn, starting with Tsana, took the beater from Jhadel and struck a single beat to honor the passing of the old woman. Now it was Ban-ya's turn. She shifted little Ea-ka's weight upon her hip and moved forward to take the beater. She did not look at Jhadel lest the old man see the truth in her eyes when she struck the drum not in mourning or respect but in triumph.

Now, old woman, no one will ever know your secret about the boy Warakan. You were right to entrust it to me. My baited meat has silenced you forever. The preparation is an old favorite of mine. Sage pounded into the meat along with small, tightly coiled slivers of sharpened bone.

When ingested and moistened in the belly, the coils,

having been meticulously dried as though for wolf bait, expand to pierce the gut! In the same way did I cause Atonashkeh, son of Shateh, to die and also—

Ban-ya's retrospection was brought to an abrupt halt when an agitated Indeh entered the cave and slung the gutted carcasses of three antelope and several grouse onto the cavern floor. "Who has died? By the forces of Creation I have heard the mourning drum across the entire valley! By now they must have heard it, too!"

Ban-ya was amazed by the flustered countenance of the man who, along with Unai and Hrak, had been gone from the cave for several days while hunting at the far side of the valley.

"'They'?" asked Tsana.

"Shateh!" The name exploded out of Indeh's mouth. "And a great movement of people coming through the pass and into the valley!"

Ban-ya could have sworn that the world rocked beneath her feet.

Tsana was livid. He pointed an accusing finger at Jhadel. "You said that he would not seek us in the Valley of the Dead!"

Jhadel seemed to shrink to half his size, and a great confusion spread like sickness through the cave. Xanahay volunteered to take the women and children into hiding within the far hills while other warriors spread out and began forays against Shateh's advancing force.

The old shaman stood erect again, shaking his head in disparagement of Xanahay's suggestion. "Are you so eager to die?"

"I am a warrior of the Watching Star. I am not afraid to stand against my enemies!" replied the man.

"As long as we remain within this cave, we are invulnerable to attack," reminded Jhadel. "No one can come against us without moving within range of our spears. We have much meat stored here and a constant supply of water. Our people are safe from Shateh in this place."

"Safe?" shouted Tsana. "I say that the warriors of the

People of the Watching Star are sickened by the thought of running and hiding once more from our enemies. I, for one, do not want to be safe! I want the sacred stone. I want the blood of the shaman Cha-kwena. And I want Shateh cornered and in fear of me, not the other way around!"

"Then let him come," advised the old man evenly. "Invite him to council. Give him the son he wants. Make peace with him at last and allow him to go his way!"

Indeh's head swung back and forth in slow negation. "This man dares not stand before Shateh. He will name me Traitor. And despite all that has been said between us on this matter, I am not at ease with talk of peace with my former chieftain. If we do as Jhadel says, then we will allow Shateh to continue to walk strong in the power of the living man totem, Cha-kwena, and of the sacred stone. After Shateh has his son, who is to say that he will not make war upon us again?"

Jhadel responded with strained patience, "Shateh has always been a man of his word. And as both Indeh and the woman of the cave have pointed out, he is old and weary of war and has need of a son to take his name."

Indeh, clearly uneasy, was still shaking his head.

Tsana's eyes narrowed. "Shateh will have his son—but only in exchange for the sacred stone and the man totem, Cha-kwena. Then we will have Shateh *and* the stone, and we will slay the Red World shaman. After we have eaten his flesh and grown drunk on his blood, the power of the totem will be ours. All who have wronged us will fall to the vengeance of the People of the Watching Star!"

Ban-ya's arms tightened around her boy. And what would happen to her little Ea-ka, son of Shateh, after Tsana's plan was accomplished? Dread expanded and contracted within her mind, like an eye focusing upon a light that will surely blind it if it does not look away in time. The moment she had hoped would never come had come. Having offered her son as a hostage in the event of impending war, she could not renege now. Her thoughts swam, then congealed into turmoil as frightful possibilities confused and confounded her. "Ea-ka!" Ban-ya, sickened by worry, whispered the name of her baby.

Then Hrak and Unai entered the cave to offer a disconcerting distraction. Ban-ya was not the only one to stare in amazement when Hrak slung the carcass of a bear from his shoulder and dropped it hard on the floor of the cave, amid Indeh's earlier contribution of grouse and antelope. The hunter gave it a sharp kick.

"Ow!" protested the bear in the voice of a riled boy.

Ban-ya's eyes widened.

"What is this?" demanded Tsana.

He and everyone else watched as a small, badly battered boy sat up and angrily pulled the bearskin protectively around his meager shoulders. He glared out of a face that seemed to have taken the butt end of a spear.

"I saw it perched on what was left of the bones of the totem," replied Hrak to Tsana. "It must have come ahead of those who now enter the valley from the pass." He laughed. "It gave me a good fight, but not good enough. Now it is a hostage, a captive, or dead meat—whatever you like. And here—look at these fine stones it carried! They will make spearheads for warriors!"

"They are not for you!" snarled the child, fighting to speak and breathe through his broken nose and swollen split lips. He looked around with the wild defiance of a wounded animal that knows it is about to be killed by those who have captured it and has resolved to be brave and contemptuous of its tormentors to the end. "And I am not an 'it'! I am Warakan! I am son of Shateh! If you harm me, you will be sorry when he comes to put an end to your kind once and for all!"

Ban-ya stepped defensively back out of the sunlight that filled the front portion of the cave. Once again, she could have sworn that the world rocked beneath her feet.

"You are no son of Shateh!" interrupted the woman Oan, indignant as she strode forward and squinted down at the boy. She touched her scarred cheeks. "Your face may be bruised and your arrogant little nose flattened, but I have not forgotten you, Warakan."

Ban-ya saw the boy wither within the bearskin.

Oan nodded and smiled maliciously. "Yes, and you recognize me, too! I see it in your eyes. Do you like my scars, Boy of the Watching Star? When you ran away from my care, these scars were my reward for failing to keep you where you belonged." She turned to Tsana and proclaimed with rapturous satisfaction, "This is the one who betrayed us to Shateh! Ah, Tsana, this woman asks for him! This woman has longed to be reunited with him so that she might make him pay with endless pain for what his disloyalty has done to us all!"

Warakan lurched forward and made a mad run for the edge of the cave. He might have made it had Tsana not placed a foot on the bearskin and brought him down.

Ban-ya heard the air rush out of the child as he landed flat on his belly.

Tsana pulled Warakan up by his hair, appraised him out of lowered lids, then let him fall hard. "Yes, I do remember him. You are right, Oan. He must have been with Shateh all along. Can it be that a chieftain of the Land of Grass has truly named a child of the Watching Star as one of his own?"

"Then, truly, there may be hope of peace between us," said Jhadel.

Tsana shook his head. "Never. Take the boy, Oan. Tend him. We will see if Shateh wants him back after he learns that we hold his true son as hostage. If the whelp still lives after all is finished between us and our enemies, then he is yours to do with as you will."

Ban-ya, shaking, watched Oan drag Warakan off by the bearskin. The boy made to resist, but the woman kicked him into submission. Ban-ya was relieved to see Warakan slump into near unconsciousness. When she last saw this boy, he was high in the favor of Shateh after naming her as the killer of the chieftain's eldest surviving son. If he revealed the details to Tsana, she was certain to be accused of causing the old grandmother's recent death; everyone had seen her offer meat to the woman. And then what would they think? What would she say to them by way of explanation?

Ban-ya attempted to calm her fears. *Old women die all the time! No one suspects you of bringing Death to this one! As far as Warakan is concerned, there is no one alive—not even the boy himself—who knows that he is truly of the blood of Shateh.*

"At what do you stare? You know this youth!"

Ban-ya winced at Jhadel's unexpected allegation. She wondered how long he had been observing her. His expression was sharp, accusing. What had his shaman's eyes seen of her inner thoughts and fears? She stood tall. "The woman Ban-ya knew this youth," she replied unflinchingly. "He came to Shateh's people while Ban-ya lived among them. The spirit of that woman now speaks through Sheela to tell you that Warakan is, in fact, the one who betrayed you to your enemies!"

The old man smirked. "The spirit of Sheela speaks through Ban-ya? I thought it was the other way around." With a contemptuous snort, he turned on his heel and stalked away.

Ban-ya wondered if her face had gone as pale and bloodless as her spirit now felt. Everyone was looking at her.

"Come," Tsana said, drawing their eyes to him. "It is time to prepare this cave for what will appear to be a council of conciliation. Instead we ready it and ourselves for war!"

"Madness!" declared Jhadel from behind the woven protection of his feathered privacy screens.

Ban-ya's head went high. She regretted not having fed the shaman the same kind of death that she had given to the old woman. *Soon,* she vowed. *Soon!* But in the meantime did she not have a more dangerous enemy? Within her mind reason and logic were expanding and dispersing like clouds before the sun at noon on a summer day; she could not grasp her thoughts, could not find clarity within them. Still hefted on her hip, little Ea-ka was playing with her necklace again. She kissed his cheek. *You will be safe, my little one. Your mother will find a way to keep you safe from whatever enemies may come against us now.*

Shateh stared across the Valley of the Dead. The unmistakable sound of an enemy thunder drum booming in distant hills had brought him to pause and call an immediate council in the cool light of morning. To a man the vote had been the same:

"We will go!"

"We will seek the cannibal People of the Watching Star!"

"When we have found them, never again will the sound of their drumming be heard in the hunting grounds of Shateh and Axwahtal."

And so Shateh had left a handful of men behind with the women, children, and dogs and had led the majority of his warriors and those of his old hunt brother, Axwahtal, through the high pass and into the Valley of the Dead. In stealth they had come. Yet they had been seen.

And now, as he stared fixedly toward the cave-pocked hills in which he had once confronted and formed an alliance with the shaman Cha-kwena, the great drum was sounding again, this time in invitation to council. He did not like it, did not trust it. If he was placing the sound correctly, it was coming from the cave that the People of the Red World had claimed for their own.

Shateh's shaman heart began to beat very quickly. Intuition told him that someone deeply connected to his blood and spirit was in danger of death among his enemies within that cave. The feeling was incomprehensible. His sons were dead. Warakan was dead. The drumming was coming from his age-old enemies—only the People of the Watching Star used the thunder drum. If he felt any connection with them at all, it was a mutual bond of pure loathing. And yet the sense of foreboding nearly over-whelmed him.

"The People of the Watching Star." Teikan exhaled the name of the despised tribe with a sneer as he came with several others to stand beside the chieftain. "It is fitting that we find what is left of them here . . . hiding in the Valley of the Dead!"

"As we found them once before," said Ranamal.

"And fought them!" added Ynau.

"And vanquished them!" said Xohkantakeh.

"And sent them scattering out across the world in fear of us like leaves flying away, torn and broken and tattered by the breath of White Giant Winter!" proclaimed Zakeh.

Axwahtal's brows arched toward his browband. "It seems that they have been blown back to this place. How many warriors would you say you left to them? If they are all assembled within a single cave, there cannot be so many, eh? Nor can they be so eager to fight if they want to call a council?"

Shateh eyed the man with cool speculation. "Axwahtal did not choose to bring his warriors to fight in the great war against the men of the Watching Star when their numbers were as great as the star children of Moon. Their marauders raided the villages of the Land of Grass and stole our daughters for their cannibal rites, to pacify the storm spirit they name Thunder in the Sky. Many died in that war. But after years of fighting and harassment by the raiders of Shateh, this man is confident that our force will greatly outnumber any warriors who have survived the last great battle, which was waged in this place. Yet I wonder: If Axwahtal does not have the heart to fight, why has he spoken to bring his warriors to this place now?"

Axwahtal was vexed. "This man is a warrior of the Land of Grass! Big is the heart of this man for fighting! *Big!* In the days of the past great war, Axwahtal's people were on the far plains, hunting bison. No raiders of the Watching Star came for our daughters. And no runners came across the Land of Grass to the village of Axwahtal to invite him to battle! Finally word came of Shateh's war, and sorrow heaped upon Axwahtal when he learned that he had missed the chance to bloody his spear in battle. It will be a good

thing to bloody it now—in any battle! Against any enemy!
Axwahtal simply wants to know if there are warriors
enough left among the Watching Star People for him to
fight . . . or if maybe this Red World shaman you seek has
killed them all, and there are only old men and women and
children in that cave!"

"Even women and old men and children of the Watching Star are worthy of death, Axwahtal," said Teikan. "The
Four Winds and the spirits of the ancestors will sing with
joy and smile upon those who wet their spears with the
blood of the last of their kind. They are fit for carrion and
for nothing else."

"Not even for slaves?" Axwahtal seemed disappointed.

Teikan shook his head. "Not even for that."

A slow, deepening tightness in Shateh's chest made
breathing difficult. He thought of Warakan. How he missed
the boy! How he ached to have the child back at his side, as
bright-eyed as a river otter, and as quick and clever and
loyal.

No! Shateh cut off his thoughts; they were too painful.
Warakan was a bad-luck bringer whose presence among
Shateh's people had always been as a shadow before the sun
of his power, eclipsing his authority. So great was his love
for the boy, he realized, that it had, at times, unmanned him.
Now, with potential danger and possible duplicity looming
above him in a cave, he had to set aside all longings from
the past and concentrate on that which was to come.

He considered Axwahtal's troubling reference to Cha-
kwena. It was possible, of course, that the Red World
shaman had used the sacred stone to work some dark,
totemic, killing magic upon his old enemies. But was it not
also possible for Trickster to have joined forces with the
People of the Watching Star so that now, even though
Shateh came against them with a greater force, his enemies
would be invincible in the power of the totem?

"Ah, yes . . ." the chieftain spoke his thoughts aloud.
"And then this calling to council would be a trick . . . a
lure to draw us like fish into a weir."

Teikan was openly annoyed. "Or it could be exactly what it seems! A pathetic handful of enemy survivors and their women and children! What is this hesitation, Shateh? In this place or in another, we are sworn to kill our enemies and to seek the totem and the sacred stone. Surely my chieftain is not afraid?"

The tightness in Shateh's chest spanned from shoulder to shoulder and across his upper back now; it bordered on pain. It took extreme concentration for him not to react visibly to it; this alone kept him from responding violently to Teikan's provocation. With one hand pressing his breast just under the collar of golden eagle flight feathers, he eyed the man with open disdain. "Only little children who have never known war are unafraid before battle. Surely Teikan is afraid?"

Teikan's features tightened defensively.

Shateh stood motionless. Gradually the tightness in his chest lessened; he could breathe more easily now, and did so, deeply, as though starved for air, but he was strangely light-headed and dizzy and aware of Teikan's watching him out of narrowed eyes.

"I say we go forward boldly, running like wolves, howling to our enemies, mocking their call to council, and calling them to battle so that our greater numbers will overwhelm and destroy them! Come! Who will run with me now?"

The chieftain hated the man. He knew that Teikan had seen weakness in him and wanted others to see it. Shateh was determined not to give him that satisfaction. His head was clearing. The tightness in his chest was gone. Remembering past fighting tactics in this place, the chieftain spoke evenly and strongly against the dangerous impetuousness of Teikan. "Wolves will we be—cunning, not careless, in our boldness. Wise and wary and watchful, we will send one main body of warriors forward, to show our strength and intimidate our enemies—for surely there cannot be many survivors—while others of us will move unseen to cover those who seek council with whoever dwells within the cave."

"Council!" Teikan spat the word as though it soured his mouth.

"If Cha-kwena is with them, we will ask for him and the sacred stone," explained Shateh. "If they yield the shaman and the stone to us, we will give our enemies their lives . . . briefly."

"And if they are strong in the power of the totem and see through our deception?" pressed a worried warrior of Axwahtal.

Decision making had focused Shateh's thoughts. "If Cha-kwena is with them, perhaps he has set himself to be as disruptive and deadly a secret enemy within their camp as he was within ours. Perhaps they will be glad to be rid of him."

"And if he is not with them?" demanded Teikan.

"Then we will go on," he replied. "We will seek the Red World shaman and the sacred stone."

"And what happens to the People of the Watching Star?" Teikan insisted.

"They are few, and we are many," the chieftain responded coldly. "Never again will warriors of Shateh leave enemies behind so that they may gather like ravens, conspire with Spirit Sucker, and come at us with Death another day."

This said, his face was tight when he set himself to command the others in the way that he would have them assemble for their advance toward the hills from which the drum was still sounding invitation to council or to . . .

A slur of wings above the chieftain's head scattered his thoughts and left him momentarily breathless. Again his heart was racing. He looked up, shielding his eyes from the feathered flurry of a passing shrike.

While Axwahtal murmured about omens, Shateh stared after the bird. He was aware of others looking to him for comment about the hidden meaning in the appearance of the shrike. Because he was a shaman as well as a chieftain, he knew that he must now form some sort of reply, but he was not certain of the implications of this sign. Frowning, he remembered that many years before, he had heard men speak with hatred of his dead son Masau; they had called him Impaler and said that his deeds in war and ritual sacrifice had won him the shrike as totem animal.

Shateh's eyes followed the bird eastward toward the hills within which the great drum was sounding. Once again breathing became difficult, and he reexperienced a sense of knowing that someone of his blood was in danger there. But how could this be? His frown became a scowl. In a moment, he told himself, understanding would come to him. In a moment he would find words to explain the meaning of the omen. In a moment . . .

Teikan exhaled through his teeth and took the moment for himself. "When this day has passed, may we deal with our enemies in the way of Shrike—impale them and leave them hanging in the trees to mark the way of our passage through this land. Then all who would venture into this country in days and nights to come will recognize the color and markings of our lances and turn away in awe of the power of those who leave no adversaries alive as they seek the totem and the sacred stone!"

Heady words, conceded Shateh, still staring east. He could no longer see the shrike. He turned his face upward and stared at the form of a single raven circling before the sun. Seconds passed. Other winged forms joined the first, and soon there were many ravens. A living cloud of dark wings shadowed the light of day and the chieftain's mood.

"Always before a hunt or battle Raven and his clan gather in hope of a feast," Shateh intoned. "How do they know when to come?" He regretted the question immediately. As shaman it was up to him to interpret the omens, not to postulate in ignorance about them.

Shateh turned his glance from the sky to the warriors who surrounded him and quickly answered his own question. "Raven sees the color of our body paint and battle spears. Raven is wise. Many wars and hunts has Raven seen with his yellow eyes as he rides the back of the Four Winds and looks down upon the world, awaiting the flesh feast that our kind always leaves for him."

The faces of the men were set, their eyes squinting with concerned speculation and from the glare of the sun.

"I see no ravens," said Teikan.

Shateh looked to the sky again. The cloud of black wings was gone. And suddenly the chieftain realized that it had never been there. Again he felt the deep, slow tightening within his chest. Fighting for life-sustaining breath, he wondered if the shadowing omen of Death had been for him alone.

10

Deep within the primordial forest, Cha-kwena heard a raven
cawing above the broken canopy of the trees. He stopped,
looked up, and squinted from the unaccustomed bright light
of day. The woods were definitely thinning, but if a raven
was perched in the sunstruck branches above Cha-kwena's
head, he could not see it. He was glad.

"I have had enough of dark omens!" he said, and
turned his gaze down and back along the way he had come.

Mah-ree was not there.

Cha-kwena could not deny his disappointment. For
two nights and the better part of two days he had been
looking over his shoulder, expecting to see his defiant little
girl-of-a-woman following at a discreet distance, hiding
herself within the shadows, following just close enough so
that if danger threatened she could cry out to him for help,
but preferring to keep her distance as she waited for the
right moment in which to show herself and beg his
indulgence once again.

Now, Cha-kwena scanned the ever-changing forest and
was beginning to believe that Mah-ree had actually obeyed
him and returned to the village with the sacred stone. He
told himself that he should be grateful. In the absence of
their shaman and totem, his people needed its power. But

like it or not, Cha-kwena was forced to concede that he was lonely without his woman at his side. And despite his best effort to keep his mind open to the will of the spirits that called him ever deeper into the forest he could not help but worry about her and feel regret, if not for his harsh words, then for his decision to leave her alone.

"What else could I do?" he asked aloud, then suddenly became angry with himself for burdening his thoughts with concern for Mah-ree. His heart hardened toward her. "I am Shaman! She is Lawbreaker! Lest Cha-kwena risk offending the forces of Creation, this man could not bring that woman on his search for the totem!"

The justification made, he assured himself that she would be all right. Mah-ree was *always* all right! She had outsmarted or prevailed against marauding warriors of the People of the Watching Star, charging bears, and hungry dire wolves. And now she had the sacred stone . . . and her cursed lances! Who or what could possibly win against such a woman? Her shaman certainly never had! Cha-kwena shook his head. He would not go back for her—not until he had accomplished the purpose of his journey. And then only the forces of Creation could say what would be between him and Mah-ree. But he would not think of that now.

The mammoth were trumpeting again. Cha-kwena's heart leaped at the sound. All day they had been vocalizing with great excitement. He turned and eagerly faced eastward. The tuskers were moving well ahead. He could see them making their way through widely spaced trees and brush. Save for two hulking adolescents and the little white calf that walked close to the side of the great matriarch, they were huge, high-shouldered, tuck-hipped, and well shed of their winter coats. As they plodded on with slow deliberation, their tails and ears twitched, and the massive, twin domes of their heads rose and fell, making life difficult for the tiny brown birds perched upon their forelocks and feeding upon stinging gnats and biting flies that sought to

suck the blood of mammoths but ended in the beaks and
bellies of the little brown birds instead.

"Ah! Where do you lead me, Great Ones?" called
Cha-kwena, hurrying after the herd. "I have come far—so
far that I fear my people will not want to follow! Will you
not return with me through the dark wood? Will you not let
Kosar-eh and those who are losing faith in your power set
eyes upon you, so that they may know that their shaman
has led them well and that the totem has, indeed, been
reborn?"

But the mammoth plodded on.

Cha-kwena was suddenly overwhelmed by frustration,
hunger, and fatigue. "When will you stop?" he cried.

The great cow turned her pale, freckled head and
looked back at him.

Eye contact was made. Cha-kwena caught his breath.
The shock of communication with the mammoth struck him
like a physical blow.

"Are you not Shaman?" asked the matriarch. "Are you
not Cha-kwena, grandson of Hoyeh-tay, brother of animals
and guardian of the totem? Surely you must know when we
will stop."

Cha-kwena stared. He did *not* know. But without a
shadow of a doubt, he did know that, as shaman, he would
follow until he found out. Nothing else mattered. He would
go on. He would not look back or question his calling again.
He was Cha-kwena, grandson of Hoyeh-tay, brother of
animals and guardian of the totem. His people—and his
little Lawbreaker—would be strong in the protection of the
sacred stone and safe within the village until he returned.

They were gone.

Stunned, Mah-ree dropped her pack roll, clutched the
sacred stone, and stared at the deserted village of her people.

"Kosar-eh? Ta-maya? U-wa? Gah-ti? Children of my
band?" Her voice squeezed through a constricted throat and
sounded oddly disconnected from its source, as though the

very formation of the words stressed the one who spoke them to the point of breaking.

There was no reply.

Disbelieving, Mah-ree stared at the abandoned lodges. For two days and nights she had remained in the deep woods, stubbornly awaiting the return of her shaman, refusing to believe that Cha-kwena would truly leave her alone in the dark and threatening forest. At last, with the return of wolves, her resolve to wait for him had faded. Frightened and alone, she had known in her heart that Cha-kwena was not coming back for her, but she had not allowed herself to believe that he had stopped loving her forever.

So, obedient to her shaman's command—albeit belatedly—Mah-ree had returned to the village, determined to wait for him there and to prove to him by whatever means possible that she would never be Lawbreaker again. But where were her people? How could they have packed up their belongings and gone off without her or their shaman?

When Mah-ree's eyes settled on the fire pit and then drifted beyond it, she understood. Her eyes widened. Denial screamed for release upon her tongue, but when she gave it voice, it emerged as a small, tight "No-o-o . . . " that was an acceptance of the truth. She stumbled forward to the embankment of firestones and then, as she stepped to what lay just beyond, dropped to her knees.

"Gah-ti!" Mah-ree sobbed his name and reached to touch the remains of his body—charred, fleshless bones arrayed as though awaiting reanimation, limbs straight, skull facing upward in the spirit-seeking death position that her people called "looking at the sky forever," and his one arm folded upward across his chest. Tears burned beneath Mah-ree's lids, welled and spilled and ran down her cheeks, burning her to her heart as she rested her hand upon the spear that Kosar-eh had laid at his son's side in the place where Gah-ti's missing arm would have been.

Slowly, lovingly, Mah-ree's fingers traced the long, lanceolate projectile point of obsidian, strayed over the sinew bindings and bone foreshaft, and then downward along the perfectly straight hardwood haft that was incised and painted with Kosar-eh's identifying black and white striped hunt markings. This was the big man's finest spear. It was a lance—not of a Red World man but of a big-game hunting warrior of the Land of Grass. Kosar-eh had secured his battle insignia to the upper portion of the shaft—a slim banner cut from the black-tipped tail skin of the lion that had taken Gah-ti's arm, and with the black and white flight feathers of a teratorn and an immature white-headed eagle.

"Yes," said Mah-ree, smiling through her tears and sadness. She understood the significance of the spear, for surely Kosar-eh had placed it in deliberate defiance of and challenge to the laws of the Ancient Ones that had denied all happiness to his eldest son in this land or any other. "May the spirit of Gah-ti soar on the wings of Eagle and Teratorn! May the spirits of the ancestors look upon the wonderful new arm of this man Gah-ti and know that he is Warrior and Lion Stalker and Bear Baiter . . . a man of great courage, worthy to hunt with other men in the world beyond this world." Her voice broke, and she hung her head.

And now, assuming that Gah-ti had succumbed to the fever and pain of the Cannot Drink sickness, Mah-ree spoke not to the spirits but to the bones of the one-armed young man who would never look at her with love and longing again. "Forgive this woman, Gah-ti. Medicine Woman is no Medicine Woman. The healing spirits would not yield their secrets to Mah-ree. She was not worthy . . . of them . . . of you . . . of her shaman." Again her voice broke; this time she closed her eyes and wept.

The shadows of the unseen sun were growing long when Mah-ree could at last weep no more. She looked up and around the abandoned village and could not fault her people for leaving her behind. She wondered how long they had been gone; clearly they had not waited the traditional four days to mourn poor Gah-ti, and from the scent of the fire, his body must have been burned not long after she had followed Cha-kwena into the forest. If they had left soon after that, then they had been gone for two days, no doubt assuming her to be safe at the side of her shaman.

Perhaps they expected Cha-kwena and her to follow the band when—and if—he found the mammoth, for now, as her gaze strayed, she saw that they had marked the way they had gone with a strip of rabbit skin tied to a tree that already bore the notches of Kahm-ree's dagger. Or perhaps they had left no sign at all, and the poor old woman had tied the skin in yet another pathetic attempt to leave a trail by which her precious Ban-ya might someday find her.

Mah-ree sighed at the irony of the situation. The old woman might yet find Ban-ya. But surely Kosar-eh knew that when Cha-kwena found the totem, he would never consider leading it back into the country of those enemies who would hunt it if they ever learned that it had been reborn.

A rising wind moved through the forest. It was not a cold current, but Mah-ree shivered. She wondered if her band had been severed forever. Her hands strayed to the sacred stone that she now wore around her neck. Holding it tightly, she looked up at the swaying canopy of the trees. Somewhere the sun was shining—but not on the abandoned encampment.

With a deep intake of breath to steady her against weariness and remorse, Mah-ree closed her eyes again and wished upon the sacred stone, "Please, Spirits of First Man and First Woman, this woman is not worthy to ask it, but she would be grateful if you would tell her what to do now!"

A moment later she heard the huffing of a bear.

Mah-ree tensed. Her eyes flew open. She clutched the sacred stone so hard that her hands hurt. Would the talisman protect her from predators? Was she deserving of protec-

tion? Or had the spirits of First Man and First Woman
answered her wish by sending a bear to devour her? Surely
she had dreamed of this often enough! And had not
Cha-kwena told her to die? Because of her defiance of the
ways of the ancestors, her people suffered and perished and
lost faith in their shaman and in the totem. And perhaps,
because of her, the totem had left the People forever! The
concept was devastating.

Mah-ree stared straight ahead, and the many times that
she had broken the traditions of the ancestors flashed
through her mind. From the moment she had picked up the
spear of Teikan and dared make the killing thrust that
shamed the great bear, everything had gone wrong for her
band. Despairing, Mah-ree accepted her guilt and knew that
there was no way for her to undo the tragedies that had
unfolded along the path of her endless wrongdoing. Ha-xa,
Ha-xa-ree, Piku-neh, and Gah-ti had paid with their lives
and, because of her, would walk the wind forever. Cha-
kwena and U-wa had banished her from their hearts.
Because of her thoughtlessness, the band had been torn
asunder.

There was one way to be sure that she would not cause
more grief for those she loved. Again she sighed and rose to
her feet. She walked slowly, as if in a dream, to the
sanctuary and went inside. Carefully, reverently, she placed
the stone within the sacred circle. When Cha-kwena returned, the talisman would be there waiting for him. But
Mah-ree would be gone.

She heard movement in the trees beyond the sanctuary
and knew that it was not the wind.

"Ho, Bear! This woman hears you. This woman
comes. Great Paws has been waiting for Mah-ree for many
a long moon. Now she comes. Now Walks Like a Man will
see that she is not afraid!"

She swallowed hard, knowing that her dreams and
Cha-kwena's visions were about to be fulfilled. Soon she
would be within the skin of the animal that he had seen

standing before him, blocking his way to Vision along the
shaman's path of dreams.

"Never again!" she swore, and tried to be brave as she
walked out of the sanctuary and into the dark woods, where
the spirit of the great shamed Bear was waiting to consume
her.

11

"Do not worry, Oan. I want him for just a moment. You are not the only one to wish death to this one. A slow death, yes? But first we must have his silence. We cannot have him moaning and drawing attention to himself when our enemies come to the cave to 'council' with our warriors." She held out her baby to Oan. "Here, hold the son of Shateh while I do what I must do."

The woman's words drew Warakan from delirium. His swollen, blackened eyes opened hurtfully. He was still huddled in his bearskin against the back wall of the cave. Through a haze of pain he found himself staring at the woman he had seen standing in the shadows when he had first been brought to the cave. Kneeling next to Oan, she was leering at him.

"Yes," said Oan. "Let me help. I can hold your son of Shateh in one arm and help you deal with Traitor with the other."

When the woman of the shadows leaned close and took hold of his bearskin, he recognized her.

"Ban-ya!" he cried out.

She struck him.

Intense pain flared in Warakan's already battered face. He heard her laugh. It was a low, hateful sound.

Warakan felt Oan's strong hand on his right shoulder, pressing him down, pinning him down. He squirmed to be free, but his entire body screamed against the bruises and abrasions and cracked ribs that had been a gift from the man who had taken him captive by the lake. Warakan felt sick. The world seemed to be spinning. Exhausted by agony, he lay still and looked up at the women and plump, square-faced baby that they had both called "son of Shateh." His mind swam back, back, back to a long-gone winter and a wild-eyed woman begging for her life and that of her unborn child after she had been cast out to die alone within the Valley of the Dead.

"Yes, Warakan," said Ban-ya, leaning so close that he could smell the stink of sage-scented gland oil all over her. "I did not lie. I *was* with child. But you had no pity in your little traitor's heart for me and for this son of Shateh! And so now you must expect no pity from me . . . as I tend your poor battered face. Here. Your mouth is cut. Open it. Let Ban-ya see the extent of the injury!"

The sudden change in her tone did nothing to alter the hatred he saw in her eyes. He squirmed again and tried to move away. It was no use; it hurt too much, and she was straddling him now. And then, as Oan pressed more tightly on his shoulder, Warakan saw the blade. Hidden in Ban-ya's right hand until now, it was a small, palm-sized flesher of the kind he had often seen women use to scrape and slice the last fragments of muscle tissue from small, delicate skins. He stared at it, knew that she was going to hurt him, to cut him, and then—recalling the words that had awakened him—he knew that she was going to take the tongue from his mouth if he let her. A squeal of pure terror and outrage came ripping from his throat as he fought to be free of her and her eager accomplice. A sharp jolt of pain from his cracked ribs stole his breath and his strength, as Ban-ya's questing fingers invaded his mouth. He tried to fold his tongue back on itself, but his mouth was so swollen and the pain so great, he feared he would lose consciousness.

"Leave him!"

Warakan did not know who had just spoken. It was a
male voice, rasping and phlegmy with age. Whoever it was,
the command that had been given elicited an immediate
response in both women. They relaxed their grip on him,
and in that instant Warakan managed to push Ban-ya back
and twist free. He scrambled to his feet and bolted for what
seemed to be a nearby opening into the interior wall of the
cave. Bending, he ran forward into absolute darkness,
banged his head on the low ceiling of the cavern, cried out,
and stumbled. But he regained his footing and kept moving
as quickly as he could . . . deeper and deeper into the
labyrinthine hollow of the hill.

Ban-ya glared furiously up at Jhadel.

"Shateh is coming," he told her. "You are wanted at the
entrance to the cave, where you and the chieftain's son can
be seen."

She wondered if the old man had any idea what he had
just prevented her from doing. *No matter,* she consoled
herself. The boy was lost to the confounding blackness of
the inner cavern; as weak and battered as he was, he would
probably cower there like a frightened mud worm until
someone went to bring him out. And now, with the enemies
below the cave, no one would be in a mood to search for
him.

"Sheela!"

Tsana's summons brought Ban-ya to her feet. Oan
handed Ea-ka to her. With trembling hands she reached for
him and drew him close. Then, slowly, with the dignity
expected not of Ban-ya, Lizard Eating Woman of the Red
World, but of Sheela, high priestess of the People of the
Watching Star, she joined Tsana in fading sunlight as he
stood with his warriors at the lip of the cave.

"Behold the father of your son," he invited.

Head high, Ban-ya looked across the Valley of the
Dead, and then down to where Shateh and his many
warriors from the Land of Grass had stopped just out of

spear range below the cave. Her brow flexed as fear assaulted her.

"So many," she said, trying hard not to react to the well-remembered sight of them—tall and powerful and painted for war, with Shateh standing before them, tallest and most powerful and imposing of all.

Her mouth went dry. How would Tsana react to the accusations Shateh was sure to hurl against her? The question made her light-headed with dread as she felt Ea-ka playing with her necklace; she rested her hand upon his pudgy little fingers. Would Shateh accept this child as his own? What would happen if he did? Would Tsana give him the boy and let him go his way? No, she thought. He wanted Shateh dead as much as she did. But would he put Ea-ka at risk to gain this end?

Ah, my baby! I would rather die than lose another son! But no, Tsana will do nothing to risk the affection of his woman. And Ban-ya is his woman. No! Sheela is his woman. It is Sheela he loves. Her mind was whirling; everything seemed too bright. She closed her eyes and hoped that when she opened them, there would be nothing below the cave but the lake and the long, intervalley hills and shouldering snow-clad ranges that lay beyond.

"They hold their spears at a forward slant. They have agreed to council," informed Tsana.

"The Red World shaman is not with them," said Indeh, frowning.

"Not where we can see him," replied Tsana.

Ban-ya looked up at him. "You will not give him my baby?" The spoken query brought another equally frightening one in its wake. "Or yield this woman to Shateh if he asks for her life?"

Jhadel, adorned in all of his hideous ceremonial finery, had come to stand beside Tsana. He snorted in contemptuous mockery of Ban-ya's obvious fear. "Sheela would never ask for her life or care so much for the fate of a lizard eater's suckling."

Ban-ya felt her face flush. "This is Shateh's son!" she proclaimed.

"Perhaps, but surely he is yours, Lizard Woman," replied Jhadel.

"Ban-ya is dead!" Tsana's sharply disapproving statement took the smirk from the old man's face. "This woman is *my* woman! This woman is not what she appears to be."

"Ah, yes, I would agree to that!" conceded Jhadel, turning his attention to the force of men that had assembled below the cave. "It is not yet too late to council with them in truth. I tell you now that if it comes to battle, many on both sides will perish."

"Not this time," vowed Tsana with venomous purpose. "You know as well as I that Hrak has taken some of the best of our men from the cave and placed them in concealment, where they may close ranks upon those who move against us. And remember your tenuous position in this band, old man," he warned Jhadel. "I need a shaman beside me now, but later, if you do not stand with me in this . . ." He allowed the implication to settle. Then, standing tall, he called to Shateh. "I am Tsana of the People of the Watching Star. I send my words to Shateh of the People of the Land of Grass. I ask why Shateh has left the land of the totem and brought his warriors to the Valley of the Dead? Must Shateh be chieftain of all the world? Must he harry my people even in this place?"

"I seek the man totem, Cha-kwena! My people have heard the great drum of the People of the Watching Star. Its voice spoke across the land in invitation to council with old enemies. My warriors would know why," came the reply.

Ban-ya flinched at the hated voice while Jhadel and Tsana exchanged looks of surprise and puzzlement.

"The Red World shaman is not with Shateh?" Tsana shouted.

"Shateh *is* Shaman! He needs no other!" was the reply.

"Then why does Shateh seek the Red World shaman?" questioned Tsana. "And why does he name Cha-kwena totem? The spirit of Life Giver still lives among the mammoth kind and by now must surely walk as a newborn calf with its own herd in the Land of Grass!"

The ripple of startled confusion that stirred Shateh's forces was audible to all in the cave.

A few moments passed before Shateh replied, "All have seen what is left of Life Giver here, lying in the lake within the Valley of the Dead. The herd that once walked with the great white mammoth now walks eastward beyond the badlands, into the face of the rising sun with the new totem, the man Cha-kwena!"

Jhadel laughed and called out for all to hear, "It seems that the Red World shaman has lived up to one of the many names by which I have heard him called—Yellow Wolf, Trickster, for surely he has tricked us all!"

And now, while Ban-ya stood numb with dread, she saw a new tension change Tsana's posture. He was rigid. His face was livid with frustration as his head strained forward on his neck. "If the totem is not with Shateh, then he has no more power than any other man," he said out of the side of his mouth.

"He is Shaman," warned Jhadel.

"He is old," countered Tsana. "Like you. And we have all seen the extent of your power." His mouth pressed against his teeth, lengthened, and whitened as it twisted into a smile of pure malice. "We have him now!"

Ban-ya's arms tightened around Ea-ka; she knew what must soon happen.

Tsana called down to his enemies. "Let Shateh come up into this cave so that he may see with his own eyes the painting that Cha-kwena has made and left behind within the sacred cavern to mock us all!" he invited. "After Shateh sees this, he will know that the totem lives on in the mammoth herd, not in the man!"

"No, Shateh! Do not trust them!" warned Xohkan-takeh.

"Behold!" cried the voice from the cave. "We will send women to you! Hostages to assure our goodwill to Shateh if he fears for his life among those who seek only to council and make peace with those who have been enemies for too long!"

Shateh winced at the well-cloaked insult.

"Look!" exclaimed Teikan. "They come—women! *Young* women!"

Shateh scowled with distaste at the man's predictable reaction; but Teikan was right. A large contingent of females, including young girls, was descending from the cave by way of a series of shallow stone stairs that had been cut into the face of the cliff.

"Tsana sends to Shateh daughters of the Watching Star!" proclaimed the warrior who stood closest to the edge of the cave. "May Shateh and his people care for them as kindly as Tsana and his people have nurtured this son of Shateh!"

For a moment the words failed to impact on Shateh's consciousness. As he continued to stare at the cave, he saw that the man who had called himself Tsana extended his hands to the woman standing between him and a grotesquely attired shaman. Now the woman took a step back, and as she moved, something stirred in Shateh's memory. He had no chance to grasp it. Tsana took the child forcibly from her arms and held it high for all to see.

"Has Shateh so many sons among his women that he would turn his back upon this son, who has been raised by those who are no longer his enemy?"

Now the words connected. "Son? . . ." Shateh intoned the word as a prayer. Then, sensing deception, demanded, "How can this be?"

And Tsana replied, "It has been said in the tales of the Ancient Ones that once, in time beyond beginning, the People were one tribe. So we have taken this child, in the hope that one day it would be so again. If Shateh would have this son, he has only to come in peace to the People of the Watching Star. We will no longer weaken our numbers by war. Instead we go forth together against a common enemy. It is Cha-kwena who has stolen the sacred stone and driven the totem from the land of our ancestors. Together we can hunt him and together feast on the blood and flesh of the totem!"

"How can this man have a son among you? None of my women was captured in the last war."

At the edge of the cave, the woman who had held the baby was brought forward by Tsana, who, as he gripped her by an arm, declared, "This woman, Ban-ya, was left behind."

The reaction among the warriors of Shateh was instantaneous. All remembered Ban-ya. All despised her.

Shateh was speechless. His hatred for Ban-ya was so intense that, once again, he experienced a tightness in his chest that caused breathlessness. He remembered all too well how, on the day he abandoned her to what seemed a certain and well-deserved death, she claimed to be pregnant by him. He had not believed her, nor had he given her claim a second thought until this moment. But now, as Raven's invisible wing brushed his cheek to rouse the familiar fear that Death would come to him when he had not a single son left alive to take his name, he wanted Tsana's words to be true.

"Shateh?" Standing next to him, Teikan—wearing the skin of a wounded bear cub that he had come upon and slain while crossing the valley—saw the expression on the chieftain's face and shook his head. "Be wary of this, Shateh. Dark spirits clothed that woman. No man would claim a son of hers as his own!"

Shateh did not hear the warning. Instead he was remembering a vision he had seen in the sweat lodge on the night of the feast fire, when old Lahontay had taken Warakan from the village on the ill-fated quest for Bear. It was the image of Masau, the best and bravest and brightest of all his sons—a son whom he had abandoned to "certain" death, in the same way that he had abandoned Ban-ya. Masau's unlikely survival told him that Ban-ya, too, might have lived. And now, recalling that Mystic Warrior told the chieftain to look for him where he would be least expected

to be found, the chieftain wondered if it was possible that
Masau had been born again into the world through Ban-ya
by way of Shateh's seed.

"I must know!" cried Shateh, and as the women of the
Watching Star began to come meekly and submissively
toward his assembled force of men, he started toward the
cave.

"Ban-ya is the one who took the life of Atonashkeh!"
reminded Teikan sharply.

"Yes!" conceded Shateh. "And perhaps, because of
this, the forces of Creation have seen to it that she—who
has taken the life of a son—must repay that life by giving
birth to another!"

Hope flared in his old man's heart. Smiling for the first
time in longer than he could remember, he commanded all
but one of his warriors to hold their positions and found
infinite pleasure in using Teikan's words against him as he
taunted over his shoulder, "Come, Teikan! Are you no
longer a bold wolf who would run howling to your enemies?
What is this hesitation? Come, I say! Together we will go to
the cave of the People of the Watching Star! Now is a good
time to be afraid!"

Cha-kwena stopped dead. The day was nearing its end.
The forest lay behind him. He turned, looked back at the
way he had come, and marveled at how quickly the forest
had thinned and then fallen away completely. To his right
and left, long dark fingerings of trees extended to the
horizon, but ahead lay the open landscape of a great
boulder-strewn floodplain and a lake that took his breath
away.

Tired, Cha-kwena hunkered down on his heels and
stared at it. A cold wind blew into his face; he barely
noticed. Never in all of his days or imaginings had he seen
such a body of water as that which lay before him now.
Although he rested upon high ground, he could not see
across or around it. Mountainous islands of ice rose from

blue depths that stretched away and away in dimensions that added to his weariness while he watched the mammoth plodding across the floodplain and toward the water.

"Come, Cha-kwena!"

Startled, he looked up to see Owl flying out of the gathering dusk and toward the mammoth. When the bird alighted on the head of the little white calf and called again, Cha-kwena knew that he had no choice but to follow.

He crossed the tracks of wild dogs several times before he turned to see that they had circled and were following. He paused and held his spear at the ready, then looked straight at them.

"I am Cha-kwena, grandson of Hoyeh-tay, brother of animals and guardian of the totem. You should go now on your way in search of other game."

The dogs looked straight back at him.

"Go, I say!"

The dogs did not go; they growled and menaced him with a display of teeth.

The hair rose on the back of Cha-kwena's neck. He had never trusted their kind. He loathed them now. "Totem killers. Biters of children. Sharers of sickness! Be gone!"

The dogs remained where they were.

Cha-kwena knew that they saw him as meat. He also knew that one spear would not serve to drive them all away, so he turned and walked on, slowly, doing his best to appear bold and unconcerned and as unlike prey as he could. But the dogs not only followed, they moved to one side and kept pace with him, staring ahead and making him know that they were hunting other meat.

"Mammoth!"

Cha-kwena lengthened his stride, and soon, with dogs to his left and the mammoth and the lake to his right, he suddenly broke into a mad, arm-waving, howling run, turning the herd, driving it and himself into the water.

"Find other game!" Cha-kwena commanded the dogs as he followed the herd farther and farther into the shallows.

Suddenly, he lost his footing. The shock of icy water stunned him. He released his spear and made a grab for the sacred stone, then—as he saw the dogs paddling toward him—remembered that it was not there.

"Mah-ree!" he cried. "Keep it safe for meeee. . . ."

12

Fire . . . darkness . . . enemy eyes all around, staring . . . and the guileless, curious face of a child—all these Shateh saw when he entered the cave of the People of the Watching Star.

"This child has no look of Shateh!" Teikan's pronouncement was boldly spoken.

Shateh raised an eyebrow; he was growing used to the man's outspokenness, if not approving of it. But considering the intimidating circumstances, Teikan was comporting himself bravely, and that was more than any man could have asked of him. Now, surrounded by his enemies, Shateh stood tall and expressionless as he eyed the naked baby being held up for his appraisal in the hands of a scar-faced woman. He saw that Teikan was right: The boy was small and solid, a Red World child.

Briefly, his eyes scanned past the child, searched for Ban-ya amid the throng, and found her—a shadowed form standing alone at the far side of the cave. Hatred congealed like a clot of blood at the back of his throat; he could taste it, a foul thing, and knew that his features contorted in revulsion.

"Behold this fine son of Shateh!" said Tsana, standing with the shaman Jhadel, beside the scar-faced woman. He gestured to the baby. "He is Ea-ka, born from between the thighs of Ban-ya, strong and whole and sound in all his parts."

Shateh stared at the baby. There was no denying Tsana's observations. The chieftain nodded. He wanted this son, needed this son. "Shateh will accept the son—but not its mother—as his own."

Teikan, shifting his weight, shook his head and whispered from the side of his mouth, "The people of Shateh will no more accept a son of Ban-ya's blood than they were willing to accept the foundling Warakan."

The whisper went unheard by all save those who were closest to the chieftain. Of these, the scar-faced woman reacted most strongly, while the hideous old shaman visibly stiffened; but it was Tsana who spoke out.

"Warakan?" The Watching Star man turned the name with some amusement. "That boy is among us! Would Shateh have him back? Surely *we* have no desire to keep him."

Shateh flinched. "Warakan is dead! He cannot be here."

Tsana shrugged. "But he *is* here! He has fled into the depths of the cave to avoid the discipline of this good woman, Oan, who despairs of his truculence. Come. Perhaps we will find him as we seek the sanctity of the sacred cavern. Accompany me now in peace, brother from the Land of Grass, and see the truth that our true enemy has placed upon the cavern wall for all to see."

Shateh hesitated. He did not trust Tsana's easy camaraderie. He sensed the tension in Teikan and shared it. Yet he went on. He wanted to see what—if anything—Cha-kwena had painted on the cavern wall. But above all else, he had to see if Warakan was still alive.

The shaman Jhadel lighted the way, and all along the inner corridor of the cave, men followed with stone lamps. The interior of the hill glowed gold, and yet, as Shateh walked, bending low to avoid hitting his head on the damp, rough-textured ceiling, he was aware of shadows looming all around, waiting their chance, it seemed, to thicken their wraithlike substance, then devour the light and the men who walked within it.

On and on the procession advanced into the belly of the world. Shateh was aware of cold drafts moving in the darkness. Now and then he reached to his left or right to steady his passage and found his hands sinking into black hollows that evidently opened into other corridors through which he could hear the moaning of the wind . . . or the voice of Mother Below.

"I do not like this."

Shateh heard Teikan's barely audible opinion whispering at his back; he found it irrelevant. Whatever lay ahead, they were committed to it now.

And then they were there.

"Behold the truth!" declared Jhadel as he stepped forward and to the side.

Light and space opened before Shateh. Stunned, the chieftain stood staring like a gape-mouthed boy into the sacred cavern. The cave painting blazed before him, lighted by what seemed to be uncountable numbers of stone lamps.

"Ah!" Shateh saw the truth, the story of the People from time beyond beginning, the magnificent passage of First Man and First Woman from the misted realm of ice spirits into the world of the living. There, searing his eyes and consciousness, were depictions of other migrations, of wondrous hunts and battles, and of a great white mammoth rising bloodied from a lake, entering the belly of the matriarch of a small herd of tuskers, and emerging transformed into a little white calf that led a small band of Red World People eastward, over the edge of the world, into the face of the rising sun . . . not into oblivion but into a fine, green land of perpetual good hunting in which the resurrected totem would live forever.

Shateh advanced slowly, stared, then frowned as he saw the image of a shaman dancing on the wall, a blue man with the head of a coyote, wearing around his neck a medicine bag that contained the sacred stone.

"Shateh sees that Tsana has told the truth," the warrior of the Watching Star said.

"Shateh sees many things," replied the chieftain, knowing that Cha-kwena had lied to him but at last understanding why the young shaman possessed no totem-like powers and why it had been so important to him to drive the mammoth over the edge of the world, beyond reach of the spears of those who would hunt the totem, kill it, and take its power as their own. "We will hunt him now," he said and, knowing his own intentions for the mammoth totem, could not find it within himself to blame Cha-kwena for his deception.

"Shateh . . . Father . . ."

The words were tremulous whispers in the lamplight, but Shateh knew the voice. "Warakan?"

Startled, he stared down and to his left. Hope and love and yearning to be reunited with this most beloved of all boys filled the chieftain's chest until the old tightness was back. Again he found himself fighting for breath. And there, huddled against the farthest, most dimly lighted section of the cavern wall, he saw Warakan staring up at him out of the skin of the bear.

"Again Shateh sees that Tsana has spoken truth to him!"

Shateh ignored Tsana's statement of the obvious. Warakan was so heavily shadowed and bundled in the bearskin that the chieftain could not see much of his face, but he could see his eyes, swollen as though from crying. As the pain expanded across his breast and back, he felt a terrible sense of loss. He could not bring the bad-luck boy back among his people, especially after Warakan had been sheltering among members of his native tribe. He would be Outlander and Cannibal Boy until, at last, Shateh would be forced by the People to kill Warakan for the good of the tribe. *No,* he decided. *Better to leave him here, with his own.*

Shateh turned to Tsana. "Keep him. He is of your tribe, not mine. I have a son in the child that you have returned to me."

Now he looked at Teikan. "Whose scalp was given to me on the day you swore that you had discovered the body of Warakan lying dead in the river?"

Even in the tremulous golden glow of the cavern, the changing color of Teikan's face was apparent.

"Namaray's!" The exclamation came as a gasp from the boy within the bearskin.

Shateh was incredulous. "You scalped your own son so I would believe that the foundling whom I called Son was dead?"

Teikan's features tightened. The man stood as though he had just been impaled. Then, slowly, he shook his head and looked to his left and right. Realizing that there was no escape for him and that he had made a fatal error in judgment by choosing to remain at Shateh's side this day, he suddenly hissed a wordless epithet through his teeth. "And why not?" He spoke to Tsana, not to Shateh. "For too many moons Shateh's decisions have been the decisions of a weak old woman. The foundling was bad luck. It was a good thing for my people to be rid of him. What was one son more or less to this man, who has made many sons on many good women . . . unlike Shateh, whose spirit will live after him in the skin of a lizard eater!"

"Or not at all," said Tsana, smiling as he raised his right arm.

Already taken aback by Teikan's treacherous words, Shateh stared now at Tsana and felt bewildered by his cryptic remark.

A high, ferocious shout erupted from Tsana's mouth. Suddenly Shateh felt a strong arm pressing at his neck and, too late, saw Teikan grabbed from behind by two of Tsana's warriors. With his head pulled back by his hair, Teikan roared in outrage as his throat was slit from ear to ear. Blood, black in the lamplight, exploded from the wound.

Shateh arched his back, then bent forward from his waist and fought with all of his strength to be free of Tsana and the two warriors who tried to bear him back and down. He heard the grunts of their efforts as they strained to hold him and knew that they wasted their time. He was Shateh, chieftain and shaman of the People of the Land of Grass, and in that moment he called upon the power—not of totems or of sacred stones but of youth. It surged within him at his command, making him as strong and invincible against his attackers as surely as the blood and flesh of the great white mammoth could have done. When he flailed up and back and then forward with his arms, they lost their grip on him. He heard their heavy panting as they stumbled back.

Still on his feet, he whirled to face them, leering and laughing at their expressions of . . . mockery? He sneered with contempt of their cowardice. How many of these courageous, daring warriors had it taken to lure him and Teikan—two men, only two—into the depths of a cave from which there would be no escape? Ten men. Ten! A pack of dogs running to bait a bear! And the bear had driven them back! *Cowards!*

It was not until he tried to shout the word that Shateh knew why they were sneering back at him, pointing, laughing now. His hands flew to his throat. He felt the wound—wet, pumping, hot arterial blood. From base of ear to base of ear, the stem of his neck gaped wide. His eyes went round. He stared at his killers and knew that he was a dead man.

Crouching, Tsana ran through the dark, dank corridors to the lip of the cave. He looked down in exaltation. Outside, the tumult of war ruled. His shout within the sacred cavern had been relayed by his men in the outer cave, to signal the start of a major battle.

Of the female hostages sent into Shateh's ranks, over half were warriors in disguise. Led by Indeh and reinforced by the hidden, well-placed ranks of men whom Tsana had earlier sent from the cave, the warriors of the Watching Star ambushed Shateh's fighters and took them unaware just as Tsana's companions surprised and left for dead the chieftain and the braggart who had tried to save his life by speaking words that dishonored not his chieftain but himself.

"Neither man was fit to live!" proclaimed Tsana as he stalked the exterior edge of the cave. He rubbed his hands together. Everything had worked out as he had hoped it would. When Shateh's warriors now broke and fled from the Valley of the Dead with warriors of the Watching Star in howling pursuit, he threw his head back and laughed. "Would that the moon would rise higher so that I could see more clearly what I have so long yearned to see!"

Shocked and delighted, Ban-ya held Ea-ka close and, relaxing for the first time since coming to live with her enemies, rejoiced in the death of Shateh and the ruination of his battle ranks. "I . . . . Sheela has also yearned for this."

Tsana turned, gestured her forward, then embraced her. "Our days of fear are over, woman. Shateh is dead. Later, when I have feasted my eyes and grown sated on the sight of this, we will take his body and stake it high. All who see it will know and tremble at the fate of those who dare to rise against—or put their trust in—the People of the Watching Star. We are *warriors!* We do not council for peace; men have peace enough when their bones lie looking at the sky forever!"

Ban-ya trembled in the fold of his bloodied arm; she liked the smell of it and the dark promise of power that emboldened his words.

"Now the survivors of Shateh's band will be dispersed or enslaved," he promised. "And soon I will lead my own people over the edge of the world in search of the totem. The People *will* be one again, Ban-ya. Our enemies will fall before us. You will see. It will be so. Our sons will be chieftains and warriors strong in the power of the totem, in the daring vision of their father, and in the bold brazenness of their clever lizard-eating mother!"

The reference shook her. "Ban-ya is dead, Tsana. It is Sheela whom you love."

"No." He corrected her gently but firmly as he moved to take Ea-ka into his arms. "I have known for some time that you have fostered that lie to keep yourself alive, Ban-ya," he told her, rocking Ea-ka, smiling at the child as the boy reached to touch his face with open affection. "But it is all right. I hold no rancor toward you. I take pride and find admiration for the bold, brave heart of my new woman."

Ban-ya's heart swelled with relief and with joy to see her child so cared for by her new man. "It is necessary to lie sometimes," she admitted cautiously.

"As I have lied to you and to Shateh," he said expansively. "But now the time for lying is over. From this day the People of the Watching Star are reborn. From this day Ban-ya is Tsana's woman. And from this day he will not stand aside while she gives suck to this spawn of a dead enemy and, by so doing, keeps her belly unfit to take the new life that I would put into her."

"I—no! You do not understand! Ea-ka is not—"

Ban-ya's protest came too late. Ea-ka was already dead and dangling by an ankle from Tsana's hand, his skull bashed to quick ruin upon the floor of the cave. She stared in horror at her baby's brains oozing from his fractured cranium. Blood was coming now—not much. She cocked her head; the bright green light was back behind her eyes. So bright! She squeezed her eyes shut as Tsana flung the body of her dead son from the edge of the cave, as though it were of no more value than a haunch of spoiled meat.

"Now Shateh is dead forever," he told her. "Now his spirit will not rise to come in vengeance against Tsana. Now he has no sons to take his name."

As Ban-ya's mind collapsed into madness, Tsana turned and called for Jhadel.

"Where are you, old man? My people have need of a shaman to consecrate their victory! Come out of hiding and see with your own eyes that which you said could never be! Come, I say! Or I will put you from the band and take your place myself!"

"Babies . . . Ea-ka . . . Ea-nok . . . Piku-neh . . . Have you seen my babies?" murmured Ban-ya.

Tsana smiled the hungry smile of a man's awakening sexual need. "I will give you babies—sons fit for a warrior of the Watching Star!" His bloodied hands reached beneath her furs, below her collar of human finger bones, to handle her breasts hurtfully. "Yes," he said and took her down roughly, as was his preference. "Open yourself to me. Now. The smell of blood and battle is the smell of life to me. Ah, Ban-ya . . . now . . . now . . ."

He looked down into her face. But Ban-ya was not reacting to the fury of his mating. Her hips were not moving. Her legs were not wrapped around his hips. She was staring off, mindless it seemed, as if her spirit were drifting away upon the rising wind of night, looking for her lost babies among the star children of Moon.

Jhadel crouched in the darkness of the inner cavern, just behind Warakan as the boy lay across the body of Shateh. The shaman of the Watching Star put his hands on Warakan's shoulders. "Come away, boy. Come away now. I must extinguish the last of the lamps before the others return."

But Warakan would not release his grip on Shateh. "Father! Father! You must know why I ran away—to find the sacred stone, to return it to you! Father, Shateh . . . please tell me that you know this and—"

"He cannot speak to you, boy! Perhaps he has heard. Perhaps he understood before the end. Now come! If you stay here, you will die!"

Numb with grief, the boy turned his swollen, tear-stained face up to the age-shrunken, tattooed visage. "No-o-o!" he sobbed. "I will not leave him again."

"Bah! We must go, I say! Now!" The old man hefted the boy by a handful of bearskin and jerked him to his feet, half pulling, half dragging him. Jhadel went about the cavern, pinching the light from all of the oil lamps save one; this he raised by its long stone handle. "Now, look your last upon this place and never forget what you see!"

Too weak and hurting to fight the shaman's forceful insistence, Warakan followed the old man into cold, narrow corridors of darkness so intense that even with the feeble light of their lamp, the boy felt suffocated by it.

To his amazement, they emerged into windswept moonlight. Warakan was shocked to find himself on the far side of the hills, where enough food for two and traveling supplies were cached. In this place Jhadel wrapped the boy's rib cage and treated his abrasions with soothing salves.

"Even before you came," the old man said, tending the child, "and even before the wind spoke to me out of crevices in the cave and told me who you are, I knew that I must go from among Tsana's people or be killed by them sooner or later." The old man saw the question in the boy's eyes.

"What do you mean, before the wind told you who I am? I am Warakan. I am—"

"An ignorant boy!" Jhadel chuckled to himself. "The wind has a way of carrying voices through the hollow hill, from the outer room of the cave into the sacred cavern, where this old shaman kept the wicks in the oil lamps trimmed and burning as he studied the wall painting, to discern where the totem has gone and where he may hope to find Cha-kwena and steal the sacred stone."

"You are not worthy!" snapped Warakan.

"Would you rather it be for Tsana? He will seek it. Soon."

"*He* is not worthy. No one of the People of the Watching Star is worthy!"

"But you are worthy. I will teach you to be worthy. The sacred stone will be for you, Warakan, grandson of Shateh, son of Masau, Mystic Warrior. And someday you will be the greatest shaman of them all."

"You don't know what you're talking about! Shateh named me Son, not Grandson!"

A shadow fell upon the earth as a large bird flew across the moon. Boy and man looked up, surprised to see an eagle flying in darkness.

Jhadel, watching the bird soar upon high, shifting winds, spoke quietly. "Many times has Wind brought gifts of understanding to these old senses of mine. Once, Wind came like a soft, cool river of sound deep into the sacred cavern, bearing the words of an old woman whispering a great secret to Ban-ya. Wind does not lie, Warakan. Listen . . . it speaks to us now in the voice of Eagle, who is brother to Moon and Sun and alone among all birds is welcome in the upper reaches of the sky. The Ancient Ones have said that when Eagle flies at night, he carries the lost spirits of this world to the world beyond this world. Look . . . see how Eagle courses back and forth across the face of Moon."

"As though he wanted us to see him," observed the boy.

"Yes! And so we have." Jhadel was ecstatic. "The life spirit of Shateh soars upon Eagle's wings this night. Shateh calls to you, Warakan. He tells you that before his spirit left his body within the cave, he heard the words of the one he named Son. He heard you name him Father. Soon Eagle will bear him away from this world forever upon the back of the Four Winds. Quickly, Warakan! Rise! Name Shateh Father once more. Invite his spirit to live again in you! *Now!* Quickly, before it is too late for him."

Warakan was incredulous. Could it be true? Shateh had worn the skin of a golden eagle, as had his son Masau, and that bird's flight feathers as a collar. Memories flared . . . of a man with obsidian eyes, looking at him across the cooking fire of his parents' lodge, watching him, taking measure of—his *son*!

Warakan snapped to his feet. He raised his arms skyward and called to the Four Winds. "Shateh! I do not know if Jhadel speaks truth or not, for I am a most unlikely boy to be a son of your son. But once, long ago, Mystic Warrior looked at me as though he knew my spirit, and that look has followed me in my dreams! If it is true, Shateh, if your blood *is* in me through him, then Warakan is the one who will keep your life and name alive so that your spirit will walk forever in this world! Come! Live in me! Now and forever!"

The wind turned in four directions. The eagle shrieked and rose straight into the sky, then banked and flew away into the vast, shimmering sweep of the great Sky River until it was seen no more. Breathless, Warakan felt a strange and wondrous tremor ripple through his body. Then something soft fell across his face as though in loving caress. When his hand rose and enclosed it, he knew what it was even before his eyes beheld it—the flight feather of a golden eagle.

"Your grandfather has spoken," said Jhadel. "Shateh acknowledges his grandson and has given this sign as a gift of his thanks to you. His spirit will live forever in you, Warakan. Now we must go on. I do not think that anyone else knows the way through the caverns to this far side of the hills, but you must learn that not even a shaman can be too careful. Come. Can you heft your pack? We must go on."

Warakan obeyed. His injuries stressed him, but he did not complain. He hefted the deerskin pack roll that Jhadel had prepared for him, and a new resolve gave strength to his battered body. "From this moment, Warakan will honor the spirit and the names of Shateh and Masau! From this moment Warakan will seek the sacred stone! From this moment Warakan will hunt the totem and the Red World shaman who denied its power to Shateh and led my grandfather to his death!"

"Beware of what you say, boy, and of how you say it, for the spirits of darkness and light are always around us, listening . . . waiting to carry our words and thoughts upon the Four Winds to the forces of Creation, who may well turn our hopes and dreams to their own ends. And if we offer offense, not even a shaman can predict what those ends will be."

"Then Warakan asks the listening spirits of this night to take his words to the forces of Creation. May they grant this boy the gift of their power so that someday he may be the one to eat of the flesh and drink of the blood of the totem . . . not seeking this for himself . . . but for Shateh! His blood is Warakan's blood! As long as Warakan lives, so, too, will Shateh live in me! And when I am bigger and older and taller, strong in the power of the Four Winds, this boy will make Tsana pay for what he has done this day!"

Jhadel eyed the child as he hefted his own pack. "Someday is a distant time. Come now. We have far to go, you and I."

Warakan stared eastward. Cha-kwena and the sacred stone and the totem were out there somewhere. Someday he would find them. No matter how long it took.

And so, in the skin of the great mother bear whose children had been so cruelly parted from him, Warakan held the flight feather of the golden eagle pressed to his breast as he walked on in silence beside the old shaman, while Moon, mother of star children, lighted their way eastward.

13

Dawn was coloring snow-clad mountains when Warakan and Jhadel rested. They stopped only long enough to eat of the food that the old man had brought. The boy ate well-fermented wedges of fat and smoked and pounded meat, chewing carefully around his bruised mouth as he stared eastward toward the distant ranges over which the sun was rising. When the wind dropped, turned, and blew hard from the north, he was grateful for the skin of the great mother bear and silently thanked her for the gift of warmth.

"White Giant Winter will come early again this year," said the old man, bundled in his heavy traveling robe of bison hide. "Perhaps the time beyond beginning is not so long ago as we have thought. Perhaps soon White Giant Winter will be high chief of the Four Winds again, and the passes through which the great herds have always come to be food for the People will close, and mountains of ice will walk upon the world once more."

Warakan shivered. He remembered old Lahontay's sharing the same concern and accusing him of being the one to have summoned eternal winter. He started to speak a rebuttal to this, just in case Jhadel was thinking the same thing, but the old shaman had put his raven-feather-crowned head onto his bent knees and was fast asleep. Weary,

Warakan sighed, swallowed down the last of his dried meat, copied Jhadel's posture, and was soon dreaming. . . .

He saw himself as a young man, clad in the skins of all animals that were food for the People. Across the neck of an ice-clogged mountain pass, a shaman dressed entirely in white fur whirled and danced and displayed serrate-edged, wolflike teeth as he howled to the leering face of a watching moon. Somehow Warakan was both men. And then, simultaneously, he became yet a third—a man clad in the skin of a black-maned lion, kneeling on a vast and snowy plain that undulated like water as he incised magical patterns into a bludgeon fashioned from a rib taken from the nearby skeleton of a fish that was larger than a mammoth.

Who is to say where the spirits of any of us resided in time beyond beginning? Predator . . . prey . . . men . . . beasts . . . all who live now lived then in different skins.

Memories of Lahontay's disturbing premise woke him. The sun was well risen above the crests of the eastern ranges. Jhadel was already up and hefting his pack. A solemn Warakan rose, stretched, relieved himself, donned his own load, and with the golden eagle feather braided into a forelock, followed Jhadel toward the edge of the world.

On a long, rolling downslope he was aware of being watched from behind and turned at the unmistakable high huffing of a worried bear cub.

"Little Bear Brother!" cried Warakan with a sob of joy as he raced toward the animal.

A moment later an astonished Jhadel saw the boy lying on the ground, embraced by the gripping limbs of a tawny creature that was bawling with delight.

"Aiee!" exclaimed the old man in confusion as he grabbed for a short spear and, frightened for his life but more concerned for the safety of the youth, ran to save him from what turned out to be a loving, licking, sloppy embrace.

"'Bear brother,' did you say? W-what? . . . H-how? . . ." Still confused but no longer afraid, he relaxed as he commanded, "Get up, Warakan, this is not seemly! What will the spirits of the ancestors say if they see a future shaman and a son of Masau and a grandson of Shateh sucking muzzles with a bear!"

With great reluctance Warakan managed to be free of the transcendently happy cub. As he got to his feet, he explained, "I am Warakan, son of Masau and grandson of Shateh, but I wear the skin of the one who bore this cub, and since I have taken her life, I have become Boy Mother of Bears. This one's brother perished in the Valley of the Dead. This bear is my child, and I will not leave him behind or kill his kind again."

Jhadel, scowling, thought about that and then shrugged. "If this 'child' grows to be a 'man' and considers us to be his parents, this man will walk more easily, with him to protect us against the dangers that must surely lie ahead for us."

And so they continued on, an old man, a bearskin-clad boy, and an orphaned cub. Now and then a shrike was seen and heard. Warakan smiled and named it Friend. The sun rose and fell many times. The travelers crossed badlands that sobered them to the dimensions of the journey that lay ahead.

The old man frowned and brought Warakan to pause at the crest of broad, boulder-strewn dry hills. Hidden within tall, summer-dry grasses, he pointed below and ahead to a small band of people trudging out of the distance.

Warakan's eyes widened as they came closer. "It is Cha-kwena's band!" Disappointment suddenly shadowed his rising excitement. "But the Red World shaman is not with them as they journey toward the hunting grounds of the Land of Grass."

"Hmmm . . . ." Jhadel watched the little group, studied it, shook his head. "They walk into danger. Death or slavery awaits them if they blunder into Tsana's path."

Warakan felt pity for them. "My heart feels no hostility for the one named Kosar-eh. We should warn him before he—"

"No," interrupted Jhadel. "For whatever their reasons, they have chosen their path. We cannot help them without risking ourselves. Come. We will seek Cha-kwena and the sacred stone. The totem will be with them."

Again they went on. It was Warakan who first found mammoth sign, old and dried but unmistakable. Jhadel's aged but practiced eyes were the first to note odd little piles of stone and notchings in trees and shrubs.

"This is the way they have gone," said the old man.

And soon the badlands fell away. They crossed a fine, mixed-grass prairie and came onto highlands, then through a great gorge that led them into a land of many unfamiliar trees. At night, they sat close together and looked up at the high canopy of the forest. When the wind stirred the treetops, Warakan and Jhadel could see the Sky River flowing brightly against the black cloak of Father Above, and now and again they could pick out the Great Bear and the Twin Brothers of the Sky and the Watcher looking down at them out of the configuration of stars that they both knew as the Great Snake.

"Do you think our enemies will follow us?" asked Warakan.

"Perhaps in time they will come, but not for a while, because soon White Giant Winter will return to the land. Tsana will be chieftain of a great tribe now, with many women, children, captives, and warriors to feed; he and his hunters will have to seek meat and settle into a winter camp if any of them are to survive until spring. In the meantime, you and I and Little Bear Brother must continue on this path that the spirits have made for us until we find a suitable place in which we, too, may settle in and prepare for winter."

And so, three days later, still following the "spirit" trail and drawn ever forward through the dark wood by a strange wind that wept like a woman in the night, they came through the forest to discover an abandoned village set amid fallen trees.

"I do not like this place," said Warakan.

Jhadel frowned as he looked around. The wind was shifting restlessly—a cold wind, a north wind. There was the smell of snow and storm in it. And once again the low sound of distant weeping was coming through the woods.

"Is it a spirit?" whispered Warakan.

Jhadel shook his head. "A woman. A grieving woman somewhere far away."

That night the first snowflakes fell. And though the wind dropped and the wailing in the wood was not heard, Jhadel awoke with a start.

"What is it, Jhadel?" asked Warakan, bundling with the cub in the skin of the great bear.

The old man shook his head. "Do you not hear it? Somewhere a shaman weeps, but only the Four Winds and the forces of Creation will ever know why."

Cha-kwena raged against the snow and interminable distances of shoreline and waterways that had been confounding his attempts to return to his people ever since he had awakened half-drowned on a bleak, boulder-strewn spit of gravel somewhere along the deeply indented shoreline of the ice-islanded lake.

"I must get back!" he declared to the moon and stars, even though he could not see them above the clouds. "But how?"

For endless days and nights, since being dragged unconscious by the mammoth from the frigid deeps, he had been desperately trying to find his way back to the place where he had first emerged from the forest—but every cove and inlet appeared much the same, and the shoreline was so vast, it confused his senses. And all the while mammoth and the little white calf had watched him as they grazed on stunted spruce and alder. Now, finally, in the deep dark of this cold, snowy night, they were moving on again.

"Wait!" he cried. "I can follow you no longer. Surely you must know this! I have left my woman alone and the sacred stone of the ancestors in the keeping of my band.

Now, Life Giver, you must return with me! You are the strength and spirit of the People. You are their courage. You are their heart. They *must* look upon you and know that you walk within the world once more, or they will lose courage and faith in all that you have been to them since time beyond beginning! Please, I have followed you to the edge of the world and beyond! Now you must help me to return to my people!"

But the mammoth kept on walking.

In frustration, Cha-kwena followed across a cold, windswept, stony plain. Dawn found him walking upslope under clear skies, with the mammoth stopped well ahead, atop the crest of a long, massive hill of stones. Breathless and tired, he followed until at last he stood atop the hill and stopped, stunned. Ahead lay the canyon of his dreams.

There, across yet another stretch of plain, dark ice-scoured walls soared against the sky. A river flowed within the great cleft in the earth. The canyon floor was forested, and waterfalls, frozen by the sudden early freeze, plunged in glistening white translucent silence from the heights. And showing above and beyond the canyon was a mountain range of solid ice, stretching as far as he could see. It was the most singularly glorious and desolate vista Cha-kwena had ever set eyes upon.

"I cannot follow you there! Not alone . . . not without the band . . . not without my people!" he exclaimed to the mammoth. His hand went to his throat, seeking solace and understanding from the sacred stone. Its all-too-familiar absence caused a hollow, sinking feeling in his gut. Ahead, close to the mammoth, he could have sworn that he saw old Hoyeh-tay materialize and Owl swoop from the sky to land upon the old man's outstretched hand.

"Ah, Cha-kwena, Grandson of Hoyeh-tay, look with the inner eye of a shaman's Vision, and you will neither fear nor rebuke the way in which you must now go! Behold the edge of the world! Is this not what you have always longed for? To discover new lands that no living men have ever seen before?"

"Living?" Cha-kwena was suddenly uneasy as well as afraid. Strange things were happening ahead of him. The mammoth were no longer the only animals standing at the entrance to the canyon. Horn Nose was with them, huge and granite gray and arrogant even though Teratorn, in all of his fine-feathered condorlike magnificence, perched on Horn Nose's rump. A herd of small, broad-bellied striped brown horses stood close to the rhinoceros. There were camels, too, and sloths and a pair of mastodon. And among the browsers, as though their presence was the most natural thing in the world, were a pair of leaping cats, a great spotted lion, and an enormous short-faced brown bear that stood upright and seemed to speak to Cha-kwena in the voice of a man.

"The world is changing," said the great short-faced bear. "Few of our kind remain in the world. Are you no longer our brother, Cha-kwena?"

"No!" he cried, realizing what was being asked of him. The world was changing, and many of the animals that had walked the hunting grounds of the ancestors would soon walk within this world no more; but wherever they were journeying, Cha-kwena had no wish to journey with them. For now, at last, he realized that his love for Mah-ree and for all the members of his band was greater than his love of the totem or sacred stones or his need to wander endlessly in search of unknown lands. He had found the totem! He had followed it without question! But for what purpose, if all that he loved was lost to him forever? "I will not go on! I must go back!"

"You cannot return to the land from which you have come," informed the great short-faced bear.

"We will see about that!" declared Cha-kwena as he turned and ran back toward the lake and the floodplain and the forest and the village of his band that lay somewhere . . . and back, most of all, to the loving embrace of his little lawbreaking woman, Mah-ree—if she would ever forgive him and welcome him into her arms again.

"Stop!" demanded the great short-faced bear.

Cha-kwena did not stop.

"You must return to us!" cried the animals of the dying age.

"We will see about that!" shouted Cha-kwena, refusing to listen, refusing to die with them.

On and on he ran until he reached the shore of the great lake. Exhausted, he sank to his knees upon the unforgiving glacial rubble of its stony beach. A strong, subfreezing wind beat into his face. Miles of deep, open water and islands of ice stood between him and the storm clouds that hulked over the far shore. White Giant Winter was not only coming; he was here. Without the power of the spirits, Cha-kwena knew that he had no hope of finding his way back to his band.

"The People have chosen to go the way of seeds upon the wind. The sacred stone is for another. Soon the predators of your nightmares will follow. Who will guard the totem when the sacred stone is taken and the People are one no more? Here . . . beyond the edge of the world . . . the little white calf will become the great white mammoth, and Life Giver will dwell safe in the care of Guardian of the Totem. And although there will be many in the world of men who will say: 'Come! Let us hunt him!' Guardian of the Totem will answer: 'We will see about that! I will stop you! I will make sure that in this world beyond the world, he is not easy to be seen!' "

Cha-kwena flinched at the well-remembered words from the story of bold Jay and his hapless adventures in the blue land of Sky. And, suddenly, Vision flared, and beneath his eyelids he saw the carnivores of his nightmares: wolves, lions, cougars, bears of kinds and colors that he did not know, and dogs . . . slavering, treacherous dogs. He gasped. The images shifted. The animals became men: warriors of the People of the Watching Star and of the Land of Grass and—was it possible?—of the Red World. They came like wolves across the country of his vision. Into the land of his dream they came, lean men and youths tattooed and painted black and red and white with ash and clay and ocher. And then, as suddenly as they had come, they were gone.

Cha-kwena sat alone on the shore of the great lake. He stared toward the past—toward all that he had loved and lost and would never see again. The sun was rising to claim the height of noon before he at last found the courage to rise and turn toward the future—toward a new life, he wondered, or to death?

He sighed, acquiescing to his fate, whatever it would be. He was, after all, Cha-kwena, grandson of Hoyeh-tay, brother of animals, guardian of the totem, and Trickster, Yellow Wolf, for in the end it seemed that he had succeeded in tricking himself more than any other.

The mammoth were moving on again, linked trunk to tail, plodding with slow deliberation toward the great, sunstruck canyon and mountains of ice that lay beyond. Cha-kwena followed, his mood as dark as a night without Moon and her star children to ignite the shimmering fires of the Sky River, which, in turn, illuminated and gave heart to the passage of all who walked below.

It was the distant chattering of raucous jays in the canyon far ahead that brought him to pause. There, on the ground at his feet, a fluff of downy feathers caught his eyes. He knelt, picked them up, held their soft blueness in the hollow of his hand, and remembered a night when he and Mah-ree had lain close together, sheltered from the storms of life, warmed by their love and the fire that she had kindled.

"Let her be safe!" Cha-kwena shouted to the Four Winds and the forces of Creation. He rose and looked back at the way he had come, westward to where the sun had roused Rainbow from the gathering storm clouds that were building over the country of the ancestors that he had left far behind.

"We will see about that!"

Cha-kwena turned. Who had spoken? The mammoth were entering the canyon, and with the sun shining brightly upon the back of the little white calf, Life Giver turned its head and raised its trunk and spoke in the voice of the totem, "Come walking in the path of the rising sun, Cha-kwena! Come now and do not be afraid! You and I will live and grow strong in the tales that Mah-ree will tell of us. And as long as we live so, too, shall the People live . . . always and forever."

AUTHOR'S NOTE

This novel has been drawn from a wealth of ongoing scientific research in the fields of North American archaeology, paleoanthropology, geology, meteorology, and ever-expanding studies in Native American prehistory, lifeways, and mythology.

The use of blue-jay feathers by Native Americans as a traditional kindling is well documented; hence the inspiration for the story of Jay's misadventures in the blue land of Sky. The tale, however, is my own.

Some might ask why I have chosen an owl to be the helping animal spirit of the Red World shaman, Cha-kwena, when in most Native American mythologies, that bird is often synonymous with death. Precisely. As Cha-kwena follows Owl, he walks the path of a dying age, the Pleistocene.

And it has been out of consideration of those long and lingering Ice Age winters that I have presumed to put "winter coats" on Mammuthus imperator; since modern elephants often possess vestigial body hair, I believe this would have been the case.

For those readers who may ponder the location of the great glacial lake and placement of forests and wetlands where there are now grasslands and badlands, please note that eleven to twelve thousand years before the present era, the world was a very different place.

Wipe from your mind, if you would, all images of the North American continent as it is now. Visualize it as it was midway toward the ending of the Age of Ice. . . .

The considerable remains of the miles-thick Cordilleran ice sheet still holds the Pacific Northwest, Canadian Rockies, and the massive Alaskan and Brooks ranges in deep freeze. Meanwhile, on the far side of the ice-free corridor that extends across the heartland of the Yukon and then down along the eastern spine of the Rockies, the Laurentide ice sheet continues to cover much of northeastern Canada and the northernmost United States. In its retreat northward, this larger of the two melting continental ice sheets has not only reshaped the land and redirected the course of many a mighty river, it has also created Lake Erie and Lake Ontario. At this time, much of Lake Superior has yet to emerge from beneath the ice sheet, and Lake Michigan and Lake Huron—hosts to the leading edge of the glacial massif—are one huge body of water.

Incredibly, these "two" Great Lakes are not nearly so huge as the nearby lake that drowns most of neighboring Manitoba, Minnesota, parts of Saskatchewan, and the entire northeastern half of North Dakota. Prehistoric Lake Agassiz is so enormous that it has overflowed the Continental Divide and, at its maximum extent and depth, covers some one hundred thousand square miles! At this same time— while a frigid tundra belt extends southward approximately thirty to one hundred and fifty miles into New England and all along the margins of the retreating ice sheets—in some portions of the West, Midwest, and Southwest, parching summers and long, dry, excruciatingly cold winters are creating badlands, grasslands, and deserts even as remnants of the vast boreal forests of the Ice Age continue to stretch from the Atlantic to the Rocky Mountains, southward through the Carolinas and deep into today's great plains.

This was the world of the People—a world in which changing climate was affecting everything upon the planet, a world in which the Age of Ice was not ending overnight but dying slowly, albeit not always subtly, during long periods of benign warmth that were often followed by resurgences of extreme cold. The world's weather patterns mystify and challenge to this day. Indeed, even as I write, an "unprecedented" southward shift in the Canadian summer storm track brings snow to the Rockies and causes the rain-engorged Mississippi and Missouri rivers to reestablish dominance of a vast Ice Age floodplain. If this weather pattern were to remain constant for only another few years, massive glaciers would return to the mountains, ice sheets would spread from the poles, and the great wetlands and lakes of Pleistocene midwest America would no longer be of the past. It has been my intent to re-create this world through the story line and characterization presented within this novel. If I have succeeded, thanks are due to so many who have helped in the research and given encouragement along the way.

Once again, the author is indebted to Dr. Richard Michael Gramly, Curator of the Great Lakes Artifact Repository, Buffalo, New York, and Clovis Project Director at Richey Clovis Cache in Wenatchee, Washington, for his gracious and continuing interest in this project. The description of the bone "shoes" used to protect the wooden runners of sledges used by the People in this novel has been made possible by Dr. Gramly's generous sharing of hypotheses based upon the most recent analyses of certain mysterious bibeveled rods of proboscidean limb bones found in the Richey Clovis Cache. The descriptions of dietary habits and some of the lifeways of the People of the Watching Star, Land of Grass, and Red World have also been made possible through Dr. Gramly's sharing of the most current analyses of natural pigments and of human and animal blood residues found on nearly all of the flaked tools inventoried in the Richey Clovis Cache.

Thanks also to John E. Mosley, Program Supervisor of the Griffith Observatory, Los Angeles, California, for supplying the sky charts necessary to assist this author in placing the polestar and constellations on their proper prehistoric pathways.

More thanks to all the fine scholars whose works have lighted this author's way into antiquity and along the shaman's path, especially to Dr. Joan Halifax for her exceptionally insightful book *Shaman, Wounded Healer* (the Crossroad Publishing Company, NY, 1982) from which the epigraphs from *Seeking Life* were taken; to Charles Cline, whose sleuthing in the "halls of the learned" on this author's behalf saved invaluable time; to Laurie Rosin, Senior Project Editor; Marjie Weber, copy editor; and Pamela Lappies, Elizabeth Tinsley, Meredith LeClair, Sally Smith, and all of the incomparable staff at Book Creations Inc., for getting this project to deadline on time.

And last but not least, thanks to the forces of Creation for leaving "the Mac" (and me!) and most of this manuscript intact and in hard-drive memory while shaking the earth so explosively beneath this author's home in Big Bear Valley, California, on the morning of June 28, 1992, and every day and night thereafter for many a long moon.

WILLIAM SARABANDE

Fawnskin, California